P9-DDZ-556

CS 10/20

WV Jan 2021
RT April 21
TH Jan 22
SC June 22

THE
ACCOMPLICE

ALSO BY CHARLES ROBBINS

Life Among the Cannibals *with Senator Arlen Specter*

Passion for Truth *with Senator Arlen Specter*

THE
ACCOMPLICE

***

CHARLES ROBBINS

THOMAS DUNNE BOOKS
NEW YORK
ST. MARTIN'S PRESS

THOMAS DUNNE BOOKS.
An imprint of St. Martin's Press.

THE ACCOMPLICE. Copyright © 2012 by Charles Robbins. All rights reserved. Printed in the United States of America. For information, address St. Martin's Press, 175 Fifth Avenue, New York, N.Y. 10010.

www.thomasdunnebooks.com
www.stmartins.com

ISBN 978-1-250-01051-3

First Edition: September 2012

10 9 8 7 6 5 4 3 2 1

In memory of my father,
Melvin Lloyd Robbins (1928–2004),
who taught me that the two greatest sins
are hypocrisy and naiveté.

ACKNOWLEDGMENTS

***

Thanks, first, to Tom Dunne and his stellar team at Thomas Dunne Books, including Karyn Marcus, Katie Gilligan, and Margaret Sutherland Brown, and to my magical agent, Victoria Skurnick, for bringing *The Accomplice* into the world.

Two other brilliant writers, Pinckney Benedict and Melanie DeCarolis, also helped me shape and smooth the overall text.

Kevin Mathis, my public policy "answer man," helped concoct or integrate key elements, especially some of the more sinister and cynical moves.

Former Senate chiefs of staff Scott Hoeflich and David Urban, now premier lobbyists, and veteran media consultant Chris Mottola, helped flesh out political maneuvers.

Ken Bovasso, a former Omaha Police detective sergeant and criminal justice professor, helped craft logistics for the murder investigation.

Ashley Turner and Aura Dunn, and one friend who asked to remain anonymous, helped flesh out nuances of Elizabeth's relationship with Peele.

Howard Robbins, a partner at a major international law firm, helped craft legal flavor and language.

Many others provided vital guidance, including David Brog,

Anne Cheng, Lawrence Cheng, Warren Dym, Richard Hertling, Adam Inselbuch, Catherine Larkin, Fred Leebron, Daryl McCullough, Naeem Murr, David Payne, Dan Renberg, Patty Sheetz, Robin Sparkman, Abigail Thomas, and Paul Weinstein, Jr.

THE
ACCOMPLICE

1

★ ★ ★

THE DANCE

Henry Hatten shifted on the anteroom sofa, the dog-eared sheaf of printouts in his lap beginning to blur, a picture of Senator Tom Peele coalescing in his head from excited blue underlines, arrows, and phrases. The warm leather grudgingly released and then reclaimed his suit pants, and Henry was about to begin another pass through the folder when a mass flashed toward him. He looked up to see Mike Sterba take two final bounds. Before Henry could shield his papers, Sterba lifted him off the couch.

The chief of staff nearly crushed him in a bear hug, then dragged him past a receptionist who shot a distracted glance. Sterba pulled him down the corridor into an office that looked like a combination tea parlor and trophy room. Dodging the doorframe, Henry brushed an accent table, rattling framed photos of a younger Sterba in a West Point football jersey, in camouflage fatigues, and on the ski slopes with a blonde. He settled against a barrister bookcase, beneath a bill with the President's signature.

Sterba was sizing him up again, wondering whether this had been a good idea, after all. Henry could tell. He'd seen that look before, of hope, forced kindness, anxiety. He first saw it fifteen years earlier on James, a dean's list student who had volunteered, maybe been assigned, as his escort when Henry applied to Trinity. Henry had been so proud that day, arriving at the Manhattan prep school in the new outfit his father had bought him, a slate-blue windbreaker with fabric so crisp it swished when he walked, a white dress shirt, brown EZ-Waist poly-blend trousers, and white Pro Keds low-tops. He had gotten a haircut the day before on Steinway Street, a short pompadour. James had swallowed at meeting him, then tried to cover it with schoolyard gusto. Other kids came up to them, James was popular and Henry was a curiosity, and James introduced him repeatedly as a "prospective." The others took the cue, became oh-so-polite ambassadors for Trinity and the next generation of *übermensches*. A girl in a cable-knit sweater pointed at him and grinned, then cupped her hand over her mouth, eyes wide, when she realized he had seen her. Still, somehow, Trinity had taken him.

And now he was a prospective again, this time a refugee from the House of Representatives and a busted campaign trying to crack the big time, maybe with the stench of small-time sorrow and failure soaked into his best gray suit.

Sterba, posted by the door, watched the corridor. "Boss is about to file paperwork at the FEC to form an Exploratory," the chief of staff said. "You do the interview walking to the garage. You get, maybe, two minutes with him."

Henry nodded. His temples throbbed and the pulse at the hinge in his jaw pounded, the way they had half a lifetime earlier as a Trinity wrestler, when his name blared across a gym and he snapped on his headgear and trotted onto the mat. "Talk about getting in on the ground floor," he said, just to say *something*. He had been ready to gamble that Tom Peele would run for President. The Nebraska senator was the only moderate Republican positioned for a serious bid. Hell, Peele was about the only moderate Republican. But he hadn't expected action so soon; the first voting, the Iowa caucuses, were fifteen months away. Forming a presidential exploratory committee would give Peele license to raise money and hire staff.

Sterba leaned in, inches from Henry's face, the azure eyes studying him, searing him. Sterba had a stake in this now, too. The chief of staff had interviewed Henry a few days earlier, and apparently recommended him. If Peele nixed Henry, or he got the job and flamed out, Sterba would catch the heat. "If he takes you on the ride to the FEC, that's the second interview," Sterba said. "He invites you into the FEC, you own the job."

Henry nodded again. So two minutes would spell his destiny; whether he got profiled in "up-and-comer" *Washington Post* and Politico columns and helped shape history, or crawled back to his father for a bridge loan.

A Bronze Star medal glinted at Henry from a triple-matted frame. Sterba's ego wall, even the photos with Peele, revolved around the chief of staff, a howl of "I am!" in a world where aides' identities subsumed into the boss's. Nothing here or, for that matter, in the anteroom to suggest Peele's earlier on-screen persona as keeper of America's Marlboro Man idealism. Not a magazine cover or even a photo from the TV show *Parkland*.

"Game on," Sterba called.

Henry felt a hand clamp between his shoulder blades and shove him into the corridor. To his right, a column was closing on him. The Senator was in the lead, head forward. For an instant, Henry froze. Peele, in person, exuded an aura that the photos didn't capture. Henry's eyes caught first on the chin, broad with a deep cleft, vintage Hollywood. Then the hair, thick and graying progressively down the sides, the top still mostly dark; just the way Henry had hoped his own locks would one day gray, before they began thinning. Under a forehead that looked plains-etched, Peele's intense blue eyes scanned the corridor above a chiseled nose and dimpled cheeks. Tom Peele looked like a senator, with a mien that said "Trust me, I'll save you."

Squinting to erase the gray and the lines, Henry pictured a younger Peele, as TV's Ranger Roy, flashing an aw-shucks grin as he fought forest fires, rescued tourists and bears, and made a generation of teenage girls swoon.

Then, for a moment as Peele advanced, Henry met the blue eyes. Despite himself, he wilted. He'd met plenty of senators, sometimes over big stakes, and some of them pulsated with power, while he didn't notice others until he was introduced. It's something inside that a senator either has or doesn't. Size can augment the effect, but can't create it. With Tom Peele, it seemed to flow from the eyes. Peele wasn't that big, a shade under six feet and maybe 190 pounds, but he seemed massive stalking the corridor, even with a giant behind him.

The bald giant's double-breasted suit, a lustrous charcoal with beige chalk stripes, looked like it cost Henry's House press secretary salary. As the man swaggered, a gold cuff link glinted. Henry glanced down at his steel-gray Jos. A. Bank two-button, which used to make him feel cool, with its pinstripes that met at sharp angles where the lapel sections joined. His tie was creased, a gash across the meat of the silk.

Henry fell in behind Sterba and the bald man, Sterba's lineman's shoulders shifting in cadence before Henry's nose. Did

Peele schedule meetings when he planned to dash, posse in tow?
Maybe stagecraft picked up in Hollywood.

They cleared the anteroom and passed into a corridor, a
herd of cap-toes and pumps slapping marble. Sterba trotted up
on point and made the introductions.

Up close, Henry noticed that Peele hadn't shaved the back
of his neck, leaving stubble that extended from hairline to collar. The guy wasn't perfect.

"I've been a fan, Senator, since your speech about the fringe
turning the Republican Party into a regional right-wing cult,"
Henry said, sliding between Peele and the bald man. He focused on forming the words flat, not slipping into a Queens
accent.

Peele nodded. "I'm looking for true believers." The Senator
eyed the bald man. "Too many mercenaries in this town."

The giant scowled. Cass, the man's name was, Sterba had
said. Henry had seen the name before, maybe in a news story.

"Senator," Henry began, but Cass stepped between them and
whispered to Peele.

At the elevators, Henry studied the metalwork, the way the
brass molding blended into the marble frame. He had a month
to land another Capitol Hill gig, before the sergeant at arms
locked Tyler's House office and seized the staff's I.D. cards. After that, he'd be just another outsider trying to claw in. For now,
fellow Hill rats were helping, like Tyler's health-care aide, who
had tipped him about Peele's job opening. They all knew that
the guy down today might be up tomorrow. They all knew the
stories, like Kansas congressman Dan Glickman, unseated and
shunned, and then Clinton named him secretary of agriculture, and all those guys who hadn't taken Glickman's calls
were begging him to take theirs. Henry had fantasized about
landing a top spot on a top-tier presidential campaign, once

nearly missing his Metro stop. And now it might actually happen.

The brass doors parted and Peele's crew marched in, Henry last. The descent and a short march took them to the Russell Building garage, where a silver Lincoln was waiting, a grim young aide at the wheel. A Buick SUV idled behind the Lincoln.

Sterba jumped in the Lincoln's shotgun seat. The rear door opened, and Peele stepped toward it. The word "Senator" formed on Henry's tongue, but no breath came to expel it. He tried to make contact with the blue eyes, but Peele was angling into the cabin.

"Take a ride, Henry," a high, nasal voice said. He spun toward the sound and found Cass. The voice seemed too small and tinny for the big frame.

Henry squeezed between Cass and Peele in the backseat, his feet on the driveshaft, shins pressed together. Cass scowled. The glare suggested deep secrets, that Cass knew how the game was played, and could invite you in or throw you under. Cass's talc and aftershave scent both singed and soothed his nostrils.

As the Lincoln flew up a ramp into daylight, Peele propped on a pair of reading glasses and plucked Henry's résumé from a leather briefcase. Up close, Peele had pretty good skin, but a few tiny purple blood vessels scored a cheek, like lines on a map. Henry realized he was playing a game with Peele that he usually worked on the subway with dauntingly beautiful women, finding flaws to make them more approachable. Still, purple capillaries and all, the former "Heartland Heartthrob" radiated an anguished decency that made you want him to like you.

"You got the best possible recommendation," Peele said, reading a yellow sheet. "From the opposition."

He felt himself glow. It must have been the Iowa governor's campaign manager, with whom he had sparred on camera after a debate, and who told him, "You spin well." Or maybe the media guru whose ads he had debunked.

"Thank you, Senator."

Peele sifted papers. Henry squeezed his thumb in a fist.

"Dartmouth, English major," Peele said, reading. "Founded and ran the Student Pizza Delivery Agency. You worked your way through?"

"Partially," Henry said. Almost completely, actually. His father's warehouseman's pay barely covered his used textbooks.

"Trinity School before that, in New York City," Peele said, swaying as the Lincoln bounced over a pothole. "Guy who runs Morgan Stanley, his kid goes to Trinity. You were on scholarship?"

Henry felt his face heat. "Yeah."

Peele nodded again. "Five years on the Hill as a press secretary. First for Morris from Alabama, then Tyler from Iowa. Then handled press for Tyler's run for governor. We're going to need people who know Iowa."

Henry forced a quick smile. *God, whatever else, don't ship me back to Iowa.* When he began with Tyler, a veteran reporter told him, "If you ever find out you have six months to live, spend it in Iowa; it'll feel like ten years."

"Hey, I'm just a kid from Mead, Nebraska," Peele said, maybe reading Henry. "Had dirt under my fingernails till I was eighteen." The Senator swept an arm at Constitution Avenue. "This town's just a giant theme park of federal government. Most weeks when we adjourn, I can't wait to get back to the real world."

Peele was spouting the Washington blather that you'd rather

be back with your constituents, the real people, at hog roasts and pancake breakfasts, than stuck in this Sodom suffering through the National Symphony and four-star dinners with CEOs. Henry felt himself smile. Peele's bottom lip curled, saying the Senator saw that Henry knew the dance. But Peele had also seen through his Knickerbocker society guise.

Henry had to keep the conversation going. What to say? "Yeah, I guess 'true believer' says it. Congressman Tyler called for enlightened, progressive Republicans to rise and stifle the shrill cries of the extremist right that hijacked the party. Well, this isn't the time to be modest; I wrote that."

Peele nodded again, only slightly this time. Cass rolled deep brown eyes.

"What went wrong with Doug?" Peele asked.

"Nothing," Henry said. "We nearly took out a three-term governor in a Republican primary."

Peele seemed to be waiting for him to say more. To say what? An image of Tyler's primary-night party at the Des Moines Holiday Inn filled his head, the melting ice sculpture after Tyler's concession speech, the thinning crowd hitting the ballroom bar.

"We knew it was uphill from the start," Henry said, "basically asking Iowans to fire a guy who hadn't done anything wrong just because we said we could do better. That's a tough trick without a scandal."

"Without a scandal?" Cass's nasal voice bounced around the cabin. "The Governor's son was selling dope in a Laundromat in Denison. You needed someone to draw you a picture?"

Henry's face fizzed, sending white rays up through his eyes. How could they know about that? He had agonized for two days, recalling decent neighborhood kids who shoplifted or worse as rites of passage on Astoria's streets. By the time he called the Denison police for the incident report, nobody there seemed to know the Governor even had a son.

He never told Tyler, who also surely would have sat on the dirt; you don't ruin a sixteen-year-old's life to win an election. Two weeks later, he told Fran. She scoffed. No absolution, no sympathy. Later that night, when he invited himself to her hotel room, she told him, in her opposition researcher snarl, she didn't feel like it. That was the last time he had seen or spoken to her.

But Fran wouldn't have said anything, wouldn't have betrayed him. Would she? No, it must have been Tyler's Crawford County chairman, who had given Henry the tip. Peele was exploring Iowa for a presidential run; the Senator's people had probably run into the Crawford guy, an electrical contractor also plugged in politically.

Henry looked at Cass. "We couldn't get anything solid on that."

Cass raised an eyebrow. Sterba swallowed, maybe worried about Peele chewing him out for wasting his time.

Sterba looked like a solid 240 or 250 pounds. If Henry had to take him out, right now, he thought, the move was an eye gouge. Henry had conjured these scenes since Trinity, to ease tension when he felt bullied or stressed. The fantasies grew more complex when he began aikido training. Yeah, he'd spread his fingers, bend the joints slightly, then jab his hand like a fork at Sterba's eyes. That way, one or two fingers would hit an eyeball, and the others would bend back safely against bone. From there, once Sterba was blinded, he'd clench Sterba's hair with one hand and ram the base of his other palm into Sterba's nose, repeatedly.

He felt his breathing deepen, and his eyes narrow. He sat straight. The look had flashed for only a second. Nobody could have seen it. He scanned the faces. Cass was staring at him.

The Lincoln whipped past 6th Street. The FEC was at 10th and E, as Henry recalled.

"Senator, I assume your staff flagged CNN and C-SPAN about your filing papers," Henry said. He could still feel Cass's stare.

Peele turned to him, the blue eyes narrower. Peele's breath cut through Cass's talc musk, slightly sour and hot.

"Well, you probably want some cameras outside the FEC," Henry said, "to at least catch you going in or coming out."

"Mike," Peele called, and waved a finger. Sterba reached for a cell phone.

Maybe Henry really could play at this level. "Senator, we did move the poll numbers in a big way on the issues. Mr. Tyler's bill to tie the minimum wage to inflation jibes with your plan. The unions and small businesses both hate fighting every few years about raising the rate. But the key to doing the whole en-chilada, after you get a workable formula, is selling it to the American people as the least bad option."

Peele clasped his hands, as though in prayer. "Well, Henry, we'll need more than snappy slogans to index the minimum wage." Henry knew Peele had been leading the talks, trying to rally centrists in both parties, in both chambers. He had marked a *USA Today* story in which Peele quipped, "Once a week, our outcasts meet with their outcasts."

"Henry," Cass said, "even Ivory Soap is only ninety-nine and a half percent pure. You know what's in the other half percent? The unholy, keep-it-off-the-label shit you don't want to talk about. The stuff that gets the job done. The dope-selling in Denison."

The Lincoln bolted off a stoplight at 8th Street, pressing Henry into the leather. Peele was giving him a soulful look, like his wrestling coach's gaze after he got pinned. It was over. In a moment, they would reach the FEC, and Peele would thank him for coming by. He'd ride back to Capitol Hill in the Buick staff car. And he'd have to tell his father, after boasting about the interview, that it was another bust.

"Senator," he said, "if you're looking for a cowboy, I'm not your guy." He tapped his folder of notes. "I nail stuff solid, and then when I do shoot, I blow the target out of the water. It's not squeamishness. It's strategy."

In the corner of his eye, he saw Cass shift toward him. Henry kept his gaze on Peele. He couldn't invite any distractions. He felt his breathing quicken again. "And like you, Senator, I'm ambitious—nothing wrong with that. When you were at Columbia, I'm told, you brought women back to your room, and when you were going at it, you told them, 'Call me governor.'" He shrugged. "Twenty years later, the whole state of Nebraska was calling you governor."

Peele blanched, as though he had been punched. In the shotgun seat, Sterba's big head slumped. A hot, throbbing silence pressed Henry's eardrums. He swallowed.

Cass glared at him, then grinned.

The car pulled to the curb and Peele slid out. On the sidewalk, aides swarmed the Senator. Henry climbed out, his legs heavy, and studied his Florsheim cap-toes. Glass shards in the pavement shot rays at him as they caught the sun.

Peele stepped toward the FEC doors, then paused as Cass took his elbow. Cass leaned down to the Senator's ear. Henry could hear the giant whispering, but couldn't make out the words. Cass stepped back and crossed his arms.

Peele's tongue extended, as though in thought. The Senator turned toward Henry, the eyes wider. "You coming?" Peele angled toward the FEC.

Henry, in the corner of his eye, saw Sterba looking as stunned as he felt.

"We can use you here in D.C., maybe in Iowa," Peele said. A smile spread on the Senator's lips, for the first time.

Back at Tyler's House office, across the Capitol from the Senate buildings, autumn dusk cast sliding shadows across the barren rooms. Henry did a double take in a mirror by the receptionist's desk. His face looked older than its thirty-one years, blood vessels scarring his eyeballs, the lids purple and puffy. At least the dark pillows had shrunk, so heavy during the primary he could shift them by squeezing his eyes shut. The receding corners of his thick brown hair were leaving him with a more pronounced widow's peak, as though he'd been shaved for a lobotomy. A few silver strands glinted above one ear.

A few feet away, a young legislative correspondent moped amid stacked cartons and dark rectangles on a wall where festive and triumphant photos had hung. Doug Tyler would soon become a face on archived class pictures and a name in *Congressional Record* minutes. The kid glanced at Henry. Envy, maybe. Word of job interviews spread in Tyler's shop like adoption tryouts in an orphanage. And he had landed Daddy Warbucks.

Peering into the private office, Henry watched Tyler trudge from the desk to the window. Doug had increased his shrink sessions to twice a week, still bewailing the voters' rejection and dreading life without the first name "Congressman." The moping was new.

Henry had also thought Tyler would pull it out, until the final counts came in. Until one A.M. on election eve, he had scrubbed and polished a victory speech, as much for himself as for Tyler. He needed to spew, while it was fresh and raw. To shout why he had left his friends, freedom, and Upper Northwest D.C. condo for eighteen-hour workdays and a Des Moines dive. He had modeled his style on Tyler, eaten Christmas dinner with Doug's family, imprinted on the Brahmin. He had poured out, his own voice mixing with Tyler's, why pragmatism had to conquer self-righteous, know-nothing intolerance. Who were those cavemen to call Henry a squish and a RINO, *Republican in Name Only?*

When they lost the primary, Henry's father told him to get a real job, get married, and get on with life. But the presidential cycle was heating up, and Henry had already paid his dues. Now he could peddle statewide Iowa campaign experience. Maybe he could advance his ideals on the national stage—do good and do well.

He knocked on Tyler's doorframe. Beckoned in, he approached the pedestal desk with none of the augur he had felt an hour earlier across the Capitol. Tyler was wearing a jaunty check sport coat and khakis with a rep tie, but the cheeks were sunken, gray bags. The almost-governor must have shed ten pounds since the election.

"It's a gamble, Doug. Peele offered his top press job to the Republican National Committee communications director. That was three weeks ago. The guy has a newborn and an offer from the insurance association for a senior VP gig that pays four hundred K. And I hear his wife's going to leave him if he signs on with a campaign. So I take the number-two job, run things, the RNC guy passes, and pretty soon I'm the man."

Tyler shook his head. "At this stage of your career, you shouldn't be taking hind tit."

He looked away. He hadn't really wanted Tyler's advice, he realized; he had just wanted to crow. He should have anticipated Tyler's response. He had run Tyler's statewide press shop, and now he was going to staff another statewide official. Never mind that his new boss was running for president. "I'll be in charge. It'll just be a while before it becomes official."

"Okay, then. At this stage of your career, you shouldn't be taking middle tit."

Henry felt an artery throb against his collar. "It's all front tit, Doug."

He scanned the bare office. So this was how it would end. He and Tyler had begun in this room three years earlier. The office had seemed so much larger then, bursting with hope and promise. At the time, Henry was flacking for Morris, who had just lost a reelection bid. Henry had landed in D.C. figuring he could hawk any member, like a lawyer defending any client. After a few months, he had trouble spewing the Mobile congressman's John Birch agitprop. In one interview, he could sputter only a string of one-word responses, prompting a reporter to ask whether she had offended him. He had vowed never to work for another right-winger. Tyler had rescued him.

When Henry mentioned Cass, Tyler nearly lunged across the desk. "Wait a second. The Angel of Light?"

"The Angel of Light?" Henry repeated and laughed.

"Yeah, press boy. Gil Cass. One of his fans dubbed him the Angel of Light, and the name stuck. Or just 'the Angel,' for short." Tyler sighed. "Not too up on your Bible, eh? The Angel of Light was one of Satan's disguises. Cass chaired some big campaigns, but got radioactive after some dirty tricks went south."

He nodded, picturing the bald giant.

"Cass makes most of his money lobbying. You heard of Joachim Azullo, the Central American rebel leader? Kind of a modern-day Zapata. Killed about fifty thousand people?"

Henry shrugged; another name from old newspapers.

Tyler sighed again, louder. "He was one of Cass's clients.

Cass has kind of specialized in dictators and corporate sleazes. Word gets around in that crowd, who's willing to handle them, and the Angel became one of their go-to guys. For big coin." Tyler eased back behind the desk. "Listen, Henry, you're going places. But Peele, and Cass, may not be the place you want to go."

Henry dug a finger under his collar and tugged to loosen it. He knew the words were wrong before they left his mouth. "Doug, are there any sour grapes here?"

Tyler shoved back from the desk and raised both hands. "Go with God."

2

★ ★ ★

AMATEURS

Henry marched up the escalator from the Union Station Metro stop amid a parade of suits, all of them too busy, time too precious, to wait for the folding metal stairs to deposit them on the Senate side of Capitol Hill. As he emerged, a November breeze slapped his cheeks and he found his landmarks. He could even see a wedge of the office building, gleaming slabs of dark green glass, a couple of blocks over. He angled past human obstacles, meandering tourists, homeless men with cups and cardboard signs, hustlers hawking watches or sunglasses, bureaucrats stealing time from Uncle Sam for a morning smoke or stroll.

Henry enjoyed the tattoo as his gleaming black Florsheim Imperials slapped North Capitol Street, whisking him past limos, cabs, and other sharks. At the building, the revolving door gave grudgingly, adding to the augur of Peele's Presidential Exploratory Headquarters that lay beyond the stolid guards and card-key turnstiles.

Peele's campaign shop looked like a start-up insurance

agency, a windowless main space feeding into a long office-lined corridor, all low-pile beige carpet, Formica desks, and bare walls. But to Henry, the North Capitol Street suite radiated like a global nerve center. In his Sheetrock cell, Henry was wrestling with the desk chair's height lever when a smack against the doorframe jolted him. He looked up to see Cass, resplendent in a blue pinstripe suit that folded at the elbow like velvet. Henry had been working out a script to ask about his status and title. Cass's glower said now wasn't the time.

Cass lurched toward Henry. For a moment, he thought the Angel was going to knock him to the industrial carpet. Instead, Cass clapped two newspaper printouts onto the desk.

"This ran in the *Omaha Globe-Times* yesterday," Cass said, shoving one of the pages. "About a Teamster in Omaha getting tuned up." Cass locked deep brown eyes on him. "Real mess. They ripped his ear off, just about, knocked his teeth through his lip." Cass shook the bald head. "*Amateurs.*"

Henry felt a grin rise on one side, not sure whether Cass was joking.

"This," Cass said, drumming a thick finger on the other printout, "ran in the *Globe-Times* today."

Henry angled his head to read. "Rumors of Assault Cover-Up May Hurt Peele Campaign," by Bill Burr, *Globe-Times* Staff Writer. The story said the battery recalled an earlier Teamster beating involving one of Peele's close supporters.

"You know this reporter?" Cass asked.

The Omaha paper boasted the second-highest daily circulation in western Iowa, and Henry knew several of its political writers. But not Bill Burr. He shook his head. He began to read, and Cass shoved the story aside and perched on Henry's desk.

"The head of the Omaha Teamsters is a guy named Ed Zabriskie. Good friend of Tom's, good supporter. Nine years ago, another Teamster accuses Zabriskie of cooking the books. Next day, the guy shows up at an emergency room looking like a semi ran him over. D.A. is about to charge Zabriskie. Tom assures the D.A. that Ed wouldn't hurt a fly. D.A. has political ambitions." Cass locked the brown eyes on Henry again. "And he drops the case."

"So now the paper's blaming Peele for setting a thug loose?" Cass hung his head.

"Sorry," Henry said. "Go on. Please." He crossed his arms.

Cass scowled. "A few months after they drop the case, the Nebraska Teamsters pension fund donates one-fifty large to the state Republican committee, which then spends exactly that on Tom's Senate reelect. That was more dough back then. There's noise about a quid pro quo; never amounts to much. Fine. Everybody forgets. Until now." Cass flicked the story into the maw of Henry's stapler.

Okay, he got it now. The Omaha paper did seem to be taking a cheap shot, using recent union thuggery as an occasion to revive rumors about old union thuggery. But the headline almost suggested Peele was the assailant. Henry willed himself to feel the fury of injustice. But something was off. "The way this story reads," he said, "this reporter must have been digging into the old beating for a while. He didn't just stumble on it when a fresh body turned up."

Cass shot him a glare. "I want you to tell this reporter, Burr, that he's just stirring up malicious old gossip. You warn him it's damn near libelous. You shut this down, you understand?"

Henry waved his arms. "Mr. Cass—"

"Gil."

"The Senator's a public figure. The press gets more license. The standard is actual malice or reckless disregard of the truth or falsity. I mean, this stinks, but it doesn't seem like libel."

Cass stood. "You got talent for keeping dirt out of the news, Hatten. Just think of this as dope selling in Denison." Cass stepped toward the door. "Freedom and prosperity."

After Cass left, the talc-and-aftershave scent lingered, like a cloying cloud. Cass's order was absurd, unrealistic. But who was Henry to second-guess Gil Cass? Cass faced the world on his own terms, ran with bad boys, got drummed out of the establishment; they had done their worst and he was still here, needling them, maybe now about to topple them. Cass, from what Henry had learned, had money, homes, cars, clothes, offices, and a staff. The Angel arrived and the world paused. It was certainly one way to define success.

Henry googled Bill Burr. The reporter, three years out of college, was on his first major newspaper job. Fresh off the night cops beat, Burr had been detailed to the *Omaha Globe-Times* political team. Henry phoned the paper and left a voice mail for Burr. Urgent but not desperate. While he waited, he set out his pens and a framed photo of his father and him, taken half a lifetime earlier in an Astoria playground, and of Walter, the orange tabby he had adopted when he got back from Iowa. The cat's look of strained tolerance made him smile.

Another rap hit his doorframe, softer than Cass's. He looked up to see a shaggy middle-aged man straining a striped button-down and wool slacks, like a Woodstock groupie gone business casual.

"Ira Fogel," the man said. "I'm doing media for the campaign—ads."

So this was the artist who crafted footage sharp enough to impress their Hollywood boss. Fogel, like Cass, seemed to promote himself as much as his clients, his scripts and his quotes constantly popping up in news stories. From what Henry had read, Fogel had studied film at one of the big California programs, done some independent producing, then signed on with the National Republican Senatorial Committee, and then with a series of senators and governors and an occasional big-city mayor. This was his second or third presidential campaign.

Fogel lowered himself into a chair by the door. "Need you to make sure I get any news clips that could be useful, on an ongoing basis. Although today's clips'll probably be more use to the opposition."

Henry was about to protest, reflexively, then checked himself. Anything published or posted before he began work that morning was somebody else's fault.

"You seem like a nice kid," Fogel said. "You sure you're ready for all this?" The media man swept an arm at the suite beyond Henry's door.

"The Senator wouldn't have hired me if he didn't think so."

"Listen," Fogel said, taking a deep breath. "Next November and December, life as you know it will end. It'll be a pressure cooker that's going to claim half the senior people. There'll be terror in the office. This is the national press corps, not just statehouse hacks, and they'll be howling for blood, some of them looking to make their names by taking down a presidential contender. Like this tool in Omaha.

"The competition is for the most powerful job in the history of the world." Fogel shifted in the chair, giving the belly more room. "If you screw up, it's there for the world to see. But if you succeed, if you make it through the early primaries, you get your boss's picture on the cover of *Time*, you've got it made for life. You can walk into anybody's office with a résumé and say, 'Where's my desk, motherfucker?!'" Fogel paused, the big torso bobbing with each breath.

Henry felt a smile spread. "Peele's already been on magazine covers," he said. "And I'm hoping to do better than the early primaries."

"Yeah, *macher*? Well, first see if you can get through a week here."

He'd get through it. The night before, he had drifted to sleep picturing the White House press secretary's office, the way he had pictured the Iowa governor's media suite during Tyler's campaign. He had seen himself at the podium behind the White House seal, briefing the press, lecturing the world. Next time he heard about a governor's kid peddling dope, he wouldn't think twice.

He heard aides shouting. "Senator's coming!" Then, a minute later, "He's in the lobby! He's in the elevator!" Henry joined a gaggle in the main spaces.

Peele sauntered in, wrapped in a gray houndstooth suit and red tattersall shirt that didn't quite work together. The others, grinning like paparazzi, didn't seem to notice, or care. What it must be like to be so self-assured, so comfortable with power, so damn good-looking, a TV star turned governor and senator, your staff along with the rest of the world falling over itself to kiss your ass.

Peele smiled and shook his head like the guest at a surprise birthday party, both pleased and embarrassed by the attention. "Don't you people have anything to do?"

Peele met Henry's eyes, projecting a gaze that said Henry was the focus of Peele's world. Part of a politician's arsenal, but Henry still felt the warmth.

"I'm going to testify on the House side at two," Peele said, looking at him. "You come with me."

"Yessir." Henry felt his face flush, as though heated by the others' glares.

Peele squinted at a middle-aged couple standing toward the back of the room. "Do I know you?" he asked. It was a polite way of asking, *Who the hell are you and why are you in my top-secret operations center?*

The man took a half step forward. He looked like a Nebraska farmer in his Sunday best, maybe the only suit he had ever owned, "to be married in and buried in," as one Iowa farmer had once described his own Sunday attire to Henry. The woman, thin and sinewy in a print dress and a turquoise and silver necklace, the kind sold at Indian reservation gift shops, reached for the man's hand.

A young woman jumped in front of the couple. "Senator," she said, her voice almost breaking, "these are my parents. It's their first time in Washington, and I just wanted to show them where I work. It's my fault for bringing them here."

Peele nodded and looked at his watch. "It's Wisconsin day at the Senate Dining Room. I hear they've got a decent cheese soup. Do you all have lunch plans?"

The daughter looked about to cry. Senators took top VIPs to the Senate Dining Room in the Capitol. Henry imagined sitting with his own father and Peele in the ornate sanctum, the old man taking it in, impressed.

Peele headed toward the back, where Diane Spriggs, the campaign manager, was standing outside an office. Pushing forty and puffing out on a big frame, Diane had adopted the matronly look, a shorn afro and frilly blouses and neckerchiefs, in blue and salmon that day.

Shortly after Peele left, Burr phoned. The reporter sounded wired, firing words in staccato bursts.

"Bill, how can you print rumors that even you acknowledge everybody denies?" Henry asked. "The *Globe-Times* get bought up by the *National Inquirer*?"

"Hey, we're a newspaper of record. What people say about a candidate for president is news. It's news!" Burr's words raced ahead of the thoughts, clipping final syllables. "I let Peele give his side. So don't try to shoot the messenger."

"Next time, call *me*," Henry said.

He padded down the corridor, a thirty-foot strip of carpet that felt like a mile, to the big offices at the back. He knocked on Cass's doorframe, waited for the bald head to look up from the desk, and reported on Burr's call.

The Angel scowled. "Get your old boss to write a letter we can use to build an Iowa steering committee. You've worked for both these pinkos. You know their lingo. Vile race of quislings. Put something together that sounds like Tyler, but hits the points Peele wants to make. You know, the country needs to be governed from the center, extremism is unhealthy, all that subversive liberal crap."

"Subversive liberal crap. Got it." He smiled, but Cass stayed deadpan. "What does a steering committee steer?"

"You kidding?" Cass grinned. "Doesn't steer anything. Doesn't do anything. We put a checkbox on fund-raising letters inviting donors to join the committee. They feel important and we look like we got a wide, deep bench."

3

***

WAYS AND MEANS

At a quarter to two, Tom Peele halted at a receptionist's desk in his Russell Building anteroom to grab a ringing phone. It was the main number, probably a constituent. Good to keep your fingers on the pulse of the people.

"Senator Peele's office," he said. Sterba and Hatten stared at him from the doorway. His receptionist, a beef-packing scion, gawked.

A young man's voice, the words caked in a heavy drawl, began a saga about losing veterans benefits and getting put on the street; he was a Gulf War vet, fought for his country in Iraq, now couldn't use one hand, Purple Heart.

"Wait, slow down," Peele said. "Where are you calling from? Lexington, as in Lexington, Kentucky?" He sighed. "You want Senator Paul's office. This is Senator Peele's office."

He looked at his aides. Sterba was in a topcoat. Nobody had time for this. But the guy on the phone was real, unlike the rest of this theater. "No, I'm not going to pass you off," he told the man. "Go through it again for me, but slowly this time." He snatched a memo pad off the receptionist's desk and began scribbling notes. "Okay, Ben, we'll see what we can do. Hang in there, buddy."

He stepped through the great mahogany doorway, framed by his brass-embossed name and the Nebraska state seal, and into the marble corridor. Sterba shut the door, like a disapproving parent. Hatten fell in, at a respectful distance.

"Dartmouth!" he called to Hatten. "You're not the footman. Come here."

Hatten trotted up, smiling.

Peele handed the scribbled note to Sterba. "Fix this VA problem for this guy," he said. "If you need me to call the secretary of veterans affairs, I will."

"I'll see you tomorrow, Tom," Sterba said, sliding the note into a pocket.

"Big high school football game on public access this afternoon?" Peele asked. "Walk with me a minute, Mike."

"This isn't just some acting scene," Sterba said as they reached the balustrade. "You've got to watch your six, Tom; your back."

"Performing, not acting," he corrected. "Acting is when you play somebody else. Performing is when you play yourself. In Washington, I perform."

Sterba made a face.

"Have a good day, Mike," he said. "Dartmouth here can . . . watch my six."

He liked to take at least one aide when he walked through the Capitol complex, as a buffer against the aging groupies and autograph hounds and the tourists, reporters, protestors, lobbyists, and gadflies. Either that or stride, head forward and jaw tight, as though rushing to a summit on nuclear strikes. It might have been easier just to drive across the Capitol to the

Longworth House Office Building, but he enjoyed navigating the network of tunnels and trams that connected the three Senate office buildings to the Capitol, and the similar network on the House side.

Mike made a great escort. Despite cuff links, pocket square, and wingtips, the guy looked like he could rip your head off. He didn't like to stand with Mike in public, though; his chief of staff dwarfed him. Hatten was a little smaller than he was, and radiated an earnest zest; he'd make a good traveling aide.

With the first steps down the Russell Building corridor, Peele found his breath growing short. He inhaled hard, his chest swelling, but couldn't fill his lungs. Asthma. Again. He reached for the ProAir rescue inhaler in his jacket pocket, gripped the metal cylinder, but he'd just taken a hit before lunch, and you weren't supposed to overdo the thing. A morning blast of Advair, a bronchodilator, usually got him through the day, but he'd been sucking more on the rescue inhaler recently.

The tightness came with changing weather, stress, exercise, secondhand smoke, even thirdhand smoke, breathing the heavy metals that clung to nicotine addicts. Sometimes his breath tightened for no apparent reason. It was maddening, not being able to fill your lungs; you couldn't concentrate on anything else. Peele pictured his airways swelling like a moist, lumpy pink life raft, inflating in on itself. Must be stress; his body knew even if his mind thought he was controlling it.

Even before the sound of Sterba's massive wingtips tapping the marble had faded, they hit the first roadblock. A dowager from Potomac, Maryland—rocks, gold, and face paint—waved and lumbered into his path. He'd chatted with her about Beckett at an Arena Stage opening a few months earlier, tried to explain nihilism.

"I was on my way to your office," she warbled, and he knew

this would cost him at least two minutes of his life. She was trying to line up sponsors for a fund-raiser. "It's a wonderful cause," she said with a continental lilt. "And I know how much of a friend you are, Senator, of natural preservation." He didn't say anything, and she went on. "And the historic park is only a half hour from Capitol Hill."

"So you're looking for remarks, not just a drop-by."

"Oh, yes," the woman said. "Certainly, we'd like you to speak." She paused. "And could you wear your uniform from television, or at least the hat?"

"Excuse me," he said, and stepped around her.

Maybe Ranger Roy was his natural role, and governor, senator . . . president were the stretches. He angled his head toward a flowing marble staircase; they would walk the three flights to the basement. They moved in silence, rounding a corner into a Dirksen Building corridor that had been sandblasted to expose redbrick walls. They passed a display case outside the Senate library. Warren Harding, in a detachable Windsor collar, glared in glossy black-and-white from a hardcover.

"Harding was elected president because he looked like a president," Peele said, his breath coming easier now. Peele's hair looked at least as good as Harding's white mane, his jaw was just as strong, and his chin was better. The lecher, maybe best known for siring a bastard daughter on his office couch, was the first sitting senator to win the White House, and a Midwest Republican. In two years, Peele could be the next.

"People don't vote for you," he said, turning to Hatten. "They vote for the character you play. For the image, the icon, the Mattel action figure." The worst part was, after a while, you never really knew if what you were doing was you or the role you were playing.

He spotted a men's room. After ten years in the Senate, he knew every head in the complex. He always carried a bottle of hand sanitizer, but a good scrub with soap and water worked best. The hands he routinely shook had probably picked noses, wiped bottoms, held doughnuts, and clasped other filthy mitts.

"First rule of politics," he said. "Never pass a men's room; you never know when you'll get another chance."

He stepped to a sink, washed, and pulled out a pocket comb. His salt-and-pepper hair was turning all salt. Distinguished, or just old? By the time he planted his feet at a urinal, Hatten had stepped away, giving him a respectful berth.

"Henry," he called, unzipping, "you should always wash *before and after* you go." He relaxed, and released a stream, not a river. It took him longer these days.

Over the splash, he said, "Mike's kicking mostly because Gil arranged today's adventure."

Hatten came closer, to hear. Not close enough to see; the kid had manners.

He inhaled and pushed, accelerating the stream. "Sterba's a good goose-stepper; keeps the trains running on time." He breathed. "But I need everybody to drink the Kool-Aid now."

Hatten gave a faint nod. Peele had hoped for a "Yessir!" At a sink, as he was rescrubbing his hands, Hatten stepped close.

"Mike Sterba would take a bullet for you, Senator. Tom. Not that you need me to defend your chief of staff to you." Hatten's face was pink. What passion. Could he also count on that loyalty?

"Maybe." He turned off the faucet and reached for a paper towel. "Everybody has an agenda." He balled the soggy paper, shoved it into a refuse slot, and shook his head.

Sterba smelled something wrong, some connection between Peele's testimony today and the Omaha Teamster stuff, but hadn't yet asked, or pressed, maybe didn't really want to know. Or maybe Mike was just assuming some sinister connection.

Sterba's antenna went up anytime Cass stuck that bald head into Senate stuff. "Cass," he said, as much to himself as to Hatten. "Sometimes I wonder who's working for whom."

He closed his eyes and concentrated, an old acting exercise he liked to run when he found himself in spots like this. He took a step outside of himself, now a disembodied presence hovering atop the tile wall. He asked himself, like a viewer watching a cliffhanger television scene, "How is Tom Peele ever going to get out of this one?" He smiled, eager to watch the rest of the episode. Because somehow, every devoted viewer knew, Tom Peele always escaped.

He pulled the rescue inhaler from his jacket pocket, took a deep hit, and held it. He'd had asthma as a kid, seasonal, bad during the summers, okay after the first frost. When the asthma came back a year ago, after a balls-out, ninety-minute workout on a treadmill and weights in a dank Atlanta hotel basement, he should have stopped at the first sign of tightness, but he'd gutted through the workout, and gone back to the dank gym the next morning for more. After that, he couldn't walk a flight of stairs without gasping. He should sue the hotel, but that would mean making a public stink about his condition, not what you need in a presidential campaign.

The doc had put him on Advair 500/50 twice a day, the highest possible dosage. But the meds did something to his vocal cords, making his voice faint and high. Giving one speech, he sounded like he was going through puberty. They had gradually lowered the dosage, and he was now at the minimum, one morning blast of Advair 100/50, which he insisted, as much to himself as to the doc, was just fine. When he had pressed for a cure, the doc told him, "Once an asthmatic, always an asthmatic." The doc said he might outgrow the symptoms, but they just didn't seem to be going away.

He turned to Hatten. "Yeah, Ranger Roy has asthma. All that jumping out of planes and wrestling bears, who'd believe it?"

On the tram to the Capitol, alone in a car, Hatten asked, "Is there anything I need to inoculate us against?"

"Stick with me, kid," he said. "You'll be farting in silk."

From the Capitol, the trip felt like traveling from Beverly Hills to East L.A. On the Senate side, they walked a crimson-carpeted corridor lined with gold-framed oil portraits. Faint scents of brass polish and linseed oil tickled his nostrils. The scent of royalty. Past the rotunda, entering the House side, they hit institutional-yellow walls plastered with entries in an annual high school art contest.

"Make you feel homesick, this side of the Capitol?" he asked. "I always thought LBJ had it right; the difference between the Senate and the House is the difference between chicken salad and chicken shit."

Hatten met his gaze. "Mr. Tyler said, 'Same circus, bigger tent.' That's why he ran for governor."

Peele smiled. The kid needed a civics lesson. The House and Senate were two completely different circuses. The House, with 435 members, was a zoo that had to run by strict majority rule to keep any hope of order. The 100-member Senate was a bastion of gentility that glorified the individual and enshrined minority rights, allowing any senator to speak as long as they liked in debate, and to filibuster, holding up the Senate, the Congress, the entire federal government, if they chose.

The Senate oozed history, and he savored his part in it. On the floor, he sat at a mahogany desk with a snuff box and ink-well and a drawer in which his predecessors had carved or scrawled their names, going back a century. He had actually gotten chills the first time he stepped onto the floor and got a number—his place in the continuum going back to the Founders, heir to Daniel Webster, Henry Clay, John C. Calhoun.

Really too bad, though, he came to the Senate in the worst possible way, as a former governor. You just can't enjoy being a junior senator after being chief executive of a state, with an army of staff, a massive budget, a mansion, even a state police escort. Now at least he had some seniority, but he was still pursuing an agenda, not setting one. A CEO spot, and the top one, that's what he wanted. Plenty of history there, too.

He was about to tell Hatten that he had yearned to be governor, a chief executive, since a sixth-grade trip to Lincoln. He had tried it out for the first time that night, chanting to himself in his boyhood bedroom, "Governor Peele." But then he remembered that Hatten knew about the "Call me governor" bit with the screamer in the Amsterdam Avenue flat; one of his roommates must have been talking. He had been tempted a few times, for kicks, to ask Susan to call him "Mr. President." But he already had enough friction with his wife.

He breathed deep, expanded his chest to that satisfying point when the air sacs filled. "Just saying the words, 'I'm running for President of the United States' is an awesome act. The sheer gall, to stand up and say you can lead the free world better than anybody else."

"I wouldn't have signed on if I didn't think you could," Hatten said.

"Don't be a suck-up, Dartmouth. But if you're going to be, go all the way. You're damn right I could. That's a fact; no 'think' about it. The world needs me. They just don't know it yet. That's your job, convince them."

Hatten smiled, as though half agreeing, half humoring him.

"Executive action?" Peele said. "Look at my record as governor. I was way ahead of the curve on restoring felons' civil rights, creative use of tax policy to go green, health insurance expansion. Add it up, Dartmouth."

"You know, the way you call me 'Dartmouth,' it's as though you're amazed I got in there." Hatten was glaring at him.

He wondered, every day, how his life would have turned out if he'd graduated from Columbia. Instead of dropping out midway through sophomore year, after his father's accident, when the farm went bust. He might be like those Ivy Club, Porcellian, and Skull and Bones assholes in the cloakroom. But then, his agent never would have discovered him hustling chess in Washington Square Park, and he never would have been cast Off Broadway as Hap Loman, and the rest of it.

"Don't be so serious," he said, softly. He put his hand on Hatten's shoulder. "The only way we're going to get through this is to have fun."

As Peele stepped into the Longworth Building hearing room, a young House committee staffer led him to the witness table. A sensuous Ways and Means water pitcher, gleaming in black-and-white enamel with contrasting deco type, sat before a laser-printed nameplate. He turned and scanned the audience until he spotted the woman he had invited. In a muted print dress, wire-framed glasses over her weathered face, her hair pulled back, she looked like she'd stepped from *American Gothic*. He raised a hand in a half wave. She nodded, a hint of a stoic smile crossing her lips.

"It is my privilege to introduce our first witness, the distinguished junior senator from the great state of Nebraska, Thomas Pritchard Peele, Jr.," the subcommittee chairman, a wiry Idahoan, gushed from the dais. After reading Peele's letter in the *Washington Post* pushing for off-label coverage, to allow Medicare patients to take drugs for ailments beyond those for which the drugs were strictly intended, the chairman said, he knew his hearing to examine cost containment within Medicare on prescription drugs wouldn't be complete without the Senator's testimony.

The chairman had invited him, Peele knew, for the same reason chairmen generally invite high-profile witnesses: to get their hearings on TV. C-SPAN and CNN cameras were shooting from the wings. A gaggle of photographers crouched beneath the dais, clicking away. The chairman glowed. Peele nodded, almost a seated bow.

"Before seeking elective office, Tom Peele inspired a generation to public service as Ranger Roy Hearst in the television drama *Parkland*. The Forest Service actually saw a twofold increase in applications the year Senator Peele was nominated for an Emmy."

Jeez, why mention that? He didn't win the damn thing. The nomination was kind of maudlin, anyway. For his emotive mourning in a Very Special Episode in which a hermit character with whom he had a volatile, fraternal relationship refused to leave a mountain and died in a rockslide.

Finally, the chairman wound down and the green light went on.

Peele shifted and pointed at the graying woman. "Mr. Chairman, Margaret Mayhew traveled all the way from Mead, Nebraska, to be with us today. I've known Meg all my life. Her husband, Herman, used to fix me ice cream cones at the general store they ran in town. He'd always add a little extra, especially on the pistachio, which was my favorite. Six months ago, Herman died of cancer."

He turned to Meg. The stoic face was beginning to quiver. "Herman's doctor wanted to give him a drug called Ganadex. Ganadex was designed to fight stomach cancers, but a smart doctor found it also fights other types of cancer, like the one Herman had. The FDA told us Ganadex was safe. This drug can prevent our mothers and fathers, husbands and wives, sons and daughters, from suffering and dying one of the worst deaths you can die. The death Herman Mayhew died. With a stroke of a pen, we can fix all that."

He glanced back. Meg's jaw was trembling. "But a bunch of bureaucrats don't want to use that pen. They told Herman that Ganadex was off-label as far as his cancer was concerned. Medicare now covers cancer drugs, but it doesn't cover off-label drugs." He scanned the panel, making eye contact. "Now CMS—the Centers for Medicare and Medicaid Services—has the discretion to allow off-label coverage for a given drug, if there's peer-reviewed science to demonstrate that drug's effectiveness."

He looked at Meg. Tears streamed down one weathered cheek and then the other.

"Do these faceless bureaucrats have no sympathy, no understanding, that these drugs can actually save lives?"

What he didn't say was that if CMS takes a drug like Ganadex, intended for a fringe cancer with a small potential patient pool, and allows it to be prescribed for a mainstream cancer, it can mean a windfall for the drug maker, because a whole lot more people can now take the drug. And megabucks for anybody who has stock in the company. But the bureaucrats don't want to grant off-label coverage, because then the government has to reimburse a slew of patients and providers for experimental use of the drug.

The chairman tossed a couple of fawning questions, and the

ranking member and a couple of others tossed a few more. When the light turned red, and Peele stepped into the aisle, Meg Mayhew lurched over and hugged him, her bony body hard and light.

The chairman nodded to him; the C-SPAN cameraman was zooming in. Now, if the Ganadex scheme blew up, he'd also embarrass Ways and Means. The chairman wouldn't be so genteel about that.

4

★ ★ ★

PAW PRINTS

Asmack against the doorframe of his office jolted Henry from a chat with Fogel. He looked up to see Cass, wearing a chesterfield topcoat as a cape, the sleeves hanging at the sides.

"I wanted you to know, we—" Cass began, then stopped. The Angel pointed at a framed photo on Henry's desk. "That your cat?"

"Yeah, that's Walter."

Henry had gone to a shelter looking for a beagle, under Harry Truman's dictum that if you want a friend in Washington, get a dog. But Henry's work hours would give a dog separation anxiety, the shelter told him. So he took Walter. The tabby kitten seemed half-canine. Every night, he clipped a leash to the cat's collar and walked him along Connecticut Avenue, to the zoo and back. The wide orange head sniffed the air and the turf. He had named the cat after Walter Johnson, the Washington Senators' mild-mannered ace who hurled thunderbolts.

"I had a cat," Cass said, gazing off somewhere.

Henry waited.

"I got this big gas outdoor grill, fifty KBTUs. A lid it takes both hands to lift." Cass's face contorted into a baleful mask. "Some whack job lit the burners and threw Plato inside. You can see claw marks all over the inside of that lid."

Henry felt the silence pulsate off the walls.

"I have Plato's ashes in a rosewood box, in my living room," Cass said, seeming calmer now. "With a lock of his hair and a cast of his paw print."

A bell went off, piercing the silence, breaking the spell. Cass reached into a pocket of the Chesterfield coat and produced an iPhone.

As Cass jabbered into the phone, in what sounded like Italian, Fogel leaned toward Henry. "He still uses that grill," the media man whispered. Henry stifled a snort.

Cass soon flipped the phone shut and turned to Henry. For an instant, Henry thought Cass had overheard, and froze.

"Anyway, what I came for," the Angel said, the voice back to its usual high timbre. "Congratulations. You're officially communications director of the Peele Presidential Exploratory Committee."

The RNC honcho must have passed. It had all paid off. Henry had made it; he was The Man. The exploratory committee would become the presidential campaign as soon as Peele announced. And Peele would announce; the exploratory phase was just one step in the dance. Reporters quoted people at his level, producers put them on the air, and not just for what their bosses thought, but for what *they* thought. He wished somehow this scene could be broadcast, real-time, to all the banking scions who had scorned him at Trinity, to the little prick who had called him "Meathead" when he learned that Henry lived in Astoria, Archie Bunker's neighborhood. He saw Cass was looking at him, waiting for a response. Fogel, too. "Wow, Gil. Thanks." It was all that came.

Still, Henry thought, he hadn't necessarily dazzled Peele and Cass. They needed to fill the communications director post, to show progress and momentum, and may have settled for him, rather than making the effort to court another dream staffer like the RNC honcho. The campaign had short lists for at least a dozen senior staff jobs, people they needed in various states and at HQ. And a lot of the other presidential campaigns were going after the same pros.

Maybe Peele and Co. also figured Henry was safe, a Boy Scout who wouldn't even narc on an opponent's dope-selling son. A lot of prized staffers came with baggage, having alienated various groups in various states, sometimes just by sleeping around or copping an attitude. Whatever the calculus, it didn't matter now. They had chosen him.

"There are only a few jobs on this campaign that can get you laid, and you've got one of them," Cass said, turning to the door. "Don't waste it."

As soon as Fogel left Henry alone in his office, he pumped a fist. Then again, harder. He slid into a crouch and let out a guttural, atavistic, throat-scraping "Yeah!" And then another. *Yeah!*

He lifted the phone. He wanted to hear Fran's voice, had wanted to hear it for months. An image from their second meeting formed in his head, from a hotel bar where they plotted a budget hit against the Iowa governor. She wore a yellow T-shirt without a bra that night, nipples showing through cloth pressed tight against firm, slightly oval breasts. A trim but solid waist that flowed into wide, muscular hips. Cobalt eyes reading him as she told him to come up to her room to get some documents. He thought of the way she leaned into him as she unbuckled, the way she cried against his neck once, showing her face only after she had put her mask back on. And then, how she shucked him after the Denison drug-selling fiasco. He felt the rush fade. He wouldn't call. To Fran, their thing was just campaign sex, more release than romance. Her contract, in the end, had been only a contract.

An hour later, Henry was sliding folders into his desk in Peele's Senate press office in the Russell Building suite. The campaign shop would become his primary residence, but campaign and congressional would split his paycheck and, in theory, Henry would split his time between the North Capitol Street and Russell Senate Building suites, a few blocks apart. The desk phone blared with his first Senate call.

Tyler's former district director, Mary McCormick, spat his name through the receiver. Cass had assigned Mary to Peele's Des Moines campaign office, after Tyler had demanded a job for her and another aide as a condition of signing the endorsement letter Henry had penned. His smile died; his ear had expected lilting gratitude.

"Gil Cass waited until Doug's letter went out, and then he fired us," Mary said.

He rubbed his temple.

"Doug also gave you his donor lists, which he could have sold for eighty grand," she said, as though charging him with a crime. "And I know that because I was the one who sent them to you."

A minute later, as he was trying to figure out how to confront Cass, Henry got his second call on the Senate line, from the campaign scheduler. "The Senator wants you downstairs in fifteen minutes, in front of this building." She meant North Capitol Street.

"What's up?" he asked, more casually than he felt.

"He just said you should be downstairs," she said. She didn't seem to relish the intrigue, just wanted to move on to her next task.

Henry grabbed his suit coat. Minutes later, the silver Lincoln pulled to the North Capitol Street curb. A young aide whom Henry hadn't seen before, about thirty and African-American, sat behind the wheel. Henry met Peele's eyes through the glass and climbed in beside him.

"Just wanted to talk to my communications director," Peele said.

"Senator, I really appreciate your confidence."

"In Hollywood, the first person any actor hires is his press agent."

A wail sounded and Peele lifted a cell phone from the seat.

"You work fast, Larry," Peele said into the device. "That's terrific." The Senator cupped the phone and whispered to Henry, "Write this down."

Henry pulled out a pen and a copy of Peele's schedule. Since his first House job, he'd folded a copy of the boss's daily schedule into his shirt pocket. According to the sheet, Peele's next event, in ten minutes, was a speech to the National Ready-Mix Concrete Association.

Peele put the phone on speaker. A deep voice, as though from the netherworld, filled the cabin.

"Okay, in Seattle you call Mort Goldstein, and Mort's going to do sixty-five thou for you. And you're going to do a dinner with him." As Henry scribbled, the voice gave names and numbers for San Francisco and Los Angeles. The voice said it had talked to all these guys, and they knew they had to come through.

Peele flipped the phone shut. "That's AIPAC's top political guy. Larry's okay. I called him a couple of hours ago, told him about our West Coast trip, said we needed sixty thousand dollars in each city."

Henry knew the campaign was going after Jewish support. The American-Israel Public Affairs Committee seemed a good ally, and a step up from the Iowa Pork Producers Association that Henry had courted for Tyler.

Peele asked Henry for the San Francisco number and dialed, the cell phone back on speaker. Peele pantomimed to Henry to keep taking notes.

"Fred, you know, I'm going to San Francisco," Peele said into the machine, "and I'd like you to put together a lunch for me."

"Well, sure," a new voice said, higher than the first one. "You want it to be a fund-raising lunch or a get-to-know-you lunch?"

"Oh, you tell me," Peele said, innocent. "Do you think it's too soon to do a fund-raising lunch?"

Henry looked at Peele, who winked.

"*No*, you know what," the voice said, "I think I could do one for sixty K for you."

"That's great, Fred."

Peele's coalitions director, Henry knew, was already mailing to AIPAC's donor lists and had nearly locked a speaking spot for Peele at the group's annual convention. Peele's political team had been dissecting the electorate, figuring out which groups to cultivate. Peele was differentiating himself in the GOP primary field as a fiscal conservative and social libertarian, so Jews were a natural. The campaign was also going hard after moderate Republicans, especially in the Northeast, business groups, African-Americans, even labor.

The Lincoln pulled to the curb outside the downtown Marriott. Peele told the aide to leave the car with the valet and come along. Downstairs, in a burgundy and cream ballroom, Peele delivered a ten-minute version of his business stump speech. Peele was ad-libbing as he went along, Henry could tell, sprinkling references to concrete and heavy industry. But it was smooth. When Peele finished, meaty hands crashed together and pounded tables.

As they headed for the ballroom doors, Henry saw what looked like a burly guy in a corduroy blazer laying into Peele's driver. As they got closer, Henry heard the guy tell the kid, "I don't give a damn *who* you're waiting for, you don't block the damned door." Henry was about to slide between the two when Peele asked the aide, "Joe, what's the problem?"

"This kid's blocking my way, that's the problem," the man said. The guy was nervous, even scared, now facing Peele, Henry saw, but couldn't back down and lose face.

"I wasn't talking to you," Peele told the guy, keeping a kindly gaze on the driver. "What's the problem, Joe?"

"Well, Senator," the aide said, "I knew you were late for your next appointment, so I wanted to get you your briefcase, in case you wanted to call somebody. I was waiting for you at the door, but I didn't block the way."

By this point, several other concrete men had gathered. Henry wondered whether Peele would sacrifice his aide, now that all the goodwill was at risk.

Peele turned to the corduroy blazer, for the first time. "My man was doing just what he's supposed to do. *You* move out of the way."

Back in the Lincoln, Peele pored through a stack of newspapers. "Come to lunch," the Senator said, turning to Henry after plopping a copy of the *New York Times* on the floor. "You might find it interesting."

After watching Peele defend the driver, Henry felt an almost physical need to rescue Mary McCormick. He pulled Peele's schedule from his pocket. An entry in small bold type read "1 P.M.—Senate Dining Room—Chet Hopkins, Rae Karnes." Chet Hopkins was a hard-line televangelist with a national empire, part of a key bloc in the GOP. The guy railed about scheduling prayer in schools, restoring "traditional" marriage, and putting creationism at least on par with the hypothesis of evolution. But Hopkins's main crusade was outlawing abortion.

"Would you like me to call the Senate Dining Room and ask them to leave the knives off your table?"

Peele grinned. "I have lunch with these guys at least every couple of months. Did you see my legislation cleared committee to resettle Jews in Israel?"

Another light went on in Henry's head. Yeah, Peele had arranged close to $100 million, under a Health and Human Services program for displaced persons, to sponsor Jews who wanted to settle in Israel, mostly Holocaust victims and their descendants. Jews liked the program, but evangelical Christians loved it. Many evangelicals believed that Jews must return to Israel and rebuild the temple before the Messiah could come.

Henry had met the other name on the lunch list, Rae Karnes, at a fund-raiser. She was Peele's new conservative outreach coordinator. Cass had snapped her up when the right-wing senator she had been working for retired. By hiring her, Peele also adopted her book of business, or at least her Rolodex. At the fund-raiser, and presumably around the country, Karnes was telling her friends that she was with Peele now, and that she was okay with it because all those things they had worked on before were consistent with Peele's positions.

"Hopkins has an army," Peele said, shifting in the car seat to face him. "Forty thousand people go to his annual convention in Kentucky, and just spout off—conservative, pro-life values stuff. Then Chet tells them to go out, and those forty thousand people reach out to forty people each, and you have a national movement. We need to tap that movement."

Okay, it made sense. But how many evangelicals could they really convert? Then again, Peele seemed to be making progress building a coalition. The week before, Peele had announced an endorsement from a fireballing Arizona Diamondbacks pitcher turned Republican congressman, enlisting a serious African-American conservative with a massive e-mail list of supporters. Meanwhile, Henry could chart Peele's inroads with business by the burgeoning pack of trophies on the Russell Building credenza from the Chamber of Commerce, National Association of Manufacturers, Citizens Against Government Waste, Watchdogs of the Treasury. If it all went south, Henry wanted the huge marble eagle with wings spread.

In the Senate Dining Room, they settled under an oil portrait of John Nance Garner, FDR's first vice president, nicknamed "Cactus Jack." Finished in crimson carpet and drapes and sculpted crown molding, the chamber suggested an upscale private club, which Henry supposed it was. Hopkins spoke softly and gestured in tight, precise motions, suggesting senior executive more than TV firebrand.

When the menus arrived, Rae Karnes turned to Hopkins and recommended the glazed bacon and scallop salad, which she called "new-vayle cuisine." "The executive chef calls his style 'progressive American,'" she said, dropping the twang and narrowing her eyes. "You won't regret it."

Hopkins laughed and ordered the scallop salad.

Over Senate bean soup, Peele said, "Chet, I'd love to have a thirty-minute speaking spot at your annual convention. Just come down and meet those people and let them know what we're doing in the Senate. I think your members would be interested in what I have to say."

Within fifteen minutes, Peele got his speaking spot. Eventually, Hopkins offered, "We don't expect to endorse in the presidential contest this time, at least not before the early primaries."

"I appreciate that, Chet," Peele said, and reached for the bill.

Henry and Peele walked back to the Russell Building aboveground; Peele said he wanted some air. Waves of delight and despair crashed in Henry's head. Yeah, it was all so heady, as Fogel had promised. But Henry was supposed to spin these nuances, and he couldn't even grasp some of them. "Senator, I'm not sure I caught the whole thing about the endorsement."

"Hopkins is never going to endorse us," Peele said as they crossed Constitution Avenue, clearly pretending not to notice a pack of gawking tourists. "That'd be blasphemy. But one of my biggest donors, major Nebraska beef producer, is also a huge Catholic and a big Hopkins donor. So my guy called up Hopkins a few days ago and said, basically, 'Hey, Chet, that ten million I give you every year . . . that's from me, and my guy in this race is Peele. Take a hint.'"

"And your speaking at his convention, that wouldn't be a mortal sin for them?"

Peele shrugged and let Henry reach for the handle to a

heavy Russell Building door. "Hopkins can say, 'I didn't endorse Peele, but he asked to come speak, and I thought it was a
natural thing, given that the annual convention this year is in
Omaha.'"

Late that afternoon, as the taxi swung onto K Street, Henry
turned to Fogel in the backseat and said, "I'm going to tell Cass
that what he did with Tyler's people was bogus, and he needs to
make it right."

"No, you're not," Fogel said. "Or you can get out right
now."

Henry met Fogel's glare. This was the first time he had pissed
off the media man, and he wasn't sure how far to push it.

"Gil's just a power-hungry weasel," Fogel said, in a more
soothing tone. "Either he's doing something creepy or he's just
a creep. All campaign chairmen are Machiavellian."

Tyler's gubernatorial campaign, he realized, hadn't had a
chairman, just a manager who handled the daily grind and a
pack of rabid consultants who devised strategy, cut ads, and
gnawed off a chunk of whatever the campaign raised or spent.
Welcome to the big time.

"That doesn't mean Cass should get away with dicking over
some staffers," Henry said. He raised his hands as if to say, But
I won't make a stink about it in front of you.

Fogel's lip curled. "Gil may not even be in this campaign for
the reason you think."

"How's that?"

"He may have signed on with Peele to hurt Dagworth, just to
help Sadler." The media man wedged a hand into a jacket pocket,
apparently fishing for a wallet. "One of Gil's partners is running
Sadler's campaign, for Chrissake."

Three senators now formed the Republican field's first tier: Peele; Cliff Dagworth, a hard-right, Old South Virginian; and Jackson Sadler, son of a rodeo bull breeder turned Texas attorney general. Henry had trouble telling their two main rivals apart; only their accents seemed to differentiate the conservative dogma they each spouted. Both were essentially career politicians, now with the clout that came with Senate seniority; Dagworth chaired the Agriculture Committee and Sadler chaired the Environment and Public Works Committee. As Fogel had put it, "They're like Burger King versus McDonald's; it's fast-food politics. For consumers, it's the same stuff, no nutrition value at all."

"So you think Cass is some kind of double agent?" Henry asked.

Fogel yanked out a wallet and exhaled as though he had just extracted a bullet. "I got to get some bigger suits. Maybe Gil really does have Peele's best interest at heart," Fogel said, pulling out a ten. "Or maybe he's just waiting to see how the field shakes out before he commits."

"*Before he commits?* He's our general campaign chairman."

Fogel shrugged again, the big body heaving. "Hey, look, Gil is running this campaign about as well as it can be run. Even if he wants Peele to do just well enough to help Sadler beat Dagworth, he can't fine-tune the polls; it's not like fixing a basketball game."

"And you think the Senator's okay with that?"

"Peele figures he's so smart, he can just take Gil's good advice and ignore his bad advice."

The cab pulled to the curb outside a gleaming glass-and-limestone building. Another power corridor, but this one reeked of money, not just juice.

"You behave when we get upstairs now," Fogel said.

Henry nodded.

Upstairs, in the anteroom of Cass's political affairs shop, it was Fogel who got raw, as they stewed in matching leather chairs. After fifteen minutes, Fogel said, "Chairmen make you wait just to burn your ass. With a chairman, the only thing you have to figure out is whether you don't trust the guy because he's not trustworthy, or because that's just part of the adversarial process within a campaign. When I get off the phone with a campaign chairman, I assume the *gonif* is talking to four other people who are undermining me."

Henry smiled. Watching Fogel seethe somehow calmed him, as though the media man was absorbing the ambient heat.

A few minutes later, a receptionist with a British accent dispatched them down a corridor. As they reached Cass's office, the Angel stood behind a desk in the twilight glow of corner windows, a corona around the bald head. By a table piled with baubles, the campaign's finance chairman, in wire rims and a navy chalk stripe, was sipping a cloudy yellow drink over ice.

"Get you something?" Cass asked, coming around.

"No, I'm good," Fogel said.

Cass eyed the media man, as though he'd never before seen Fogel turn down food or drink.

Cass showed them some photos, including one of himself with the first President Bush on a yacht and another with former President Ford on a golf course. "Hold on a second," Cass said, and pressed a button on the desk phone.

A moment later, a twenty-something man appeared in a double-breasted suit, blond hair parted in the center bouncing as he strode.

"This is my aide, Skip," Cass said.

Fogel turned, found Henry by the far wall, and beckoned. As Henry stepped forward, Fogel said, "This is my aide, Henry."

Henry met Cass's eyes, half expecting an explosion. The Angel grinned.

Sitting before Cass's desk, Fogel reported on focus groups and scripts he was drafting and shooting. Cass mostly nodded and asked a few questions.

The finance guy sipped cold yellow syrup and admired the cityscape out Cass's windows. At one point the man turned and said, "Ira, your stuff all sounds kind of negative."

Fogel's neck reddened. "There was a news report, some archaeologists found a wall in Pompeii with the slogan, 'Vote for Vaddeus: All tax collectors are whore-mongers.' What was Pompeii, two thousand years ago? People were running negative spots in Pompeii!"

Fifteen minutes later, Cass stood. "Okay, Ira, thanks for coming by."

Henry stepped around toward the Angel. "Do you have a quick second, Gil?" Henry glanced at Fogel, like a pitcher checking a runner. The media man stayed at the desk.

Looking up at the V of bone under Cass's chin, Henry said, almost whispered, "Gil, Doug Tyler's former district director, Mary McCormick, is very upset at being fired from the campaign. She may make a stink—Tyler, the Iowa media, local buffaloes, she's plugged in out there." Henry could feel Fogel's stare. But he wasn't challenging Cass, which Fogel had forbid; this was all very polite.

Cass shifted and scrunched his lip.

"Here's what I propose," Henry continued. "Let's get Phil Eggert to tell Mary it was all a miscommunication—Eggert was the one who actually told her she was fired, after all—and that she's back on the job. Mary's really very good, and we can use the help in Des Moines." Eggert was their Iowa campaign director.

Cass shrugged, then waved a hand in a do-what-you-want gesture. "Anything else?"

"No, thanks much, Gil." Henry pivoted and rejoined Fogel.

As the oak-paneled elevator doors closed on them, Fogel reached into a jacket pocket and pulled out a beveled glass disc about the size of a hockey puck. The media man turned it so Henry could read the inscription: "Richard B. Cheney, Vice President of the United States."

Henry was pretty sure he had seen the paperweight on Cass's desk, beside a silver fountain pen. "What are you going to do with that?" he asked.

"I'll show you," Fogel said. When they reached the lobby, the media man found a large Chinese evergreen and slid the paperweight between the pot and the planter.

"I just like to think of Cass turning that spiffy office upside down searching for it," Fogel said as they headed for the exit. "I had to do something; it's like emotional graffiti." Fogel gave him a knowing look. "Thanks for the diversion."

5

★ ★ ★

GROUNDERS

As the Amtrak Acela climbed out of the Philadelphia station and into daylight, Peele dropped a newspaper from his lap onto the growing mound at his feet, removed his reading glasses and turned to Henry.

Henry was ready. He felt loose beside the boss, their knees inches apart. He could still feel the honeymoon glow; he should still have one free foul-up, which gave him some license.

As Peele began to speak, a "jumper" landed in the aisle by Henry's arm, a fortyish woman actually bouncing with excitement as she ogled the Senator.

"Tom, I'm your biggest fan," the woman gushed, gripping one hand in the other to still herself. "I watched every episode of *Parkland*. My favorite was when you saved that bear cub." She pulled a postcard and a ballpoint from a jeans pocket. "Could you sign, to Dawn?"

"I've got a new gig now," Peele said. "Saving the world."

Dawn just stood, quivering.

"Don't brag about a misspent youth, Dawn," Peele said, and handed back the card with a chicken-scratch salutation and signature.

Dawn squealed and dashed off.

"Senator," Henry said, "the whole world seems to know you from *Parkland*, and I've never seen the show. Do you have a tape I should watch?" He figured his unfamiliarity with Ranger Roy would earn points.

"Nope."

He met Peele's eyes, which stayed fixed, medium-wide.

"Try the network, or the Library of Congress," Peele said and turned to the *Times* business section.

Actually, Henry had watched most of an episode a few weeks earlier on a nostalgia cable station. He had cringed at the opening credits, when a young, grinning Peele snapped a salute to the brim of his Smokey hat as a caption popped, "And Tom Peele as Ranger Roy Hearst." But he found himself cheering as Ranger Roy bounded a Jeep after drug runners.

"How come you left?" he asked. Might as well spend his capital.

Peele looked up, the eyes narrowing. "Not getting the Emmy was a bummer. Until I realized it was more about L.A. politics. I decided if I was going to play politics, I'd play it for real." The Senator shrugged. "They made it easy. They gave me a script for a three-episode arc where Roy goes native, loincloth and all. I canceled my contract." Peele smiled. "Show went off the air the next year."

Before Henry could speak, Peele grimaced. "Tell me why I need to do this barking head's show tonight on CNN."

Henry chased the Ranger Roy image. "Carmody reaches a key demographic, the hip, politically tuned-in, underthirty set. It's CNN, so you get big exposure, buzz on Politico, The Hot-

Line, if you make news. We'll blast out tweets and texts, before and after, post on Facebook. And it shouldn't be too painful; I'm pretty tight with Carmody's producer, and she's a fan."

Peele clasped his hands. "And what news do you suggest I make, Mr. Hatten?"

"You told me you were thinking about holding a hearing on distributing condoms in Africa. You can talk about that."

Peele sucked his lip. "We make too much noise, we risk riling the Neanderthals, losing the funding."

"Then why hold the hearing?"

"To see whether it's the right thing to do."

Henry felt his forehead scrunch. "You know it's the right thing to do." All the science showed that condoms were the best way to stop third-world HIV transmission. And Peele was passionate on the AIDS-in-Africa issue. As chair of the State, Foreign Ops Appropriations Subcommittee, he had been pushing to increase shipments of HIV drugs to Africa, with bipartisan support.

Peele raised his eyebrows.

Henry exhaled. "Okay, I get it." The right-wingers wanted to ban U.S. funding for condom distribution. Peele was going to placate them by holding a hearing about the perils of sending rubbers to the world's poor. Then he'd quietly allocate the money.

"I agreed to do CNN, Dartmouth—Henry—because I don't like to turn down staff when they come to me with a request that's important to them."

He nodded. Now he was just "staff."

"Come up with something for me to say, and let's talk about it on the flight back."

Henry cleared the hot seat for the finance director and settled next to Peele's wife. Susan Peele glanced at him, then

dived back into a CEO's nostrum for corporate growth. On
the jacket, a relic in a yellow power tie pointed like Mussolini.
Susan sipped red wine and worked to steady the glass on her
tray, next to an empty one.

"Are you going to the meeting at the Plaza?" he asked, wanting to talk to her, not sure why. Peele was going to pitch some
money men that afternoon in New York.

Susan smiled and looked over. "No, I need to meet with the
rating agencies, for my job." She was CFO of a Midwest grain
company. "Tom said it would be nice to take the train together
to New York . . ." She motioned toward Peele, who was circling entries on a spreadsheet the finance guy was holding.
"I might as well have flown up last night."

Susan Peele reminded him of somebody. Then he realized
who. She was Fran Blackburn twenty years later. Taller and
more angular, but the same basic face. And the same passion
and drive in her eyes, but tempered by age or adversity. Susan
was Fran, domesticated.

"The *Monitor* spread was a big hit," he said. "Maybe we can
do more media." The *Des Moines Monitor* had run a profile of
Susan, Nebraska's former first lady and maybe the nation's next.
The paper's photo of Susan behind a power desk, an admin
handing her a folder, went over big in a focus group with the
sensible pantsuit crowd.

"Fine," she said. She took another slug of wine.

"We can put together a press kit for you. We can staff you
on the road, set up interviews remote, whatever you like." He
hadn't asked the Senator about drawing Susan further into the
campaign, but the Peeles could work that out between them.

She returned to the corporate titan's tome and they sat si-
lently for a few minutes.

"Did you know the Senator when he was doing *Parkland*?" he asked.

She looked up. "No, Tom and I got married a year after he became governor." She gave a pained smile. "Right before I met Tom, there was a big catfight at the Eppley charter terminal. One starlet arrived on a private jet as another was leaving; made the papers. Tom decided it was time to get serious. Or his campaign handlers told him it was time." She twisted the stem of the second wineglass, now empty. "Enter the stable corp fi junior exec. 'And Susan Clymer Peele as the first lady of Nebraska.'"

Two hours later, Henry gazed out a taxi window at Steinway Street, Astoria's main shopping strip, feeling like a returning conqueror. The car glided past screaming neon, discount banners, aging econoboxes, and slogging locals.

At the curb, he stretched a cap toe over a litter-strewn gutter, scraping its leather sole against the concrete. When he stood, the cuffed pants of his new blue pinstripe slid into place, with only the barest of a break. The suit was Brooks Brothers, a step up from his Mexican-made Jos. A. Bank, though not quite Cass's finery. Still, it was running up interest on his Master-Card.

He gripped the Cross Key Tavern's door handle, thumb poised on the latch. He peered through the old glass panel. Too filmy to see more than shapes. He breathed and yanked the door open. The bar looked unchanged since the seventies. Chipped paneling, Police Athletic League and American Legion trophies lining a shelf, letters and notices taped to the walls among framed photos of local sports teams. The air was stale and heavy with cooking grease. A few regulars hunched over shots and beers. One looked up and glared.

Henry walked the aisle, the old oak planks creaking, toward the burly figure in a flannel shirt and faded jeans.

His father pried a nacho chip from a mound slathered with congealed Monterey Jack and sour cream, wedged it in his mouth and licked two huge fingers.

Henry settled onto a bar stool. "Hey, Dad, you may want to take it easy on those chips. That's a heart attack on a plate."

His father swiveled to face him, squaring broad shoulders. "Jack's fresh out of broccoli." The old man gulped a glass of beer and eyed Henry's suit and starched white shirt. "Who died?"

"Good to see you, too, Dad."

The old man nodded. "Been what, six months? Let's hope your new boy doesn't blow up like your last one."

"Tyler didn't blow up. Anyway, Peele has a real shot."

"A *real shot*." His father snorted and leaned forward. Veins and sinew mapped the old man's flesh. In a few years, when his father retired, it would all sag and shrivel, leaving a turkey neck and knobby knuckles circled by dark green cords. He could see two cables in the neck already beginning to protrude when the old man talked, stretching folds of skin no longer elastic. His father wiped broad palms against denim thighs.

A bartender in a soiled apron and seen-it-all look came over.

"A Manhattan, please," Henry said.

"We're in Queens," his father growled. "Jack, get him a Miller." When the barkeep turned away, his father said, "Next time you meet me, lose the tie."

Henry checked his watch. "Dad, I can only stay half an hour. We're on the six thirty shuttle back to D.C., from LaGuardia."

"You just got here, you're already making for the door." His father dug fingers into the nacho pile, producing a large, jagged chip laced with cheese and sour cream. The old man had to angle his head to cram the shard in his maw. His father wiped his hands on his jeans again.

Henry leaned over and shoved the nacho platter down the bar, the ceramic bouncing along the scarred wood.

His father turned to him, eyes wide. "What's the idea?"

"Oh, I thought you were finished."

Henry spotted a vintage Air Aces pinball machine in a corner, with a red biplane on the backglass, mechanical score counters, and massive pop bumpers. He stepped over.

"Hey." His father beckoned like a traffic cop. The old man had been using that gesture for thirty years, since Henry was an infant, and it usually preceded a hug. Something triggered inside him, making him want the boyhood comfort of the big arms and the grizzled chin. When he didn't move, his father stood and waved again, this time mouthing the words "Come here." He pushed off the machine. The old man had four inches and fifty pounds on him, and draped a heavy flannel arm around his neck, letting a hand dangle past his shoulder.

"Listen," his father said, leaning in, breath all nachos and beer. "I watched your boy on a talk show. You want some advice from an old shop steward, he's gotta *relax*. It's like he's trying too hard to sound smart, make up for all that time on TV with Yogi and Boo-Boo." His father shrugged, which tightened the hold, a flannel shoulder rubbing Henry's chin.

Their faces were inches apart. Henry tried to smile, but couldn't, not in the old man's grasp. Where was his rage at having his movement restricted, after all the years on the mat? Maybe he had softened in Washington. Political fights weren't physical. He dipped his shoulder, creating space, and took a deep breath.

His father kept the grip. "You couldn't swing it for me to meet your boy, as long as he's in town? I could have put on a tie."

"The schedule's tight, Dad. I was barely able to get away while he's meeting with some money guys."

"What is it, you ashamed of your old man?" His father brought the dangling hand to life and squeezed the cap of his shoulder.

He pivoted out of the hold and walked back to Air Aces. His father's glare seared his back. Every campaign trip put him in a battle for Peele's time with the finance and organizational directors, as Henry pressed to slot news conferences, interviews, and editorial boards and they pushed for fund-raisers and heavy-hitter meetings. If he'd asked for ten minutes for Peele to meet his father, after they finished laughing, they would have made him trade CNN.

"Hey, I asked you a question!" His father was still standing.

One of the regulars looked over, white hair over red jowls.

"You never invited me to Washington to meet your buddy Tyler," his father said, softer. "Now your new boy comes to New York, you don't invite me to meet *him*."

Jack plopped a mug of beer on the counter.

Henry stepped over. "Dad, I don't want you to see me as anybody's lackey, even a senator's."

The old man brightened and nodded. "All right, I can understand that. See, when we talk things out, we can understand each other."

Henry felt all the worse for his lie.

"You know," his father said, "this career of yours, you're like that cartoon guy in a lake, jumping from one alligator's back to another. You're past thirty. You think maybe it's time to find something stable, get vested?"

"Nature of the game, Dad. What do you want me to do, climb into some corporate hole, just to make a buck?"

His father shrugged. "Like I always told you, do what you want. Just don't come to me for handouts when I'm on a pension."

"Dad, I'd rather starve than hack away at some nothing job."

His father shot a look that would once have meant the promise of a backhand. "I'd left you in P.S. Eighty-four, you'd be lucky to *get* a nothing job. Taking off from work, dragging my ass all over the city taking my *gifted and talented* boy to *prep school* interviews."

Henry rested his head on a fist, waiting for his father to wind down.

"Awright," his father said, waving a hand as though to clear the air. "But I don't see it, you in politics. You knew Ray, lived down the block, used to be a district councilman—until he copped to skimming construction money. And he wasn't any worse than anybody else; he just got caught, poor dumb dago bastard. But you, you've kept your skirts clean your whole life, except a few schoolyard scraps. You won't even sneak in the back of a move theater."

He breathed. "Dad, it's about the president signing a bill that has language in it that you wrote. It's about picking up the *New York Times* and seeing yourself quoted on something you believe in. And no offense to your neighbor Ray, but the Senate and the presidency is the major leagues, and it's different from the bushers."

His father gave a dismissive snort. He wondered if he had inherited the gesture and made a mental note to stop using it. He checked his watch.

"Betcha haven't had a real slice of pizza in years," his father said. "There's a good place right down the block. Come on, you can be on the road in twenny minutes."

"Twen-*tee*," Henry whispered, louder than he intended.

"What's that?"

"Twen-*tee* minutes. Not *twenny*. Just trying to help you out."

His father gave another family snort. "Yeah, now I can see you in politics. Son, it's what you say that counts, not how pretty you say it."

He stepped up to the old man, close enough to smell the nacho breath. "Yeah, you sure do say it straight, Dad." The words were bursting out. "Remember when Mom found out you were banging some skank, and she told you to take your whores and go to hell, and you yelled back that it'd be an improvement over our place. Remember? You didn't come back for a week that time."

That was the last time Henry had heard his mother shout. After that, she lay mostly silent in her hospital cot in the living room, gazing at the television, an unkempt mass giving off an odor of balm and meds. She died a few months later, on a rainy fall morning, when he was twelve.

"You don't know the whole story," his father said, the voice mostly air. The old man stepped back. "And I'm not going into it, out of respect for your mother's memory."

"Well, that's fine," Henry said. He hopped off the stool and turned toward the door.

"Wait a minute, where you going?" His father's paw was on his upper arm.

Without looking, he reached his free hand across and laid it on his father's, his thumb finding the groove between the bones leading to ring finger and pinkie. Gently, he twisted the meaty hand back against the wrist, a basic aikido move, breaking his father's grip.

As he reached for the doorknob, the old man called, "That's right, leave. Quit. Just like when you were a kid."

What was his father talking about? The grounders? A generation earlier, his father had taken him to the 28th Avenue playground on Sundays and drilled him on dribbling a basketball, tossing a spiral, snapping a curveball, hitting, fielding. Henry was lousy at gloving the skidding baseballs his father tossed at his feet, and the old man just threw them harder, telling him he'd be picked last when the other kids chose sides for a game, until Henry finally threw down his mitt, in tears. When he got home, his father told him that quitters never win, and that he was a loser. He vowed then never again to cry, and he hadn't.

Henry dropped his arm from the doorknob, sighed, and turned back to face the old man. They wound up in the pizza place, which had been a Greek take-out joint when Henry was growing up, splitting a peppers-and-onions pie that had been reheated too often. Across scratched Formica, the old man told him stories about neighborhood characters, maybe hoping to channel a formative time.

The old man did awaken memories, as they gnawed dough. As an escape from Astoria, Henry had turned to wrestling. The practices kept him at Trinity until past five, and the strain was cathartic, the sweat and tension and pounds burning off, the thrill of his growing power to dominate others. He had the build for it, a long, powerful torso and relatively short legs on a five-ten frame; a lithe ape's body made for the mat. Winning the starting 148-pound spot in tenth grade also gave him cachet on campus, which grew as he placed third in the state. He even developed a wrestler's swagger, his heavy arms swinging at his sides.

He had never brought friends from Trinity to the Newtown

Street row house. When his father asked why, he said his class-mates lived in Manhattan and couldn't make the trek. When he was a junior, his father got four tickets to a Giants game and insisted on taking him and two of his friends. He invited a couple of fellow wrestlers, kids who had little personality off the mat, were into sports, and would probably appreciate the invite.

They piled into his father's Chevy Impala wagon and headed to the Meadowlands. The 129-pounder laughed at his father's horn-honking highway bluster. Then the Giants blew a fourteen-point lead, launching the old man onto his feet with a cigar and trooper cap, hollering at the Giants and their quarterback, "You bums! You hear me, Simms, you're a bum!"

For days at Trinity, kids leaped at him, shouting in mock bass voices, "You're a bum! You hear me, Hatten, you're a bum!"

When Henry visited friends' houses, the biggest difference was the quiet. The other kids' parents never shouted. The other dads wore broadcloth shirts and silk ties at dinner. They ban-tered about Hampton homes and a couple of them, especially after cocktails or port, spewed a smug, playful sarcasm that said they ran the world and so, one day, would junior.

And, of course, the Central Park West and Park Avenue co-ops made the Newtown Street row house look like the dive it was. And the artwork. Oils, framed charcoal drawings, ab-stract sculpture. Henry's mother had bought their living room centerpiece, a floral still-life print, at a Bombay Company fac-tory outlet because the color matched their carpet. Henry could tell some of the West Siders didn't have real money, but they all seemed to grasp the art of living, and he wanted—needed—to learn if he was going to get anywhere at Trinity, and beyond. And eventually, he did. A couple of years ago, another neighborhood kid who had made good introduced him, saying, "This is my friend Henry. He used to be from Queens."

Over a third slice, Henry glanced at his watch. He felt a blinding flash and pulse. A minute later, at six oh five, he was trotting up Steinway Street, debris scraping and gouging his cap-toes, as he waved down a cab. He had twenty-five minutes until Peele's shuttle left. By the time the taxi lumbered onto the Brooklyn-Queens Expressway, he had seventeen minutes.

"I gotta make dis flight," he begged, the stress sliding him into Queens-speak.

The driver, a fiftyish Indian or Pakistani on a beaded seat cushion, seemed moored in an inner peace. "I am going as fast as we can," the man said. "It is rush hour, you know."

He expelled air and yanked his BlackBerry from its holster.

The campaign receptionist couldn't seem to grasp his message. "So you're not going to make the flight?" she asked. "You were supposed to staff the Senator, but you're not going to?"

"That's right," he snapped, doubling over in the seat. "Please just tell him I have some ideas for what he can say on CNN tonight, and I can call him, or I'll have my BlackBerry and he can call me."

"O-*kay*," the aide sang.

Arriving at Reagan National, Henry jogged into the terminal, his pulse pounding in his ears, his throat dry, his legs straining as though plowing through water. He found a lounge just beyond the gates and begged the bartender to tune the TV to CNN. He checked his BlackBerry again. No messages from Peele. He had left three for the Senator.

When members of Congress yelled at you, Henry had found, at least they thought you were redeemable. Stupid but trainable. When they ignored you, or beseeched the heavens for reprieve from your failures, you had to worry about your clout, and even your job. He ordered a Manhattan and chewed his index finger until the drink arrived.

The show came on in a couple of minutes. Carmody lobbed softballs, which Peele could have whaled in any number of directions. Instead, Peele answered as though under cross-examination, then sat with hands clasped, waiting for the next question. Carmody asked about alternative medicine, and Peele replied, "You can't treat alternative and complementary therapies as monolithic, equating faith healing with chiropractic. Some approaches have more promise, and more basis in science, than others." It was as though Peele wanted to blow the interview.

Well, the honeymoon was over. If he was lucky, the marriage was still intact. He yearned to talk to Peele, to salvage his standing, and dreaded it. Around nine thirty P.M., just as Henry stepped into his Cleveland Park condo, the call finally came.

"Tom wants to rip off your head," Cass began. "But I told him we just needed to slice off your balls."

"Yeah," he said.

"You're running with the big dogs now," Cass said. "You're just a communist intellectual amateur, but you got to try to act professional."

"Yeah," he said.

"Consider your balls cut off. Freedom and prosperity."

6

★ ★ ★

GANADEX

At his campaign office desk, Tom Peele waited for his chairman to sit. Cass, like a lot of big men, seemed to enjoy glaring down at the world, and especially at patrons.

"I don't know why you got your panties in such a wad," Cass said, folding into a chair, careful not to bruise a lustrous blue pinstripe suit.

He inhaled deeply. A test. His chest swelled until he hit the satisfying lungs-full point. "Zabriskie is concerned," he said. "Some other Teamsters are concerned. I told a Ways and Means subcommittee, basically, that Medicare should cover Ganadex for every cancer known to man. Any day now, some trucker in Omaha with an ear hanging off his head may march into the *Globe-Times* or the county attorney's office and say the whole thing's a scam. Which it isn't, because the drug actually works, but nobody's going to care about that. And the only silver lining, maestro, if it happens this week, is that then I won't have to go to the fund-raiser for your nitwit client from Arkansas."

"Tom, will you calm down?" Cass shifted in the chair. A buzzer sounded from somewhere within the blue suit, and Cass reached into a pocket. The Angel produced an iPhone and held up a finger.

"*Oui, Jacques,*" Cass said into the device. "*Alors, dites lui, trois cent mille, ou rien. Oui. Liberté et prospérité.*"

Peele rolled his eyes. Cass had been grousing that the campaign wasn't paying him enough to drop other clients.

Cass pocketed the phone. "If somebody does connect the dots, nobody but Zabriskie has any proof." Cass scanned the office, a Sheetrock box slathered in generic off-white paint, and lowered his voice. "And he won't say anything, right? Old Ed is *your* nitwit buddy."

He smiled at a memory. "Ed arranged for me to load sandbags during a flood when I was governor, and rescue evacuees. You can't buy that kind of publicity." He shook his head.

"Nobody in the union is going to squawk," Cass said. "They're sitting on a boatload of Western stock. The company crashes, the union pension fund goes belly-up."

"I'm going to have to meet with the Teamsters in Omaha, calm them down," he said, Zabriskie's nervous growl rattling in his head. "The carpenters, the plumbers. Everybody that reporter has been spinning up."

Cass shrugged.

"Maybe I shouldn't have testified before Ways and Means," he said. "To that point, all I'd done was write an op-ed in the *Post.*" He grimaced before Cass could say anything. "Nah, a no-show would have raised even more questions, made it tougher to get the off-label coverage."

A beep went off inside the rich blue suit, and Cass pulled the iPhone and waved and jabbed a finger at the screen.

"Not that you care," Peele said, "but it would actually help a lot of people, letting them get those meds. Poor people. Sick people." He pictured Herman Mayhew, and Meg.

"Sure," Cass said. "You'll be a hero. Everybody's gonna be grateful. Western Pharmaceutical execs are gonna write us some big checks. And they're gonna put your lovely and charming wife on their board of directors." Cass leaned in. "That's right. Susan will make twenty G's a month for doing not much. That'll get her off the rag, and off your back."

And the Omaha Teamsters would sell their Western stock and write a big check to a 527 corporation, which would spend the funds on Peele's reelection. A win-win-win. He waved an arm. "None of it matters, anyway, maestro. Everything we do, in the grand scheme, it's all bullshit."

Cass sucked his lip. "You took Hatten with you to Ways and Means, right? Next, you take him with you when you meet with the Nebraska union guys. Then, if it blows up, we say Hatten set up the whole thing. He's tight with that fat slob Iowa AFSCME president, guy practically bankrolled Tyler's whole pinko campaign."

Peele groaned. "Let's hope it doesn't come to that. And by the way, being to the left of Attila the Hun does *not* make somebody a pinko."

7

★ ★ ★

RETURN TOUR

On a crisp March morning of banners, signs, bullhorns, and buttons, of hope and jubilation, Henry stood at the front of the crowd as Peele mounted a riser before the Washington Monument and prepared to end the four-month kabuki and declare his candidacy. They had prolonged Peele's "exploratory travels" foreplay as long as they could. For Henry, the dance had grown absurd and almost obscene, as he coyly refused to say when or if Peele would decide to run, mostly because campaign finance rules would then limit their spending.

Henry felt a tug on the sleeve of his new Brooks Brothers trench coat and turned to see Miles, a bearded wire service stringer who fed Washington process stories to the *Lincoln Star* and a few other Nebraska and Kansas dailies. An hour earlier, he had refused to grant Miles a solo interview with Peele. Now, as the band swelled, the guy bleated that he had covered Peele dutifully, religiously, for two years. Now the national media had descended, and it wasn't right for Henry to favor the bigfoots over the stalwarts. Miles's face was crimson, and Henry noticed, first with surprise and then revulsion, that the man was crying. The guy wouldn't last a day on the other side, in Henry's line, doing what Miles now critiqued and criticized. Miles wiped a sleeve at the stream, before it reached the thick facial hair.

"All right, Miles, afterward come walk with Peele to the car. How's that?"

The newsman sniffled and nodded.

So far, so good. The generators were sending enough juice for all the TV lights and mics, the multiboxes hadn't melted down, and the cameramen weren't shoving each other off the risers. The rain was holding off, and no terrorist attack or other breaking news had diverted the reporters.

Henry counted some forty TV cameras and figured at least four thousand heads in a sea that stretched across the mall, all the groups of their coalition represented, accented by bobbing blue-and-orange "Peele for President" signs. Bankers and business types stood here, Jews there, blacks there, doctors and nurses, union guys and regular Joes there, Republican soccer moms, and *Parkland* fans across the social spectrum, all taking an hour off from the job or the kids, a seemingly spontaneous outpouring orchestrated by weeks of calls, e-mails, tweets, texts, and Facebook postings.

"America has always been governed from the center, and we forget that at our peril," Peele intoned, his voice booming across the mall on speakers the size of Volkswagens.

The phalanx of cameras snapped and rolled.

After the speech at the press gaggle, Henry edged close to Peele, to try to get into some of the shots. In the crush of a campaign, you collected mementos where you could, stepping out from the shadows occasionally to take a bow for all the sweat and stomach acid. He wasn't a whore about it, plastering his walls with clippings and photos the way some flacks did. And this was the big time; the world would see these images, maybe even Fran. He'd send the best one to his father.

They jetted to New Hampshire, Iowa, and Nebraska to repeat the ritual. The blogosphere flooded with "@PeeleforPres" tweets: Henry and his New Media whiz, a first-generation Taiwanese woman just out of Berkeley, pushing out message. The Peele-palooza dominated newspapers and newscasts. Shots and scenes from *Parkland*, including a still of Ranger Roy staring down a bison, filled the web.

Everywhere, Peele was mobbed. The Senator signed autographs without scolding, and grinned more the week after the announcements than Henry had ever seen any man grin. The euphoria was infectious. The North Capitol Street suite took on a festive air—except for Cass, who paced, scowling and muttering about complacent Bolshevik amateurs. When the Angel called a staff meeting, Henry tensed.

"We aren't building quickly enough in Iowa," Cass began in the high voice, a gray-blue herringbone suit giving in gentle folds as he moved. "We need to win the caucuses, or at least place second, by capturing the communist vote while the rest of the field splits the God-guns-and-guts-made-America-great *real* Republicans." Cass scratched a fingernail along the gleaming skull. "The way we're going, we're going to run out of time, or money."

Diane stepped forward, in what seemed a choreographed tag team. Cass folded his arms and waited.

"Dagworth and Sadler are lining up more bigfoot fundraisers and Iowa county chairs," Diane said. "We may have a stronger, broader message and greater affinity with the mainstream media, but they're building bigger organizations and war chests. And they're both also still beating us in the polls."

A fearful quiet filled the room. Something was coming, and the staffers knew it, like forest creatures sensing an earthquake or predator.

Diane wasn't painting the whole picture, Henry knew. For starters, they weren't playing a zero-sum game, pursuing only Republican votes. On top of activating moderate Republicans, they were running drives to register Independents and Democrats, who could vote in the Iowa caucuses and in many state GOP primaries, if only by switching to Republican for a day. They were targeting states that already offered incentives to Independents and Democrats to vote in a Republican primary, usually a popular Republican gubernatorial or senatorial candidate also on the ballot. Some Republican leaders were grousing that they wanted to keep the contests in the family. Peele replied, "I want an extended family."

When Diane cued Cass, the Angel leaped forward. "Iowa's the key; has been since McGovern in '72," Cass ranted. "Talk all you want about a compressed schedule. If we generate buzz, make a big score in Iowa, New Hampshire will follow, and so will the money. *Then* we can worry about Florida, South Carolina, California, the rest. We bust in Iowa, game's over." Cass's cadence accelerated, and Henry could see the Angel wasn't going to yield the floor again. "Basically, Tom's got to move to Iowa until January."

An image of a flat, brown expanse filled Henry's mind. "Excuse me, Gil," he called. "Are you talking about Tom operating out of actual Iowa, or out of Omaha?" If Peele worked from his home base of Omaha, just across the Missouri River from Iowa, they could rely largely on local staff.

"*Actual Iowa*," Cass said. "I like that. Yes, my Bolshevik friend, actual Iowa. Tom's going to spend at least a day or two each week for the next nine months in actual Iowa. And you get a ticket for at least that. We've reserved rooms at the Rigsdale Hotel in Des Moines. The hotel owner's a fan, gave us a break. The 'Presidential Suite.'" Cass smiled. "And while you're there, make sure there's plenty of booze in the cupboard. Dewar's, Glenfiddich, whatever swill Peele drinks. Can't have our candidate getting bombed at the hotel bar."

Acid rose in his throat. He had braced for a one- or two-month Iowa tour, not eight. Could he appeal for leniency, citing Walter? The tabby hissed when Henry left for even a day.

"Leave the strategy to me," Cass told the group, the bald head rotating on the thick neck like a gun on a turret. "You're a bunch of amateurs, intellectuals, and communists. Freedom and prosperity."

As the others filed out, Henry walked up to Cass. The Angel's silk pocket kerchief had a muted skull-and-crossbones pattern.

"Will you be joining us at the Rigsdale, Gil?"

Cass stroked a cashmere lapel. "I don't do Iowa."

That night, just after ten, the deskman at Henry's building phoned to tell him he had a visitor. "Jeannine, a friend of Mr. Cass." Maybe one of the Angel's retinue, delivering some "unholy shit" for him to tweet or plant in an op-ed.

He opened his door to find a blonde at least his height, maybe twenty-five, tanned and shapely in a long chocolate dress, breasts pressing out a low neckline. Her skin was all silk and pillows, except maybe for a bit too much rouge on the chiseled cheeks. She smiled, showing an expensive cap job. The woman reached out a long, delicate hand and rested two gleaming fingernails on the groove between his shoulder and chest, sending a shock through him.

"Can I come in?" she asked, in a whisper soft and husky. She smiled again, more broadly, but he could see it was forced, the kind of political smile she affected, using different muscles from those in a natural grin. Her eyes were projecting warmth, but there was something missing: the vulnerability, the tension, the tingle. This was business.

He thought of Eliot Spitzer, the disgraced New York governor, immortalized as an escort service's Client Number Nine. But Henry wasn't paying Jeannine. Still, if he went through with it, he'd have to perform; she'd probably report back to Cass. He felt himself stir as she worked a nail against his chest.

Cass had said Henry had a job that could get him laid. So why send Jeannine? As consolation for shipping him to the romantic desert of Des Moines? Or was the Angel just sucking him deeper into the morass, making his collusion physical as well as moral? Should he send Jeannine away, on principle? Then Cass would call him a communist amateur intellectual *pansy*.

He probably stank by now. He showered at night, before going to sleep, so it had been twenty-two hours. And he was pretty sure he was wearing boxers with little red elephants. He stepped back and opened the door, his body making the decision before his mind finished sorting the angles.

"Come on," he said, leading her down the hall to the bedroom. She was all business; so was he. The key here was being in charge. He turned to make sure Jeannine was following. She was sauntering along, as though amused by his ardor. She had probably seen and done everything he could imagine, and then some. The only edge he had was physical. She was alone with him in his place, and he was bigger and stronger, even if his once-strapping wrestler's body had atrophied and gained a coat of campaign flab. He shoved the bedroom door shut, hard and loud, behind her.

She stepped to the side and crossed her arms, which pushed up her breasts.

He realized, above all, that he didn't want to touch her. Didn't want to have to perform. Didn't want to get naked in front of a pro and get judged. And then judged by Cass. Who had probably been with Jeannine, too; ugly image, sloppy seconds. Didn't want her in his home, in his bed. He was tired, stressed, wired. He just wanted to go back to his e-mail and his Neil Young CD. And that made him angry. Annoyed at Cass for invading his home. No warning, no barriers. Annoyed at himself that he didn't want her; why shouldn't he want a beautiful pro like that, experience of a lifetime, literally knocking on his door? What was wrong with him? He felt himself deflate, and now he knew he couldn't perform.

He eased into his rocking chair, a JFK inspiration, in his khakis and untucked button-down, across the room from her. He began rocking, gently, off the balls of his feet, trying to figure an escape.

She stood looking at him for a couple of moments. She raised an arm, pulled her hair loose and shook it, now shoulder-length ash blond, falling partly over her forehead. He could almost feel the strands as they brushed the tanned swell of her breasts, settling in her cleavage.

He found himself in pain as an erection pressed against his zipper. He shifted, crossing one leg partially over the other, to give himself room to grow sideways, like a plant that hits a ceiling.

She dropped what looked like a velvet scrunchie on his

THE ACCOMPLICE | 75

dresser and swung one leg forward, beginning a rolling gait, toward the center of the room and him.

He was breathing heavily now. He stood, slowly, sliding against the khaki, and stepped to meet her. He leaned forward to kiss her, but she moved her head away.

"No, baby," she whispered, and slid her hand down his front, the long fingers finding and working him through the cloth.

He reached for her, and she let him cup one of her breasts. He waited for the warmth to radiate through his palm and the soft give as he pressed, and searched with his thumb for the nipple, to stroke it until it jutted through the cloth. But instead, it felt like he was gripping a water balloon. Jeannine was a silicone sister. That had always been a deal-breaker; he couldn't even get off to a stripper whose telltale orbs stood round and full even when she lay on her back.

"Oh, Jeannine," he said, dropping his hand and stepping away. "We're in the same line of work. Let's both of us call it a night."

8

* * *

THE BANKER'S BARBECUE

Des Moines felt at once familiar and eerie as Henry steered his long-term lease, a Ford Fusion, out of the airport and onto Fleur Drive. After eight months with Tyler he didn't need a map. The Ford rattled along Grand Avenue, prompting him to christen it "The Blue Bucket."

When the Rigsdale Hotel came into view, granite and brick towers lit against the night sky like a fortress, Henry couldn't help smiling. The Blue Bucket felt like a child's toy as he steered through an arch into the hotel garage. After all his bitching, this might not be so bad.

On the tenth and top floor, he opened the heavy wooden door of the Presidential Suite. A faint mildew odor pinched his nostrils. Lifting a switch, yellowed lamp shades cast the living room in shadows, showing worn aqua carpet, a sun-faded recliner, and cracked seams in the crown molding where Midwest extremes had stretched and shrunk the wood.

Two nights later, Henry returned from the Des Moines campaign office after ten. He smelled the soiled socks before he saw them in the dining room, along with the congealed remnants of baked salmon in dill mustard sauce. An amber bottle of hand sanitizer sat on the dinner table. The master bedroom door was shut, light filling the crack at bottom. Peele had arrived.

Through the thin door, he heard the Senator's phone calls to his wife, his daughter, and to someone named Barb who was apparently trying to lose weight despite Peele's assurances she was a "babe" just as she was. The voice took him back to the Newtown Street row house, his mother's shouts and his father's door-slamming departures.

The next night, Henry trudged back to the suite around nine thirty. Peele was home in Omaha; he should have the place to himself. Opening the front door, instead of mildew, stale tobacco assaulted his nostrils. He stepped onto the carpet with a crunch. Lifting his shoe revealed a shattered potato chip. He stepped to the bathroom in the hall, off his small bedroom, and turned on the tap. The soap dish was empty.

He called the Des Moines campaign office and finally got one of the organizational directors. "Yeah," she said, "Phil used the place to meet with some union guys." Phil was Eggert, their Iowa director.

"Looks like he set off a grenade."

"Well, they'll clean it before the Senator gets back. What's the problem?"

"The problem is, I'm living here."

"Oh, yeah," she said.

He slammed down the receiver.

Thankfully, Eggert's crew seemed to have let the small bedroom alone. The place was beginning to feel like home. He had bought some cheap plastic picture frames and set two photos on the dresser: a boyhood shot with his father in the 28th Avenue playground; and Walter, eyes hooded, head cocked, bored and smug. Poor Walter, now a ward of the pet co-op at his D.C. building, billeting in neighbors' apartments during Henry's Iowa sojourns.

Saturday was a road day with Peele, driving as far as Sioux City, on Iowa's border with Nebraska and South Dakota, for a banker's fund-raiser. Eggert, hauling them in a Jeep Cherokee that was overdue for a wash, was soft and pudgy, with straw hair and aqua eyes that looked faded like the hotel carpet. He gave off a stale-tobacco musk, magnified in the closed car.

Peele, riding shotgun, opened his window, beckoning the summer steambath.

"I've got the AC on, Senator," Eggert said.

"Smells like a fucking ashtray in here, Phil," Peele replied. And that was the last conversation for forty minutes.

Henry slouched in the backseat, which he had to himself. Eggert, trapped a few feet from Peele, dabbed a handkerchief at sweating temples and jowls as they ground along an endless strip of interstate.

Peele, as usual, seemed blissful on the road, away from the Capitol Hill crush, with throngs awaiting him at events throughout the state. Halfway through the leg to Sioux City, though, Peele began leaning out the window, then asked for his jacket. Henry passed up the blue blazer, and Peele patted it frantically, finally pulling a metal cylinder from a pocket, shaking it and inhaling.

"Phil, we going to clear fifty thousand?" Peele asked as they passed a sign for Avoca.

Eggert gripped the wheel and nodded. "Should be at least that, Senator."

"I wouldn't go to Sioux City to raise money," Peele said.

"But if you guys are going to put me on the road, I want you to put together some events I can drop into for forty-five minutes and leave with at least fifty thousand. Is that too much to ask?"

"I think we'll be okay," Eggert said.

Peele nodded. "Anything less than that isn't worth my time."

Henry rolled his eyes in the backseat. They certainly did have to raise money in Iowa, if only so they could say they had raised money in Iowa, and Peele knew it.

"Yes, sir," Eggert said.

Peele breathed. "You talk about squeezing blood from a stone—raising money from moderates. The biggest problem with moderates is that they're *moderate*." Peele turned to Eggert. "But we don't have to worry about any of that today. Since I've got your guarantee, Phil, if we don't raise fifty thousand, I expect you to make up the difference out of your own pocket."

Eggert didn't say anything, maybe not sure how to respond.

"Phil," Henry called over the seat, "why don't you agree, as long as the Senator lets you keep anything above fifty thousand?"

"That's a very good answer, Dartmouth," Peele said. "Maybe you'd like to join Mr. Eggert in the arrangement, and put up half of any shortfall."

"Phil, how confident are you about raising fifty thousand?" Henry asked. In the rearview mirror, he watched Eggert's eyes dart in the bloated face.

"I think we'll do well today," the Iowa man finally said.

Studying the back of Peele's head, Henry tried to muster the same electric awe that had hit him that first moment he'd seen the Senator in the Russell corridor. Nothing; just a handsome cascade of hair. You don't have to approve of everything this guy does, he told himself. You just need to approve of his agenda overall, believe that the world would be a better place if suddenly, everything the boss advocated came to pass. Henry figured he approved ninety percent of Peele's positions. That was well into his comfort zone, about where he'd been with Tyler. And way beyond where he'd been with Morris, probably around fifty-five percent, not even at his tolerance level. You want one hundred percent agenda approval, run for office yourself. As for Peele's philandering, he told himself, the guy's not his father. One time in Tyler's office, the scheduler was bemoaning the adultery epidemic among congressmen, and a legislative aide said, "Why do dogs lick their balls? Because they can."

Northbound on Interstate 29, they passed a series of signs for a scenic overlook. Where could there be a scenic overlook in Iowa, which Tyler had called "the original level playing field"? The next sign noted the overlook was open from seven A.M. to seven P.M. How can you close a scenic overlook? Five miles later, Henry found out. They passed a five-story wooden tower, which looked like a giant gallows.

"These guys want to buy a senator, and they want to buy one cheap," Peele said as they approached Sioux City. "Every four years in this state, the Kiwanis and Rotary social chairmen get to be players."

They parked in a circular driveway atop a winding street in a leafy subdivision. Peele strode into the house, tasseled loafers clicking against the terra-cotta floor. Henry could tell that Peele was enjoying the moment, as guests who noticed their arrival elbowed and hushed others. Peele smiled, giving the crowd a flash of white teeth, and stretched the grin until the cheeks creased into dimples. The right hand rose in a shoulder-level wave.

Henry felt a tingle as the crowd genuflected to the Senator.

He couldn't help enjoying their gazes as guests sized up this aide to the beautiful solon. He had been staffing Peele at events like this for seven months by this point, and had staffed Tyler and Morris before that, and it almost bothered him how comfortable he had become invading strangers' homes, examining their books and family photos, and using their bathrooms, dripping suds on their marble basins and floors and fouling their sculpted soaps and potpourri. The banker had an elegant old home on a landscaped slope and the furniture was generally both tasteful and comfortable, but the cultured air was spoiled by too many golf knickknacks, unread leather-bound mail-order classics, and Ansel Adams prints.

After studying the living room through the open archway, he noticed a woman at the greeting table, once some arrivals had cleared. Her russet hair was pulled back in a ponytail that fell over a pink oxford shirt. The shirt was opened to the third button, exposing a string of pearls around her faintly freckled neck, and straining around full breasts before tapering and tucking neatly into a khaki skirt just below a small roll of flesh. The corners of her eyes wrinkled in an outdoorsy way when she smiled, showing perfect teeth. The hazel irises, behind oval titanium-framed glasses, gleamed above a slightly oversized nose and angled jaw.

The nose, coupled with the easy smile, made her more interesting. Sitting upright in a lacquered chair behind rows of self-adhesive name tags, her poise and warmth seemed worlds beyond the former dairy princesses and 4H queens in designer armor who clutched their husbands' golf club blazers and slurped cocktails. He glanced at her name tag on the pink shirt: Elizabeth Walmsley.

He wanted to talk to her, beyond just telling her his name and having her hand him his preprinted tag, and was trying to craft an opening when Peele asked, "Where's mine, Elizabeth?" and leaned over the table of name tags.

The woman gave another natural smile. "I don't think you need one, Senator."

Peele flashed the grin. "I don't know; I feel kind of naked without one."

The woman took a blank adhesive rectangle and a marker and wrote "Senator Peele" in a neat blue hand, the letters curved and cheery. When she was done, the Senator took the name tag, his fingers brushing hers, peeled it and pressed it to his lapel. Then Peele smiled and turned to work the room.

When Henry's turn at the table came, he spotted his name tag, took it, and nodded at the woman. The second line of his tag said "Sen. Peele's Staff," so she'd know he belonged to Peele, even if she had missed his entrance with the Senator. Any banter he might try now would seem predatory. Even so, she gave him a toned-down version of the smile as he stepped past.

He trailed a few feet behind as Peele weaved through the crowd. The Senator squeezed hands, clapped shoulders, and allowed men in pastel jackets to whisper into his ear with onion-dip breath, all while continually flashing the grin.

Peele gave each guest enough time to feel important, but not a moment longer. The Senator made no amateur mistakes, like looking over a guy's shoulder for somebody more important, or bungling a name or some feature of local geography.

"What the hell's going on with the farm bill, Tom?" a paunchy man in a cord jacket asked, gripping Peele's upper arm. "They're looking to gut the CRP, stiff us on our acres."

Like a good New Yorker, Henry saw the Conservation Reserve Program as welfare for farmers, paying them to keep their acres fallow.

"Henry, make a note of that," Peele instructed. "Make sure

you get Bill's name and number." The Senator fixed the blue eyes on the man and assured him, "We'll look into that for you, Bill, get back to you." Peele clapped the man on the shoulder and moved on. He scribbled the number in a pocket notebook and scurried after the Senator, playing his role.

Peele covered the living room, kitchen, and den in about fifty minutes. "Too hot to work the backyard," the Senator whispered to him, looking through sliding doors at a few men in shirtsleeves sipping drinks on the lawn. On that day's schedule, the banker's barbecue was one of twelve speeches, meetings, news conferences, and fund-raisers wedged in ten-point type on an index card. He had risen before five A.M. and would go until ten P.M. or even midnight before returning to his little room in the Rigsdale suite, traveling three hundred miles in Eggert's Jeep.

For the hosts, a tall guy in wire rims and his beaming wife, whose worlds extended from the Sioux Falls Bridge to the Sioux City Mall, the barbecue probably culminated months of planning, drafting, and refining invitation lists and menus; printing and mailing reminders; riding herd on caterers, gardeners, valet parking attendants, and other contractors; and overhauling the house. When it was over, and Eggert had collected the checks, the hosts would probably feel that they had survived an ordeal together, triumphed and bonded. Peele had delayed their arrival ten minutes to buy a Depression glass bottle for his wife at an antique store they saw on the way, and would probably want to leave early. Henry's own biggest concern was whether the hors d'oeuvres would be any good, with dinner still a couple of hours off.

Returning to the living room, the Senator was ready to wrap up. Peele motioned to Eggert, who took the banker aside.

"People, people!" the host called, waving an arm as though

hushing tellers. "Senator Peele was gracious to join us today, but he has to get to a TV interview. So please, everybody, come into the living room."

Peele flashed the smile. "I just spoke to Majority Leader Mathis, and he told me the State Department and Foreign Operations bill may get held up in the House-Senate conference because some of our friends on the other side of the aisle want to subsidize foreign terrorist organizations with your tax dollars." The Senator shook the silvered head.

Frowns creased some already weathered faces. Some guests seemed thrilled at the inside gossip from Washington. They would probably tell their clients that they were friends with the Senator, even confidants. "Yeah, Tom's my friend; sure he's my buddy," they'd say. "I had dinner with him the other day in Sioux City, and he told me just how tough it's going to be to pass that foreign-aid bill . . ."

He hadn't written anything for Peele for this event; he didn't have to. Peele handled these by feel. After establishing tough-on-crime bona fides and taking a few bows for fiscal restraint, the Senator launched into a harangue about how the Republican Party was going to forever lose the soccer moms, the Northeast progressives, and much of the rest of its base if it dived further toward intolerance and isolationism. Peele didn't name the hot-button social issues: abortion, immigration, public funding of religious schools, gay marriage. They were understood. The words flowed as the face reddened and the hands wagged.

Peele called for an America in the spirit of Teddy Roosevelt, where government boosted a laissez-faire market but busted trusts, where government valued and preserved the environment, and where government exported its ideals and protected its partners by speaking softly and carrying a big stick.

Peele called for an America that balanced national security with civil rights. "America has always been governed from the center, and we forget that at our peril. Barry Goldwater put it best: We've got to get government out of our boardrooms and bedrooms."

He felt another tingle; he was hard-wired to melt at stump speeches the way most people cued to weddings or school plays. Peele had delivered in Nebraska; why not on the national stage? The Senator *could* make America stronger, better. The sense of decency that Peele projected with The Look was integral, an affinity with the average guy and the clubhouse set alike, that we're all in this together.

Henry waited until one of the guests clapped and then beat his own palms in resounding applause. Several others joined in, including one woman who nearly spilled a Bloody Mary. Peele glowed in the adulation. Eggert seemed to be fighting sleep.

As Peele's crew left the house, Eggert stopped at Elizabeth Walmsley's table.

"The Senator wants to send you an article about a book you were discussing with him," Eggert said. "*Main Street,* I think he said. Do you have a card?"

The woman wrote her name, address, and phone number on a blank name tag in her neat, cheery blue hand. Eggert took the name tag in greasy fingers. The Iowa director seemed giddy; they must have made the $50,000.

Henry had seen Peele work lobbyists, agency execs, and Senate aides at fund-raisers, touching their elbows, flashing the grin, and some of them soon landed on the Senator's schedule for private afternoon meetings. Those women all brandished a wary Washington edge; let them take their chances. But Elizabeth Walmsley radiated innocence, and he didn't want her to get hurt, or used. As Henry stepped toward the door, he leaned toward her to whisper the word "Careful." It's all he would have time to say, and maybe she'd understand. As his lips neared her ear, she tilted her head, as though to receive a kiss on the cheek.

As he was about to voice the word, Eggert tugged his arm. "Hey, did you get any of the sesame chicken skewers?" the Iowa man cawed. "Really good."

9

★ ★ ★

FRAN

Henry felt a presence hovering in the Des Moines Community College auditorium. He shifted in the folding chair and listened. He scanned the chamber. Political aides tended to their bosses, coiled to spring at any order. A sea of dark suits studied the pol at the lectern, some taking notes. A gaggle of reporters, including two TV cameras, filled the front row.

Then, against a wall, Henry spotted a whelp panning a cell phone camera past him to Peele, and to the other candidates. Fogel's guy. The media man was collecting footage for ads and web postings. Fogel had recruited a couple of tech-savvy college kids and sent them to events around the country armed with flip phones, and occasionally called on Henry to dispatch aides and volunteers. Cell phone video was now broadcast quality, Fogel said.

Fogel had devised the tactic on a campaign a few years earlier, comparing video of an opponent from morning and night events to show the guy was an alcoholic. The media man was essentially running a parallel opposition research operation. "You can tell a lot about a guy on a shoot, and working a crowd, especially when they think the camera is off," Fogel had told him. "You kind of figure out who they are."

The Iowa Taxpayers Association forum, a command performance for Republican presidential candidates, affected the air of an academic symposium. Sadler was at the podium now, arms wagging. The Texan was vaporing about creating a climate in which Americans could prosper, unshackling businesses and individuals from regulation, taxation, and litigation.

Around Henry, hands scratched noses and ears or hid yawns, and fingers worked BlackBerrys and iPhones. Peele's speech should go over better, when the time came. Henry had reworked the business aide's pabulum, with a Medici prince's quote for a finale.

He felt the hovering presence again and heard a familiar voice. His head snapped to the right, toward a group around Cliff Dagworth. And there she was, sitting by the Virginia senator, in a mocha skirt suit with a gold brooch. Looking harmless and demure. Fran.

He had known, somehow, that he'd see her during the race. She wouldn't miss a presidential. They were like two asteroids in erratic orbits around the same sphere, bound to collide. Or maybe like two flies buzzing around the same turd. He had been looking forward to seeing her, daydreaming about it and dreading it.

He watched her, mostly out of the corner of his eye, as she scribbled on a pad, joked with Dagworth's staff and occasionally whispered to the Virginian. She didn't seem to notice him, or didn't care. A wave of depression hit him, settling as a dull ache in the base of his jaw. Watching her with Dagworth's people, onto a new chapter with new characters, oblivious to him even when he was only thirty feet away, felt like watching the world go on after he was dead.

He had first met Fran eighteen months earlier, on a blustery December day a mile from where he was now. Des Moines had been frozen so long that icicles hung from icicles. It was early in Tyler's gubernatorial race, and he had been sitting with their campaign manager, Pat Mallory, in a musty, froufrou coffee shop on Grand Avenue sipping hot spiced cider, chewing an organic blackberry muffin, and waiting for the oppo they had hired to arrive.

Finally, she walked in, fifteen minutes late, and strode to their booth. At least she showed some savvy; she had immediately picked out the two Washingtonians in an Iowa café. For her first meeting with her new boss, Fran wore faded jeans, hiking boots, an Icelandic sweater, and a ski parka. Up close, he could see she wasn't wearing makeup, and didn't need any. Her cobalt eyes accented her flushed cheeks and chestnut hair, which hung to her shoulders in waves. Her handshake was firm and dry.

He let Mallory do most of the talking. The manager launched into a lecture that they were up against a sitting governor, this wasn't beanbag, and they expected initiative and results. Her stuff had to be sharp, and Mallory had no time to babysit her.

Fran unzipped her parka as Mallory talked and coated her lips with cherry balm. Shifting to pull an arm out of the parka, she angled her shoulder back, which had the effect of pointing a sizable breast sheathed in furry Icelandic wool toward the campaign manager. Mallory's words stalled, then flowed again.

When Mallory finished, she began, in a crisp monotone. "I plan to focus on two broad avenues," Fran said, locking cobalt eyes on the manager, pinning him in the chair. "First, the Governor is weak on taxes. Any governor who's been in office twelve years is going to have a boatload of taxes and fees buried in legislation that's going to look enormous when you add it up. Second, he's vulnerable on crime. Iowa may not have a high crime rate when you compare it to New York or Florida, but he's done nothing to put away violent offenders while other states are passing three-strikes-you're-out."

As she talked, Mallory squirmed. She gave Henry a quick glance, to see if he would jump in. He just watched. Fran rattled off a list of agencies and public records she would tap and outlined a schedule for submitting her material. Then she reminded Mallory that the first month's fee, $7,000, was due at this first meeting. Mallory wound up sliding a post-dated personal check across the table.

"I'm assigning you to oversee that woman," Mallory told Henry as they stepped out of the coffee shop into the Iowa frost. The manager wedged his hands into pants pockets.

"Okay," Henry had said, smiling.

"You think she's hot? Don't even bother. That woman is a classic career-bitch ice queen. She's going to wake up one day in a hotel room in Oklahoma when she's forty and alone, and she's going to realize she never had a life, and it's going to be too late."

Over the next few weeks, he called Fran a few times to ask her to check records or to track down particular tax increases, budget votes, or appointments. She called him twice, once when she found a budget message in which the Governor touted a grain subsidy he would later veto, and the second time, more excited, to say she had discovered a book-cooking scheme. The Governor was debiting expenses in the next fiscal year and in capital accounts to make a bad year, the one before the election, look better.

They wound up meeting in the Holiday Inn's Heartland Café. That was the night of the yellow T-shirt.

Henry squirmed through Dagworth's folksy empowerment-over-entitlement speech. Dagworth, Richmond gentry who traced his ancestors to the *Mayflower*, crammed Skoal in his face to play man-of-the-people. When the Virginian finally finished, Henry broke for the water fountain. By an oil portrait of a nineteenth-century academic with mutton chops, he found Fran. She was facing away, maybe avoiding an exchange. She made a living observing, catching details others missed. If she hadn't noticed him during an hour at the forum, she wasn't very good at her job. "Hey," he said, touching a mocha elbow.

She started and turned. She looked the same after a year. Maybe the face was a bit fuller and the crows' feet a tad deeper, but he couldn't be sure. No gray hairs streaking the chestnut, the way he had imagined, and the cobalt eyes were just as bright.

"Wow, talk about a blast from the past," she said, giving him a broad smile. "How you doing, bud?" He liked the way she called him "bud"; the New York cabbie's term carried punch in her throaty alto.

He stood with his arms at his sides, waiting for her to step in for a hug or a kiss. She stayed planted. She also hadn't asked why he was at the forum. Maybe she already knew.

"Congratulations," he said. "Looks like you're with Dagworth. Opposition research?"

She nodded.

"I was wondering what brought you to this part of the world, who your target is."

Her eyebrows rose.

"There's only one Midwest Republican running."

She cocked her head.

"Peele."

He held her gaze, and she eventually broke a smile. She must have been digging through records from Peele's term as Nebraska governor. The Taxpayers Association event was probably a chance to connect with Dagworth and some of the Virginian's top aides.

"Fran, you're not really surprised to see me, are you? I mean, you're checking out my guy; you must have expected to run into me at one of these things."

A grin played at the corners of her glistening lips. "I did hear you were with Peele. I don't mean to bruise your ego, pal, but I don't track the staff."

He smiled, reflexively. Actually, he knew she was lying. She had told him she always looked at her mark's top aides, to check any connections, whether the aide gave the candidate access to a particular group, and of course whether the aide had a dark past. She had probably filled a file on him from memory, maybe replete with intimate details, and billed Dagworth for at least a day's work. So she owed him royalties on their time together. "You're still taking on clients, like Dagworth, doesn't matter what they stand for—or don't stand for?"

"You're still the conscience of the campaign?" The cobalt eyes narrowed.

He waved an arm, as though to start fresh. "You look great, Fran. Really." What the heck. It was true.

She nodded. "Thank you. You, too."

"Maybe we can grab a bite, catch up. I'm in Iowa about half the time now. I'm assuming you're in Omaha or Lincoln, doing your . . . work."

She stepped back, weighing him. "Call me," she finally said. "You still have my cell number?"

He nodded.

"See you, Henry." She strode back to the chamber, her firm hips shifting under the mocha suit with each step.

Now that she was targeting Peele, he should stay away. Far away. But he couldn't even stop watching her. A brew of emotions washed over him, aching for her, but not wanting to want her, wanting to tame her, but admiring her spirit and spunk. Mostly, to somehow ease the tension and try again.

10

★ ★ ★

DIRT

Big Jim Bauer was aptly named. The head of the Nebraska Plumbers & Steamfitters may have been the biggest human being Henry had even seen. When Big Jim opened the trailer door, Henry's eyes caught first on the forearms, two hams protruding from a black knit shirt. The wrists were the size of Henry's biceps. The gut was the size of a beach ball. The man must have stood six-four, maybe six-five, and weighed at least four hundred pounds.

Big Jim led them into a combination office and game lodge, a menagerie of stag and boar heads, shellacked Alaska salmon and blue Marlin, all glaring amid the rifles and fishing rods that must have done them in. Six other men sat on orange-and-green-plaid couches, all with hard, weathered faces.

Henry's eye caught on a man, maybe sixty, with a broad head under thinning gray hair combed back, and a scar that ran from a lined forehead to cheek, pressing one eye partially shut. Milky caramel eyes glared at no one, and at everyone. The two other men on the couch hugged the armrests, giving the scarred man the meat of the cushions.

Henry didn't know any of the names listed on the schedule under "Nebraska and Iowa Labor Leaders." But Peele clearly knew them all. The Senator gripped the scarred man in a two-handed shake and called him Ed. Now Henry recognized the man, from some campaign brochures, "Working Families for Peele" and "Democrats for Peele." So this was Ed Zabriskie, head of the Omaha Teamsters.

Henry felt like a stiff in a poplin suit as Peele introduced him, nodding like a bobbing head doll at the union men as they eyed him. He settled onto a folding chair beside Big Jim's desk, within reach of a glass bowl of Crackle and Nestlé Crunch mini bars.

Big Jim eased into an oversized desk chair, sighing like a truck releasing air brakes. Peele thanked them for mailing copies of his letter to their memberships, and told them the campaign was going great, but that funds were tight. Politicians always tell potential donors that money is tight.

"We can transform the presidential contest if we can convince twenty-five thousand Iowa union members to become Republicans, if only for one night, to vote for me in the caucuses," Peele said, focusing on the Iowans. "You can send a signal to the Democrats that there's somewhere else for Labor to go. And if you get a choice between me and the Democrat in the general election, you can't lose."

The Iowa Carpenters boss squirmed on a sofa. "That's a tough sell, Tom."

"The AFL-CIO endorsed me in my last Senate reelect," Peele said. "I'm the only Republican who's had a union card. And I'm the only one who can walk out of a union hall alive."

A few of them chuckled. Henry nibbled a bite-sized chocolate bar. The candy didn't dent the hunger pang in his gut, but loosened the low-blood-sugar vise on his temples.

"It's an even tougher sell with these stories in the *Globe-Times*," the Iowa Carpenters boss said from a plaid couch.

Henry swallowed. Cass, piqued at Bill Burr's continuing reports, had told Henry the night before, "Union guys have their panties in a wad because you can't control some Jimmy Olsen gossip-mongering prick."

"The *Globe-Times* is going nuts on the presidential race," Peele said. "They're not just looking under every rock, they're looking under every pebble. This is the first time a Nebraska boy had a shot at it since Bob Kerrey, or maybe William Jennings Bryan." Peele panned their faces. "I don't need to tell you, there was nothing to those rumors ten years ago and there's nothing to them now."

"Well, we gotta stand for election just like you hotshots in Washington, and this doesn't help," the Carpenters boss said. "It surely does not."

Peele nodded, sober. We're all victims, his look said; we need to stick together.

Bauer hoisted himself out of the chair and promised to let Peele speak at an upcoming Plumbers & Steamfitters membership meeting. The Ironworker pledged to print "Another Ironworker for Tom Peele" bumper stickers. Then meaty, calloused hands clasped and patted broad polyester backs and Big Jim opened the door, letting in the summer heat.

Henry stood, slightly light-headed, with a dull sugar ache in his molars and a chocolate slick in the back of his mouth. He sidled toward Peele, and wound up near the Senator's sidebar with Zabriskie.

"The stock price is going to go through the roof once the drug gets approved," Peele whispered. "You're sitting pretty."

Zabriskie shot Henry a glare and leaned toward Peele. The Teamster whispered something Henry couldn't hear.

"No, no, no, Ed, for God's sake, not to my campaign," Peele hissed. "You send the check to a 527 corporation—we'll get you the details—and they'll make an in-kind contribution."

Ninety minutes later, marching in a Founders Day parade in Cherokee, Iowa, Henry gripped one end of a Peele banner, with Phil Eggert on the other end and a couple of volunteers between them. Peele was riding in a red 1966 Mustang convertible toward the head of the procession. Iowans and their parades. On any summer weekend, the campaign could find at least one. Italian parades, German parades, Swedish parades, Polish parades. City parades, business district parades, Jaycee parades.

All the pieces fit now. Peele's crusade to get off-label Medicare coverage for Ganadex, replete with the weeping widow at the Ways and Means hearing, was all to advance a stock scam. Peele and Cass weren't worried about Bill Burr digging into the old assault stuff, or not chiefly. They were worried mostly about the reporter discovering the scam, maybe through some spooked union guys. With his right foot, Henry barely sidestepped a glistening, chocolate brown chunk of dung. A caravan of sorrels, at the front of the pack, had strewn the road.

Peele might make the cover of *Time*, after all. As for him, instead of walking into any office and demanding a desk, he might have to beg for some *nothing job*.

Henry had made a friend shortly after arriving on the Hill,

Pete, a press secretary for a New Jersey congressman. Pete needed money to raise three kids, and hocked his Boy Scout looks and résumé for a job as spokesman for the payday lending industry, the storefront banks that attach workers' paychecks to collect on steep loans. Shortly after Pete signed on, states began banning payday loans. A few months later, the House Banking Committee called Pete to testify. Pete was harpooned in the Star Chamber and lampooned in the media. The last Henry heard, Pete was selling real estate out of a storefront office in Hoboken.

Well, maybe the drug actually would help poor cancer victims. And Peele didn't seem to be taking money himself; it would all go to the campaign. Was Peele's scam any worse than some of Henry's? Taking the SAT, he had finished the first verbal section early; words had always come easier than numbers. He spied the other students still buried in their booklets. He flipped back to the first math section, a cardinal sin. By the time the verbal section ended, he had marked the four open questions on the first math.

Those four answers had probably boosted his total SAT score above Dartmouth's average and gotten him in, at the expense of some more deserving applicant, and delivered the cachet and bounty that continued to flow from an Ivy League diploma. In that sense, his whole adult life sprang from a cheat.

Should he resign from Peele's campaign on principle? What principle? The first principle of politics, he knew, was to win office. Alben Barkley, the Senate Majority Leader turned Vice President, was asked what makes a great senator. "To be a great senator," Barkley replied, "first you have to get elected."

Well, Henry was already soaking in the half-percent impure. What was next?

He let his mind drift, to ease the pounding on his temples,

amplified by the heat. Images of Elizabeth Walmsley, the russet-haired woman handing out name tags at the Sioux City barbecue, danced across his mind. He'd track her down and call her. And say what? I'm the guy who was staffing Peele when he was hitting on you? No, not the guy who took your phone number; the other pimp, the younger, dark-haired one. Maybe he could arrange to have her staff a press event, and meet her fresh.

His left foot slid, as though the loafer had hit a grease slick, and he looked down to see that he had stepped on a ball of moist, rich dung. The manure covered a corner of his foot, climbing up the sole and nearly lopping over onto the leather. He shuffled, scraping off the excrement against the pavement, but couldn't reach the edge of the sole. Maybe the sun would bake off the dung.

By the time the Cherokee parade ended by town hall, his shirt clung and sweat was streaming down his temples. He hung back in the parking lot, as Peele climbed in Eggert's Jeep with a couple of volunteers. Peele liked to ride with different aides, doling out snippets of precious face time.

He climbed in the front seat of Mary McCormick's Chrysler. He worked his BlackBerry, sending updates to their New Media woman about the parade and next stop, for her to bombard the blogosphere. Mary's firing and rehiring hung in the car, but he didn't want to talk about it, it would mean spewing more lies, and she apparently didn't want to hear them. So they sat in what was actually a comfortable silence, watching Iowa roll by. He'd always liked Mary; she gave off a disapproving but slightly amused vibe, like a homeroom teacher.

The schedule gave them forty-five minutes to drive forty miles from Cherokee to the figure-eight races in Primghar, along two Iowa state roads. Iowans prided themselves on their state highways, a network of two-lane blacktops slicing through swaths of fields. They would be lucky to make it on time; politicians had to obey speed limits.

He breathed, slowly and deeply, as Mary's Chrysler rolled north on State Route 59. The road puckered and bowed, stretching the macadam and cracking the edges like piecrust. On the shoulders, an occasional raccoon or possum lay with legs splayed. On either side, cornfields floated past, endless rows of stalks and leaves and tassels.

He soon drifted into sleep. He was living in perpetual exhaustion, racing on adrenaline and anxiety, and often found himself nodding off when the merry-go-round slowed. He was at the gate to an obelisk, and the guard asked for his watch, maybe to scan it, but the guard unscrewed the back and began turning and removing gears, and before Henry could object, the watch lay open to the sun, like a gutted fish.

He woke to see a sign on the road: "Welcome to Primghar— The Only Primghar in the World." Stones pinged against the Chrysler's wheel wells as they bounced toward the racetrack. Muscle cars and pickups filled the parking lot, a couple on massive orange shocks.

Near the ticket gate, Peele was shaking hands. Several reporters and one camera crew jostled amid a throng of aging fans. When Henry arrived, Peele was telling an older man in a tank top, "Hi, I'm Tom Peele, I'm running for President."

"Well, I'm running for the shithouse," the man said and brushed past.

After shaking a few hundred hands, Peele stepped to the side and went through nearly a bottle of amber hand sanitizer. The race managers let Peele speak from the tower and then take a lap around the track, standing through the sunroof of Eggert's Jeep.

As Henry and Mary settled into the bleachers, the announcer explained that cars to the right had priority at the ingrade intersection of the figure-eight track. But points were awarded to any car finishing the race, not just the first three.

"Kind of like politicians," Henry said. "Scrambling for the finish line, cutting off and smashing everybody else." He shrugged. "At least these guys do it in the open."

Soon a dozen cars lined up, a column of battered, day-glo Detroit muscle, all glass removed. They sprayed turf as they spun through turns. By the fourth lap, the first three cars were interspersing with the last two. Two laps later, the yellow lead car was crossing the hub at full throttle. In the other direction, a green Ford was swerving around a laggard and accelerating into the intersection. They collided, head-on. Both cars flew up on their rear wheels, as though in an embrace, and fell to the turf. A woman in a "Garlic Breath Pizza Racing" T-shirt screamed from behind Henry, piercing his eardrum. The drivers climbed out open windows and hobbled to the pits. A Mack wrecker dragged the crumpled hulks from the track, like bull carcasses from a ring. The race resumed.

Henry climbed down the bleachers and stepped behind the grandstand. He unholstered his BlackBerry and dialed from memory.

"Hey," he began, with a lilt. "Henry. You said to give a shout."

A pause. "Good to hear from you, bud," Fran said, flat.

"There's this *Globe-Times* reporter writing about a Teamster getting beaten up, and airing some old rumor involving Peele. You know what I'm talking about."

She didn't say anything.

"Just seems too much of a coincidence. You show up, looking at Peele, and then this reporter starts digging into this old dirt."

"Hey, life's strange."

"Not that strange."

"Henry, I think somebody spiked your hot chocolate."

"No, this has you written all over it. You stumble onto this old crap, but you can't get some salty Nebraska cops and prosecutors to open up. Not right away, anyway. So you recruit this cub political reporter, Burr, who's fresh off the cops beat. Guy should have all the contacts you need. And you get him to do your digging for you. And you rattle the enemy while you're at it, even if he doesn't find anything—which he won't, because there's nothing there. Pretty smart."

"Henry, I've got to go."

Might as well go all the way. "I was also wondering," he said, "what you're giving the reporter in return."

The line went dead.

11

★ ★ ★

FIRST AMONG EQUALS

Elizabeth squeezed her eyes shut as the assured voice on the phone told her he'd been thinking of her. She had been longing for the call, but also dreading it. The spark between them was unmistakable at the fund-raiser a couple of weeks earlier, and he was drop-dead gorgeous. But she'd also seen his wedding ring.

"Caught you at a bad time?" the voice asked. She tried to recall the Senator's timbre. Maybe one of her faculty friends was playing a gag; she had mentioned Peele at a lunch.

"No, no," she said. "What can I do for you, Senator?" He had introduced himself as "Tom Peele," but she didn't want to invite intimacy, or make this too easy. And if it was a gag, let her friends think she routinely took calls from senators.

"Well, I've been looking for some ideas to really boost our operation in western Iowa, and you seemed to have a pretty good feel for the landscape. I'm going to be in Des Moines tomorrow, and I was wondering if you were available for lunch."

She expelled air to the side, so it wouldn't vibrate in the mouthpiece. It actually was Peele. No academic could fake that tone. It was authoritative, driven by brio, ego, and testosterone, but with that adorable little catch of vulnerability, when he asked whether she was available. But what a transparent pretext; western Iowa campaign tactics. Or was he assuming that, as a professor, she had smarts and community connections?

Well, she had to accept his lunch offer, if she wanted to stay on the campaign. But if Peele suggested anything more intimate than western Iowa outreach strategy, her answer was: not with a married guy. Anyway, it was only lunch.

"Sure," she said, quickly adding, "but I have to be back in Ames by one forty-five."

Could it really be all business? Maybe he was one of those older guys who liked to talk to younger women and be seen with them. Much thunder, no rain, as a local Indian saying went. They made a date—an appointment—for noon the next day at an Italian restaurant in Des Moines she had never heard of.

Ironically, she had volunteered on Peele's campaign mostly to expand her social network, but hadn't been targeting the candidate himself. The only men she was meeting at Iowa State wore corduroy jackets with leather elbow patches and rubber-soled Rockports and granola crumbs lodged in their goatees. The Jaycees women were vicious Midlands snobs, where the ultimate academic cachet was a University of Iowa degree and the Ivy League was a decadent Eastern cult. When she mentioned her doctorate from the University of Pennsylvania, she drew a boast that Iowa State would crush the Nittany Lions. Since the divorce, she'd connected with friends mostly through Facebook and her cell phone, often while sitting alone in her living room.

She dialed her old college roommate Ursula, now a recently divorced investment banker. "Okay, I got one for you."

"Yeah, go ahead."

She gave a summary. "The whole thing makes me sort of . . . uneasy."

"No, it sounds pretty cool."

"Cool?"

"Yeah, sure. It's a first-among-equals kind of thing. You get to be a favorite on the job. And he's married, so you still keep your freedom. And I'm assuming you don't really care much about this campaign work, so if it all goes bust, there's no huge downside. Is he as cute as he was on TV?"

She'd never seen Peele's TV show. Growing up, her father had limited her to an hour a day at the tube, and *Parkland* hadn't made the cut. Peele was seventeen years older than she was, not that she was hung up on age, or race or religion, for that matter. "Yeah, he's pretty easy on the eyes."

"Go for it."

Well, she wasn't ready to Go For It with a married man. But her career and her life were sliding into Iowa muck, and she needed to find some reprieve. She'd been trying for two years to publish her book on religious symbolism in Chaucer, and was pretty sure the growing pile of rejection slips had cost her a promotion to full professor. Publish or perish. A mediocre teaching eval couldn't have helped, either.

She hadn't been going after publishing houses in the most strategic way, she knew. When her dream list turned her down, she asked some Iowa State profs, who told her, Oh, send it off to this press or that press. But those houses were also passing. When she checked with one publisher who was reviewing her manuscript, the editor asked whether she had thought of doing

a comparison with Boccaccio. Then somebody told her she
should cultivate senior profs who sit on the major university
presses' editorial boards. But those people come from all over
the country—and none from Iowa State.

Okay, her tome would never make the bestseller lists, but
she'd thrown herself into the thing and it was really pretty
good. Or was it? She couldn't even tell anymore. Who else really cared what an ass's jawbone might have symbolized in
fourteenth-century England? Or about anything else she had
to say?

Maybe Peele had some advice. If you can figure out how to
win a Senate seat, and maybe the presidency, you can probably
figure out how to publish a book. She could also use a break
from wine-and-cheese socials with the elbow-patch set. She
had never cheated on Evan when they were married, even when
it all soured. And not for lack of chances. A full English prof
had cornered her at a faculty cocktail mixer and run a hand
through her hair, his breath ripe with Merlot and brie. "Had we
but world enough, and time, this coyness, lady, were no crime,"
he had murmured, quoting Marvel and leaning into her. "But
your quaint honor will turn to dust, and into ashes all my lust."

"Fuck off," she had replied, and shoved past him.

She arrived first at the restaurant. The place looked frozen in
the 1940s, with a floor of small patterned tiles, a curved wooden
bar with a brass rail, and casks of wine on shelves. The air was
warm and heavy with cheese, garlic, and grilled fish.

She needed to use the restroom, to freshen up after even a
short walk in the sultry Iowa summer. She swept some stray
hairs behind an ear and adjusted the tortoiseshell clasp on her
crown. With her hair pulled back and the blue oxford tucked

into a khaki pencil skirt, the look was a tad severe, if shapely. Ovid would have approved: "Act in such a way as to instill him at once with hope and fear."

At the table, absorbed in an ice water with lemon, she didn't see Peele until he was standing over her. He was beaming the same confident smile he had flashed in Sioux City. A younger man was standing beside and behind him in a gray suit, scanning the restaurant. The man was a boy, really, the age of her students, but looked older in the suit.

"Thanks for coming, Elizabeth," Peele said, waving his hands as though to press her back in her seat. She hadn't thought to rise, but she supposed his stature warranted it. American royalty, elected officials. When he pivoted toward her, she tensed, thinking he might lean down and peck her on the cheek. Instead, Peele angled his head toward the younger man. "I don't know if you know Mitch; he works on our Iowa team. We've got a packed schedule this afternoon, and I asked him to join us." He wasn't asking for approval, just stating fact. Mitch would join them.

Peele slid into the chair next to hers. At the other end of the circular table, the boy pulled out a sheaf of papers and began marking them with a pen, which seemed rude. Then it hit her. The boy was doing exactly what he was supposed to. His role was to be there but not to be there: a live prop to give Peele cover for taking her to lunch.

"I've been thinking about you since the fund-raiser," Peele said. "That was a fabulous house, wasn't it, tucked into that rise? It was like stumbling on a gem—all the more wonderful for the surprise." He caught and held her gaze. She felt herself blush.

How much was Mitch hearing? Would the boy schedule a second date with her afterward, the way Phil Eggert had taken her number in Sioux City?

Over house salads, Peele leaned back and said, "Tell me about yourself." He seemed to have all the time in the world.

She glanced at the boy, who seemed to be tallying columns of numbers.

"I grew up in Portland, Maine, right off Casco Bay," she said, feeling like she was applying for a teaching grant. "I was an only child. My father was a Navy oceanographer, my mother was a researcher."

Peele looked as though he felt cheated by the mere facts.

"I'd sit alone for hours with books, spinning fantasies, on the oak floors in this big old colonial where my father had hoped to raise a brood," she said. "That's how I discovered classic lit. I came to Iowa five years ago, right out of grad school. There's not a lot of call for medievalists, so you take what you can find. Not that Iowa State isn't a great place to be. And we were able to find a colonial in Ames—about a fifth the size of the one in Portland."

"You professors sure move around a lot. Do you find it tough, lonely?"

She shrugged. "It's part of the game. But there are worse things than being alone—like wishing you were alone." She pictured her ex, then her cozy cocoon of a living room.

Peele seemed so damned interested, leaning toward her, his big blue eyes wide. Over linguini and clams, she wound up mentioning her divorce. That also seemed to intrigue him.

"I still care for Evan," she said. "But the divorce was a relief, like death after Stage Four cancer." Thoughts of Evan tended to dim her mood, but she didn't feel as blue as Peele looked.

"I'm blind in one eye," she said, to jar him and gauge his reaction.

He looked stunned. "Really? Which one?"

"Oh, come on," she said. "Just look. You can tell."

He studied her. "I can't. Really."

"The left one. The shaft of the optic nerve is only partially formed. I'm fine in the library, but I'm a hazard on the tennis court. No depth perception." A memory popped up and stung her. "Evan said I look retarded, the way the blind eye just kind of floats."

"Elizabeth, the guy sounds like a prick. And a liar." Peele pulled a red-and-white inhaler out of his jacket pocket. "Without this, I sound like an obscene caller when I breathe. We're all flawed specimens." The attentive blue eyes still held her, still just as warm.

"I joined your campaign because you seem to have the right ideas on the environment, civil rights, and some other key issues—for a Republican," she said, something inside her trying to create distance. "And because if I worked for a Democrat, Dad would disown me."

"So you bought a colonial?" Peele asked, pushing a bread plate aside. "With a front porch? We had a front porch, growing up. Used to fall asleep Sunday evenings on this old bench swing reading used paperbacks I'd buy at the general store."

Yeah, her colonial had a porch swing and an oak in the yard. The house also had a small upstairs bedroom with a circular window that she thought would work perfectly as a nursery. The room now served mostly as storage.

Peele was so different from Evan. He was a politician, not an artist; a Midwesterner, not a Californian; voluble where Evan seethed and brooded. Peele seemed comfortable commanding other men, unfazed even at using an underling as a shill at his table. He was like her father, in many ways.

Just as she thought he might open up about himself, he looked at his watch, made a mock-pained sound, and said he was late for an appointment, but it was wonderful seeing her.

He slid some bills into the check folder and stood. Then he smiled at her, reaching out a hand and cupping her cheek with it, his palm cool and dry. For a moment, she thought he would lean down and kiss her, but he just smiled and brushed his fingers against her cheek as he withdrew them.

Two days later, Tom—he said to call him that—phoned. "I'd like very much to see you again," he said.

She wanted to exult, then told herself to calm down, and wound up not saying anything.

"You've got me intrigued about your house," he went on. "It sounds like you've done a wonderful job fixing it up. I tried once, in an earlier life, to fix a hardwood floor. Made an awful mess. Took a contractor two days to undo the damage—busted nails, gouges—and cost four times what he would have charged me in the first place. I'd love to see your place, see what you've done."

She pictured Peele in her foyer, her sanctuary, and felt pride, then fear. This time, the silence got to her first. "Sure," she said. Then, with as much exuberance as she could muster, "The floor's due for a fresh coat of wax; this is a good occasion."

They made a date—no denying that's what it was—for three nights later. To this point, it had all seemed removed, abstract, word games at fund-raisers and restaurants, but now Tom was coming to her house. To her home, where she kept her treasures and trinkets, where she rarely invited a man until she knew him well, or better than she knew Tom Peele. She'd need to clean the place, rotate some rugs, polish her grandmother's silver.

She thought of Tom periodically, at odd moments in her office or among the tomes, and found herself smiling. She told herself to be careful. It had been so long since she was interested in a man that she might just be smitten by the idea of being smitten, without really having any of the underlying passion.

Tom arrived fifteen minutes late, on a sweltering Iowa evening as field crickets chirped a screeching assault. There was the awkward, nervous tingle that she had always enjoyed, when she opened the door for a first date, and he was standing on her doorstep trying to look his best. Her heart would pound, her palms moisten, her throat dry, her stomach fizz, all the clichéd responses. She had savored these moments since junior high in Portland.

Tom didn't seem nervous or swept by the moment, though. He flashed his smile, standing loose as though the scene, if it were choreographed, would be titled "Tom Enters." He reached into a leather briefcase as he stepped through the portal and, without breaking stride, produced a bottle of burgundy, pivoted, and presented it to her. The label had a drawing of a medieval chateau. Was the choice deliberate, or had he stumbled on it?

Tom stepped into her foyer, which opened to the dining and living rooms. "This place is magnificent, Elizabeth," he pronounced, scanning the off-white walls, Moorish arches and antique tables, cabinet, and barrister bookcases. "Absolutely magnificent." His eyes passed over some sixteenth-century woodcuts on one dining room wall and caught on three white plates with blue country scenes mounted on brass arms. "There must be a story behind those plates," he urged. "Tell me."

"Actually, there's a pretty good story," she said, smiling at his enthusiasm. "It's kind of a long story, though."

He shrugged and smiled.

She told him the story, as her mother had told her. A notorious fox hunt had inspired a master Sussex artisan to paint the plates, which had circulated among English country folk for

generations and then languished for years in an Irish bootleg-
ger's shed. Her grandmother had spotted them at a flea market, recognizing the craftsmanship and value. Her grandmother
gave the plates to her mother as a wedding present, and her
mother gave the plates to her to adorn her first home.

She felt herself running on, and was surprised Tom still
seemed interested, even mesmerized. His smile never sagged,
though the story sounded a bit flat, even to her ears. She wondered whether this was one of his techniques. Every time he
goes to a voter's house, does he find something they're obviously
proud of and exclaim, "There must be a story behind it, tell me!"

Tom's wine, a grand cru burgundy from St. Emillion—
God knows what he paid for that in Iowa—would go well with
the marinated roast lamb and baked red potatoes simmering in
the oven. It was one of those simple but elegant dishes, if done
right, that showed you knew how to cook and how to eat well.
And it was kind of a primal dish, a hunk of red meat surrounded
by potatoes, that said you knew how to feed a man.

He handled her grandmother's acorn-pattern silver deftly,
scooping a mound of vinaigrette-laced greens for her by working a fork and spoon with one hand. His posture was perfect,
back straight and head back. Watching his jaw flex, she was
tempted to count whether he chewed each morsel the textbook
twenty times.

"You're very proper," she said. "Grandmother would approve."

"You too, professor." He gestured around her dining room
and dabbed a corner of his mouth with a napkin.

"I wasn't always," she said.

"No?" A faint leer crept across his face.

She shrugged again. "In high school, I fell in with a clique
of bohemians and nihilists. You know, elf boots, black stock-

ings, leather skirts. Sneaking clove cigarettes in the woods. I moved on after I'd riled my dad enough, but he got the last laugh. They hung a photo of me wearing so much black eye shadow I look like a raccoon."

He smiled. "I hung out with some of those characters at Columbia, on the literary magazine, sort of beat-poet wannabes." He stopped, as though recalling a painful memory. "But my views were pretty fixed by then. There weren't too many rebels in Mead, Nebraska, when I grew up, so I kind of missed my avant-garde phase."

He took off his suit coat and draped it around the back of his chair. Poor thing, she'd made him feel like a stiff. But maybe he was also showing off. He was in good shape for his age: broad-shouldered and solid, with only a slight roll above his belt under his white shirt, not much bigger than her muffin top, she had to admit.

She wondered if he got invited to White House balls, like the one in the sappy romance *The American President,* which had made her misty. Did Tom wield any heft in that world, or was he just a big fish in a small Midwest pond, on whom lonely women projected environmental hopes and schoolgirl fantasies? "Are you on a first-name basis with the President?"

He smiled. "Yeah, my first name. With him, it's 'Mr. President.' Gotta show respect for the office."

"But you talk to him fairly often?"

"Once in a while. When I want something, or more often, when he wants something."

This man forking watercress salad at her grandmother's table wanted more than to talk with the president, she reminded herself; he wanted to *be* the president. He seemed almost sure of his prospects, to judge by the grin. What would it take to jar him, to pierce his plastic shell, even for a moment? She wanted to slide her foot out of her pump, reach it under the table and rub the ball against his shin. But that seemed too Monica Lewinsky. And she needed to make him work for it a little more, partly because he seemed to take it too much for granted. But first, there was still the elephant in the room.

"You've got a wife and a daughter," she said. "What are you doing here?" She fixed a stare on him, the one she used on unruly students. They didn't know she was seeing them with only one of the two narrowed eyes.

He didn't say anything for a moment. Good. At least he was thinking of a response, instead of spouting a canned line.

"My wife and I have an open relationship," he finally said.

She smiled and shook her head. "I'm not looking to get involved with a swinger."

He exhaled. "This needs to be strictly between us."

He was waiting for a response. At least he had dropped the grin. She nodded.

"I wanted kids; Susan kind of resisted. Then Agatha was born with a spinal disorder, needed surgeries, therapy, rehab. I swear, we must have paid off more medical school loans than the NIH. Susan handled most of the running around. She figures it set her back five or ten years in her career, while I hopped up the political ladder."

He was still making eye contact, the dark brows furrowed around the blue eyes. She waited.

"My wife comes from an old Nebraska family, Knights of Ak-Sar-Ben—that's Nebraska spelled backwards, kind of their Skull and Bones and Masons rolled into one. Daddy's little girl wasn't used to adversity." He looked down. "Ten years ago, Susan had . . ." He glanced up. "What she called . . . a miscarriage. But I'm pretty sure. It was. An abortion. We kind of drifted apart."

He looked up and returned her gaze, hopefully now, like a puppy who had messed the rug begging forgiveness, or at least understanding.

She shrugged. He was playing her like a violin, continuing a concerto that had begun with admiring her plates. But part of it, clearly, was sincere. How much? "Tell me about the secret passageways in the Capitol you always read about. Sounds like something out of *The Count of Monte Cristo*."

He flashed the grin. "Nothing secret about them. But they wind all over the place. If you don't know where you're going, no telling where you'll end up." He seemed to cue on her interest in the trappings of high office. He described meetings with prime ministers and a private audience with the Pope. He described how his police escort in Tbilisi nearly sideswiped a cheese peddler while rushing to the Georgian president's palace.

"I'm filibustering," he said. "What do you do for fun, Elizabeth? Besides volunteering on political campaigns?"

Most of her spare time recently had been going into revising the book on religious symbolism in Chaucer, getting it ready to pitch to another batch of publishers. Should she ask for advice? No, too soon. Should she tell him about trolling antique shops for porcelain figurines? She'd sound as though she'd skipped a generation and turned into her grandmother. "I'm a movie junkie," she finally said. "I've already worn out one DVD player. I'll watch almost anything, but I'm a sucker for a sappy love story."

He told her he liked some of the same stuff, musicals especially, to escape the political grind. He backed it up, too, reciting lines from *My Man Godfrey* and *Gigi*. When she tried to recall a scene from the Garbo classic *Ninotchka*, it was he who remembered the names of the three Russian advance men. He even described the camera angles and scene breaks.

As she talked, he locked his blue eyes on her, once even resting his chin on his fist, as though such an intense act of listening required physical support. When he told his stories, his smile spread, his hands fluttered like a schoolboy's. She enjoyed storytelling as seduction, a tradition going back at least to *The Odyssey*. An intelligent, powerful man, interested in her interests; it was all very alluring. And very rare.

"Ultimately," he was saying, "we're in the communications business. We sell ideas. And, yeah, we sell ourselves. But there's no place for poetry anymore, or even a complete sentence, with the YouTube generation."

"You like poetry?" she asked.

"I saw the best minds of my generation destroyed by madness . . . angel-headed hipsters burning for the ancient heavenly connection to the starry dynamo in the machinery of night."

Well, at least he knew the landmarks. "'Howl,'" she said.

"Very good. But then you do this for a living. Allen Ginsberg wrote that in 1955. The fifties, in the postwar complacency, were a time of conformity. *Leave It to Beaver*, Levittown, crew cuts." He paused, as though deep in thought. "The poem's still just as relevant today."

"So what does the poem mean to you?" She leaned across the table toward him, letting her breasts rest on her upper arms, lifting them.

"Apart from the drugs and sex, I've always seen it as a cry for individuality in a world that's becoming ever more cold and repressive."

Well, she'd give him a B-plus, maybe an A-minus. He'd answered her question, telling her what "Howl" meant to him, though not how it had moved him. She had been hoping for an example of how Ginsberg's plea had spurred him to action. She was tempted to ask whether he took the poem's anticonformity as a license to indulge his libertine impulses, or, like Frost, to take the path less traveled by. But at least he had tried, giving her a glimpse of his soul on her turf. That must have been tough for him. He was waiting now for her response, the eyes still bright, but his jaw tightening as he braced for her critique.

Pressing one heel against the other, she slid off a pump and stretched a bare foot until her toes found his shin, and rubbed against it.

He smiled and put down his fork. Grinning like a fox that snared a rabbit, he pushed out his chair and came around the table toward her.

12

★ ★ ★

THE DEATH PENALTY

Peele phoned for Henry at the Iowa campaign office, setting off what sounded like an air-raid alert. "Senator's calling! It's the Senator!" aides screamed, until the headquarters hushed, as though Peele could reach out from the phone and see who was working and who was lolling.

"Tom?" he asked, his pen poised above a yellow pad like Moses over a clay tablet.

"I've arranged a private meeting at the hotel room tonight. So I'd appreciate if you wouldn't come back before nine, if that's not too much of an inconvenience."

"That's fine." He hadn't had a request like that since college.

"Okay, good," Peele said, crisply. "While you're there, you need to beef up our news conference for tomorrow morning." Peele was going to call for restoring Iowa's death penalty, flanked by a cadre of cops in Cedar Rapids. "The script needs work. You don't even have how many Iowa cops have been killed. Cop-killing is a prime capital offense in a lot of other states."

"We've never gotten into that level of detail before."

"Well, don't you think those numbers are relevant?"

He sighed. "Sure." The death penalty news conference was a standard criminal justice hit they had been trotting out across Iowa and in other states that banned capital punishment. You lined up a few uniformed cops outside a police station and railed about career criminals literally getting away with murder. Why did Peele want to puff it up now, the night before a show?

"Get with it," Peele said. "This is the big leagues." The line went dead.

He stepped out of his office to find the Iowa press secretary. Let Kyle track down the statistics. No, Kyle was in Cedar Rapids, doing advance work on a rally next week. He would have to track down the numbers himself. He didn't like being banned from the Rigsdale, and didn't want to set a precedent, even if he rarely got back to the hotel before ten. Peele's call also jeopardized the exciting evening he had planned, featuring a workout at the YMCA on 4th Street, where he had renewed his membership from Tyler's campaign, and a roast beef club platter at the diner up Ingersoll Avenue.

Peele wouldn't be satisfied with just the Iowa numbers. The Senator would want to know how many cops had been killed in states that had capital punishment versus in those without, to make an argument for the death penalty as a deterrent. It was already past five P.M. in Washington, so the Congressional Research Service couldn't help. During business hours, an army of CRS issues experts at the Library of Congress stood by to answer any question or prepare any material a congressional aide requested. It was like having a private research firm and trivia team, all courtesy of the taxpayers. He could ask Sterba to task Peele's Senate staff. But some of this stuff was Iowa-specific, and the aides might not be able to find it, or might bristle at doing campaign work. They had already overloaded the former House Judiciary Committee staff director the campaign had hired to draft crime-control policy. He looked at his gym bag in the corner, bulging with workout gear.

He stormed over to Lynn, who handled Peele's Iowa scheduling. Lynn was a no-nonsense farm girl turned out-of-work executive whose whole being grated, from her clipped sentences to her itchy tweed blazers. She seemed to enjoy making men cringe by telling stories of castrating horses and tossing their testicles onto the barn roof, counting the bounces.

"The Senator told me he has a meeting tonight at the hotel," he said. "What's it about, do you know?"

"Yeah," she said, flipping through a notebook. "He's meeting with a volunteer about education."

"Who's the volunteer?"

She looked back at her notes, as though he was pressing her patience. "Professor Walmsley, from Iowa State."

Elizabeth Walmsley. He felt like an ass. There he was, sliding in horse dung in Cherokee, Iowa, obsessing about a woman while Peele was lining her up for a session in their hotel room. He stepped over to the refrigerator, an aging, humming Amana where he kept some pints of orange juice. Elizabeth. She had smiled so innocently at Peele, with those dimpled cheeks and white teeth, like showing a Rembrandt to an art thief. He tugged at a juice container's paper seam, but the two ends wouldn't separate into a spout. After a few more tries, he jammed a finger into the seam and ripped one side, sending up a sticky orange spray.

"Something wrong?" Mary McCormick was standing beside him with her schoolmarm stare.

"Nothing," he said, shaking the juice off his hands and onto the carpet.

She gave him the glare again.

"I've got to track down some crime stats," he said and angled toward his office.

"We have a Des Moines police detective who's offered to help the campaign," she said. "I can get you his number."

"Appreciate it, Mary, but this stuff is complex."

"Jeff Rensi has a Ph.D. and he teaches criminal justice at Drake." She strode to her desk and came back with a number on a yellow Post-it note. "He works evenings."

Did all of Peele's Iowa volunteers have doctorates and teach college? Back in his little office, he dialed the number. What could he lose?

"Homicide, Rensi," a deep voice barked in what sounded like a New York or New Jersey accent.

"Sergeant Jeff Rensi?"

"Speakin'. What can I do for you?"

"Save my career, or at least my evening."

Rensi, over the phone, sounded like a cross between a professor and a stevedore. Rensi sounded, Henry supposed, the way he might have if he hadn't gone to Trinity and Dartmouth. The sergeant, it turned out, was a Newark transplant. Rensi had served in the Air Force at Strategic Air Command headquarters in Bellevue, Nebraska, married a local, and settled in Des Moines.

"Come over to the squad room at six thirty and I'll have the stats for you," Rensi said.

"Sergeant, no offense, but we've got to do this news conference early tomorrow morning. It's going to be ugly if we count on you and you don't come through."

"Hey, Hatten, be here at six thirty. And wear a tie. We got standards."

Was Rensi joking, or had somebody told the cop that Henry didn't dress well? He shook his head, as though to clear it.

A wave of loneliness swept over Henry, pressing in on him as though gravity had doubled in his small Des Moines office. He lifted his phone, smiled, and dialed. Fogel answered on the third ring, an abrupt "Yeah?"

Mostly, Henry just wanted to hear a familiar voice from home, or what had become home. He told the media man he was checking in, wanted to give these crime hits more punch. It didn't take long for Fogel to launch into a monolog.

"A lot of times you get into these landlocked campaigns, where just nothing moves," Fogel said. The race had slipped into stasis, Sadler and Dagworth generally scoring first and second in national and Iowa polls, with Peele filling out the top tier and occasionally breaking into a poll's top two. Neither Sadler nor Dagworth projected an aura of inevitability.

"I feel like Admiral Peary," Fogel said, and Henry vaguely recalled the turn-of-the-century arctic explorer. "We're doing focus groups every other week, and pretty soon we're going to do them every week, because nothing is working.

"No, it isn't like taking a hammer and chopping through ice," Fogel corrected himself. "It's like being a thief, a safe-cracker—and listening until you hear the tumblers fall."

Henry leaned back in the chair, exhaled, and let Fogel's words rush through his head.

"For now, we have to be counterintuitive. We have to do things in focus groups and write scripts that we know are wrong, that we know won't work, in the hope that they'll tell us something that gives us a thread of an idea that *will* work."

"That's tough," Henry said, just to prime the pump.

"You spend a lot of your time writing shitty scripts and doing shitty spots, and burning through Peele's money, and Peele's not happy about it, and then Gil takes me aside, and he's not happy, and I say, 'You've got a better idea, you let me know. If not, I'll be in the fucking studio.' How's that for an update?"

Henry smiled. "That's great, Ira."

"Hey, chin up," Fogel said. "The tumblers *will* fall."

At six twenty P.M., in the Des Moines police headquarters lobby, a uniformed sergeant buzzed Henry through a Plexi-and-metal door, and he boarded a stainless-steel elevator. The whole place felt cold and antiseptic, metal panels joined at right angles, as though designed so cops could pound prisoners to pulps and easily wipe up the blood and gore. On the third floor, which housed the Criminal Investigation Bureau, or detective squads, a receptionist buzzed him through.

The squad bay looked more like a newsroom than a cop shop. Clusters of desks filled the main area. Detectives sat scribbling on forms or tapping on keyboards, a lot of wide poly-ester ties, oversized belt buckles, and rubber-soled shoes, the occasional older detective showing a swath of white athletic sock. The few women wore their hair pulled back or bobbed. Most of the men wore mustaches. Among the several in shirt-sleeves, grips of 9mm semi-automatics jutted from leather belt holsters. There was something eerie about being in a police station, walking among armed detectives trained to spot crim-inals, with licenses to lock you up.

He passed a series of glassed offices lining the squad bay walls, blinds running from floor to ceiling inside. At the third office on the left, he peered through the open door. A tall man was leaning back on a swivel chair, feet on the desk, legs crossed at the ankles. The man was dressed like a senator, in a starched white shirt with silver cuff links and rich navy wool suit pants cuffed above black balmorals. The dark hair, graying at the temples, looked freshly cut. Tortoiseshell reading glasses perched on the nose, which was angled slightly back to read the *Wall Street Journal*. The only inconsistency was a shoulder holster that gouged the crisp cotton.

"Sergeant Rensi?"

The man looked up from the newspaper. "Hatten!"

"Yes, sir."

Rensi put down the paper and stood, extending a large hand. The detective had a good cop handshake, firm, dry, and quick. "Have a seat." Rensi indicated a vinyl-cushioned chair against a wall.

He glanced at his watch and perched on the edge of the chair. The office was tidy and spare, essentially a glass-walled cubicle with commercial carpet and a bookshelf in one corner. *Bartlett's Quotations*, the *Oxford English Dictionary*, *Roget's Thesaurus*, the *Columbia Introduction to Contemporary Civilization*, and a textbook on criminal justice sat next to a volume of "Far Side" cartoons and a rotisserie baseball guide. "That's an eclectic set of books."

Rensi glanced at the shelf. "Oh, yeah. The thicker ones are mine. I share this office with the A-shift and C-shift sergeants—the morning and overnight guys. Actually, the C-shift sergeant used to have a couple more books on the shelf, but he took them home to finish coloring them."

Henry smiled. Copies of half of those books sat on his shelves, back in his Cleveland Park apartment. "I used that textbook at college, the contemporary civilization one. Even used it to quote Castiglione for a House floor speech. Good princes, noxious princes." He shrugged. "Mostly, it made me wish I'd been a knight in the days of chivalry."

"Actually," Rensi said, "the chivalric code was designed to

control a bunch of bored young noblemen who were tearing up the countryside, raping women, trashing farms. That kind of deterrent doesn't seem to work so well today."

He squinted at the cop. "Sergeant, don't take this the wrong way, but you don't seem like a typical police officer."

"Worst part for me was uniformed patrol," Rensi said, wincing. "Had to buy off the rack."

He laughed. Rensi, he noticed, was wearing a woven tie, gold and white ellipses stitched on a maroon field. Where had an Iowa cop picked up such fashion sense? If you're going to go to all that trouble on the wardrobe, though, why not also fix the accent? Maybe because Rensi fancied finery for its own sake, not as a guise.

He looked at his watch again. Nearly seven. By now, Peele was probably in the hotel suite with Elizabeth. He pictured them on the faded couch, Peele's hand unbuttoning her blouse.

"Sergeant, you have any luck with the statistics?"

The cop's lips parted as though about to speak, but then clamped. Reaching into the desk, the detective pulled out a manila envelope and tossed it like a Frisbee, corners spinning, into Henry's lap.

He smoothed a corner of the envelope, opened the flap and slid out a dozen pages of charts, graphs, and text printed in crisp colors. The material covered not only the statistics he had asked for but also trends, such as Iowa's growing murder rate using guns, which played into Peele's crusade against repeat offenders caught with firearms. The report looked like a term paper for an applied physics class. They could hand out copies of the graphs and charts.

"That's terrific."

"Glad it's up to your standards."

He tucked the envelope under his arm and stood. "Really

appreciate all your help, Sergeant. I'll make sure the Senator knows what a contribution you've made." He eased toward the door.

Rensi stiffened. "Hey, Hatten, I get patronized enough by the brass around here; I don't need it from some snot-nosed politico."

13

★ ★ ★

POACHED BASS

Henry thought a blood vessel might burst in Cass's head, the way the Angel's eyes bulged as they scanned the table in the Boston law firm conference room.

"We've learned that Zach Lowe is going to skip the Tennessee Straw Poll next weekend to campaign at a Republican picnic in Washington State," Cass said. Lowe was New York's libertarian governor. "I've told Diane to hire an airplane to drag a banner that says 'Lowe Means Higher Taxes' right over the picnic for an hour. I'm going to get some guys to distribute 'Lowe Is a Taxer' flyers at the picnic—guys who won't be intimidated."

"Intimidated from what?" Brian Natter, their New Hampshire chairman, asked from the seat next to Henry.

"Intimidated from exercising their First Amendment right of free speech," Cass said, looming over the table. "I've got a couple of guys in mind from the karate dojo where I train."

Natter made a face. The New Hampshire chairman was supposed to be a top Manchester corporate lawyer. He seemed

brainy, but wore a bit too much gel in his brush cut. Natter had
joined Peele's campaign largely to build his own political stock,
Henry figured. The guy probably wanted to make and keep
friends, including those on Lowe's New Hampshire team.

"We've got to, one, establish that we own the socially centrist, antitax position," Cass said. "And two, send Lowe a message that we won't just roll over; we'll flame-broil him."

Cass didn't mention it, but Henry knew the Angel was also
trying to enlist Sadler's campaign in the effort to torpedo Lowe.
Cass had shown selected results of Peele's polls to a top Sadler
aide, suggesting that Lowe was an even bigger problem for
Sadler than for Peele. Cass wanted Sadler to ask his maxed-out
donors, those who had already given the Texan the $2,500 fed-
eral limit, to write checks to Peele, on the understanding that
Peele would use their money to attack Lowe.

Cass turned to Diane and then to Henry. "I'll teach you
communists yet how to win a campaign."

The war council in the law firm conference room would
kick off a six-day New England swing. Throughout the week,
amid a crush of meetings and media hits, Peele scrawled and
scratched out words on yellow legal pads until the pages were
so soaked and smudged and stiff with ink that they crinkled
when the Senator pulled them from a pocket. Peele was drafting a Saturday-night speech for Harvard's John F. Kennedy
School of Government, which he had come to call the "Kennedy School Address," as though that's how historians should
refer to it. Peele asked Henry to track down quotes from Theo-
dore Roosevelt, Oliver Wendell Holmes, and other Harvard
alumni, then crammed further scribbles onto the pages.

Twice Henry asked Peele if he could help with the draft.
The Senator wouldn't let him or anybody else even see the yel-

low pages. "It'd take me longer to explain it to you than to just do it myself," Peele insisted.

Part of him didn't really want to tackle the scrawled mess. But Peele was breaking their compact, to let him weigh in on all the Big Think. Tyler had let him draft victory and concession speeches; Peele wouldn't even let him touch a text for a gaggle of geeks. Even if Peele was the best writer in the office, a pro who had penned scripts for *Parkland* and other shows, any text could benefit from another set of eyes.

"You sure C-SPAN is going to cover the speech?" Peele asked him.

"Yes, Senator, they covered Sadler's speech at the Kennedy School last week; they'll cover yours, if only as a matter of fairness."

"Should we release an advance text to the press?"

"Only if you're going to make news, Tom; nobody's going to reprint your white papers."

Cass was less diplomatic, loping alongside them after a meeting with the *Boston Herald* editorial board. "What are you doing, pissing away that kind of time writing sixteen drafts of a speech for a bunch of eggheads who are going to vote for the most liberal fucking communist pinko Democrat on the ballot, no matter what you tell them?"

Peele halted in the parking lot and glowered at Cass, like a football coach at an overgrown lineman. "Hey, maestro, in the end, we got to be about ideas. *Ideas.*"

Peele had set aside Monday morning for a meeting at the Copley Hotel with Carlton Hires, a former Massachusetts State Senate majority leader. Massachusetts, and especially Boston, was key to the nomination. Many New Hampshire voters read the *Boston Globe* or *Herald* as their primary paper and tuned to Boston TV news. A Boston media ad would let Peele reach them without depleting his meager allocation for New Hampshire.

At ten A.M. Monday, the hour for the Hires meeting, an older woman in a sharp tweed suit stepped toward their alcove off the hotel lobby. The woman's bobbed hair had gone gray, but she still projected power and attitude, like a hotshot litigator. Her calves flexed when she walked, and Henry pegged her for a runner, maybe a swimmer.

Henry was about to intercept the woman, when Peele jumped up and gave her a kiss on the cheek. In the flurry, Henry hadn't seen the briefing package on Hires. He had assumed Hires was a man, because the only other Carlton he knew was a high school wrestler. The woman's full name, it turned out, was Victoria Carlton Hires.

Hires said she was flattered by Peele's interest and wanted to give the Senator the courtesy of personally telling him thanks, but no thanks.

Peele said he hadn't come to Boston for a No.

Hires said she was looking forward to a peaceful retirement with her grandchildren and her garden. "This is the first summer I haven't worked on a campaign in nineteen years."

"Summer's almost over," Peele said. He told Hires she had a chance to be part of something big, that she was too young to go out to pasture, that they needed her. Henry thought Peele was going to tell her that the country needed her, too, but the boss had a good governor on his BS.

All the presidential campaigns were going after a lot of the same people, Henry knew, and Hires was probably on the list. There were certain staffers to get, certain chairmen to get, both for their names and their networks.

Hires leaned back on a couch and nodded as Peele pressed. If her No had been firm, she wouldn't have agreed to meet. But if Hires was going to sign on, she would demand a price. Henry eased back in a blue leather wing chair, crossed his legs, and watched to see if he'd developed any instincts.

Hires had a no-nonsense style and a matching alto, and it didn't take long. "Well, Tom, as you may know, I've been spending a lot of time pushing for The Cure." The Cure meant the fight against breast cancer, Henry knew. Pretty good PR in a world where advocates competed for funds to combat a plethora of deadly diseases.

Peele nodded in tight motions and crossed his arms.

"There's a bill going through the Senate right now that should be a lot stronger on our grant channels," Hires said. "Just really a squandered opportunity. It just got reported out of the HELP Committee." The Health, Education, Labor & Pensions Committee authorized all federal health care programs. "What I'd really like, Tom, is to get the bill back-burnered until I get a chance to talk to the Majority Leader." The U.S. Senate Majority Leader, Scott Mathis, controlled the Senate calendar, and could bring bills to the floor for debate and votes when he chose, or bury them.

Peele was nodding again, the head strokes longer now. "Well, Carlton, let me see what I can do."

Word at Peele headquarters was that the Majority Leader was leaning toward Sadler in the presidential, though still officially neutral, which meant Peele wouldn't have much juice with Mathis. But maybe Peele knew something about the bill, and thought it wouldn't be a big ask. Or maybe these were just the first steps in a dance.

Within thirty seconds, Peele and Hires were on their feet planting cheek kisses.

That night, while Peele worked some money men, Cass took Henry to dinner at an upscale steakhouse on the harbor. The Angel was wearing a three-piece Donegal suit that looked like something out of F. Scott Fitzgerald. If money didn't matter, Henry thought, he'd like a suit like that.

"One adult, one child," Cass said as they approached the maître d'.

Henry felt like a student with the teacher all to himself. He sniffed for the Angel's familiar talc and aftershave scent, and found it, faintly. He held it in his nostrils until it turned saccharine.

They settled under a white linen tablecloth. A waiter in black tie glided by with a wine list, bound in gold-etched leather, like a rare volume. As Cass studied the columns, Henry glanced at the prices. At least a dozen were in triple digits.

Cass looked up. "We'll have a bottle of the Chateau Lafite-Rothschild, 1996," he said, handing back the book.

The waiter nodded, gave a short bow, and glided off.

"I think you'll like this," Cass said. "Lafite was sort of the house wine at Versailles under Louis XV."

A metallic ring blared from below the table. Cass reached down and came up with an iPhone. "I got to take this." Cass clutched the phone to his mouth. "*Oui, Jacques. Oui. No, ce n'est pas necessaire. Dites lui, seulement le quatre vingt mille. Oui.*" Cass snapped the phone shut and returned it below the table.

"Gil, what is it you do, when you're not helping us communists?"

"I fix problems," the Angel said. "That was a guy in Brussels; you don't want to know. Monday, a steel company CEO calls me, very upset. The FAA was going to impound his Gulfstream V. That plane, by the way, costs more than you'll earn in your lifetime. The steel man, we'll call him K, flew the Gulfstream to Long Island for the weekend, which he likes to do. The local airport barred planes over a certain weight from taking off or landing after midnight. Seems the locals were complaining about the noise. But that doesn't concern K. He figures his Gulfstream is quieter than half the rickety, bargain-bin Cessnas on the airfield, so the rules shouldn't apply to him. The FAA didn't see it that way."

"Did you save his plane?"

Cass smiled. "Yeah."

The waiter, now joined by a sommelier, appeared with the wine. Expert fingers wielded elaborate silver tools, peeling the metal sleeve and popping the cork. The fluid looked almost black when a sample sluiced into Cass's glass.

To Henry, the wine tasted rich, with a silky texture and a lingering aroma of mint and bitter fruit. "Pretty good," he said.

"Glad you appreciate it." Cass looked up, as though summoning a memory. "It's art that *makes* life. Art is power." He smiled and looked at Henry. "The problem in our business is, you make your art well, so few people ever know it."

Henry sipped the wine. He tried to identify the flavors, and thought he could pick out almond. He buttered a pumpernickel roll. "So why does a big guy like you go for karate? In my experience, it's mostly little guys who go into martial arts, to compensate for their size."

"That's why," the Angel said. "I was a geeky punching bag as a kid. Six-five, one fifty, when I got thrown out of my last prep school, Coke-bottle glasses and an attitude. Every Napoleon-complex little prick smacked me around."

Henry smiled. In his high school wrestling days, he had relished opponents with Cass's build. With their lanky limbs, they had less upper-body strength and little leverage once you tied them up. "You think the Kennedy School speech is a waste of time?"

Cass made a face. "Good old Tom Peele from the Nebraska cornfields. He's going to mix it up with the Big Thinkers."

Henry chewed a chunk of the roll. "He's the boss."

Cass shot him a staff-meeting look. "You don't work for him; you work for me. Remember who butters your bread."

The pumpernickel tasted slightly bitter and coarse, even buttered.

A few hours before the Kennedy speech, Henry sat in the backseat of a bouncing Dodge studying Peele's stubbled neck. The Senator, bracing against an armrest, head bobbing, was making some final tweaks to the sacred draft as the car sped past Boston Common toward their final meeting of the day.

Henry felt an urge to whip his left arm around in front of Peele, dig the thumb between Peele's collar and neck, on the far side of the Adam's apple, and raise the hand under Peele's chin, jerking Peele's head back. Then, and Henry could almost feel it, he'd whip the right arm through the gap the left had made, and dig the right thumb under the other side of Peele's collar. Then he'd pull his arms in and back, still gripping Peele's shirt, twisting his wrists into the neck, turning the Senator's collar into a noose. He'd lean forward and press his head against Peele's, skull to skull, cheek to cheek, and listen as he cut off the air and the blood.

He exhaled and let the image go. This was the first time he had ever targeted Peele in one of his psycho martial arts fantasies, and he knew he had crossed a line. He'd never pictured hurting anybody precious to him, never dared lay even an imaginary finger on his father, not even after their worst fights.

He felt an emptiness, and realized that he'd been forgiving and overlooking all of Peele's downsides and disappointments—drug scams, bloody Teamsters, adultery, surly condescension—because he was smitten, and each seemed trivial against the greater whole. Now the collective weight of all of Peele's foibles and failings was crashing down, and Henry was no longer smitten. So that left him, essentially, in a bad romance. Well, more like a mediocre romance with a generally decent partner capable of occasional sin and cruelty. That might describe most marriages. It certainly described most politicians. Anyway, the stakes were too high to get out now.

"Senator," he asked when Peele leaned back and rubbed his eyes, "you ever think what your life would be like if you'd stayed in show business?"

"I am in show business. Washington and Hollywood are both one-industry towns, fueled by gossip." Peele leaned over the seat. "Probably a few more years on *Parkland*, until we all got too long in the tooth, then character roles, maybe some stage work."

"Doesn't appeal to you?"

"I'm already living in the house that Roy built." Peele turned further, fixing the blue eyes. "Henry, you don't take any chances in life, nothing good or bad will ever happen to you."

After the meeting, Peele went to nap in the hotel room the Kennedy School had provided across the street. "I'm going to skip the cocktails and dinner," the Senator told Henry. "Wake me at seven." Peele never ate before a performance.

An hour later, the front desk called Henry's room. "Mr. Hatten, can you come downstairs at once? There are two security officers who say they have to talk to you." He threw on his jacket and trotted to the elevator. Two Harvard External Affairs men in black blazers and rubber-soled cop shoes were pacing in front of the reception desk. "Where's Senator Peele?" one asked, rushing toward him. Cocktails had begun half an hour earlier. The university had already alerted the Cambridge police that the Senator was missing.

"The Senator *must* go to the dinner," the other officer pleaded. "It'll be a disaster if he doesn't."

He waited fifteen minutes, until seven, to phone Peele's room. Peele asked him to come over with a cup of black coffee, two sugars. Clasping the steaming Styrofoam cup in the corridor, he wondered what his college classmates would think if they saw him, and what they were doing then. A few were probably barbecuing on spacious lawns, savoring the long summer evening. Some were probably at the office or in the studies of their Hampton homes, negotiating ten-figure banking deals or preparing court cases. Others probably performing surgery. Maybe a few on distant battlefields, commanding companies or battalions. And he was toting coffee, black with two sugars.

The Senator was in the bathroom working an electric razor when he arrived. He sat on a chair at the desk, reading the dialing instructions on the telephone's faceplate. Eight then zero then the country code for an overseas call, and so on. He turned to the bed, where Peele had tossed a briefcase and some papers. Among the pages he noticed a name tag, white with ornate blue borders. Looking closer, he saw the name written in flowing blue marker was not Peele's, but Elizabeth Walmsley's, along with a phone number. The name tag Elizabeth had written at the Sioux City fund-raiser.

He summoned the image, now etched inside his head, of Peele and Elizabeth on the Rigsdale couch. He began to reach for the name tag, wanting this piece of her and wanting to deprive Peele of it. Maybe he'd even send the Senator tearing through his bags for the missing name tag, frazzling him before the big speech; Fogel's ploy. But Peele might emerge from the bathroom at any moment, and he didn't want to get caught with his hand in the boss's papers. He memorized the number, then walked back to the desk, wrote it on a hotel memo pad, and folded the slip of paper into his shirt pocket, behind Peele's schedule.

Stepping into the room, Peele slipped a navy suit jacket over a white shirt and favorite tie, a maroon-and-aqua swirl. "Let's go."

Henry felt small walking into the Kennedy School banquet hall, like a valet using the guest entrance. Dartmouth, alas, was second-tier Ivy League, not the Big Three. Ornate sconces gave dim light, largely absorbed by dark wood wainscoting and trim, lending an aura of Camelot. He hadn't seen so many vests, bow ties, and watch fobs outside a 1930s film, and had never heard the word "indeed" tossed around so freely. At a table toward the front, he pecked at a plate of poached sea bass while Peele chatted with the dean and some professors.

Minutes later, they were in the wings of an adjacent auditorium, broiling under a C-SPAN camera. When the dean introduced Peele, for an instant that most would not notice, the Senator breathed, gathered himself, put on a grin, and walked onstage. Placing the battered yellow text on the lectern, Peele gazed out at the rows of seats and at the camera. Seconds passed and Henry wondered whether Peele was going to be able to perform.

"I grew up on a farm outside Omaha, Nebraska," Peele began. "We had some itinerant help, but it was basically, literally, a mom-and-pop operation. When I was seventeen, a small-bale forage baler—a machine that has since been phased out, for good reason—dropped a six-hundred-pound bale of hay on my dad. Now, when hay is packed tight, it's hard as concrete. The hay bale crushed my father's right arm. He couldn't use it much after that."

Henry had never heard that story. Peele was clearly reliving it, reaching into himself, the voice nearly choking on the memory. The Nebraska farm boy bit was part of The Story that staff weaved into the Senator's bios and speeches, but not Papa Peele's injury. He thought of his own father and boyhood fears of a falling carton or pallet that would leave him an orphan. He could have told Peele that a crowd like this might respect you for rising above humble roots, but wouldn't want to hang out with you or hear your opinions.

"My father went to a lawyer in town, and they wound up settling for ten thousand dollars, which barely covered my dad's medical bills. And left nothing for my college tuition."

Peele, still riding the memories, said his father had to sell the farm eighteen months later. "He finished up managing a farm-equipment store, working for somebody else for the first time in his life, and he died bitter, and too young. And I wound up leaving Columbia. Eventually, I got a degree from UCLA, taking evening classes." Peele smiled at the crowd. "Not quite the same thing."

From the wings, Henry scanned the audience. They all seemed to be paying polite attention, if occasionally checking a watch or whispering to a neighbor.

Peele segued to the manifesto, laying out a vision for an America where the little guy who was willing to work hard could prosper, or at least get by. That didn't mean handouts; it meant a safety net. Peele hit the core points, calling for a fiscally responsible, environmentally conscious, internationally engaged America that balanced national security with civil rights.

These were the kind of lines that could make Henry tingle, but tonight the words just faded in his ears. Peele may have been trying too hard. Or maybe Henry had seen the show too many times.

Henry noticed a woman in the front row who looked like Elizabeth, with the same voluptuous shape and wire-rims, though her coloring was darker. She projected the same intelligence, though with more of an edge. He noticed Peele's eye catch on her, causing the Senator to miss a beat. Then Peele found a cadence and rhythm. Finger stabbing the air, the Senator barely glanced at the inky script. Peele cited Teddy Roosevelt's "man in the arena" line, invoked Goldwater on keeping government out of our boardrooms and bedrooms, and closed with the refrain that America must be governed from the center. Pocketing the text, Peele stood straight and square behind the lectern, arms extended, chest out, like a gymnast awaiting the judges' scores after nailing a routine.

A few hands clapped and then the rest joined in, producing a respectful din. A couple of heads rose as though to rally a standing ovation, but then looked around and eased back down. From the wings, Henry beat his cupped palms in booming thuds.

When the floor opened for questions, a thirtyish grad student with a goatee stepped to the mic. He cleared his throat, covering his mouth with a hand, and in a soft voice, said, "Senator, clearly, you're affirming *Roe v. Wade* in calling to get government 'out of the bedroom.'"

"No," Peele snapped. Then, more calmly, "Government needs to focus more on the other end of the birth canal, on adoption and neonatal care."

Peele looked to Henry in the wings, as though for rescue. The blue eyes were almost plaintive, and hit Henry's core. There was still a connection, apparently. But there was nothing he could do to halt the barrage or hustle Peele off the stage. He raised his palms in a shrug. The Senator turned back to the gauntlet.

A tall, drawn academic in a tweedy suit took the mic. "I'd like to posit a theory," the man began, singsong. Then, for several minutes, the tweed blathered that elected officials would always push government bailouts, on homes and businesses alike, to the point of moral hazard. He began to step away. Then, as an afterthought, he leaned toward the mic and asked, "Do you care to comment?"

That was how senators treated witnesses at hearings. Peele smiled, waved, and walked off the stage.

14

★ ★ ★

PROVERBS OF HELL

Lounging in the mottled recliner in the Rigsdale suite, Elizabeth caught the end of a racy Doris Day film on HBO, from an era that Day had described as "before I became a virgin." When the credits rolled and Tom had still not arrived, she stayed planted in the chair, without the energy to search for another program, and let HBO's next offering wash over her.

American Pimp, a documentary on urban flesh peddlers, came on shortly. The show opened with a montage of fur-lined, tricked-out Cadillacs and an album of black men adorned in zoot suits and fedoras, one with lightning bolts emblazoned on his bicuspids. She watched until a pimp named Rosebudd boasted of seducing poor women from broken homes. "I steal a bitch's mind."

Was Tom Peele so different? She had begun to feel like a musical instrument he was playing. Tom still radiated genuine interest in her, but mostly on his schedule, and too often she couldn't reach him when she needed him, or wanted to talk.

The worst part was the pace, intensity alternating with voids. Tom would disappear for ten days to Washington or Omaha or to campaign somewhere, and never phone. Then he'd get back to Iowa and call, desperate to see her. "You're so amazing, I've got to see you now," he'd gush, and beg her to meet him at the Rigsdale that evening. Then he'd arrive two hours late and tell her, "You don't understand; I'm a slave to my schedule. I don't control it; it controls me."

It was always hot or cold; there was no medium tempo. Also, she resented being only a compartmentalized part of his life. She'd see him when he was in Iowa. She didn't know much about his life in Washington, and nothing about his life in Omaha, with his . . . wife. She didn't share that, couldn't share that. It was as though there was a parallel universe she was excluded from. Tom had this intensity with her about one universe, but stone cold silence about the other. She got little glimpses, like his mention of a big maple tree in his yard, but he never invited her there, even though it was only a couple hours' drive.

She sometimes wondered whether he had other women. Does he ask them about the plates on their walls? She had been sitting in the suite for an hour now, alone. In fairness, Tom had said he doubted he could get to the hotel before nine thirty P.M., and much as he wanted to see her, maybe they'd better try another night. She had insisted, telling him they needed to talk.

They should be alone, once he arrived. Tom had said that his aide, Henry, who sometimes slept in the suite, would be in Washington that night. When Henry was around, he usually kept to the small bedroom, except to use the hall bathroom every couple of hours. Tom didn't seem to mind, any more than he had minded the young aide at their table at their first lunch. But she felt tawdry, like a courtesan, not worthy of privacy.

What made it worse was the way Henry looked at her. She wasn't flattering herself, but there was no mistaking it. Whenever their eyes met, it was as though the love arrow pierced his soul, like a reenactment of *The Romance of the Rose*. She had been waiting years for a man to look at her that way, to want her that way, and now it was the wrong man at the wrong time, in the wrong place. Okay, Tom occasionally gave her that look, too, but those moments were too few and far between.

She had never exchanged more than brief small talk with Henry, but one thing she liked about him was the way he stood up to Tom. Henry was matter-of-fact, not fawning like so many other staffers. All Tom would say about Henry was that "his press guy" had "a good handle on Iowa."

She shifted in the recliner, causing the old chair to groan. She leaned her head on one stained arm and dangled her legs over the other, gazing at the tube. Rosebudd was parading in a bright red suit and white Stetson. Maybe Tom would arrive with candy, flowers, or some other consolation. He was big on trinkets and tributes. A week earlier, glowing with pride, he had given her a fifteenth-century clay bowl that he said he had bought in Egypt on a congressional trip. When she said he must have paid a fortune in entry duties, he said, "Nah, I brought it through the diplomatic pouch; nobody ever checks what a senator brings in."

But don't senators have that privilege, she had asked him, precisely because they are expected not to abuse it? He had changed the subject and she thanked him for the bowl, but the incident had shaken her. He seemed diminished after that. It had nothing to do with their relationship. But his flexible morals killed her white-knight image of him. She wasn't going to display the bowl, but she wasn't going to toss out a historic artifact, either, so she buried the thing at the top of a hall closet.

She palmed the remote, weary of the preening pimps, when she heard two thuds against the suite's front door. She hit "mute" and sat motionless in the recliner, not breathing. Tom never knocked. Maybe he had forgotten his key. Henry was in Washington. Maybe it was a maid or maintenance man. But if it was somebody from the campaign, how should she explain her presence in the suite? She'd just say she was waiting to give the Senator a report about an upcoming fund-raising event. If the person didn't believe her, it was a bigger problem for Tom than for her.

She slipped on her loafers—no point looking too much at home—and walked to the entrance. Up close, the door had the texture of an old candle. The latest layer of semigloss off-white covered countless earlier layers, along with scattered lumps, bristles, scars, chips, and drips. "Yes, may I help you?" she called.

"Yeah," a deep voice called back. "Edzie . . . looking for the Senator."

"The Senator's not here right now." What kind of name was *Edzie*? "Who's this?"

"Ed Z," the voice said more slowly, with a hint of annoyance. "Ed Zabriskie."

"The Senator's not here," she called again. This was getting silly. She turned the knob and cracked the old door a few inches.

A wide, meaty, weathered face was staring at her through the divide, less than a foot away. A scar ran from its forehead to cheek, pressing one eye slightly shut. It was like a film noir scene, when the heroine opens the door and finds herself inches from a menacing villain. She could see the pores at the bottom of the broad, slightly skewed nose and tiny blood vessels in the whites of the milky, caramel eyes. She realized she had not slid the door chain, and that there was nothing keeping the man from bursting in. The expression was kind, but the man still radiated raw strength.

"Howdy," he said, softening the deep growl. "I'm Ed. Old friend of Senator Peele's. Mind if I come in?"

She pulled the old door open and stepped back. The man minced onto the faded carpet, smiling like a gentle beast who knew he scared strangers. He seemed less threatening a couple of feet away, when she could see all of him. For one thing, he looked at least sixty.

"The Senator should be here any minute," she said, more for safety, but realized it gave Ed Z an opening. Christ, where the hell *was* Tom?

Zabriskie panned the suite, taking in her wineglass on the coffee table and the pimp show on the television. Then the milky eyes scanned her, from ponytail to loafers. The big head nodded. "That case, I'll just wait, if you don't mind. Drove all the way from Omaha, I guess few more minutes won't make much difference." He smiled, showing rectangular teeth, stained at the bases by either tobacco or coffee, and pushed the door closed with the back of a heavy, tanned arm. The sound of the latch catching shot a pang through her, annoyance and angst. Zabriskie pulled out a latticework chair from the dining table and eased into it with a sigh.

Though Zabriskie seemed gentle, she still wanted to keep her access to the sole escape route, the paint-smeared old door. That left two options: either move to the kitchen, where she couldn't stay long, unless she began baking, or sit at the dining table in the chair nearest the door, next to him.

"Place looks a lot better than the last time I was here," Zabriskie said, completing his inspection.

"You've been here before?"

"Yeah. A bunch of us union guys came over one night to meet with Phil Eggert and some of the other campaign people." Zabriskie snorted, apparently at the memory. "Popcorn, beer, potato chips everywhere you sat. Place was a sty."

Zabriskie, despite his fierce features, was actually quite tidy. What was left of his graying hair was combed back neatly, the creases in his sport shirt were sharp, and the belt buckle, shirt placket, and pants seam all lined up, military style, the way her father had taught her. "Keep your gig line straight," the Captain had instructed. Zabriskie must have been in the service. He had missed a couple of white chest hairs that sprouted from the collar of his plaid shirt, but aging men were always sprouting hairs.

"You got something to drink around here?" Zabriskie asked. "Soda, beer, juice, anything, even water? The air wasn't working too good in my car; Freon's low, I think." He gave an almost sheepish smile. "I promise not to make a mess."

Does he think I'm a junior aide who doubles as a housekeeper, she wondered. Maybe he thinks I'm a senior aide, but he's such a sexist throwback he'll ask any woman to wait on him. No, this man can smell sin, the way a dog smells food. He saw the wineglass and the TV; he knows what I'm doing here. She felt the milky eyes on her and reflexively crossed her arms over her chest. She walked into the kitchen.

"There's some Mountain Dew, Diet Coke, and some beer, Heineken," she called.

"A Heiney sounds great."

Sure, the beer; why wasn't she surprised? She grabbed a green bottle by the neck. She didn't take a glass; he didn't seem the type who'd care. She didn't even check to see whether the bottle had a twist-off cap; he could probably open it with his teeth.

"Is the Senator expecting you?" she asked, putting the bottle down in front of him.

He looked up at her. "Yeah. Well, we've both been wanting to sit down and talk, so I thought I'd try to catch him."

"Well, I'm not sure when he's going to get here. I mean, it could be any minute. But it might not be for a while." How did this man know Tom was supposed to be at the hotel tonight?

Zabriskie smiled. "I make you nervous?"

"No. It's just, I don't know you, and it's late. You know."

He laughed, the eyes softening. "Relax. I'm a pussycat. I been working with the Senator to organize some union support in Nebraska and Iowa. I'm with the Teamsters. We got some details to discuss, that's all."

Zabriskie resembled a big, lovable, snorting bulldog. Ed Z. He wanted to discuss more than details of union support with Tom, she was pretty sure. But he wasn't going to hurt her; she could tell by the way he looked at her. It was more a paternal look. Maybe a disapproving paternal look. Zabriskie looked like the kind of man who spent his days with other men, rough men, and who venerated women, or at least women close to him, by some primitive code. He might not accord women much opportunity, but he'd protect them. He was wearing a wedding ring, she noticed, a worn, scuffed, plain gold band. He probably had a little fireplug wife who ordered him around and a daughter or two who ran up his credit card bills. She exhaled, long and deep, and felt her tension melt.

"You need a bottle opener, Mr. Zabriskie?" she asked.

"Yeah. And it's Ed. And get a beer for yourself, or some wine, whatever you're having. I don't like to drink alone."

What the heck. She pulled another Heineken from the refrigerator and returned to the table. She preferred to drink from a glass, but couldn't take one for herself after failing to offer him one.

Zabriskie popped the bottle cap with a massive thumb. The man's feral, physical aura was different from anything she had found at Iowa State. The faculty athletes were squash players or runners, graceful antelopes, not grizzled, battle-scarred bears. Even the football players and wrestlers among her students radiated a youthful innocence.

"So what's your name?" Zabriskie asked. "What do you do?"

She took a swig of Heineken. The first swallow was cold and sharp, the heavy carbonation burning the residue from her throat. "Elizabeth. I teach at Iowa State, but I'm volunteering on Senator Peele's campaign." She could see Zabriskie wanted more. Maybe he was giving her a chance to save face, to offer an alibi for the record. He was probably lying about the purpose of his visit; why should she bare her soul? "I'm sort of in charge of an event that's coming up in Council Bluffs, and the Senator wanted some information about it."

Zabriskie nodded and wiped his mouth with a thick wrist. He seemed disappointed, as though her lie were unnecessary and insulting. They drank in silence, Zabriskie taking a long pull of beer, his Adam's apple bobbing in his thick, corded neck.

"You teach college, huh? My youngest boy goes to University of Northwest Iowa. Majoring in business. First one in our family to go to college." He beamed, then shrugged. "Me, I never got past tenth grade. Wasn't much of a student."

"UNI's a good school," she said. Well, it rated high among Midwest public colleges.

Zabriskie seemed to enjoy the praise. "I tell my guys this country's shifting to a service economy; you want a future today, you need an education." He shrugged. "They don't listen. I was their age, I didn't listen, either. Joe, that's my son, he's got one more year. I told him he can do anything he wants when he graduates—as long as it's honest and it's productive." The milky eyes glared at her.

She took a slow sip of beer.

"You don't mind me asking, how'd you get involved in the Senator's . . . campaign?" She felt Zabriskie looking her over again, pausing at her curves, but like a father inspecting his daughter before allowing her to go out on a date.

"You mean what's a nice girl like me doing in a place like this?" Enough of this blue-collar, prairie paternalism.

Zabriskie shrugged. "Hey, like I say, Tom Peele and I go way back."

Ed Z, it occurred to her, was the first person she had met who had known Tom for decades, and knew about his life in Omaha. The other Iowa campaign hands had all signed on recently. Here was somebody who could offer insight on Tom's other world.

"You've probably been to Tom's house in Omaha," she said. "What's it like?" She realized, after she said it, that referring to Tom by his first name and asking about his house killed her late-working-campaign-aide alibi. It made her sound just like what she had become, a jealous mistress. *Steal a bitch's mind.*

Zabriskie shrugged. "Nice little bungalow. Three-story brick job in West Omaha, yard big enough to raise cattle."

Did he think she wanted to case the place, like some stalker girlfriend? "So how has the Senator changed over the years? You must have known him before he was even a senator."

The mouth puckered. "We all get older. Hopefully, a little wiser, too."

"Come on, Ed, that's not much of an answer. I'd give a C-minus for that." That was the first time she had used Zabriskie's first name, she realized.

Zabriskie shrugged. "Like I said, I wasn't much of a student."

"So what's his wife like?" In for a dime, in for a dollar.

Zabriskie splayed meaty fingers on the table. "Elizabeth, first you tell me a little bit about yourself. You're not wearing a ring. You're not married?"

This was the first time he had used her name and it gave her a childish rush, as though she had won the attention of a powerful adult. Now she knew whom Zabriskie reminded her of: her father's older brother, an oil company engineer who used to visit them in Maine during her childhood, his face weathered and hair coarse from desert sun, sea salt, maybe arctic blasts, wherever his work took him. She used to giggle as Uncle Paul hoisted her above his head in massive hands. That had been twenty years ago; Paul was retired now, living on a pension in Corpus Christi.

"I'm divorced," she said.

The Teamster leader's nose curled. "People don't work on their marriages anymore, like you have to. They get married, they're not happy after a few years, they get divorced. Your generation thinks everything has to be easy. Marriage isn't easy. It takes work every day. Believe me; I been married thirty years. You Catholic?"

She shook her head.

Zabriskie shrugged. "Well, I hope you give it another shot. I hope you find somebody you love, somebody who loves you, treats you right, somebody smart like you, and you get married again, and you make it work. Marriage, a man and a woman, it's the natural state. You agree?"

She felt tears welling. "It's not so simple."

"No? You young people think everything is complicated. You just make it complicated."

"Maybe," she said, breathing and gathering herself. "Now tell me about the Senator. What was he like when you first met him? How has he grown over the years?" When Zabriskie said nothing, she asked, "If you had to pick one word to describe him, what would it be, and why?"

Zabriskie grunted, a chuckle muffled in the thick throat. He thought for a while, his eyes narrowing with the effort. "What it all comes down to, maybe, is guys like Tom Peele and me, we're willing to do what it takes to get what we want."

"Yeah," she said, softly.

Zabriskie gazed up. "Drive your cart and your plow over the bones of the dead."

"What's that?" she asked, shifting toward him in the chair. "You know Blake?"

He raised a hand, as though to fend her off. "Just something my father used to say. What, it means something to you?"

"William Blake. *Proverbs of Hell.* 'Drive your cart and your plow over the bones of the dead,'" she said. "'The road of excess leads to the palace of wisdom. Prudence is a rich, ugly old maid courted by Incapacity. He who desires but acts not, breeds pestilence. The cut worm forgives the plow.'"

A sad half-smile played on Zabriskie's lips. "When I was a kid, my father bought these old poetry books at a yard sale. Had red covers and gold sides. I thought he just liked to have them around, to class up the house. But he must have actually read them; I never knew."

She nodded. "You're saying Tom is willing to hurt people, or to let people get hurt, in pursuit of his goals," she said in a professorial tone.

Zabriskie breathed. "Like I say, he goes after what he wants . . . and he understands certain business realities." Zabriskie looked at his watch.

Elizabeth looked at her small, octagonal gold watch, a college graduation present from her parents. It was pushing nine thirty, the beginning of Tom's arrival range. Whatever Zabriskie wanted to talk about must be pretty heavy. Part of her hoped he would stick around until Tom arrived, if Tom arrived, so she could watch the two of them together, see who led when they danced. How much longer would Ed Z wait? He had a two-hour drive back to Omaha.

Zabriskie looked at his watch again, a minute after the last time, and shook the big head. He drained his Heineken in a long swallow. He was kind of ugly-cute, with his bulldog features all scrunched, the grooves in his forehead running into the groove that scarred his face.

She offered Zabriskie another beer, but he just shook the big head again. "I'm glad Senator Peele is working with the unions," she said, to break the silence. "If you have any doubt about how important unions are, you just have to read *The Jungle*."

Zabriskie scrunched his features.

"It's a classic novel by Upton Sinclair, who was a bit of a communist—I'm not suggesting there's anything communist about organized labor. The book's about the Chicago meatpacking plants around the turn of the twentieth century, and the ghastly conditions. The foul condition of the meat, also; it put me off hamburger for months, the first time I read it."

Zabriskie nodded. "Yeah, I think I heard of it." He held her eyes with his, trying to read her. Her blind eye may have thrown him. He slid his chair back and crossed one leg over the other thigh, straining his blue chinos. A swath of calf showed above a nylon ankle sock, thick but mottled by purple veins—an old man's leg.

"You know, Elizabeth, you can be book-smart but not people-smart, and that can be a very dangerous thing to be."

Behind them, she heard a bolt snap and a latch slip. She turned to see the old door open and Tom step inside, dashing in a bone-colored summer suit and cordovans. A puzzled look crossed his face as he took in the tableau of her and Zabriskie at the table.

Zabriskie stood, but not quickly like a subordinate. "Senator, have something I wanted to see you about, so I thought I'd drop by," he growled, extending a huge hand. "Was just chatting with the professor here." He turned and gave her an avuncular bow of the big head.

Tom nodded, flashing that wary look he got when she mentioned marriage or his wife. He turned to her, a silent question. She gave a slight shrug. Wasn't Tom going to give her some cover by telling her something like, "We'll go over the plans for the fund-raiser in a minute"? No; he turned back to Zabriskie. "Sure, Ed. What's up?"

"Ah, it's kind of private," Zabriskie said.

Tom turned back to her. "Elizabeth, would you excuse us a couple of minutes?"

Why don't *you two* go into another room, she wanted to say. It was pushing ten, too late to sit at the hotel bar by herself, like a tramp. She could either retreat into Tom's bedroom, like a whore, or step into the hallway like a flunky. She wasn't going to go into Henry's room.

She strode toward the master bedroom without saying anything. Zabriskie had figured it out, anyway. He was "people-smart." She pushed the door open and was about to slam it shut, then caught herself. She eased the door against frame, letting it come to rest with about a half-inch gap. She stepped to the side and angled an ear.

"You should have called, Ed," she heard Tom say. "You know I'd make time for you. This is awkward."

"Won't take long; it's pretty simple," she heard Zabriskie growl. "We're out on Western Pharmaceutical."

"What do you mean, 'you're out'? I'm counting on you."

"Too many people watching, too many people talking. Especially with that reporter nosing around. It's just too hot, just not worth the risk."

"Aw, come on, Ed. The stakes are a lot bigger for me than they are for you, and you don't see me getting cold feet."

"Western Pharmaceutical is up twelve percent since your Senate hearing," she heard Zabriskie say. "Do you ever check the chat boards?"

"The what?"

"The message boards," Zabriskie's voice said, now with an edge. "My son Joe showed me about it. Don't your hotshots keep up in Washington? On the Internet, every public company, just about, has its own message board, Yahoo Finance, sites like that. All day long, people yack back and forth about the companies. And a lot of them really know their stuff.

"Well, the talk on the Western Pharmaceutical boards is about how you're trying to get that cancer drug on the Medicare list, and how the stock's going to go up another ten points if you do."

"Good. So?"

"So we bought in right *before* your hearing," she heard Zabriskie shout.

"Yeah?"

Zabriskie laughed. "If we sell right after the drug gets covered, and then we make certain donations, it's going to look a little fishy to anybody who can put two and two together. You were going to keep this quiet."

Neither one of them said anything for a moment. Had they caught her listening and were they now heading toward her? It was hard to see through the crack with her right eye. She tip-toed backward into the room.

When they began talking again, they spoke more softly. She heard Zabriskie say something, Tom say something, Zabriskie say something else, and by the time she positioned her ear better, they were exchanging good-byes.

"All right, Ed, I appreciate your taking the time to come here and tell me."

She heard the old front door open and close. Well, why should she be shocked? Ethical lapses were a slippery slope. That's part of the reason many universities had zero-tolerance policies for academic fraud. Tom was a cheater. He cheated on his wife, no matter how he justified it. He cheated on customs, sneaking in the Egyptian bowl. How much of a stretch was it to cheat on the stock market?

A wave of nausea began under her jaw and spread to her head and stomach. She eased onto the bed and thought for a moment she might puke. But she breathed a few times—slow, deep breaths—and the feeling passed.

She heard Tom putter around the kitchen, opening cabinets. After another minute, he called, "Elizabeth!"

She would end it tonight, right now, tell him they were through, that he wasn't the man she thought he was; that he wasn't the man he pretended to be. She stood, still a bit wobbly, and reached for the door. Then she stopped. She had learned not to make major decisions in anger. She'd wait a day or so, maybe give Tom a chance to explain, although the explanation might be some of the smooth spin he was so good at.

15

★ ★ ★

THE RIVER CITY

Henry spotted a strip of bright red cloth peeking from behind the linens in the Presidential Suite's hall closet. Standing on his toes, he reached up, pinched a corner, and yanked it down. He found himself holding an Iowa State canvas gym tote, red with white handles. The bag was light but rattled when he shook it. He opened the zipper. He found a blouse; a toilet kit, which was making the noise; a pair of white silk panties; and a paperback copy of *Pilgrim's Progress*. Elizabeth Walmsley. She taught at Iowa State. He ran the back of his fingers over the panties, feeling like a pervert.

As Henry was firing off a final e-mail at the Des Moines office before trotting out to the parking lot, his phone rang, showing a familiar 703 number. Cass's cell.

"Get the word out to our 'liberal' list," the high-pitched voice ordered. "Zach Lowe is tight with a guy who runs the worst chain of gay-prostitution, child-exploitation bathhouses in the village. I just e-mailed you a story by a bigfoot *Atlanta Journal* reporter, Jacobsen. Link to it in your nasty-gram, get it on the web."

Henry scrolled through his in-box. "Gil, why do you have such a hard-on for Zach Lowe?"

"Never mind."

He found the Angel's e-mail. "Hey, Gil, this story says the guy sent a hundred-dollar check to Lowe, and Lowe's giving it back. They don't even know each other."

"Don't be a weenie. Just send something out. Gotta go. Freedom and prosperity."

Henry sat for a minute, finger against his forehead. He cranked out a missive headlined "Gay Prostitution Magnate Gives to Lowe." Technically true, at least. He enlisted their New Media woman to send texts and tweets and call bloggers.

As he stepped out of his office toward the rear parking lot, he noticed a figure at the reception desk. A tall man in jeans and sport shirt was balancing a lawn sign against his leg and filling his arms with brochures. Jeff Rensi. The sergeant looked fit and agile, but out of uniform in the casual togs.

"You're not going to shoot, are you?" he asked, walking up with hands raised.

Rensi made a face as though considering, then shook his head.

"You switch to bunko? Impounding evidence?"

"Nah. The boss sent me on some errands, so I figured I'd pick up some of your propaganda on the way. Snow the neighbors."

"What kind of errands does Des Moines's finest run?"

"Whatever the wife wants. Today, picking up gnocchi at the Italian deli on Fourth Street. They make them fresh, sell them in vacuum-sealed packages. You just bake them, add brown butter and sage, and you're in business."

"You're a man of many talents, Sergeant."

"Call me Jeff. I tell you, I prefer *strozzapreti*, with a spinach-and-ricotta flavor. Legend is, they're so good, a priest choked to death cramming them down, which is why they're called Priest Stranglers."

He stepped closer and lowered his voice. "Listen, Jeff, you really saved my bacon with those murder stats a few weeks ago. I just feel kind of lousy about the way we left things."

"Forget it, Hatten. For me, torturing politicians is a fringe benefit."

Henry's BlackBerry rattled as he climbed into Eggert's Cherokee.

"Can't do it; I'm in Iowa," he said. "Yeah, Gil may be around; you can try." He grinned and looked at Eggert. "Our ABC embed wants to have lunch, off the record, for an update. Cass can't stand her."

Racing toward Omaha on I-80, Henry's BlackBerry rang again as they passed Adar, showing a 404 number. He found himself on the line with a livid *Atlanta Journal-Constitution* columnist. Apparently, a pundit on their liberal list had forwarded his "Gay Prostitution Magnate" missive to Jacobsen.

"You want to know the saddest part of all this?" Jacobsen said. "Your guy's really elevated the debate, but you pull this Mickey Mouse shit, and it all goes out the window."

The words hurt, more because of what he now had to do. Affecting an earnest tone, he said, "There was no intent to mislead. We linked to your story because we wanted to let folks decide for themselves." The words were rolling, on their own.

"If we'd wanted to twist things, we could have simply cited your piece, or taken some words out of context. . . . Okay, fine . . . Yes, absolutely. All right. Thanks . . . You too." He rubbed his eyes and sighed.

Approaching the Missouri River, the Omaha skyline rose above the prairie, soaring above the expanse. Here was Tom Peele's hometown and the seat of the Senator's power.

Eggert's phone blared, a tinny version of the theme from *Jaws*. The Iowa man flipped open the phone as though it were contaminated. "Okay," Eggert said. "Okay, no problem. Okay." He snapped the phone shut and grimaced. "We got to pick up some 10W-40."

"Cool ring tone."

"I got it programmed to do that when Peele's wife calls."

So he'd get another chance to see Susan.

Eggert steered the Jeep off the L Street exit, at 120th Street in West Omaha, wound through a subdivision, and took a long driveway toward a three-story redbrick federal with black shutters and white trim. The manse, in its traditional simplicity without even a porch, was a clever choice; it wouldn't carry much punch in an opponent's thirty-second spot about a rich actor turned politician.

The screen door opened, and Susan stepped into the doorway, in khakis and a pink Lacoste shirt. Her hair was shorter over her angular features, making her look even more like an older, taller Fran.

"Tom just went for a run," she said, giving him a smile and letting Eggert pass with the carton of motor oil. "You're welcome to wait in the living room."

He followed Eggert to two oatmeal-colored couches flanking a glass coffee table. Susan came in carrying two hexagonal glasses of lemonade.

Eggert gulped the drink, clutching the glass in two hands like a squirrel. When he had drained it, he announced that he was going to make some calls from the car. Eggert stepped wide around Susan on the way out.

"This all must be very heady," he said.

"Very headachy, more like. And very expensive."

"Yeah, we're raising close to $150,000 a day."

"Well, your biggest donor has given a lot more than that. And he's still writing checks."

He nodded. He knew Peele was loaning money to the campaign.

"I'm going to get more involved. Protect my investment." She angled her head toward the door and Eggert outside.

A childhood memory flooded Henry's mind, of his own parents arguing over family finances. Then arguing over what to watch on the living room set, Monday-night football or a special on the World's Fair. These were the days before TiVo, when videocassette players were a novelty. His mother had been reminiscing all evening about the 1964 New York World's Fair, which she'd attended as a girl with her father. She had dug up a souvenir belt buckle, with the space-age logo outlined in gold. They wound up watching the Jets play the Patriots.

Henry drained the lemonade. "Sorry to intrude on you like this," he told Susan. He looked at his watch. "The Senator said to be here at one. He's got an editorial board at the *Council Bluffs Nonpareil* at two."

Susan shook her head. "Tom goes by his own clock. He was late to our daughter's graduation."

"That's a poignant story: the way your daughter overcame all those . . . health challenges."

Susan raised her eyebrows. "That's just what it is, a story. A story Tom likes to tell, and I wish he wouldn't. Agatha had one surgery when she was two, to fix a common spine curvature. Well, one follow-up procedure a year later, but that was it. She was in ballet class by the time she was five. Tom makes it sound like she was the girl in the plastic bubble."

He heard a metallic snap and turned to see Peele standing in the doorway. The Senator was wearing a red UNL T-shirt and gray shorts, both soaked, and breathing hard.

"You sent this CBS producer to watch me ask two questions at the Harris confirmation," Peele panted, seeing him. "But you don't send anybody to my hearing on medical malpractice. What planet are you on?"

"Leave him alone," Susan commanded, rising from a couch. "Stop being a bully."

Four hours later, as Henry was strolling downtown Omaha, his BlackBerry shook, showing the familiar 703 number.

"How did that pest from ABC get my cell number?" Cass demanded. "Now she wants to have lunch."

"No idea, Gil."

Cass grunted. "You did a good job handling that twit Jacobsen."

"You being sarcastic?" Had the columnist complained up the chain?

"No, I'm serious. He called this morning screaming for blood, so we sent him to you. Whatever you told him worked."

When Henry said nothing, Cass grunted. "When you get back to Des Moines, there's a little token of appreciation in the hotel garage."

In the background, he heard an amplified female voice announce a final boarding call for Gate Nine.

"A V-eight Mustang, five-speed, three hundred horses,"

Cass continued. "Zero to sixty faster than you can pull out your pud. Key's at the front desk. It's an exchange; take back that beater you leased. Gotta go. Freedom and prosperity."

Henry strode into Rheinlander, a German tavern-restaurant in the Old Market, Omaha's Greenwich Village, all dark wood and beer steins. He scanned for a restroom sign. But she was already at a booth.

Fran stepped into a long hug, pressing herself against him, firm and full under a green cotton blouse and jeans. Whatever had hung between them at the Taxpayers forum had dissolved.

A waitress came by with laminated menus featuring swords crossed over a coat of arms. "You folks from around here?"

"Des Moines," Henry said. Technically true.

"Oh," she said, chipper. "Well, Des Moines is like Omaha without the glitz."

He studied Fran's face as the waitress went through the day's specials, heavy on schnitzels and bratens. She *was* Susan Peele twenty-five years younger.

"The *Globe-Times* hasn't run anything recently on that old BS about Peele and the Teamster boss," he said. "Should I thank you?"

She shook her head. "Henry, you've always given me too much credit."

He smiled at the menu.

"I'm staying at the Doubletree, a few blocks from here," she said.

He looked up. The cobalt eyes were wide, playful.

"I've got to get back on the road in twenty minutes," he said.

She sucked her lip. "Too bad."

When Henry opened the Jeep's door outside the restaurant, Eggert was leering. An odor of stale cigarettes, and maybe booze, hit him. "You look a lot giddier, Phil, leaving the boss than you did coming."

"Yeah, and your old college buddy looks pretty hot."

"Didn't know you were watching, Phil."

And now the whole campaign would know.

16

✳ ✳ ✳

LUCKY DRAGON

Henry reached the Presidential Suite shortly after six P.M., his laptop in one hand and a takeout bag from the Lucky Dragon Chinese Restaurant in the other, a grease slick already darkening the bottom. Opening the door, he found the lights on and canned laughter cackling on the television. In the living room, about twenty feet away, he saw a dark-haired form with metal-framed glasses sitting sideways in the recliner, dangling penny loafers over one arm of the chair. Elizabeth Walmsley. His head fizzed. She hadn't seemed to notice his arrival. He closed the door. When the hasp clicked, she bolted to her feet, losing one of the loafers.

"Oh, hey," she said, sliding back onto the chair. "I thought you were Tom—the Senator."

"Nope, just me." He dropped his stuff on the dining room table.

Peele hadn't told him she was coming over, though his roommate no longer always gave notice. He fetched some silverware, a plate, and a can of diet root beer from the kitchen. He took his dinner and went into his hole. He sat at the little wooden desk for half an hour, mostly listening.

Getting up and peering out, he saw Elizabeth had moved to the dining room table, where she was sitting on one of the wicker chairs prying with a fingernail at the label on a bottle of chardonnay. He watched her for about a minute as she poked at the label, sipped wine, refilled her glass, and rested her head on her hand. Her blue sweater clung to her curves, including the thin roll that he had always found endearing, now riding above her beige slacks. A pearl necklace and earrings added an urbane touch, accented by her hair, which looked freshly cut in a pageboy.

He stepped quickly past Elizabeth into the kitchen, the pounding of his heart causing the glands in his throat to throb and his temples to pulse. He took a wineglass from the cupboard. "Do you mind?" he asked.

She looked over and shrugged. He stepped around the kitchen doorway, sliding heavy legs forward, and sat on a wicker chair next to hers. He inhaled her perfume, a fruity scent that tickled his nostrils, and noticed faint green veins on the underside of her tanned forearm, where the sweater was rolled up. He filled the glass with chardonnay and took a long sip. The wine warmed his throat, radiated heat through his chest.

"I didn't know you and the Senator were getting together tonight," he said, the syllables struggling off his tongue.

She winced. "Yeah, he was supposed to be here at six." She looked at her watch. "I'm sure he'll have a good excuse. Maybe you can write one for him."

He pretended not to notice the edge in her voice. "How's that?"

"Well, you write the words Tom speaks, or sometimes the words you claim he spoke. He says you're pretty good at it." She smiled, showing even white teeth.

That was his first compliment from Peele in weeks, even backhanded. He felt a smile play.

"And when Tom screws up, you take the heat. You're his flak catcher, and you get Mau-Maued." She inhaled and affected a deep voice. "'What Senator Peele meant to say . . .' Seems like it's always 'What Senator Peele meant to say.' And it seems like somebody around Tom is always getting Mau-Maued. One way or another." She ran a finger around the stem of her wineglass.

He felt anger rise. Poor teacher lady, all dressed up, cashmere and pearls, waiting for Tom to come and fuck her, but Peele was standing her up. Love hurts.

"Last week, I tweaked a speech for Peele on steelworkers losing their jobs to tariffs and dumping. He was giving off vibes like he really cared, and it hit home with me, so I poured my soul into it. Turned out he just wanted to squeeze money from some labor group." He shrugged. "On a lot of issues, you never know how engaged he really is." Jeez, maybe that wasn't too smart, bad-mouthing the boss to his mistress.

She kept staring at her wineglass. Then she fixed her hazel eyes on him, cold behind the titanium frames. "You plan to spend your whole career whispering lines in the emperor's ear?"

He felt himself blanch, even under the blanket of wine. In her world, maybe, he was just a bureaucrat with a bachelor's degree.

"Do you think the White House press secretary is just a mouthpiece?" That was his holy grail, if Peele made it all the way. Worst case, he'd crawl back to the House side and find a flack job. Well, absolute worst case was a cell in Leavenworth.

She hollowed her cheeks and widened her eyes, in mock awe.

He took a long sip of chardonnay and breathed. He felt his right foot rise, his body trying to return him to the safety of his cubbyhole. Why prolong the pain, his mind seemed to be asking. He planted the foot on the carpet and met her gaze. "Elizabeth, I've had a lousy day, and I think maybe you're having a lousy day. Let's not take it out on each other."

She sat back and crossed her arms. "Fine," she finally said. "I don't mean to be a bitch. But I really am curious: I'm quite fond of Tom, but I don't think I could work for him. I've volunteered for your boss and for one other politician, a congressman, and I'd never want to be bound to a job like that."

She had no idea. The purple sacs had reappeared under his eyes. He was bolting awake at four and five A.M., his heart pounding, his mind spinning over a call he should have made or a word he should have deleted from a tweet.

"The best day in my career," he said, "one of the best days in my life, Doug Tyler was holding a town hall meeting, and afterward, I was standing with him in the parking lot, and this big burly guy, I can still see his plaid shirt and his beard, he looked like Paul Bunyan, he charged at Tyler, like a lineman after a quarterback. At the last second, I got my shoulder in and deflected some of the impact."

He turned, to see if she was still listening. "And I saw," he went on, "as the guy grabbed Tyler, that he was crying. He was hugging the congressman and he was bawling. And he told Tyler he just wanted to thank him for saving his job. The guy worked at a meat-processing plant, and had four kids, and Tyler had gotten a federal loan to keep the place from going bust. Actually, I was the one who had arranged the loan—well, I hadn't exactly arranged it, but I'd made sure it happened. And we did it so we could jump up and down and say, 'See, we saved the plant—vote for us!' But it was the first time that I saw that what I do can actually, directly, save somebody."

She was looking at him, listening. He let the words flow, which felt strange and dangerous, and cathartic. "I had this image of this Paul Bunyan guy in his plaid shirt lying on his back on his living room rug, it was light-blue shag, don't ask me why. He was playing with his kids, tossing the smallest one in the air, and the sun was streaming through the windows, and they were all smiling. And that image sort of printed on my brain. And sometimes, when there was a chance to save some jobs or clean up some polluted watershed, or get medical care for some underserved area, I'd picture Paul Bunyan on his rug with his kids, and I'd try to do the right thing. Playing the game and slinging the BS is a blast and a rush, but I found it's vacuous unless, at least once in a while, you can help some poor soul that nobody else can help, or will help." He breathed in and then out, spastically and audibly. "That's why I do what I do."

She smiled. "So I'm not the only wide-eyed idealist on the campaign."

"Don't tell anyone," he said. "I'm supposed to be a giant cynic. I even laughed at *Hamlet*." He'd borrowed that line from Fogel, and immediately felt tawdry. Take off the filter, he told himself; let it go.

"When I started with Peele," he said, "I used to fantasize what it would have been like to have him as a father, with his movie-star looks and swagger, coming to school for parents days, wrestling matches. What the other kids would have thought of that." He looked down. "Then I'd feel rotten, being ungrateful for all my own father did for me."

"I sometimes imagine him coming to pick me up at Iowa State," she said, "bursting into one of my lectures and lifting me in his arms, the way Richard Gere picked up Debra Winger in *An Officer and a Gentleman*. Even though I know it could never happen."

She placed a hand, with long delicate fingers, on his wrist. He had longed for her touch, fantasized about it. Inches away, she didn't disappoint. He wanted to touch her, as much now as in his daydreams. But an alarm lit his head, and he worried about Peele finding out, maybe by just seeing through him. Peele could read people pretty well, and that would be the end of his career, of his dreams. Would have to be. But then he thought, let Peele catch them drinking together. Peele was so full of himself, he'd assume Henry was just keeping her primed.

Over the next hour, amid stories of New York and Maine, of politicians and professors, and a second bottle of chardonnay, Elizabeth's shoulders and voice loosened. Her whole face beamed when she smiled. The oversized nose, amid the delicate, sculpted features and exquisite eyes, made her face interesting, not merely beautiful, and made her somehow vulnerable.

She glanced occasionally at her little octagonal watch. The next time he looked, the kitchen clock said seven forty-five. "Doesn't he usually call you if he's going to be this late?"

That drew another flinch. "Sometimes," she said. "Sometimes he just figures I'll wait."

"You deserve better." He drained his glass. "I feel a little guilty about your situation. I wish I'd warned you."

"Warned me?"

"Yeah, I saw it coming, at the banker's thing in Sioux City, when Peele asked for your number." His jaw tightened, looking at her. He poured another glass of wine.

She seemed to think for a while. "I knew what I was getting into . . . sort of." She took off her glasses to rub the bridge of her nose. "Anyway, why should you warn me? What do you care?"

His jaw tightened again. "I liked you, the moment I saw you," he said, the words sliding off his wine-loosened tongue. "You weren't just another prom queen on the come."

She looked at him and then cocked her head. "Thank you, I think."

"You're welcome." He took a deep breath. "Peele abuses the people close to him, because he can, while he charms the world. If you've got only so much decency, spread it with the people who matter."

She sucked her teeth. "It's not so simple. Tom's in pain. He's spent his life playing roles, and he doesn't know who he is anymore, if he ever did. It's an American tragedy, cutting to the heart of our national need to reinvent ourselves. What does the self-made man do when he didn't make himself?"

Henry smiled. That was pretty deep.

"Well, would you tell Tom, if he ever shows up, that I couldn't wait anymore." She stood and smoothed her sweater. "Mind if I use your phone to get another room? I don't want to drive home tonight."

The thought of her leaving plunged him into a dark, lonely sadness. "I'll walk downstairs with you," he said, standing. "You're going to have to go to the front desk to get a key, and I know those guys. I'll make sure you get a good room."

She opened the closet, reached up and pulled the red canvas gym tote off the top shelf. He felt himself blush. He dashed into his small bedroom, stepped into a pair of topsiders and returned to the dining room to find her standing by the door, canvas tote in hand. She was silent in the creaking elevator on the ride down. He studied a web of scars in the faux-wood paneling.

At the desk, he told the clerk, "She's an aide in town for a morning meeting. Bill the room to the campaign, please."

She still hadn't said anything when they got back in the elevator for the ride up. She pushed "8" and the cables heaved. He pushed "10," which lighted right on top of hers, separated by a slice of brass. In fifteen seconds, they'd reach her floor. "It must be a pretty big shift, from Maine to Iowa," he said.

"Not as much as you might think. Ames is actually pretty hip; it's like a counterculture oasis. It's about the only place around here when I can show my tattoo."

"A professor with a tattoo?" He looked her over, as though to spot the ink through her clothing.

"Three small roses," she said and shrugged. "On my left hip."

He pictured her bare flank, the golden freckled skin, the flare of her hip, and three red roses with short stems curving over it all.

The elevator whined to a stop and the "8" button went dark. She shouldered her canvas bag. The door opened, the thinner panel sliding into the thicker, and she stepped toward the doorway. The door would close in a few seconds, and she would be gone.

"Take a walk with you," he blurted, both a question and a statement.

She said nothing, so he followed her into the corridor. Her room was a few doors down. He stood by the wall as she slid the plastic card into the lock.

"You mind some company, just for a few minutes?"

She looked at him for a long moment, and finally gave a faint shrug. "Sure."

They stepped into a square chamber done in coral and beige, dusk fading outside a draped window. She dropped the canvas tote and her small handbag on the desk and the key card on the night table. She turned to walk past him, and he took her hand.

He held it loosely and left her a path to the bathroom or the door, if she wanted to take it. She stopped and looked at him, her face soft in the golden-purple summer twilight.

He eased forward and kissed her, gently taking her top lip between his. Her hand brushed the side of his head, her fingertips coming to rest on his neck. Her skin was smoother than he expected and he felt her small paunch against his waist, swollen by the sweater. She was gentle, and seemed a bit self-conscious. She held the kisses too long, apparently content to stand in the middle of the room, arms around his neck, lips locked. She loosened, once on the bed, arching as he nuzzled her neck and lifted the blue sweater. She shifted on her shoulder to let him slip a hand beneath her to work the hooks on her bra. Once freed, her breasts, full and round, flared slightly, the areoles wide and pink.

He thought she would stop him, maybe clamp a hand over his. But she shifted again to let him work her belt, which was pressed tight by her little paunch. He eased down her slacks, the cloth bunching against the quilted bedspread. Her tan line ended at mid-thigh and at her upper arms, suggesting T-shirts and shorts instead of bikinis. The revealed flesh was soft and pale, and reddened under the slightest pressure. Faint perfume on her neck and chest mixed with a talc scent under her arms. She kissed him hard and deep, with little grunts.

Her neck and ear grew hot as he worked and she cooed. Her hips were fleshy but still firm. The three bright red roses, the size of pennies, hugged her hip, accenting her paleness.

"I don't have anything," he said. He almost hoped she'd stop him. There was always the risk of failure, after so much wine. And the alarm was sounding again, though fainter now. A horror scenario was brewing—fury, disgrace, exile. He knew if he let it play in his head, he'd kill the moment, and probably the

evening. And he wanted nothing more than to be with Elizabeth Walmsley in the snug little room. It seemed like all he'd
ever wanted. If you're not going to stop, then don't spoil it, he
told himself. He shook his head, to clear it.

"It's okay," she whispered. "I'm on the pill."

She was passive, waiting, lying back and stroking his stomach with glossed nails as he tugged off his own clothes. If she
hesitated, occasionally pulling her legs together or her arms in,
if she had any fear, it seemed more of pain than of intimacy.
He tried to be slow and gentle. He pressed her pace a bit, but
not enough to jar her, and let her guide him in with the long
fingers.

"I want to hear you," she whispered into his ear, as she felt
him draw close to climax. He was a quiet lover, generally avoiding primal moans. But he gave a few deep grunts, more like
muffled martial arts *kiai,* which seemed to amplify her own soft
moans and prompt her to clutch his shoulders, the glossed nails
gripping his flesh and pulling him deeper into her.

He didn't think she had climaxed, but she relaxed her grip
and seemed to have a contented smile. He rolled off. Lying
beside her, he lowered a hand lightly onto her soft white belly
and massaged it in slow, thoughtful circles.

"I liked you, too, the first time we saw each other," she said.
"You looked like a little boy, with an expression of such fierce
determination, like you were doing the most important thing
in the world." It hung over them, unspoken, that he had been
staffing Peele at the time. "I thought about you sometimes."

Stroking her hair, he wanted to believe her. But he didn't
think affection was her only reason for letting him stay with
her. He thought she had tired of his wolfish glances and scorn.
She may have wanted him to share her shame, to turn him from
her judge into her accomplice. And she may have half-wanted

Peele to find them together, or figure it out, to punish Peele, maybe to punish him, and to force an end to all of it.

He felt his body loosen and his senses fade, swaddling him in a darkening softness. A bell blared from somewhere above their heads. He jerked out of a stupor. She reached over, opened her black bag and pulled out a cell phone.

"Uh huh," she said. "Fine . . . No, I understand . . . Bye." She closed the phone and turned to him. "Guess who?"

"*El Cappo di tutti Cappi.*" From the Great Plains, Peele had reached into the eighth-floor nest, invading and permeating the space. Acid rose in his throat. He had left his BlackBerry upstairs on the dresser in his little bedroom. Had Peele phoned the room and then his device, gotten no answer, and only then tried Elizabeth's cell? Had Peele left an urgent message? The Senator left no other kind. He felt desperately naked without his electronic leashes.

"He said something came up and he had to go to Omaha," she said, monotone.

He laid an arm across her soft middle. "Whatever."

"I don't know," she said. "I was kind of hoping he'd show up, so I could hear his excuse for being three hours late. And then he could buy me dinner. Of course, then he'd think everything was even—that a good meal is all it takes."

17

***

RED ROSES

Elizabeth's face was puffy in sleep, the skin mottled and textured without makeup, the eyelashes finer and paler, the russet hair lying unkempt across an ear. Henry watched a sliver of dawn play across her cheek. He listened to her breathe, the sheet rising and falling over her back. Her morning scent, leaning closer, was sweet and a little stale, like overripe strawberries.

She looked peaceful lying there, warm and trusting. She had slept on the other side of the bed, a foot from him, angling away even in sleep when he tried to wrap an arm around her or snuggle his head against her shoulder. He studied her eyelid and two thread-thin, red capillaries at its edge. She would probably not welcome such an inspection. Who would, except maybe a politician willing to expose his pores, lesions, and wrinkles for an extreme close-up, as long the photo ran on the cover of a national magazine?

The alarm clock on the nightstand said five fifty A.M., ten

minutes before he had set it to blare. He had to be at the Des
Moines office by seven, which was eight Eastern, when headquarters would awaken. The bed creaked and bounced as he
slid out, and she woke.

She sat up and reached for her bra, which was slung over the
chair back. Saying nothing, she slipped on her cream underwire
armor, fastened the hooks behind her with a deft fling of her
arms, and then hoisted the harness by the shoulder straps. The
gesture was cold and mechanical, done with some urgency,
like a teacher putting toys away after playtime had run long.
She reached for her titanium glasses on the nightstand, shook
her hair, and slid them on.

He sat next to her on the edge of the bed and put a hand on
her thigh as she worked her gold watchband over her hand and
onto her wrist. "What's the rush?"

She stood, shedding his hand. "I've got an early class."

She couldn't have a class before nine A.M., three hours later.
He rolled off the mattress and padded to the bathroom. The
wall tiles were the same off-white ceramic with graying grout
as in the Presidential Suite, the tub the same beige composite.

When he came out, she was standing in the sweater and
slacks, her bag over her shoulder. She took a few steps toward
him and leaned to peck him on the cheek. "Bye," she said. Didn't
she even need to use the bathroom? She strode toward the door.

"Wait a second, will you?" he called, exasperation tingeing
the words.

She stopped and turned her head, her body still angling
toward the door.

"What?" he called. "What's your concern?" Not quite the
right words, but a last-instant save from What's your problem?

She studied him through narrowed eyes and cocked her head
as though debating whether to issue formal grievances.

His anger cut through his angst and he raised his arms in a "Bring it on" gesture.

"Okay," she blurted, shifting to face him. "When Tom's wife was in Phil Eggert's Jeep, she found a printout of an e-mail I sent him, Tom, with directions to my house." She studied him.

He shrugged. In this nest, her intimate use of Peele's first name burned him.

"Now, as you can imagine," Elizabeth said in a lecture-hall voice, "she wasn't particularly pleased, and it didn't particularly help things between Tom and me." She wagged a finger, as though she'd discovered some clue to the universe. "But the thing is—and Tom says he's double, triple sure—he swears he never printed out that e-mail."

He liked the idea of Susan catching Peele, unloading her wrath on him. But he could see where Elizabeth was going. Her anger was clawing his empty guts. "Okay," he said. "So?"

That seemed to make her furious. "So? So somebody else put that printout there. So somebody hacked into Tom's e-mail, which wouldn't be very hard to do, his secretary has the account open all day. And then that somebody printed my e-mail and planted it."

Now he narrowed his eyes. "And you think *I* did that?"

Now she shrugged, mocking him. "Well, you've got a motive. Get Tom out of the way, and I'm all yours—the woman of your dreams, smitten the first time you saw me, I think you said last night. Very David and Bathsheba."

He spent the next ten minutes giving her an alternatively pleading and pissed-off denial, until she finally shook her head, as though to clear the subject, and said "Okay." Then, without looking back at him, she left the hotel room.

———

Forty-five minutes later, when he reached the Des Moines office, his shirt was sticking to his back and his neck and temples were dripping. Steam pouring off the Mississippi or Missouri River, or wherever it came from in central Iowa, had swallowed the city. Mopping himself with a handkerchief, and ignoring the message light on his phone, he found a national florist on the Internet. Red roses were for love and passion, right? But she had red roses tattooed on her hip. Would the English prof think he was overcompensating for guilt? Don't overthink it; just send the roses. The flowers would say—shout—that last night wasn't an alcohol-induced blunder; that they did click; that he was true and cared about her and wanted to see her again, soon. With a few clicks, he sent a dozen red roses to her office at Iowa State. He pictured a vibrant bouquet in full bloom, filled out with greens, arriving in a giant cone of gold rice paper. He pictured her reading the card, and smiling.

He checked the florist's website twice to make sure the roses had arrived, and checked his voice mail throughout the day. No word from Elizabeth. That afternoon, as he was about to board an O'Hare connection to Washington, his Black-Berry trembled. The screen showed an international call, which had to be Cass. The Angel was always calling from the Caribbean, Paris, Frankfurt, Rome, Micronesia, wherever some dictator or financier client took him, or from an airport on the way there. "Hey, Gil."

"Comrade Press Secretary," Cass panted. "Look, I've only got a minute, so listen up." The Angel had begun calling Peele aides Comrades. He was Comrade Press Secretary. Diane was Comrade Campaign Manager. "I'm eighty-sixing CityVote right now," Cass said. CityVote was a nonbinding referendum organized by a dozen cities to press the presidential candidates to address urban problems. Peele figured his tough stances on crime and drugs coupled with his libertarian bent would sell well in metro areas.

"I hear you're calling reporters about it," Cass said, sharper now. "You stop that immediately and you check with me before you do anything like that again, or you'll be flying baggage class."

"Gil, you've got me confused. The Senator's the one who wants to talk it up."

"Okay, Politics 101. CityVote is a bad idea because, one, talking up liberal urban issues is not what we want to do while we're trying to win votes in Republican primaries in Iowa and New Hampshire. And two, if we're going to make a big deal about CityVote, then we have to do well in those cities, and that takes a boatload of money that we don't have right now, because we have to spend what cash we do have on Iowa and New Hampshire, not on New York and Philadelphia. Can you grasp that?"

"Yeah. Fine," he said. "But you might want to take it up with the Senator."

"Hey, Henry, how many times I got to tell you? You don't work for him; you work for me. Now cut out those fucking calls. Freedom and prosperity." The line went dead.

The next day, Fogel invited him to an evening focus group in Alexandria, Virginia, across the river from D.C. He was sure that Elizabeth would call or e-mail soon, and wanted to be free when she did. "I've got something I've got to do."

"No, you don't," Fogel said.

By the time he climbed into Fogel's Mercedes, he was

grateful for the distraction. The media man looked as rough as Henry felt, the face puffy, the graying hair uncombed. They parked outside a low-rise office building. Inside, the place seemed a cross between a banquet hall and police interrogation chamber. A dozen average Joes and Janes milled in a large room, each with a rheostat, a dial to register their feelings, one way good and the other way bad. They gorged from a buffet of tortellini alfredo, chicken à la king, and other comfort food swimming in rich sauces. A giant screen at the front showed TV ads Fogel was developing. Henry and Fogel stood behind the rear wall, watching and listening through a one-way mirror.

Henry checked his BlackBerry voice mail, in case he had somehow missed a call. Still nothing from Elizabeth, nearly thirty-six hours after the flowers arrived.

For an hour, Fogel shoveled tortellini alfredo. When a waiter circulated, Fogel insisted on a Diet Coke.

"That's good, Ira," Henry said. "Watch those calories."

"Hey," Fogel said, a maw full of pasta slurring his words, "This whole process for me is like a broken glass catheter, pissing blood for a week. It ain't fun to sit here for four hours a night, three nights in a row, seeing the shit you just worked on for the past month flagged." Fogel forked in more tortellini.

Henry nodded, but couldn't help smiling.

"I go up two suit sizes during a campaign, sometimes three," Fogel said, reading Henry's mind. "I start out thin and wiry, right where I want to be—thinner than *you*. A few months of grinding, mostly sitting in editing studios and offices and eating junk food and moo shoo pork at two in the morning, you pack on the pounds." Fogel slugged some Diet Coke.

Inside the chamber, their pollster, in tweed sport coat, played neutral arbiter, posing questions. Behind the glass, Fogel raged, paced, cursed, and exulted. And ate.

"Hell, yeah, that's right, I knew that was going to do well!" Fogel hollered when an ad comparing values registered strong positives.

"Shit," Fogel said at another point, "I didn't realize how tough it may be to tag Dagworth as a wing nut. Most people want some limits on guns, like not giving Uzis to terrorists. Dagworth's idea of gun control is a steady bead in a strong wind."

In the car after the session ended, Fogel told him, "We're going to make a quick stop; I want to show you something." Fine; Henry had nobody else waiting to talk to him.

Ten minutes later, they pulled in front of a row house on an Old Town commercial street. Inside, as Fogel opened the studio door, an odor of cardboard and coffee hit Henry's nostrils. Boxes of tapes and discs, folders and flyers lay everywhere. Carts rested against cartons, their contents marked with what seemed Fogel's current projects, including a "Tom Peele B-Roll" and "Jobs/Indiana."

Henry sat on a stool in the rear of the small, dark studio as Fogel worked the console. Images of Peele and other pols appeared and raced through the three screens.

"This is for a spot called 'Junkets,'" Fogel said, bringing up an image of Dagworth's smiling, disembodied head wearing a beret by the Eiffel Tower, then a bowler on a London double-decker bus, then a sombrero at an Aztec ruin. "Hey, we throw it out as chum, see if people bite. But you need to see this, so we stay consistent on messaging."

Henry checked his BlackBerry. What the heck; hope springs eternal.

"Hey, you watching?"

"Yeah."

The spot wrapped with a narrator intoning, "Tom Peele . . . in tune with Iowa's values. In tune with America."

"This is raw footage now," Fogel said. An image of Peele at a dais came up, which Henry recognized from a New Hampshire forum two weeks earlier.

"Ira, how can you possibly keep track of all the video you're collecting on Peele?"

"I go through it when it comes in, save the good takes. Here, I'll show you." Fogel clacked at the keyboard. The machine fast-forwarded through Peele's speech, making the Senator squawk like Donald Duck. Fogel slowed as the camera panned the audience. "Here, watch this." The large screen atop a metal stand soon showed Cass and another man huddling in a corner. Cass pulled an index card from a jacket pocket and showed it to the man.

"The guy with Gil is Mark Boggs," Fogel said. "He's Dagworth's pollster. They're working together on an Ohio Senate race."

"Chummy." What would Fogel say about him and Fran? Did the media man have footage of them at the Iowa Taxpayers forum?

"Gil Cass deals in people," Fogel said. "He collects them, catalogs them, then rents them or sells them. Hell, half the top people in Peele's campaign came from Cass's network. He got a bunch of them their last five or six jobs."

"You saying Cass placed this guy Boggs with Dagworth?"

"No," Fogel groaned. "The people he can't own, Cass sees as potential trading partners. He can walk into a room and see ten deals. The deals don't have to be for today, or even for tomorrow. They can be for five years down the road."

Henry pictured Cass sizing up the crew at that early staff meeting.

"You're not seeing the forest for the trees, *boychick*."

Shortly after he returned from Fogel's studio, Henry's office phone rang, showing a number that shocked him.

"Dad?"

"Yeah. How you doin', big shot?"

"All right. What did you tell me, if you can't be good, be good at it?"

"Yeah. Listen, I've been following this stuff, and I think maybe you finally picked a winner."

"You're following politics now?"

"I'm not saying your boy's going to be president, but maybe he gets on the ticket as veep, or gets appointed health secretary or something."

He thought, but nothing came to him. Finally, he said, "Thanks, Dad."

"Yeah." The old man sounded deflated, disappointed.

The phone line crackled a couple of times in the silence. When Henry was eleven, his father bought him a football, a "Duke" model the pros used, since his hands were big enough to throw a full-sized ball. The ball probably cost his father half a day's pay. Henry's first time with the ball, he left it on a bench on the 28th Avenue playground while he ran to the water fountain. It was just for a minute. But when he turned around, the ball was gone. He looked everywhere, asked everyone. He was going to buy a replacement as soon as he saved up enough money, before his father found out. But his father wanted to toss the football that Sunday. He said he had lent the ball to a friend. The old man saw through it. He thought his father was going to belt him, or holler, or ground him. But his father just shook his head and walked away.

Henry took a deep breath. "If you want to come to D.C., I can introduce you to the Senator, show you the setup. It's three hours on Amtrak."

"Well, I tell you what I'd rather do," his father gushed. "You're mostly in Iowa these days, right? I mean, that's where the action is. I'd rather see that. If I'm going to take off from work, drag my ass out of state, might as well go where it's happening."

"Dad, I'm not going to have much time to entertain you."

"Hey, big shot, I can entertain myself."

The next afternoon around two thirty, Henry dialed the Ames number for the fourth time that day. He waited for the now-familiar voice mail message to kick in. Instead, the peals cut off halfway through the second ring. "Liz Walmsley." He didn't know she went by "Liz."

"Hey," he said, "I sent you some roses, I just wanted to make sure you got them."

She seemed to need a second to place the voice. "Yes, they're beautiful. I was going to call you."

"I'd really like to see you again. I'm back in Iowa Saturday, should be able to break free that night. Peele won't be around." That last line hung over the phone.

After a long pause, she said, "I've got to tell you, this whole thing has me a little confused."

He closed his eyes. He heard a noise outside his office door, but whoever it was continued past. "Let's sort it out Saturday."

She paused again. "Okay," she finally said. "Can you get here by seven? There's a good Thai place a few blocks away that does take-out."

18

★ ★ ★

HOG ROASTS

Peele was pacing the Presidential Suite living room, still in his shoes, when his press aide roommate returned around eleven thirty. He had finally gotten a few minutes to think, without phones blaring or aides shoving papers at him.

"I don't know how to run a national campaign," he called at Henry, as much to sharpen his thoughts as to get a reaction. "So I leave the command-post stuff to Gil and Diane. But I do know how to run a statewide campaign." Was he slurring his speech? He'd had four Dewar's. He used to need only one or two to take the edge off.

His press aide looked worried. Good. Let somebody else also worry for a change. He knew that look, though. Henry wasn't cowed; he was worried about getting caught at something. He had seen that look a week earlier on Agatha, after she knocked over a planter with her bicycle. What was Henry up to? What were any of them up to? Like him, they were all playing roles. Saintly Senator, loyal staffer. An old adage came to mind: "Beat your child every day; if you don't know why, he does."

Henry put down a bag and stepped into the living room, toward him.

"Iowa looks weak."

"Well, we're just coming off New Hampshire," his aide said. "Maybe Iowa just looks weak compared to New Hampshire."

"Iowa looks weak compared to Puerto Rico." He had come back a few days earlier from a thirty-six-hour fund-raising swing on the island, meeting with some rum moguls.

"Anything in particular?"

Was Henry playing bureaucrat? If the problem wasn't lousy press coverage, did his press guy feel exonerated? He laughed and looked away. *I'm alone, after all.*

"The Iowa Straw Poll, right?" Henry asked.

He turned back. "Phil Eggert doesn't have it. He's in over his head." He felt his breathing tighten, and prepared for a test breath, to see if he could hit the lungs-full point. The hell with it. "The rest of you, the jury's still out."

"Well, Senator, you let us know when the jury's in."

His press guy had some juice left after all; good. He savored the verbal sparring; it was invigorating, like doing improv before a big scene.

His Iowa team had spent August preparing for the Iowa Straw Poll. At least he'd enjoyed watching Eggert actually work for a living. And Hatten had cranked out a pretty good speech. The poll, probably the biggest event of the state's political season, was now three days away.

But the Iowa Straw Poll still boded disaster. He was never going to win the thing; it was a carnival for religious conservatives, not for his people. He just had to show some support among the Shiites, beat expectations. He didn't need the reports from his K Street consultants; he could read his chances from Eggert's cuticles, pink and raw from constantly pulling off shreds of flesh. The media and the money guys treated the straw poll like an actual primary. The *Des Moines Monitor* political editor, who postured like some oracle, said Peele couldn't afford a flop. No kidding.

For two months, he had considered boycotting the thing. He knew Dagworth and Sadler were trying to buy the poll. They were getting their maxed-out donors to buy blocs of tickets and busing in supporters, including out-of-state kids enrolled at Iowa colleges, enticing them with free barbecue and live bands. The thing stank. And this was the new, cleaner Iowa Straw Poll. Before 1999, campaigns bused in supporters from around the country.

In the end, he let Gil talk him into at least showing up, with all the attention the poll was getting. He would speak but withdraw from the voting, even if his name stayed on the ballot. Actually, Gil was ready to play as dirty as anybody else, no surprise there. But Sadler and Dagworth got a jump, and by the time Eggert let them know how far behind he was, it was too late to catch up.

By two weeks out, his wizards had shifted strategies and told him they needed to inoculate him against what seemed a sure drubbing. Which meant he had to inoculate himself. He had been bouncing across Iowa, from the Black Hawk County Republican Hog Roast to the Knoxville Nationals Parade, chanting that the straw poll wasn't a referendum on Iowa Republicans' choice for president, but an exercise in big-money manipulation. Aping their lines for the press, like a marionette. Who worked for whom? At the Iowa State Fair, chewing a corndog at the sport horse and pony auction, he called the poll a "fraud" that might cost Iowa its first-in-the-nation voting status.

Now his guru-scripted complaints were pissing off the Iowa Republican Central Committee, which was sponsoring the poll. To those guys, the poll was the season's biggest fund-raiser. The state party chairman accused him of sour grapes and poor judgment. Which only stoked the media pyre.

And what did he get from his team? His handlers assured him he would be president, vice president minimum, if he did it their way. Meanwhile, they bled him. That fat Fogel was taking 13 points on ad buys, thirteen percent off the top. They'd keep bleeding him until he either caught fire or bled out. And his loyal staff? All he got was a hangdog look from Eggert and some snotty retorts from Henry, as though they were doing enough, hacking away, A for effort. Well, he got judged by results. That's what an election was.

If he blew up, his staff would just move on. "Gee, bummer about old Tom Peele," they'd say. They'd look bereft, but they'd get over it as soon as they signed a new deal. Just as Henry had, crawling to him after torpedoing Doug Tyler.

He didn't have that recourse. He'd come to Washington the same way he'd gone to Lincoln, Hollywood, and everywhere else, with his own name on the door. He wasn't going to be anybody's anything. These guys who worked for him, even Mike Sterba, had limited horizons. They were employees, not owners. Stand-ins, not stars.

He had gotten where he was by himself, by putting himself out there in front of the people and the press, the critics and the rivals. Alone, mostly. And he could get by alone now, if he had to. But look what it had cost him. Compared to his old publicity shots, he looked like the Picture of Dorian Gray, all the deceit and calumny etched into his face. He could see it, even if nobody else could.

"You know, a lot of people respect a U.S. senator," he said, turning to Henry. "Not you, but a lot of people do."

His aide cast a reverent look. "Senator, when I die, *your* life with flash before my eyes."

He laughed. He'd have to remember that one. "Hey, I think I might have left my running gear in your car," he said. "Go check, will you. And if it's there, get it to the laundry. Can't win an election in dirty shorts."

19

★ ★ ★

THE STRAW POLL

This is torture," Henry said. It came out a slurred moan. "I'll give you anything you want."

Elizabeth gave that wonderful, tittering laugh. From the back of her throat, throwing her head back and showing her even white teeth. She was gripping him, her thumb pressing his swollen, purple tip, keeping him at that excruciating, pounding point just before release. He figured he would shoot any moment, a body-wracking explosion. He didn't have the control to keep himself at that point; he didn't know his body could survive that point for so long. But the delicate white fingers knew him better than he knew himself, applying just the right pressure and movement to maintain the moment. That was a rare and wonderful thing, a woman who knew you like that. And a frightening and horrible thing.

Finally, she had mercy, and in two quick strokes the explosion came, like an artillery shot that blinded him, rang his ears, and shook him with its recoil. She stood and stepped away. A moment later, he heard the kitchen tap go on, the water running hard. He dropped his head on the faded couch, sank into the soiled cushions. When she came back, he zipped up and slid to the side, making room.

"I'm going to be a delegate at the straw poll," she said. "Maybe we can see each other there." She skimmed some fingers across his buttoned, deadened crotch.

He sat up. "How did you arrange that?"

She straightened and shifted away from him on the sofa, as though preparing for a class. "Tom arranged it. It's right there at Iowa State, five minutes from my house."

"You're not still seeing him, are you?"

"Don't push me, Henry."

She didn't have to confirm it. He knew already. He had figured it out by interrogating Lynn, the Iowa scheduler. Peele had spent two nights in Ames over the past month. Where else but the tidy little colonial could the Senator have been? Well, the straw poll was in two days, and maybe Peele would lighten his Iowa schedule after that, at least for a while.

They watched the old hotel TV for an hour as he sent e-mails on his laptop. She surfed the channels, flipping among old movies. He said nothing, just watched whatever she turned to. He filed first into his little room. He half-expected to hear the front door close. But half an hour later, a shadow crossed the doorway and she slid into the little bed beside him. He lay there, breathing her scent. That usually sent him drifting into oblivion, but not now. He reached for her and nuzzled her neck, the soft, warm area behind her ear, clearing a few fine russet hairs with his lips. "Come on," he whispered.

"You serious?"

"Yeah. I'm ready."

"You need to use a rubber," she said. "I'm off the pill."

He tried to figure whether that had some meaning. As though anticipating him, she said, "My gynecologist said it was too many chemicals for too many months."

He shifted, leaned over the side of the bed, and opened a night table drawer. His hand found the glossy cardboard carton at the back. But when he lifted it, he knew it was empty. He had meant to get more.

"Cupboard's bare," he said.

"Game's canceled."

"No, come on. I don't think there's any fluid left in me, anyway."

She resisted, but he pressed. "Well," she allowed, "I'm going into what should be the safest phase of the cycle." Women were so attune to their complex plumbing.

He reached a hand under her and tugged down her panties, gently.

On the morning of the straw poll, Henry climbed in the back of Eggert's Jeep, amid the alcohol and tobacco fumes. Peele climbed into the shotgun seat and opened the window. As they passed the Iowa State Capitol, Henry gazed at the pioneer statue before the stone steps. The gold dome rose above a neo-classical pile of marble columns, friezes, and architraves. For a year with Tyler, this had been the prize. Now it seemed a quaint stepping-stone.

From the backseat, he stared at Eggert's neck, at the twin indentations where the flesh wrapped around the spine as it met the skull. By gripping the back of Eggert's collar in each fist and twisting his knuckles into those indentations, stretching the fabric taut across the arteries in the back of the neck, he could strangle Eggert in seconds, if the seat belt kept the Iowa man in place. Or, even quicker, he could reach his arm over Eggert's scalp, plant his palm square on the forehead, anchor his fingertips in the upper orbitals of the eyes, curling the final digits to grip the inside of the skull, lift the head up and back and then jerk it down, snapping the neck. He breathed. The mental workout had his heart racing. And no qualms about this one.

"Senator, this might not be worth much," Eggert said, "but the president of the Iowa Sportsmen's Association, who's a personal friend of mine, said his people are behind you."

"You're wrong about that not being worth much, Phil," Peele said. "It's not worth anything. They don't even endorse in the presidential, do they?"

"Well, not officially," Eggert said. "But word gets around. It's a very tight group."

Peele gave a cold laugh. The Senator loosened the cellophane wrapper from a butterscotch candy, popped the sugary dollop into his mouth, and extended the wrapper, pinched in two fingers, to Eggert. Looking confused, Eggert took the wrapper, studied it, and eventually slid it in the ashtray.

At the Iowa State green, they found the Peele tent toward the rear of a pavilion village, next to an NRA booth. The structure was nice enough, with a peaked roof and color band, but dwarfed by the frontrunners' hospital-sized tents in front that pounded with rock beats from live bands.

Inside, the Iowa version of Fogel's bio spot was running on a jumbo TV, Peele's grin at full wattage. Fogel had described the ad's message as "Tom Peele's a great American, and anybody who says otherwise is a child molester." Mary McCormick and some other aides buzzed around in straw hats and T-shirts. Peele pumped hands and clapped shoulders, then went off with a head-bowed Eggert. Henry tried to concoct a way to get a barbecued pork platter and a glass of lemonade from Sadler's pavilion.

Henry gave a series of interviews, mostly pissing on the poll. A KCRG-TV reporter from Cedar Rapids was a blond blur to the left as he focused on the camera lens, keeping his eyes wide. The light pressed his retinas and broiled his forehead. He spoke at normal volume, even with the crowd buzzing his ears, knowing the mic clipped to his lapel would pick up his words.

As he was asking a *Waterloo Courier* reporter how the poll could possibly gauge Iowa Republicans' views, he saw Elizabeth walking toward him from the left. She was wearing an off-white madras dress and a matching wide-brimmed hat with a brown ribbon that would have looked silly on almost anybody else. Instead of her usual wire-rims, she was wearing tortoiseshell cat's-eye sunglasses.

"You're very smooth," she said after the reporter lumbered off.

"One of Sadler's guys told me, 'Buddy, you're slick as shit through a goose.'"

"Do you have a minute?" she asked. He followed her to a pole at the rear of the tent, away from the bustle. She twisted a silver ring on her finger, rotating the ornament several times. "I just wanted you to know," she began, "it's over between Tom and me. I'm going to tell him tonight, if I can catch him. He deserves that much."

Peele deserved more than that, and he'd like to be there to see it. He felt a grin spread across his face. He stepped forward and gave her a hug, pressing her to him, feeling her warmth as her firm breasts compressed. Once separated, he began to reach for her again, to plant a hand on each bare, tanned upper arm, wanting to hold her, to cement his possession. He caught a white mass moving in the distance and saw Mary staring from the front of the tent, hand on hip. He held up an index finger. Mary nodded and turned back to the tables.

He gave her another hug, looser this time, draping his arms over her shoulders. They said nothing, but seemed to say everything. When he stepped back, Mary was looking at him again, wagging her index finger to mock the way he had raised his.

"Guess you've got to go?" she asked. She stepped away, smiling. She had learned a tactic that eluded too many politicians: always leave them wanting more.

He wanted to pump his fist, maybe hoot. Be careful, he warned himself. If the lion finds out you've taken his meat, he'll rip you apart.

When the pregame tent show ended, he hung back among some junior aides as Eggert steered Peele into the Hilton Coliseum to a locker room reserved for them. The long chamber, lined with beige lockers and flat blue carpet, smelled of mildew, balm, and cleaning solvent. A sign by the door read "The Difference Between a Champ and a Chump is U."

Peele had apparently run into Iowa's Republican senator and was seething. "He told me he has ninety-seven percent name recognition in Iowa, but this place is crawling with youth gangs who have no idea who he is," Peele announced to the group. The Senator spread his arms, inviting them to share his outrage. Two young aides returned blank stares.

"Nobody here knows an Iowa Senator . . . at an Iowa political event!" Peele nearly screamed at the aides. "Don't you get it? The poll is rigged; the other guys bused in a bunch of ringers. We're going to get slaughtered."

Was that all Peele was livid about? Henry said nothing, straddling a bench in the back of the room.

Peele took what sounded like a couple of labored breaths and turned to Eggert. "You got my sandwich?" The Iowa crew exchanged frightened looks. "Whatever you've got—sandwich, salad, I don't care."

"Uh, Senator," Eggert began, but didn't have to finish the thought.

"You've got to be fucking kidding me."

"We can get whatever you want, Senator," one of the aides offered. Peele turned away.

Eggert dispatched an underling, who returned ten minutes later with a cardboard tray containing two shrink-wrapped ham and American cheese sandwiches, grease spotting the cellophane, and some plastic packs of mustard and mayo. Peele wouldn't touch it.

From the locker room, Henry could hear the other candidates, in turn, take the stage. They were delivering what sounded like God-Guns-Guts-and-Glory versions of their stump speeches. A deep male voice introduced each pol, staccato like a fight announcer. Leaving Peele on a bench studying scribbled notes, he walked to the wings to watch.

Sadler's intro was booming from the speakers as he turned the corner. "From the foothills of Texas, a former four-term congressman now in his third term in the U.S. Senate . . ." As a Sousa march swelled and the crowd roared, Sadler trotted out, fist pumping the air, beneath the Texan's real-time image on a theater-sized screen.

When the announcer called Peele's name, the arena erupted in boos. The Senator's words, those Henry could hear, those on which Henry had labored so long and hard, came across determined but flat. Peele was listing his platform, not living it. Peele wasn't going to bare himself to this crowd.

Hecklers shouted "Liberal!" and "RINO!" They screamed

"Boring!" during Peele's deficit-reduction exposition. The Barry Goldwater line about getting government out of the board-rooms and bedrooms drew calls for Peele to get off the stage and out of the party. He watched, bracing for Peele to turn away and storm off stage, leaving him to explain the scene to the national press corps. But Peele soldiered on, rotating a steady glare between scrawled notes and the sea of snickering faces. The Senator clearly knew the TV mics would pick up his words, even if nobody in the hall could hear. Peele was playing to the millions of viewers, not the thousands of spectators.

Peele's speech finally over, the Senator marched off the stage, catcalls following him. "Where's the car?" he asked nobody in particular. There was no point even staying for the voting. Eggert wasn't around, so Peele turned to the young, food-fetching Iowa aide. "Do you know where the car is?!"

The aide froze.

"Gary, get the car, right now," Henry ordered. The young aide dashed left, probably eager to get away, but with little idea which way to go. Henry walked the balcony looking for Egg-ert. Several delegates stopped him, spotting his Peele button, and apologized for the crowd. "This is not how Iowans be-have," one older woman told him. Even two men from a fringe right-wing campaign offered regrets.

He returned alone to the wings and walked Peele out of the building. A minute later, Eggert pulled up in the Jeep. The Iowa man was wearing a panama hat with "GOP" splashed across the band, eyes glassy, a broad grin on a flushed face.

"Okay, wait a second," Eggert said as Henry yanked him out of the driver's seat and spun him onto the pavement, using an arm bar with a fist on the shoulder blade. Henry told one of the aides to climb in the rear, to drive the Jeep back from the Des Moines airport. He waited as Peele climbed in the front.

Peele said nothing during the thirty-minute ride, sorting a pile of business cards under the dome light.

They left the Jeep on the tarmac and he followed Peele onto the Citation II for the flight to Washington. Once in the air, Peele picked up the bulkhead phone.

"I wake you? Sorry. Yeah, it was a disaster." And Peele talked for twenty minutes, whining and cooing and laughing into the ear of the woman he cheated on coast-to-coast. When Peele hung up with a "Love you, Susan," Henry felt his saliva sour.

Peele snatched the bulkhead phone and called Diane. He told her to arrange a "Come-to-Jesus" meeting for Tuesday morning. Then Peele turned to him. By this time, the plane was leveling off, and the engines were pulling back. He was going to be trapped with Peele for three more hours, like two rats in a sac.

"You're supposed to be keeping an eye on these guys," Peele said. "Why do you think I sent you to Iowa? What are you doing there?"

He returned the glare. Peele no longer churned his guts. "I've been pretty busy in Iowa, Senator," he said. "Winning more hearts and minds than you might think."

20

★ ★ ★

LEVERAGE

Henry watched from the shotgun seat as Cass glided the old Bentley to the curb at 19th and L Streets, in the heart of downtown D.C., drawing stares. The 1949 Mark VI, featuring bullet headlights that sprouted, almost organically, between flared fenders and a sculpted grill, was a voluptuous mobile sculpture finished in maroon enamel, chrome, aged leather, and turned walnut. An Asian man, maybe twenty-five, scurried from a storefront and stood by the curb. Cass unfolded his frame and stepped out. The man rushed forward, and Cass handed him the keys.

Henry followed Cass into a small shop, paneled in dark wood. To his left, bolts of wool hung on brass rails against a wall, swatches stacked on a counter. To his right, sheets of crinkly brown pattern paper lay folded in loose stacks. He stepped around two featureless mannequins, their ivory torsos darkened by years of use.

An older Asian man came through a curtain in the rear, in a lustrous navy suit and white shirt, gold reading glasses on his nose. The man couldn't have been more than five-four, but stood ramrod straight with a dignity that belied his peasant features.

"Henry, meet Mr. Yang."

The man extended a small hand with a large gold ring.

"Mr. Yang is a magician. He brings cloth to life."

The man gave a short bow.

"Ah," Cass said, leading Henry to a counter, where a bolt of rich, charcoal-gray pinstriped wool had been partially unrolled. The fabric glowed like a Fabergé egg he had seen recently in a shop window; you knew immediately it was precious.

"I bought too much of this," Cass said. "Should be enough left for a suit about your size."

Henry ran the back of his fingers over the cloth. The wool gave like rabbit fur. He pictured himself in a suit from the bolt. It would make his Bank pinstripe look like a rag. "It's great, Gil, but I've got a mortgage."

"My treat."

"No, I can't do that."

"I told you, I bought too much fabric. I've already got seventy-five suits in storage; I don't need another one."

"Well, I'm not sure I can afford even Mr. Yang's magic."

"No, the first suit costs what you'd pay at Macy's. He's like a heroin dealer; he hooks you with a freebie, then makes his money on the fixes."

Mr. Yang smiled.

Henry scanned the shop and the rich wools, linens, and silks. His eyes settled on Mr. Yang's navy sleeve, then on Cass's glen plaid lapel. "Okay."

Mr. Yang draped a yellow tape measure around his neck, and steered Henry toward the curtain.

———

Fogel found Henry at the photocopier. "I heard Uncle Gil took you shopping."

Henry ripped open a ream of paper. "I felt like I was being measured for my burial suit." He dropped the wrapper into a trash bin, where it settled on the rim.

Fogel leaned over, grunted, and shoved the wrapper fully into the bin. When the media man stood, his face was red. Henry smiled.

"A place for everything, and everything in its place," Fogel said. "Like you. *Schmuck*. It's an audition, not a funeral. Cass is training you up, see if you can be of use to him." Fogel took a deep breath, exhaled slowly.

"But I'm a communist," Henry said. "A 'head-up-my-ass, squish RINO egghead do-gooder.'" He smiled again. "I know Gil has this Michelangelo complex, but I didn't think he was looking at me beyond this show."

Fogel shook his head. "You *are* an idiot. Gil knows what you're worth. Peele, too. Why do you think Peele does the in-your-face news conferences, the serial releases, seeding the dirt in speeches? It's your playbook."

Henry felt himself beaming.

"Don't get cocky," Fogel said. "You're like most people with talent; they waste it or give it away."

"Henry," the scheduler called. She was beckoning him, the way his father did. He raised an index finger, his new gesture, and stepped over to her desk.

"The Senator asked me to tell you this," she said. "There's a woman who used to volunteer on the campaign in Iowa, a Professor Walmsley."

"Yeah." He tensed.

"She's no longer on the campaign. As such, she's no longer authorized to stay in the campaign's room at the Rigsdale Hotel.

If the Professor calls, you are to tell her that the Senator is unavailable and that you'll inform him that she phoned." She caught his glare. "Those are the Senator's exact words."

An hour later, just as Henry was about to head to Peele's Come-to-Jesus meeting, a news alert flashed on his screen: "Dagworth Unveils Tax Reform Plan." Twenty-six percent top rate, no tax on capital gains, dividends, or estates. He swore under his breath. He had told Fran that Peele was working on a plan with a twenty-seven percent top rate. It was understood to be off the record. Now Dagworth had preempted them.

At ten oh three A.M., he arrived at the upstairs conference room Diane had rented. Only one chair was left at the long table, next to Peele. Staffers sitting against the wall scooted legs and feet to clear a path for him. He felt dozens of eyes on him as he slogged to the death seat and sat.

"From now on," Peele said, shoving a water glass aside, "no more Mr. Nice Guy. Everybody take your asshole pills." They would tack further right in their media on taxes and crime and further left in their mail on health care and women's rights. "Essentially, we're going to campaign like a conservative but raise money like a reactionary liberal." To the hard right, Henry knew, any leftward shift would look like a hard left turn.

Peele handed off to Cass for the details. Henry tuned in when Cass mentioned press. "It's astounding how much cover-age Henry has been able to pull off. We got more ink in the first week after we announced than Jack Kemp got in his entire campaign."

Cass often praised him in front of other aides and apparently in private with Peele, because the Senator occasionally told him the Angel had said he'd done a nice job on this or that. Cass talked him up, and let him know it, he figured, mostly to sap his resistance.

They would draw media attention, Cass said, by leveraging Peele's Senate seat. Why did Cass discuss schemes in front of junior aides? "We'll hold a hearing on violence in pro sports. Should be a hot ticket after that little Mexican boxer died in the ring last week. We'll bring in linebackers who can't remember their names after ten concussions. And I'm pretty sure I can get Bob Ostrow to testify. He's a buddy."

"The kung-fu movie guy?" Henry asked, unable to suppress a grin. "'I'll rip off your head and . . . down your neck'? That guy?"

"Shakespeare ain't for everybody," Cass said. "And it's karate, not kung-fu. Bob was welterweight champ."

Second, Cass said, they would prolong Senate confirmation of the assistant secretary of health and human services who would oversee medical devices. The medical-equipment industry liked the nominee, whose quick approval on a new defibrillator or inhaler could mean millions of dollars to a manufacturer. Industry executives would be eager to show respect for Peele's leadership. "Somebody tells them, 'Peele's having a fund-raiser on such-and-such a date. Why don't you show up and bring some of your guys and thank him?'"

Henry turned to Sterba, at the other end of the table. He waited for the chief of staff to meet his gaze, then shook his head.

"It's going to look like what it is: extortion," Sterba said, rising. "And it's a big risk, that kind of stir-fried shit. We could alienate the President by holding up his nominee. Yeah, sure, we want to run against him in the general, but any bill you want enacted into law, you need his signature." When Peele scowled, Sterba spoke more softly. "Senator, I have a suggestion on how to handle the HHS nominee. I'd like to speak to you off-line."

"No," Peele said. "I want to do what Gil outlined."

"Well, let me explain why I think we should take another tack."

"I don't have time. Handle this the way I told you."

When the meeting broke, Sterba bulled out the door.

Henry figured he had slipped to around seventy percent approval of Peele's agenda, toward the bottom of his comfort zone. Still about ten points above his tolerance level, though. What if Peele sank to that? He'd think about it if he slid closer. He scanned the room for lunch company. He kept his voice low, but one staffer asked too loudly, "Where are you going?" and Cass heard.

"Pizzeria Uno," he said, and arched his eyebrows at the Angel, by way of invitation. The Chicago-style Italian place, nestled in Union Station's mezzanine, was quick, and they should be able to get a large table before eleven thirty A.M.

Cass shrugged. "Sure."

Minutes later, they settled into chairs with a clatter of silverware on scarred wood, amid a cozy, red and white bustle. At other tables, twenty-something staffers sat with iPhones and BlackBerrys perched. They looked so young. Most of the Hill rats who had arrived when Henry had had moved on, cashing in on lobbying or corporate jobs. He got a slew of Christmas cards from his former mates, many with photos showing perky wives or paunchy husbands and a couple of toddlers.

In a few years, if Peele's campaign fizzled and he crawled to another Senate press office, he would have little in common with the other thirty-something Hill rats, who filled the high and low ends of the food chain: chiefs of staffs and chief counsels passing through the revolving door between Capitol Hill and K Street, and secretaries and schedulers inching toward federal pensions. He would be an aging apparatchik whose moment had passed. He nibbled a hunk of Italian bread. The white dough tasted soft and soggy and the crust scraped his gum.

A Concord public relations man who had just joined their New Hampshire team reached across Henry for the salt. The guy once worked for the Christian Coalition, he had heard. The Concord man seemed the type, saying through narrow lips during the meeting that at least they were staying on the right side of the abortion debate. "I'm glad the Senator understands that all human life is sacred."

Henry smiled at a memory. "The most beautiful sight I ever saw was in Washington on an idyllic summer day," he said. "There was a pro-choice rally on the mall, and thousands of beautiful, scantily clad women were all protesting for the right to have recreational sex."

"What's that?" the Concord man asked.

"Well, that's what the abortion debate is about," Henry said. "If you're going to have sex only to procreate, there's no need for abortion, or even contraception. The only reason for abortion is when you're having sex . . . to have sex."

"That's right!" Cass thundered, pounding the table hard enough to make forks dance. "That's what nobody understands. The whole abortion debate is about *fucking*!"

"Your new liberal approach is going over great," the D.C. Senate scheduler called at Henry as she hung up a phone. "That's the second Senator who canceled a tennis date with the boss." With a couple of hits on the inhaler, Peele was good for a set on the Dirksen Building roof court. "Two more senators just can't make our fund-raiser at the Monocle, even for a drop-by."

He nodded. The finance director had told him that their fund-raising letter from a pro-choice surrogate had arrived at the direct mail house the day before. A clerk who was a devout Catholic consulted her priest and prayed, and then quit Peele's account. Meanwhile, the Drill-Baby-Drill Republican caucus was needling Peele, saying the Senator's latest environmental push confirmed their suspicions from *Parkland,* that he was a closet greenie.

As Henry strode the Russell suite's main corridor, a man with a handlebar mustache stepped out of an office a foot in front of him. Henry spun to avoid a collision, brushing the wall. "'Scuse me," he said, recognizing the man's face but not able to place it. Then he realized who it was. Bob Ostrow. The karate man was a few inches shorter than he looked on film, about twenty pounds lighter, and at least fifteen years older. Up close, the tanned flesh around Ostrow's eyes was a web of creases and the neck stubble was white, not the rich brown of the mop on the head. The face was drawn, the small eyes sunk in deep sockets, the forehead deeply lined.

"No problem," Ostrow whispered, and stepped past.

Henry stopped at Sterba's office, leaned his head in, and asked about the karate man.

"Yeah, he's been squatting in our conference room, preparing for the hearing," Sterba said. "He sees these photos of the boss with the President, the king of Spain, and decides he wants to be a congressman. Schwarzenegger can be governor of California, why can't he be in the House? There's an old Dem in a New Jersey district he thinks he can bump off." With fifteen months before the general election, there was still time to launch a House bid.

"Cass wants to put Ostrow out there campaigning with the boss," Sterba said. "That's one clusterfuck that's never going to happen, if I have anything to say about it."

21

★ ★ ★

BODYGUARDS

Henry handed the typed sheet back to Diane. "You're not really going to show that to Peele, are you?"

"Boss wants to see all the hate mail before we give it to the FBI," she said.

The missives Henry had seen, since they had begun slamming the "extremists," often began with salutations such as "Dear Atheist, anti-American Asshole" or "Dear Flag-Burning Traitor." This one got blue in the second paragraph: ". . . You communist piece of shit, come for my guns, and I will kill you dead. But you won't get the chance, you backstabbing traitor, because I'm going to have you in my sights first." The writer apparently disapproved of Peele's vote for a crime bill that restricted automatic weapons. "We will accept no more gun control! The debate is over. We draw the line!"

"Peele's already a scared rabbit," Henry said. "Why don't you at least get him Secret Service protection?"

Diane shook her head. "Candidates don't qualify for a detail until January 1. We could get a team right now just by asking the Capitol Hill Police, but you've got to go on record saying you're afraid for your safety, and the boss won't do that." Diane made a face. "Wouldn't be manly."

"What does Cass say?"

Diane smiled. "He doesn't care, as long as he's not traveling with the boss."

Later that morning, as the silver Lincoln pulled into CNN's parking lot near Union Station, Peele darted his head like an owl's, scanning cars and rooftops, even leaning to look out Henry's window, then scurried to the building. After the taping, when Joe asked whether Peele wanted to be let off outside the Russell Building, the Senator told him to pull into the garage.

Henry was chatting with the Senate press secretary in the Russell Building office when Sterba barged in and wrapped a hand around his arm. "Need you for a minute, buddy." The chief of staff led him like a child toward the back of the suite. Sterba's face was set in the nose guard snarl from a football photo on Sterba's wall. They stopped by the doorway to the small conference room by Peele's office. "We need to unfuck this situation right now."

Inside the room, the table was covered with files, papers, books, laptop computers, and a speakerphone. A lean, goateed man in an ecru polyester shirt and luminous green tie was pecking at a keyboard. Another man, short and burly with a blond crew cut and compressed features, was leaning back in a swivel chair, one foot on the table, a comic book on his lap. Henry recognized them as Bob Ostrow's aides.

"The hearing was a week ago; these turds were supposed to be gone," Sterba whispered. "But Gil's pal Ostrow made this hooch into his campaign headquarters. They've got our staff looking up bills, helping them get smart on federal issues. It's bullshit."

He glanced in the chamber. "Where *is* Ostrow?"

"Who knows? Dialing for dollars at the RNC, meeting with some PAC, pulling his pud. Thing is, he leaves these shitbirds here for hours. They're from his karate school in New Jersey—his students or something." Sterba's jaw flexed. "I need to make a point."

Sterba couldn't want an actual fight. Henry regretted telling Mike a few of his wrestling stories, breaking one kid's collarbone and another's growth plate with some rough takedowns. And some bits from his later judo and nihon goshin aikido days. He had only told the stories as ante, when Sterba told tales of artillery turning Iraqi infantry into "crispy critters." Now Sterba was counting on him for some sort of backup. He nodded slowly.

"Hey," Sterba called into the room, clapping heavy hands twice. "Let's go. Un-Ass the AO. Out of here, now."

Ostrow's men seemed confused. The taller aide with the goatee squinted at Sterba, then at Henry. The short blond aide looked to the taller one.

"Grab your gear and clear out of this office," Sterba commanded. "Right now, gentlemen."

"Hey, Mike, what's the problem?" the taller aide said, standing. "We're just—"

"This isn't a debate, Gold Brick," Sterba snapped, eyes widening. "Clear out."

The goatee squinted again, like a Doberman questioning a scolding. The shorter aide slid his leg off the table and leaned forward in his chair, elbows on thighs.

Henry's heart began racing. The short one, he knew, was coiled to spring. Trained fighters relaxed their muscles before an attack; you could move quicker. The karate guys were adding a street element of feigning calm. They could have come from Astoria.

The goatee turned back to Sterba. "Bob told us to stay here. I gotta call him." The man lifted the handset next to the speakerphone.

Sterba marched into the room and jammed a heavy finger on the phone's release button. Should Henry follow Sterba into the small room? He rotated his wrists and neck, a reflexive prematch stretch. No, at this point, the chief of staff probably wanted a witness and maybe an audience more than a partner. And Henry was closer to help if he stayed in the doorway. Also, he could use the doorway as a weapon, if he had to; the thugs would have to slow to pass through. He could try to slam their heads into the narrow metal frame. Use your surroundings, his aikido instructor had taught.

"Make your phone calls on your own time," Sterba said, the huge head inches from the goatee's face. "You need some wall-to-wall counseling? Clear out."

His father had used that move a few times, looming over him with fury. It made you feel puny. Nobody spoke for what felt like at least a minute. The goatee looked at Sterba, at his shorter friend, back at Sterba, and seemed to grope for words. Finally, the karate man threw up his hands, snatched a notebook, and strode out the door, calling "Come on, Moffat." Henry jumped back to avoid them, and held his breath as the shorter man passed in a rolling-shoulder gait.

Sterba didn't budge, but his eyes followed Ostrow's men down the long corridor toward the reception area and the suite exit. The big face broke into a grin.

————

That evening, Peele glowered as Henry climbed into the silver Lincoln. It didn't take long to find out why.

"Look, Senator, those guys were getting in everybody's way," he said. "They were even hitting on a couple of the women, including interns."

"All I know, booting those guys out caused me a royal pain in the ass. I had Gil on the phone and Bob Ostrow, and I just don't have time for this crap. I *do not* have time."

Henry nodded, trying to show remorse.

"Anyway," Peele said, "we reached a compromise you may find interesting."

Henry waited for the punch line.

"Ostrow is going to handle security for the campaign. More to the point, he's going to provide protection for me."

An image flashed across Henry's mind of Bob Ostrow, barefoot in a gi and black belt, hovering around Peele at a Senate reception. "You mean he's going to be your bodyguard? Or he's going to get other people to be your bodyguards?"

"I mean other people," Peele snapped. "Bob's a big wheel these days, and he's running for Congress. Besides, the way I hear it, there's more people who'd like to shoot him than shoot me." Peele smiled. "But 'bodyguard' is as good a word as any."

"Okay." He didn't really care; this was Sterba's fight, not his. He pictured a sniper in a hedge taking out Peele. That would solve some problems, but create more.

"Gil's been talking for weeks about getting security; he finally wore me down."

If that's the way Peele wanted to spin it, no point in challenging him. "So it's a stopgap, until you get a Secret Service detail in January?"

"Yeah. Two or three of Bob's guys are going to go with us to big events, mostly in D.C., Iowa, New Hampshire. We don't even have to pay them. Just cover their expenses. It would be an 'honor' to guard me."

"Those guys aren't exactly up to Secret Service standards."

"Well, it's something, which is more than anyone else is doing around here. Besides, they can stop a bullet as well as anybody else."

"Hey, what are you doing for lunch today?"

The female voice on the phone was familiar, but Henry couldn't place it. It had a forceful, confident, authoritative timbre that belied the cheery tone. The voice hadn't made an invitation; it had issued a command. The woman also had his direct office line in Iowa; this was a voice he should recognize. It couldn't be Elizabeth; she was in Scotland for two weeks, at some medieval scholars' confab. They'd traded a couple of discreet e-mails, but she wouldn't call him overseas.

"Henry, it's Susan."

"Oh, hey!" Now he was on a first-name basis with Peele's wife? He liked that. Liked the way she had defended him against Peele, like a lioness.

"I'm in Des Moines, and I thought I'd take you to lunch and we could discuss my media rollout." Peele had finally greenlighted her press interviews.

At noon, Henry was sitting across from Susan Peele in a booth at Buzzard Billy's Flying Carp Café on Court Avenue. A red Schwinn three-speed hung from an exposed wood beam nearly overhead. She was working on a plate of jambalaya, her long, angular fingers sliding a fork under the paste of rice, sausage, and vegetables. One of those fingers wore a simple gold band that marked her as Peele's.

"We should have your business cards by tomorrow, the rest

of your press kit by Friday," he said, working a spoon in a bowl of gumbo.

"I'm putting my schedule in your hands," she said, in an executive tone. "But I don't want this becoming, 'Oh, we can't get anybody for the manure festival? Let's send Susan.'"

He laughed. "No manure festivals."

Over dessert, she confided, "I collect Depression glass." She paused and met his eyes. When he gave her a sober, interested expression, she continued. "You have to pick a pattern or two to collect, or it'll take over the whole house. I collect both Cameo and Hocking Mayfair. I'll show you, if you're interested, next time you're at the house."

"Sure." He imagined a dull green bowl, which seemed profoundly uninteresting, except for Susan's interest.

"Tom likes to buy me pieces, but he can't seem to tell the patterns." She sighed.

"I used to collect baseball cards," he said with faux cheer. "My little fingers would tremble when I opened the packs, to see if I got a Reggie Jackson or Roger Clemens." He shrugged. "If I'd kept them, I could probably make a down payment on a house."

She smiled. "It's wonderful to be young."

A mixture of elation and depression hit him. The aging lioness was being tender, tapping him with paws that could rip out his throat. In his mind, he erased Susan's smile lines and crow's-feet and tightened her cheeks. Mostly, he erased the mien of wary regret. He morphed her into the beaming newlywed in the photo on Peele's credenza. In that shot, clearly taken by an adoring mate, her head reared back, eyes and teeth gleaming, fine brown hair bouncing. If only, somehow, he could have met her then.

He looked around the restaurant, to make sure nobody was

listening. "Susan, you know anything about a cancer drug called Ganadex? There's a push to get it covered by Medicare."

She shrugged, as if he'd asked her what the temperature was in Nepal. "No idea. Ask the Senate staff."

He smiled. "Thanks."

Back at the Ingersoll Avenue office, Henry was tweaking a budget speech when he heard a woman scream, "Bloody Damned Thing!" from the common space outside, followed by a thud. He stepped around his desk and through his doorway.

Mary McCormick was curled on the carpet by the photocopier, sobbing. Her ash-blond bob bounced in rhythm with her heaves. Red and yellow lights were flashing on the copier's display. The plastic front panel was caved in and cracked. He knelt and put an arm around Mary's shoulders, which were bonier than he had expected, and lifted her into a sitting position.

"I've got to send out flyers to my chairs, and that machine is cursed, I swear," she said, in a half laugh, half cry.

"Well, you got it back pretty good." Mary laughed, her shoulders shaking, the back of her head banging the tender groove between his shoulder and chest.

A few minutes later, he walked Mary to another aide's car and buckled her into the front seat. He watched the car pull out of the lot, with Mary's blond head slumped in the passenger seat, and merge into the Ingersoll Avenue traffic. He knew he wouldn't see her again.

Fogel's warning echoed in his head. "It'll be a pressure cooker that's going to claim about half the senior people. People will implode; there'll be terror in the office." How close was he to flaming out? For weeks, fatigue made his head hum and throb, his joints ache and the back of his eyeballs burn. The purple sacs under his eyes had swollen enough that he could shift them by squeezing his eyes shut, as he did on Tyler's campaign. By evening, his speech slurred or his words tumbled out garbled. "Let me try that again in English," he'd tell reporters. He forgot papers and misplaced keys. He found himself shouting at the phone when it rang at awkward times, and cursing his computer for taking too long to download files. When coworkers called him, he often snapped, "Yeah, *what*?" A spunky Georgetown University intern at the D.C. campaign shop told him he frightened her.

Just after eight the next morning, Henry scanned the entrance to the Des Moines Holiday Inn from the Mercury's front seat as they pulled into the driveway. A couple of burly men were aiming TV cameras at them, and he spotted half a dozen regulars from the Des Moines press corps amid the throngs from Peele's coalitions. But he didn't see his father.

This was the scene he wanted the old man to see. He heard the Mercury's back doors open and turned to see Susan stepping out, curbside. She gave him a smile. Peele stepped out the other side, in Henry's blind spot. Finally, Cass unfolded his big frame out the near rear door. The Angel had deigned to stop in Iowa on the way to Los Angeles and Tokyo.

Henry stepped onto the pavement, still searching the crowd. Then, muscling through a side glass door, he saw the tall figure. The hair looked a bit grayer. His father was wearing a pale blue knit shirt that hung shapeless over tan chinos. Fine; he had said casual. Art Hatten would fit in well among the Iowans. He waved. If Peele could wave, so could he—at his own father. The old man waved back, the big face beaming.

The Holiday Inn lobby, the patterned beige carpet, the framed floral prints, brought back times with Fran at the hotel during Tyler's campaign. The late dinners at the Heartland Café, the nights in her room. He met his father's eyes and angled his head left. The old man nodded.

Falling in behind Cass, eye-level with the linen-sheathed shoulder blades, he headed down the corridor to the ballroom. The media gaggle trotted behind. The ballroom was packed, mostly with men who looked like his father's softball teammates. The government workers union had turned out most of the bodies.

He found the Iowa AFSCME president, a friend from the Tyler campaign, and thanked him for dressing the hall and filling the seats.

"If you need work, call labor," the public employees chief said.

Clearly, Eggert's crew had also worked much of the night. Streamers hung like Spanish moss from faux wall candelabra, bunting covered the stage, bouquets of balloons swayed at the tiered, tiled ceiling. Peele's name, in giant orange letters, loomed over it all. He had seen the twenty-foot vinyl banner so often, he now saw the slogan only in bits, "Peele for President/Your Choice for Change." The two Ostrow men whom Sterba had evicted from the Senate office had taken posts near the riser. The taller man's gold crucifix, tangled in chest hair, gleamed through the open neck of a tapered shirt. The shorter man's beefy arms and chest bulged in an orange knit.

TV crews bathed them in light and a woman in a severe suit shoved a mic in Peele's face. Other reporters crowded near, poising pads and recorders.

"We're here to spread our commonsense, Republican message," Peele said, "and to say thanks to the Iowans—hardworking, middle-class Americans—who are flocking to this campaign." The Senator waved at the crowd.

"I'm the only Republican running who had a union card. I know what it's like to scrounge for a living; I served my opponents' arugula salads."

Before the light clicked off, Peele strode to the stage. As the Senator belted out a pep talk, pumping a fist like Vince Lombardi, Henry scanned the seats, searching for his father. He spotted the squared head in the second row.

His father was chatting with a smaller man next to him, gesturing as though they were old buddies, as Peele thundered twenty feet in front of them. The other man looked familiar. Older, with thinning gray hair combed back above a wide, meaty, weathered face and a scar that ran from forehead to cheek. Ed Zabriskie, the Omaha Teamsters boss.

Elizabeth had called Zabriskie a sweetheart, or something like that. A pussycat. She had been convinced that Zabriskie wanted to adopt her, after their meeting at the Rigsdale. He had warned her that Zabriskie was a lion, not a pussycat. But she had given him some theory about "Ed" venerating and protecting women. Too bad Elizabeth was in Scotland. It would have been nice to show her off to the old man. Or at least point her out, since Peele was around.

Button Man stepped past him, toward a table of canned sodas at the rear. Lanky, stooped, and covered with Peele insignia, from a bumper sticker circling a straw boater to a blazer festooned with campaign buttons, Button Man never seemed to miss a Peele Iowa event. He also never seemed to talk, just stand alone, as now, sipping Sprite.

Kyle, the Iowa press secretary, sidled up to Henry. "His keepers let him out for the whole day, or just the morning?"

Henry studied Button Man's jacket, then glanced at the

Peele sticker on his own lapel. Button Man caught his gaze. He nodded. Button Man nodded back. "He just wants his flash of existence to mean something," Henry told Kyle. "Even indirectly."

When Peele finished, Henry trotted down to his father. The old man was still yacking with Zabriskie, the two of them now huddling in the aisle. At the front, the mics and cameras were on Peele again. As soon as Henry stepped in range, his father draped a big arm around his neck. He forced a smile and ducked free.

"Good to see you again, Mr. Zabriskie," he said, smoothing his hair.

"Yeah." The Teamster boss gave him a meaty handshake.

"Dad, would you like to meet the Senator?"

His father looked over at Peele, then back at Zabriskie, as if to say good-bye.

As Henry was about to lead his father toward the front of the room, his eye caught a mass approaching from the side.

"For Chrissake, what are you doing?" Cass shot in a whisper. "I got Marty Fisher here from *Newsweek*, set it up myself because you communists are as useful as a concrete canoe. And you're here jerking off while Tom's pulling tax numbers out of his ass for Marty. Get down there."

Heat rose in his face. He looked at his father. The old man gave him a glare, tacitly asking whether he wanted his pop to take on this giant for him.

"I'll see you later," he told his father and walked down to the front.

When Henry stepped into the Rigsdale lobby that night, a bow-tied desk clerk beckoned him with a raised finger. The hotel still affected the grandeur of its glory days, even amid its peeling paint, chipping plaster, and fading carpets.

"Good evening, Mr. Hatten," the clerk said. The man's heavy beard was shaved close, his hair neatly cropped.

"Mr. Seals," he said, reading the name tag on the vest, above the title Assistant Manager.

"Mr. Hatten, you should know that your associates in room 316 have been causing some . . . disturbances. If it keeps up, the hotel will be forced to take action. Perhaps you would prefer to handle this situation yourself. We enjoy having the Senator as a guest, and we'd like to avoid any unpleasantness."

"Well, I'm all for avoiding unpleasantness, Mr. Seals. But I'm not sure I know what you're talking about."

The assistant manager pursed his lips. "The Senator's firm reserved room 316 on an indefinite basis. That room has been occupied since Tuesday evening by a Mr. Moffat and a Mr. Gargano."

Ostrow's students. He smiled.

"Did I say something amusing, Mr. Hatten?" The clerk was giving him the same sneer a Trinity math teacher had flashed when Henry couldn't graph a trigonometry function, as though the Queens scholarship student was proving he didn't belong. That teacher had also called him Mr. Hatten.

"No. Go on, Mr. Seals."

"Well, these two *gentlemen* have been . . . entertaining . . . quite late. Other guests have complained about the noise and also about . . . some of the female guests. I assume you take my meaning, Mr. Hatten."

"Yeah. I appreciate your giving us a chance to fix things."

He reached the Presidential Suite shortly after ten P.M. and dropped his briefcase in the little bedroom. Since the rally, the day had seemed charmed. He'd managed to break away for dinner with his father and get through the meal without a fight. The old man was scheduled to fly out in the morning, maybe still with a smile. Peele was scheduled to stay over that night, but the light was off in the master bedroom. What the heck; this could be a fun finale.

Five minutes later, he stood outside room 316, listening to a beat thudding through the door, maybe through the walls. He rapped twice, hard. He waited and pounded again. The door whipped open and he found himself a foot from Gargano. The tall, lean goatee was wearing a sleeveless red T-shirt with faded white lettering. Curly black hairs lined the upper arms. Behind him, the room was a collage of empty pizza boxes, Doritos bags, and beer cans. Judas Priest's "Fever" was pounding from a clock radio: "You set my soul on fire . . . filled with desire." A blue haze hung at the ceiling, and the place reeked of cigarettes. Gargano looked down at him, a cocky grin fading.

"Hey," Henry said. No need to introduce himself; Gargano would remember. "The hotel's been getting complaints about the noise and some of the action around here."

"You the hall monitor?" Gargano's voice was hoarser than he recalled.

"I'm just trying to do you a favor. The manager was ready to call the Senator, or maybe the cops." He had promoted Seals.

Gargano nodded and leaned closer. He smelled a bouquet of pizza, nachos, beer, and Marlboros. The eyes were hooded and slightly bloodshot. "You're doing me a favor. You want to be my friend, huh?" Gargano opened the door a bit wider.

He stepped back, now wishing he had worn oxfords instead of black loafers. At least they weren't tassel loafers. "Where's the other guy?"

"Moffat? He's with Peele." Gargano smiled down at him. "We're alone, if that's what you're asking."

"No, that's *not* what I'm asking." He felt small and dainty in his blue glen plaid suit. How did these street punks learn such verbal aplomb? The few times he'd been mugged, the thugs always had some good lines, and were as quick on their feet as any spinmeister he'd met. "If you ain't got no bus pass, then you got to have a dollar. . . . Well, if you ain't got no dollar and you ain't got no bus pass, what you doing here waiting on the bus?"

He took another half step back and looked into Gargano's bloodshot eyes. "Behave like human beings, save us all some trouble we don't need." He turned to walk back to the elevator.

As he was about to step, he felt a hard, flat object strike the left side of his behind, and he staggered forward. It was the Trinity yard again, this time a kick in the ass instead of a sneer. He felt heat rise in his neck and head.

Before his brain could engage, his body did. He spun, dipped and shot low, off his rear foot, driving his 180 pounds into Gargano's forward knee, the point of his clavicle crashing into the patella. Instinctively, he knew a wrestling takedown from a suit would disorient the karate man. Gargano fell back onto the carpet. Henry clambered forward, toward the head. Before Gargano could regroup, he fired an open hand, catching the karate man under the chin with the base of his palm and snapping the head back into the floor. The impact smashed the jaws together, spraying him with blood, spit, and maybe a tooth fragment. Raising his right hand, thumb and forefinger splayed out, he slammed the webbing into the base of Gargano's throat, just above the collarbone. Gargano began choking, his body jerking, more pink spittle spraying.

He crouched over Gargano's face, straddling him with knees planted, and stared into the bulging eyes, waiting for the recognition to turn to fear. He raised his right hand again, slowly, twisting it into a classic martial arts fist with the thumb up, tight against his side, and angled his shoulder back. He aimed and sent the first two knuckles crashing into the bloody mouth. He stood, wiped his hand on the red T-shirt, and stepped into the corridor, unsteady from an overdose of adrenaline.

22

★ ★ ★

THE WIFE OF BATH

In the small dining area of his Washington condo, Henry raced a razor blade around the edges of the long tan carton, slicing the packing tape. He took a breath and lifted the top, revealing a sheet of gold-embossed tissue paper. Pulling that aside, he exposed the rich, thick gray pinstriped wool, now in a suit with brown tortoiseshell buttons and tight gray stitching. The fabric looked even more lustrous in its finished form. The sleeves had real working buttonholes, angled just slightly to match the arm's taper. It felt like tenth grade, when the coach issued him a navy-and-white Trinity warm-up jacket and singlet for his first varsity match. He had admired himself in the locker room mirror, thinking he'd never look any better.

Reluctantly, after a long embrace in the mirror, he slung the suit on the gleaming Yang and Co. wooden hanger. Pushing back the steel-gray Jos. A. Bank, he placed Mr. Yang's masterpiece at the front of his bedroom closet. It would be a month before the weather cooled enough to wear it.

He fired off a thank-you e-mail to Cass. The Angel had been scarce all week, since signing on as Ostrow's general campaign chairman. The karate champ had announced for a New Jersey House seat earlier that week.

Back in his small Des Moines office, Henry cradled the phone to his ear, waiting for Peele's health-care aide in Washington to patch in the business aide.

He gazed at Bill Burr's latest e-mail, titled "Western Pharmaceutical." The reporter would knock on his door in ten minutes, for a lunch interview. Sure, maybe Burr just happened to be in Des Moines. But maybe the reporter also wanted to watch Henry's eyes when he twisted the knife. He tabbed to the link, an article from a financial news website, The Partridge Report.

"Jane, you there?" he asked. "Jane?"

"The Partridge Report is a major finance blog," the business aide began. "Partridge is sort of the Matt Drudge of the finance blogosphere."

"Great," he said, scribbling notes on a pad.

"Essentially, Partridge posted a blog this morning saying Western Pharmaceutical's cancer drug, Ganadex, is going to win approval soon for off-label Medicare coverage, which is going to send the company's stock through the roof."

"Good," he said.

"You think so?" she snapped. "Why does Partridge think the drug is going to get approved? Because there was a posting this morning on Western's Yahoo Finance message board saying it will, from someone who claimed to have inside information. The person called herself, I'm assuming it's a she, 'Wife of Bath.'"

"'Wife of Bath'?" Where had he heard that name?

"Yeah," the business aide said. "The postings are anonymous. It's a screen name, like people use on eBay."

"Okay."

"The Yahoo posting was somewhat circumspect," the aide continued, now in a detached tone, as though her job weren't also ultimately at risk in all this. "Look, Partridge quotes it, midway down: 'I know people involved and have reason to believe it will happen soon. I know important people at several levels close to this.'"

"That's it?" he asked.

"Didn't you read the thing, Henry? Partridge apparently followed up with Wife of Bath and got more in an interview."

"Well, how could he do that if the postings are anonymous?" He thought he was following her lecture, but braced for a remedial rehash.

"Simple," the aide said. "Partridge posted a response on the Yahoo message board asking Wife of Bath to call him. Apparently, she did."

Now he remembered the name. "The Wife of Bath" was a Chaucer story, from *The Canterbury Tales*. He'd read it in college. It was some medieval yarn about a knight being better off marrying the grizzled Wife of Bath, who knew how to keep a home and please a man, than some sweet young thing. And the Wife of Bath turns out to be gorgeous in the end, also. He squeezed his eyes shut. Elizabeth.

Elizabeth, what are you doing? Hell hath no fury, eh, Professor? He doodled on his pad, sketching the outlines of a three-dimensional box. He drew a stick figure inside, then lined the walls with bars, trapping the figure. "The story doesn't mention the boss," he nearly yelled.

"No, not by name," the health-care aide said, as though calming a child. "But the Senator has been pushing, quite publicly, to get the drug covered."

"Yeah, I was at the House hearing," he said.

"Fine," she said. "The internal CMS process itself is supposed to be confidential, so you can see why the press would come to us when there's a leak."

He rubbed his temple. "Serious journalists don't give credence to scam sheets." He tried to match her elegant sentence construction.

"They will on this." He heard keys tapping. "Western Pharmaceutical stock is up seven percent already today. If it closes that high, business reporters are going to take a look, find the Partridge story, and then find you."

He swallowed and ran his tongue over his lips.

"The SEC and a congressional committee, maybe Ways and Means, could also get involved, and who knows who else."

At least nobody was suggesting that Peele's campaign was profiteering off the cancer drug, or that the unions were involved. They didn't seem to have that part. Maybe Elizabeth hadn't pulled the noose too tight.

He heard what sounded like the front door opening and closing. By the receptionist's desk, he saw a mop of orange hair atop a broad frame, a Viking beard curling under the chin. "Bill, be with you in a second," he called. The reporter turned around, but Henry popped his head back into his office and shut the door, like a turtle diving into its shell.

"Thanks, really helps," he said into the phone, and hit the "Good-bye" button. He dialed Elizabeth's cell, punching the keys slowly, to avoid a misdial. She should have been back from Scotland two days ago. He got a "Liz Walmsley" outgoing message. "Elizabeth, please call me as soon as you can," he implored. "Thanks."

By the time he stepped out of his office, the vise was back on his temples. "Hey, Bill, good to see you, man," he said, clapping the reporter on the shoulder.

Burr shifted a can of Jolt Cola to free his right hand for the shake. Gripping, Burr looked at him with wide blue eyes bulging from a pale, broad face. Two cellophane-wrapped cigars jutted from the reporter's shirt pocket.

Burr also looked tired, with creases scoring his face. But it was a different kind of fatigue, without the hollowed eyes from sleepless nights, bolting awake panicked over missed details or potential attacks. Burr's face just showed the wear of long hours covering speeches and crafting stories, weeding through spin, and maybe fielding a few irate phone calls from flacks and consultants after his stuff ran, all jacked up on Jolt and nicotine.

Henry envied Burr, and pitied him. No matter who won or lost, Bill Burr would go on writing articles and impaling politicians. For Burr, people like Tom Peele and Henry Hatten offered literary fodder for a time. But Burr would never feel the ecstasy of a campaign win—like the mind-blowing, body-shuddering blast of energy from deep-kissing a goddess. A few white hairs sprouted in Burr's orange sideburns, which he hadn't noticed before. Maybe it was getting to the scribe, after all.

Stepping out the campaign office's front door was like stepping into a blast furnace. Even into September, Des Moines was baking in the midday sun. By the time they walked the three blocks to the Ingersoll Diner, Henry's shirt clung. Burr was also sweating, the tips of the orange locks pressed brown and flat against the head, moisture beading the beard.

Inside the diner, the air-conditioning cut through Henry's shirt, stinging his flesh. Burr threw himself into a booth in the back. The reporter pulled out a spiral-bound pocket notebook and flipped it open. Burr poised a Bic ballpoint, chewed at the tip.

"Bill, you should ease off the Jolt. Give you a heart attack before you're twenty-five."

"I'm twenty-six."

Henry shrugged. "It's not the years, it's the mileage, right?"

Burr leaned across the table. "So what's your comment, for the record?"

He waited, holding Burr's eyes until the Bic began trembling.

"A gazillion people could have leaked about the Medicare process," he said, and shrugged. "And, contrary to your premise, this is an internal agency decision, in which the Senator is *not* involved."

"Not involved?" Burr wailed. "Your boss practically begged Ways and Means to get the drug approved."

He shrugged again.

The bulging blue eyes glared at him.

"Bill, I don't even see where there's a story here. You've got one anonymous source making an oblique, cryptic statement, reported by a financial scam sheet." *Please, don't let Burr have reached Elizabeth.*

Burr pressed the Bic into the pad, forming large childlike letters. A waitress in a yellow uniform came by with dog-eared menus. They ceased fire as Henry ordered a roast beef club and Burr a swiss-and-onion omelet. So much meat wasn't the healthiest option, but there was something atavistic about gnawing hunks of animal flesh, sinking your canines in and feeling the juice squirt into your mouth.

"So, Henry," Burr said, chewing egg, mouth half-open, "Who's the woman Senator Peele's been seeing?" Burr met his eyes, the pupils small in the blue irises.

He stared at the reporter, concentrating on the blue eyes, picturing the folded brain tissue behind them, just as he was taught to aim a martial arts punch two inches into the target. Henry didn't want his face to betray any clues. "What are you talking about?"

"The woman Senator Peele has been seeing at the Rigsdale Hotel and other places in Iowa." The Bic's point rested on the pad.

So Burr, which meant Fran, had somehow learned about Elizabeth. But they didn't seem to know who she was, and certainly not that she was also Wife of Bath. And that meant Burr didn't have enough for a story on Peele's dalliances. At least not yet. The reporter was fishing. He broke off his stare. "I don't know what you're talking about, Bill."

"I'm talking about—"

"I don't know what you're talking about, Bill. And I'm not going to listen to you smear the Senator with wild gossip, innuendo, and slander." He stood and pulled his wallet from a front pocket. He plucked out a twenty and dropped it on the table. "I've got to get back to work." He strode out of the Ingersoll Diner, each step heavy, feeling Burr's eyes on him.

By the time he fell into the desk chair back at his office, his shirt clung again and his temples and the back of his neck were wet. The light on his phone was flashing.

Fran could have learned about Elizabeth by chatting up the Rigsdale desk crew, maybe even upright, uptight Mr. Seals. But hotel clerks wouldn't know Elizabeth's name. That night Elizabeth stayed in the eighth-floor room, he had billed the charges to the campaign, and never identified her. The clerks would know only that some russet-haired woman visited Peele's suite in the hotel. But Fran made a living ferreting out information, digging up dirt others couldn't find.

His mouth went dry again. Did Fran and Burr know that Elizabeth had also visited Henry in the Rigsdale? If he hadn't stormed out of the Ingersoll Diner, would Burr have asked him why the same woman seen with Peele had stayed with him at the hotel when Peele wasn't around?

He checked his voice mail. The first call was from Elizabeth. "Hey, I just got back and got your message—" He dialed her office.

"Yeah," she said, "I put that stuff on the message board."

"And you talked to the blogger, Partridge?"

"Yup." Her voice had an edge.

"What, are you pissed at *me*?"

"Henry, the world doesn't revolve around you."

He sighed. "You have no idea what you've stumbled into."

"What, you mean about the union buying stock? No stumbling there. In fact, I also bought Western stock. And I told a bunch of my friends to buy the stock. I even told my ex."

He breathed again, into the receiver.

"What's the problem? Everything I said was true, which is a lot more than I can say for some people I know."

"I never lied—never mind, as you say, this isn't about me. Why'd you do it?"

"For the money, my dear." When he said nothing, she went on. "Evan's still got some of my stuff, so I'm either going to have to hire a lawyer, or I'm going to have to buy him off. It's a case of a man taking advantage of a woman who shared her life with him. So there's a certain appealing irony here, don't you think?"

He exhaled again, this time moving the mouthpiece out of

the way. He wanted to hold her, and he also wanted to throttle her.

"You didn't also talk to a reporter from the *Omaha Globe-Times,* did you?"

"Nope. Partridge asked me to promise him an exclusive, and I did."

"Boy, you're a media relations pro."

He checked his other voice mail messages. One was from Peele's Washington Senate office, forwarding a call from a Bloomberg reporter about the Partridge blog. The Senate crew seemed delighted to hand off the Bloomberg call, judging by the chipper intro from the deputy press secretary.

The Bloomberg reporter had left a message on the Senate press phone forty-five minutes earlier. A wire service guy wouldn't wait long for a response, not on something like this. Sure enough, Henry found a Bloomberg piece had crossed the wires fifteen minutes earlier.

His computer took forever to open the article, a tiny hourglass mocking him. Finally, the story appeared, a short process piece headlined "Medicare Close to Decision on Cancer Drug, Sources Say." Skimming it, he saw Bloomberg had combed through Peele's financial disclosure forms and, thankfully, found no tie to Western Pharmaceutical. "Peele, a vocal advocate for off-label coverage . . ." the story said. "A Peele spokesperson could not be reached for immediate comment."

Bloomberg had done them a favor. The wire service piece was more neutral than anything Burr would write. Now that the news was out, maybe the *Globe-Times* would bury or kill Burr's piece. Or maybe they'd play up the personal angles.

His desk phone rang. The 703 number.

"Comrade Press Secretary, this is not good." It was the first time in days he had spoken to Cass.

"Yeah, I know."

"That woman has a screw loose." No surprise that Cass knew about the stock scam. But how had the Angel made the connection to Elizabeth? Peele, probably. Why was Cass assuming Henry also knew Elizabeth was Wife of Bath? Was it a trap?

"What woman is that?"

Cass paused. "Whoever posted those 'Wife' messages. A lot of people are going to be very unhappy, Comrade. You get any more calls on this, you call me immediately. You understand?"

"Yeah."

"Freedom and prosperity."

23

✷ ✷ ✷

THE ROGUE RABBI

As dawn broke the next morning over the Des Moines airport, Henry gripped the railing of the Citation II's dropdown staircase and hauled himself and his bags onto the jet, following Peele. The two-day Florida swing would culminate with the Florida Straw Poll at the Orlando Convention Center, but the main mission was raising money from Miami Jews.

Diane Spriggs had rolled her eyes when she handed Henry their latest Jewish direct-mail piece, which essentially warned American Jews that the only thing standing between them and the storm troopers was Tom Peele. Since Peele's leftward fundraising shift, they had stepped up their mailings to Jewish donors, spending $3 million on letters to lists from AIPAC and the National Holocaust Museum.

Henry settled into a front-facing seat and swallowed. Arrival in Miami threatened disaster. An hour earlier, as he was brushing his teeth, Diane had phoned to tell him, "We've got a rogue rabbi." A Miami rabbi had alerted the local media that Peele was coming to town for a fund-raiser hosted by a prominent member of the rabbi's flock. The rabbi had arranged a white Rolls-Royce to pick them up outside the Miami general aviation hangar. Footage of Peele descending from the clouds in a Citation II and climbing into a Rolls, like a twenty-first-century version of Hitler in *Triumph of the Will*, could go viral.

Diane had been scrambling to cancel the Rolls and line up suitable American wheels, but nobody was taking her calls or answering her e-mails at six thirty in the morning. Henry planned to begin monitoring his BlackBerry in twenty minutes, after they reached cruising altitude. You run the device while the pilots are taking off, you can jam their instruments. Which, in this case, might offer another solution. He'd tell Peele about the rabbi later, if he had to.

Henry had been bolstering their message with the Jewish press, dispatching their New Media whiz to barrage their Jewish media list and bloggers. He put Peele on calls with reporters from *New York Jewish Week*, *Jewish Daily Forward*, and the Jewish Telegraphic Agency, the Jewish version of the Associated Press. A call with a reporter from the leading Israeli daily *Haaretz* had stretched from a scheduled ten minutes to thirty-seven minutes, as the reporter kept saying, "One more question." Finally, Henry cut in and told the guy he was asking his fifth final question. The man said, "Well, it was going to be the last question, but after the Senator just raised this fascinating point, how can I not ask this follow-up question?"

As the Citation II roared southeast, a headache chiseled Henry's temple. He put down a sheaf of papers and closed his eyes, but the pain didn't ease. Nausea and light-headedness followed. He had skipped breakfast, after only a tuna sandwich the night before, which meant his blood sugar was down. Even if they had soda on the plane, it would be Diet Coke, since Peele was watching his weight. One of the glistening wooden cabinets might hold some packs of sugar for coffee, but he didn't want to burn the energy to ask.

Peele began yammering about polls. In a *USA Today*/Gallup national poll the day before, Peele had edged Sadler and was within four points of Dagworth. Peele was blathering in a stage whisper, top-secret stuff, even though it was just the two of them in the cabin; the rest of the team was already on the ground in Florida. Henry was listening, but mostly he was releasing strategic burps, which seemed to ease the pressure on whatever was trying to expel the meager contents of his stomach. A few spasmodic breaths generally followed a burp. He tried to keep this gastrointestinal symphony quiet, nodding as Peele prattled.

Peele was saying that their own recent poll jibed with the *USA Today* results, was actually even stronger, and that they were going to begin doing their own tracking polls in about a month, coordinated with their first TV ads in Iowa. Henry released a long, silent burp. Fogel had already told him about the tracking polls. They would do them in three-day intervals. Every evening, their pollster would fill a room with laid-off telemarketers, who would dial through voter lists. They would start one poll on Monday, another poll on Tuesday, and a third on Wednesday. On Thursday, they'd get the results of Monday through Wednesday's polling. On Friday, they'd get the results of the separate poll that ran Tuesday through Thursday. And so on. And they'd begin to see what effect Fogel's TV commercials were having, and which ones.

Peele asked for the *USA Today* poll story and Henry leaned over to fish the clip from his briefcase. Immediately, he was sure he would puke. He anticipated a multicolor gush spraying the bulkhead. He closed his eyes, pushed out another burp, and felt the reflux point slide down his esophagus. He breathed and let his head loll back against the rest, vowing never again to skip breakfast.

As the Citation dived toward Miami, a different pang hit Henry. He had forgotten to turn on his BlackBerry, to check on the Rolls-Royce and any other crises. Too late now. As they taxied to the charter hangar, Henry gazed out a porthole window. He saw a horde of sundresses, pastel blazers, and straw hats and two separate throngs waving signs. One of the groups had to be the Florida team, another African-Americans for Peele. The third might have been from Democrats for Peele, judging by their youthful good looks. Their various coalitions made sure to turn out greeting parties for every Peele public arrival. Then, in the distance, Henry saw some of the campaign team, standing beside a dark blue . . . Buick.

On the ground, Henry's stomach settled a bit. Their national political director, Florida leadership team, and Moffat the bodyguard took custody of Peele. Moffat didn't give Henry any special attention; Gargano probably hadn't admitted to his buddy that he'd been bloodied by a suit.

In the hangar office, Henry fed some bills into a vending machine and pulled out a plastic-sheathed slice of yellowed cheesecake topped with strawberry syrup. He swallowed it as fast as he could, which wasn't fast, as Peele made phone calls from an office.

In the Buick, as they whisked past palm trees along sun-bleached asphalt, the Florida chairman gushed about the straw poll and how well Peele should do. From what Henry could tell, the guy's main point was that Florida was a first-class state—big, influential, and diverse—with a straw poll to match, while Iowa and its straw poll, which got much more attention, were shit. The guy had a case. Unlike Iowa, you couldn't buy votes in Florida's straw poll. Voting was limited to the thirty-five hundred elected delegates, who even covered their own $175 registration fees and hotel rooms. Still, Henry knew, that hadn't stopped Sadler or Dagworth from buying a list of delegates and sucking up to them for weeks with calls, letters, and now breakfasts during the three-day extravaganza at the Orange County Convention Center.

For Henry, the Florida trip rushed by in a blur of fund-raisers and meet-and-greets. Along the way, Peele announced that the assistant HHS secretary nominee was fit, after all, to oversee medical devices. In the five weeks since Peele first voiced concerns, pharmaceutical executives had packed three of Peele's fund-raisers, including one in Miami. Maybe Cass figured they had soaked the drug companies enough.

The second afternoon, Cass took Henry to a Cuban-American reception, where he gleaned that the Angel had been making promises to the Cuban exile delegates, offering deals on congressional legislation, and paying shills to talk up Peele. Saturday, at the finale, Henry could only watch as the delegates milked the poll results roll call for hours, introducing each of the sixty-seven counties with a description such as "home of the largest rodeo east of the Mississippi." In the end, Peele took second, edging Sadler but five points behind Dagworth—not far from the *USA Today* results.

Peele gave a few interviews outside the ballroom, then raced off to the airport while Henry stayed at the convention center to work the press. He would catch a commercial flight to Washington that evening.

"Clearly, Senator Peele's centrist message is resonating in Florida and throughout the country," Henry dictated to a big-name national reporter as she banged his quote into a story on her laptop. She was pressing a deadline, and needed a primer on the Florida process. Oh, if it were always so easy.

24

★ ★ ★

FISH FOOD

The rolling Manchester street, old redbrick mill buildings in the distance, seemed so quintessentially American as Henry marched toward the main entrance of WMUR-TV for the candidates' forum. Peele and Susan walked a few steps ahead, Susan's Burberry trench coat swishing with her strides. Moffat matched Peele's pace, a foot away. Henry hadn't seen Gargano since their scuffle.

Peele reached his hand toward Susan's. She took it without looking, seeming to sense it was there.

As they neared the glass doors, a man wearing a large YAF button jumped from a phalanx of supporters and paparazzi, wagging a sign at them: "Liberalism is dead—Let's keep it that way." Susan recoiled, but Peele kept stride. Moffat, who probably should have been marching between the Peeles and the crowd, lunged at the protester, who retreated into the phalanx. Peele seemed to have slipped into a combat calm, accepting the attacks and death threats as part of a new reality. The Senator still searched for snipers on rooftops, but had stopped dashing from cars.

Just inside the door at WMUR, a young New Hampshire state senator pumped Peele's hand and assured the Senator, "I'm with you." The man added, more softly, "I'm just not in a position to say so publicly."

Peele's new social libertarian push was also winning underground support in the Senate Republican cloakroom. Several colleagues had given Peele checks, one for the $2,500 limit, while officially pledged to Sadler or Dagworth. Some credit had to go to Peele's man who continually phoned most of the 535 members of Congress, delivering on asks and suggestions, keeping all those people happy, to siphon support from their opponents. But the senators' checks were trivial compared to their endorsements. So Henry leaked the gifts to the *Monitor* political editor, weeks before the next campaign finance reports were due. Put on the spot, the senators said they were just helping a colleague and friend.

"I feel like food in a goldfish bowl," Susan told Henry after being jostled aside by a *Newsweek* columnist reaching for Peele's arm.

He noticed a chunky man with flyaway hair. The media whiz who had cut campaign ads for the Iowa governor against Tyler. Maybe also the "opposition" who had touted Henry to Peele's people. Henry nodded and the guy nodded back, and they met in the middle. "New day, new war," Henry said. "Good to see you."

The man grinned. "You gave us a big scare."

How wonderful to be a player in his own right. One day . . .

He felt a hand on his shoulder and turned to see a beaming Brian Natter. "Senator," their New Hampshire chairman called across him at Peele, "some people you need to meet." Natter began steering Peele around WMUR.

Henry hustled outside, past the thinning ranks of protesters and paparazzi, to an alley behind the building. Breathing hard, he pulled his BlackBerry and dialed Elizabeth's number. They hadn't spoken in days, since the Wife of Bath call, and he needed to hear her voice. Craved it. He needed to scrape off the aftertaste of that last call, scrape away all the crud between them; she was free now, and he wanted her. And, mostly, he wanted some hope that twenty years from then, if he extended his hand, she'd sense it and want to take it.

The line rang a third time, and her "Liz Walmsley" message kicked in. He let the words pour out, from somewhere inside him. He told her he missed her, that she was more important to him than he had realized, that he wanted to talk to her, be with her. It was the closest he could come, he supposed, speaking to an answering machine from an alley, to telling her he loved her.

In a minute, he was back at WMUR chatting with a CNN political reporter the size of a linebacker. "You look much smaller on television," he said.

"Get a bigger TV," the CNN man replied.

Rejoining Peele, he saw the Senator had begun to stiffen at the hands that pawed his shoulders and arms. Natter gave a report on several state legislators who were on the fence. "A drink together, maybe even dinner, could push them over to our side," Natter told Peele. "You've got to show them some love."

Peele nodded absently. Then Natter leaned in. "Senator, you've got to put in more time in New Hampshire. They expect that here, and people are talking."

Peele glared at Natter, eyes now slits. Henry knew that look, like a dog pulling back its ears before lunging. Natter seemed to mistake the gesture for a cue to continue. "You can't just pop in here for a morning press conference and fly back to D.C."

Before the New Hampshire chairman finished, Peele walked past Natter to a paunchy man in a gray suit. "Hey, Jim," the Senator said, extending a hand.

Henry saw the hurt in Natter's eyes. Peele could snub the hired help, but Natter was a volunteer and a New Hampshire player in his own right, with a reputation and agenda. Not good, Comrade Senator.

After the candidates left the set, Peele took him aside. "I've got to meet with a couple of the big wheels. Take Susan out to lunch, will you?"

"You want me to take your wife to lunch?"

"Yeah, you seem to have a calming effect on her." Peele was making Susan sound like a dalmatian.

"Take her to a restaurant?"

"Yeah. Just be at the general aviation terminal by one." Peele raised a finger. "By one o'clock. We've got to take off on time, just like the New York shuttle."

He hailed a cab and took Susan to a nearby Italian restaurant that the station manager recommended, Piccola Italia. The place went for an old-world feel, with murals on the walls, a trellis with grape vines, and waiters who crooned Italian standards. They settled into a booth with a view of downtown Manchester, which bustled with New England swagger. Susan had a contented, ebullient smile, her brown eyes bright and wide.

The menu was too much, four pages. He slipped into a reverie about Elizabeth, picturing her in that slate-blue sweater from that first night at the Rigsdale, and then in a textured lace bra that looked and felt like a floral bas relief. He couldn't focus on the food. A roasted peppers entrée looked good, with fresh garlic and basil on oven-baked bread with melted buffalo mozzarella. He closed the menu.

The waitstaff buzzed and darted, filling water glasses, delivering bread baskets, reciting the day's specials.

"Senator was sharp today, on message, hit Dagworth pretty hard," he said.

She made a face. "I've heard it so many times, it's hard to tell anymore. But Tom did seem pleased with himself. Then, again, Tom usually seems pleased with himself."

A waiter swooped by, placing a medley of vegetables and cheese in front of him and a heaping platter of veal piccata in front of her. Smelling the grilled vegetables and sauce, he realized all he'd eaten that day was a granola bar at the Dulles charter terminal at five forty that morning. He waited until she raised her knife and fork, properly in her long fingers, and pierced the veal.

"That's enough to feed an army, as my father would say." He gestured at her plate.

"Would you like a bite?" she asked, with new gusto. She sliced off an oval slab, slathered the white flesh with sauce and capers, and extended the laden fork toward him. Her long hand, tanned and manicured, rested close enough to him that she was clearly offering, but still far enough that he'd have to reach across the table.

Her eyes were wide and innocent, but a smile was playing at the corners of her mouth, making her pale coral lips glisten.

Was he in heat, obsessing about Elizabeth, and spewing pheromones, or whatever signals your glands send out, his body eager for release and relief wherever it could find it? Even

Susan's hand looked inviting, the long tanned fingers and soft underside of her palm. He felt his breathing quicken and felt himself stir in his pants. A napkin covered his lap, so nobody would notice. But he didn't want to look around, to see who might be watching, maybe staring. An urge hit him to shove the fork out of the way with his left hand, and dive over the table and onto Susan. They'd land on the carpet, him on top of her. He could almost feel their bodies mesh, one of her long thighs between his. His hunger, for food, was gone. Now he wanted to touch the moist coral lips, feel Susan, taste her. Now he could hear his breathing, which meant she could probably hear it, too.

Susan cocked her head, still extending the laden fork. Whatever else, he couldn't let this scene continue. He leaned toward the fork, which also meant leaning toward Susan, extending his torso across the table. He was going to grab the meat and pull back, trying not to look like a frog in a nature show snapping out its tongue at an insect. When he got close enough to the extended fork that the orange and beige merged into a fuzzy mass and his eyes had to refocus, Susan reached out her empty hand and cupped his chin, holding him in his pose, head halfway across the table. Her touch was light and soft, but strong, the long fingers cool.

"Come on, baby," she said, softly, with a faint rasp at the low end, her voice like silk over sandpaper. He felt pain where he was pressing against his pants, now magnified by leaning over the table. Still gripping his chin, she traced a long finger, maybe her thumb, he couldn't tell, across his lips.

He opened his mouth and she slid in the veal. He bit down and felt the flesh give under his teeth and juice spurt against the walls of his mouth.

"You know," she said, releasing his chin, "you don't have to wait for an occasion to come by the house, when you're in Omaha. Just give a call."

Henry finally connected with Elizabeth around eight that night. "I just got off the phone with Tom," she said. "Or with Tom's machine. He's still not taking my calls."

This wasn't beginning as he had dreamed. "I thought you were through with him," he said. Was she one of those women who stayed friends with exes, sometimes returning to them?

"Final details, like dividing the property in a divorce. I pick up my bag from the hotel on Thursday night and leave the room key."

"I'll be there, I'll be in Des Moines on Thursday," he gushed. "Can we get together at the hotel?" He sounded like a kid begging his mother for a zoo visit. Peele would be in Iowa, also, but had dinner that night with a moneyman.

She paused, long enough to make him squeeze a fist. "Sure," she said, flatly.

They arranged to meet at the Presidential Suite at eight Thursday night.

25

★ ★ ★

THE PRESIDENTIAL SUITE

In the hall bathroom that Henry used, Elizabeth leaned toward the mirror and worked the mascara pen. Well, she'd "gone for it" with Tom Peele. It had been exhilarating, enlightening, maddening. But Tom had never eased that lonely ache. The disappointments only left her feeling emptier, even tawdry. Looking back, it was doomed never to grow beyond infatuation. Power might be the ultimate aphrodisiac, but that gets you only so far. Maybe Henry would prove different.

She heard a noise from the main part of the Rigsdale suite, metal sliding and clanging against metal. The front door opening and closing. She looked at her watch. Henry was early.

She quickly lined the other eye, blinked a couple of times and straightened her blouse. The Irish linen seemed too casual, hanging loose over gabardine trousers. The evening seemed portentous, demanding more formal attire. What would Ovid have said?

Behind her, the bathroom door squeaked. Had she left it

ajar? She exhaled sharply. Just because you were in a relationship didn't mean you abandoned all boundaries. Was it too much to ask to knock before walking in on her? For all he knew, she could be on the commode.

The door opened slowly, taking forever. She watched in the mirror.

When the door had swung about halfway, a man appeared. Not Henry. He was taller and thinner, coated in the fluffy blue fleece balls of a sweatshirt turned inside-out, as though he had been tarred and feathered. His head was a black ski mask with white outlines around the eye and mouth holes, like some comic fright mask. She spun around to see the actual man, not the reflection. That seemed important, somehow: to face the flesh-and-blood intruder, rather than his projected image. Another man stepped into the bathroom behind the first, shorter and stockier, his head encased in an aqua Neoprene mask with large white wings on the side, as though he were Mercury.

The glass had made the taller man more remote, like a car mirror that warned objects were closer than they appeared. Now, she found herself a body length from him. She scanned the windowless room for an escape, but the only exit was behind the men.

They were standing there, glaring at her, the taller man's eyes dark and liquid through the holes. She began to form a word, "What." But no sound issued, only breath.

"You been a bad girl," the taller man said, in a voice that seemed disembodied, only a flash of teeth in a long face. "The teacher's been bad," he repeated, turning to the shorter one.

The smaller man stepped forward, keeping his gaze on her. "She's been a naughty slut," he said, also in a voice from no-where, but lower.

The leering lingering on the word sent a pulse of heat up her neck.

The taller one moved toward her. She felt a fingertip ache, and realized she was still clenching the mascara pen. The man came closer, now an arm's length away, and she could see the yellow film on his teeth, the caking between a bicuspid and a canine. His irises were brown and large, like a dog's eyes, with inky pupils floating in the center.

She felt words forming again, but before she could speak, the taller man took another step, and his scent hit her nostrils. An acrid odor. Beer, cigarettes, mildew, dried sweat. She could see the dog eyes better, and their bloodshot whites. Her right hand rose. A silver-and-black missile darted at the left eye.

The brush tip struck. Her hand drove forward, grinding, painting a black wound between the eye and the skull. The head recoiled. Another horizontal flash of teeth. A guttural cry.

A wave of glee enveloped her. But then the face rose and was looming over her again. The eyes were smaller now, one pink and caked with black paste. From the corner of her eye, a beige streak flashed. A hand slammed into her throat. Fingers gouged her larynx. The air was suddenly hot and acrid, hard to draw in. A labored wheeze rattled her ear. A small gland at the hinge of her jaw throbbed.

The brown dog eyes, still narrow, moved even closer, eclipsing all but a fuzzy brightness on their periphery. As the fingers clutched her throat, pinning her head, another hand flashed and struck the back of her head, making her blink. Fingers gripped and twisted her hair, yanking her head back. She pictured filthy nails intertwined in her carefully set russet locks.

The dog eyes studied her. They seemed to be trying to read her fear, feed off it, as she grasped what was happening. Then she took flight, propelled sideways, floating. A corner of the wall raced at her in a cream blur, where it wrapped around the sink, now long and sharp, at an odd angle. She tried to raise her arms, but the wall was coming too fast. Her hand caught her toilet kit on the counter as she flew past.

She should have finished reading an essay on medieval armor days ago. She had set aside an hour that afternoon, but couldn't press through the turgid prose. Now she didn't know when she'd find the time. Then her forehead slammed into the onrushing corner, making a soft, meaty thud. A galaxy of white and gray sparkles exploded in her skull, like millions of nuclear particles bursting from a core, and everything went dark.

26

★ ★ ★

RENDEZVOUS

By seven P.M. Thursday, adrenaline aches were pulsing through Henry's head, obliterating all sustained thought. Finally, time to head to the hotel. Then the phone rang, showing Cass's cell number. He stared at the receiver for three rings.

"Gil."

"Comrade Press Secretary, need you to draft a memo pronto to the chairman of the Iowa debate commission. You tell him the format of their forum in Dubuque is nuts, and we're not going along with it. I just copied you on an e-mail to Tom; take some points from that."

A dozen aides could draft that memo, or it could wait until morning. Why did Cass need to saddle him with this now? It would take less time to write the thing than to argue about it. He banged out a draft and e-mailed it to the Angel. Finally, Cass sent back edits. He added boilerplate about Peele's fiscal conservatism—cling to those vestiges—and put the draft on electronic Peele for President letterhead. He e-mailed the missive to the commission chairman at eight eleven P.M., copying the Angel. He was free.

Henry trotted to the parking lot behind the Des Moines office and hopped into the Mustang, which he had christened the Black Baron. He peeled onto Ingersoll Avenue, leaning into the turn, feeling like Dirty Harry. He reached the Rigsdale garage just after eight twenty P.M. A few minutes later, he was on the tenth floor, jogging to the Presidential Suite.

Pushing the door open, he found the lights off. He flipped the switch and could tell he was alone. The living and dining areas looked the way room service left them. The whole place gave off a sour antiseptic scent with an undertone of mold, as though you were inhaling millions of dead microbes. He dropped his laptop and briefcase on the dinner table and headed for the bathroom outside his small bedroom.

He flipped on the bathroom light, then stopped. Acid rose in his throat. Elizabeth's toilet kit lay strewn across the floor. A mascara pen lay open against the bathtub, its end mashed in. A toothbrush and her organic toothpaste from Maine lay behind the toilet. A roll-on deodorant, its plastic ball cracked, lay by the door.

He leaned his head out the doorway. "Elizabeth!" He dashed into his little bedroom, which was dark and empty. The twin bed was made, his papers stacked on the desk where he had left them. He stormed into the master bedroom, where he had rarely stepped, and hit the light switch. Empty. The colonial made, the gold-stitched spread pristine. He ran back to the living room, looked behind the sofa and the recliner. Each breath was singeing the back of his parched throat.

He pulled out his BlackBerry and dialed her mobile number. Voice mail. He tried her house. The same. Her office. The "Liz Walmsley" message.

His stomach began to burn. What happened? Had Elizabeth decided to dump him, too? She'd already dumped a husband and a senator. Had she hurled her intimate items across his bathroom, marking his turf with her scent and colors, a kiss-off to all of them who had soiled and hidden her? Or had she been ripped from her toilette by a thug who hadn't bothered cleaning up signs of his crime? Or was there another explanation, maybe a berserk campaign aide, or hotel clerk or maid?

He stood in the doorway staring at Elizabeth's strewn and broken remnants. The red canvas Iowa State bag, with the spare clothes still inside, lay open by the tub. It was like seeing his mother's stuff, the maroon Sunday suit with large buttons, a few sets of earrings, the World's Fair belt buckle, tossed on the stripped hospital cot in the living room after she was gone, waiting for removal by a blue-jacketed Salvation Army crew. He felt his sinuses throb. Then he felt a warm tickle down his cheek and realized the tears had come, for the first time in twenty years, since the grounders.

He brushed a wrist across his face, the suit's wool scraping his cheek. He shook his head, hard, to clear his thoughts.

He bent down and picked up Elizabeth's toilet kit, by the sink. He didn't know what had happened, but he knew this was a mess, and it was his job to clean up messes. He knew this was a mess they did not want discovered, investigated, or publicized. He knew that no matter who had made this mess, or how, he would not be able to walk away from it by saying simply that he was not the one who had made it.

His palms and armpits grew moist and his throat burned as he worked. A sense hit him that something deep inside him was in jeopardy. He counted his breaths, in and out, to busy his mind. Once he picked up the first item, the mascara pen, he was committed, and darted around the bathroom gathering the rest. If anybody asked why he had spoiled a crime scene, he didn't know it was a crime scene. It was a mess. And he cleaned up messes. That was his job.

Even moving quickly, he placed Elizabeth's articles, especially the damaged ones, as gently as he could in the green case. When he finished, he zipped the case and tucked it in her bag, which he placed in the linen closet, where she had kept it. He nearly went back, to open the case and wipe his fingerprints off each item, but decided against it. If it came to it, he could admit he cleaned up her things. They were a mess.

It was not difficult to erase or at least hide all signs of Elizabeth Walmsley from the Rigsdale. By design, there was little to prove she had ever been there. He went back to the bathroom and saw that he had missed a white plastic comb against the white tile. He picked it up, but found he didn't have the energy to climb to the top of the linen closet and slip it in the canvas tote. Instead, he clutched the comb in his hand, strumming the teeth with his thumb, sawing a groove into his flesh that felt like it would eventually split and spurt. He sat on the covered commode. He must have sat there half an hour, until past nine P.M., when Peele came in.

"Elizabeth's gone," he said, the words tumbling out. "Looks like she was here and left."

The Senator leaned the graying head across the bathroom doorway and stared at him sitting fully clothed on the toilet. "Yeah, well, it's late, anyway." Peele headed toward the master bedroom. "Make sure I'm up by six, Henry, will you?"

27

★ ★ ★

STORY COUNTY

Henry was about to dial Elizabeth's numbers again around noon, for the sixth or eighth time since the night before, when the Des Moines receptionist buzzed to say their Story County chairman was on the line. Phil Eggert must have been out, as usual.

"Henry, Jim Ardmore," a voice lilted, a salesman's voice. When he didn't quickly exclaim, "Jim!" the voice added, more softly, "from Story County."

Where was Story County? He knew it was a big county, or nearby. Iowa had ninety-nine counties, and he was always amazed that Peele, Dagworth, and the other pols could rattle them off, even the sparse ones. He turned to the Iowa map on his wall to see if the little red letters would jump out at him, but they didn't.

"Jim, I went to grade school with a kid named Jim Ardmore," he said. "Did you grow up in New York, have this light blue Mets jacket covered with little round patches?"

"Henry, I'm calling on a sad note."

He missed the rest of Ardmore's utterance. He remembered that Story County was mostly Ames. "Jim, sorry, what did you say?"

"I was saying I wanted to let you know that one of our volunteers died in a car accident late last night. A very nice young woman, Elizabeth Walmsley."

Elizabeth's head, from an angle above and to the left, filled his mind's eye, as though his brain couldn't project the image properly. Elizabeth was dead? In the bathroom? No, the guy said a car. What car? Whose car?

Ardmore was still talking. "Looked like she was driving home on Route 69, fell asleep at the wheel. She went down an embankment, hit a tree, and that was it. Anyway, I thought headquarters should know. I'd like to take out an ad in the *Ames Daily Tribune*, you know, kind of saying all her friends at the Peele campaign will miss her."

An image of Elizabeth lying bloody in her Honda Civic, the car floating in leaves and darkness, played across his mind. She was bent and broken across the front seats, alone. He fixated on her hazel eyes, now both lifeless.

"I think an ad would be a nice gesture," Ardmore was saying.

"Yeah," he said. Then he realized Ardmore was asking him to cover the ad. "Yeah, that's a good idea. Have them bill the campaign."

Ardmore seemed to pick up something in his tone. "Yeah, well, I just wanted to let you know, you know."

Henry felt a cold childhood dread climb up his neck and cheeks. For a few months after the paramedics wheeled Henry's mother away in a body bag, he woke in the middle of the night and sat in a small rocking chair in his dark little room.

He tried to fathom death and nothingness until stars burst behind his eyes and he lost his balance. Then he'd crawl back into his bed and pass out.

So eight or nine hours earlier, as Henry lay sleepless in the little bedroom in the Rigsdale, paramedics were loading Elizabeth's corpse into a body bag and zipping it over her face. Now he would never see her or touch her again, either. She also no longer existed.

She didn't like to drive at night, especially with only one eye. She could have run off the road, especially if she was tired, upset, and distracted. It was possible. His sinuses throbbed and for a moment he thought the tears would come again. They didn't. Maybe he didn't cry because the tears would have been as much for him as for Elizabeth, and he knew he didn't deserve them.

So what happened, somebody attacked her in the bathroom, and wound up chasing her car and running her off the road? Or made it look like she ran off the road? So Elizabeth might have been alive, desperate, when he saw the bathroom mess, and did nothing. Well, he didn't do nothing; he cleaned the mess. He wiped away her plea for help.

The inside of his head was glowing, his brain overheating. Stop, he told himself. Think. Okay, so if something happened to Elizabeth in the bathroom, who did it? Ostrow's thugs seemed pretty good suspects. They seemed like they'd enjoy beating a woman. Did they do more than that to her? He chased an image of the dark one's simpering face. But those guys were hired apes, they didn't wipe their noses unless someone told them to. So who told them?

Peele was so calm last night. Too calm. And Peele had arranged for her to come by. Maybe she had hurt Peele dumping him, scared him with the Wife of Bath stuff, who knew what really went on between them. Cass? Sure, he was a prime suspect on anything unseemly. The bathroom scene looked like something the Angel could have ordered, he was the one who brought Ostrow's apes to the campaign in the first place. And Cass told him Elizabeth was becoming a problem, said she had "a screw loose." Maybe that was a warning, do something or Cass would. Had Henry missed two warnings? And what about Zabriskie, the big ugly teddy bear, or pussycat, whatever? He had a stake here, too, covering his various scams and assaults. Ed even had his own muscle, wouldn't have to use Ostrow's apes. Or what about Elizabeth's crazy cokehead ex-husband? He still had her stuff, was extorting her, maybe didn't want to let her go. He liked to throw books at his wife's face, his half-blind wife, liked to make messes. Maybe this was old Evan's hand. Or maybe it was one of a dozen other people he didn't even know about.

He let out a long sigh. He worked the Internet and came up with a story from the *Ames Tribune*. Ames was all sunshine and youth and promise, to judge by the page-top photo of a blond girl in pigtails on a swing, leaning back to extend an arc.

Elizabeth's obituary was accompanied by what looked like a black-and-white mug shot, probably from her driver's license or Iowa State I.D. The dead apparently didn't rate color photos. The headline read "Iowa State Professor Dies in Car Crash."

Elizabeth M. Walmsley of Ames, associate professor of English at Iowa State University, died early Friday morning when the car she was riding in apparently veered off State Route 69 south of Ames and struck a tree, officials said. She was 32.

Ms. Walmsley was alone in the car, a 2005 Honda Civic, which was apparently northbound when the collision occurred about 15 miles south of Ames. No other vehicles were involved and authorities said there were no witnesses.

Ms. Walmsley had taught in the English department at Iowa State for five years. Department chairman Alan Ainsworth yesterday described her as a "gifted scholar and inspiring teacher" respected by both faculty and students.

Funeral services are pending in Portland, Maine. She is survived by her parents, George and Margot Walmsley, and a brother, Gregory, all of Maine.

He had daydreamed about meeting her parents. They would greet him on a wraparound New England porch, the boards glossy with gray latex paint, as he reached the top of three wide steps. Her father would extend a hand, welcoming him to the home and the family. Elizabeth and her mother would look on from a bench seat a few feet away, heartened to see the men falling into such easy rapport. Her father might put an arm around his shoulder, gentler than his own father would, and walk him through the screen door into the foyer, century-old polished pine planks groaning gently under their weight. None of that would ever happen now.

He thought of going to Maine for the funeral. No, he didn't know anybody there and didn't want to meet her parents now. He didn't want to lie or spin, not over Elizabeth's coffin. He thought of sending flowers or donating to a charity in her name. But there was plenty he should have done, and he decided not to salve his conscience with some empty gesture now.

He checked his printout of Peele's schedule, tucked it back into his shirt pocket, and trotted out to the parking lot and the Black Baron.

As Henry yanked open the heavy glass door to a financier's front office, he spotted Phil Eggert slumped in a chair. He marched to the receptionist's desk, ignoring Eggert's "Hey."

"I need to speak to Senator Peele," he told the woman,

matter-of-fact. "It's urgent." He pulled out his wallet and flashed his Senate I.D. What the heck, act like it meant something.

In the corner of his eye, he saw Eggert moving toward him. He turned and shot a glare. Eggert retreated to the chair.

The woman was telling him to have a seat, the meeting should be over in ten minutes.

"I need to speak to the Senator, now," he repeated.

The woman swiveled and strutted to an oak door.

A minute later, Peele followed the woman out the door, with a guarded smile Henry had seen before, armor against an expected but not-yet-identified attack. Peele spotted him and veered over. "What's up?" The Senator's eyes, slightly narrowed, gave away nothing.

Henry angled toward a corner, and they sidled over. He shook his head at Eggert, who had stood again.

"Elizabeth was killed last night," Henry said. He thought he saw pain in Peele's eyes, but Peele was playing some part, *performing*, and he couldn't read through the mask.

"Cops said she drove off a road. But they don't know about the bathroom." He met the blue eyes, now narrowed tighter. "Do *you* know if anything more was involved?"

Peele shifted his jaw and shook his head.

"Senator, you have no idea?" he said, with an edge. He gave Peele his combat stare.

Peele locked the narrow eyes on him, matching his glare. "I don't know anything about it. And if you ever pull me out of a fund-raising meeting again, or talk to me about this in public, I'm going to ship your ass back to D.C., Parcel Post."

The Senator turned and strode back through the open oak door.

———

Late that afternoon, after tossing most of an uneaten Hardees grilled chicken sandwich, Henry shut the door to his Iowa office, found the yellow Post-it note buried in a file, and dialed the Des Moines Police Department.

"Homicide, Rensi," the deep Jersey voice barked.

"Jeff," he said, almost panting. "Henry Hatten from the Peele campaign."

"Hatten," the voice sang. "Let me guess: you need statistics on STD rates among Iowa hookers, with subsets for gonorrhea, syphilis, herpes, and chlamydia."

He forced a laugh. Just talking to detectives chilled him, as though they could read his secrets. For a moment, his tongue froze. Had he lost his mind, calling a cop? He was jeopardizing everything he had strived for his whole life. Even if the police didn't do anything else, they'd file reams of paperwork. Cops were the worst bureaucrats, and their paperwork was public, or could quickly become public with the likes of Fran and Burr trolling around.

"A woman died Tuesday night," he said, easing into a measured, assured voice. "Elizabeth Walmsley, a professor at Iowa State, and a volunteer on our campaign. There was an item about it in the *Ames Tribune,* said it looked like a one-car accident."

Rensi didn't say anything.

"Seems strange, that she'd be driving alone at two or three A.M.," he continued. "She taught morning classes. Can you keep an eye and an ear out, Jeff, if anything passes your way?"

His father had said he was like a character jumping from the one alligator's back to another. Well, now he'd churned the entire pond.

28

★★★

DIGGING DITCHES

Charging from the rear of the North Capitol Street suite, Sterba nearly knocked Henry over the printer. "Hey," the chief of staff said, grabbing Henry's shoulders as though to right him. "If Cass asks you to put out a release on this help-the-Holocaust-victims thing, don't do it. It's bogus. I don't have time to explain it to you now." Sterba spun and marched out the main door.

A couple of minutes later, Cass stepped into the common area in a gray nail-head suit that looked like Mr. Yang's work. A trench coat was folded over one arm. The Angel nodded. "Comrade Press Secretary."

He nodded back. "Comrade Campaign Chairman."

"Something I need you to do," Cass said, setting the coat on a counter.

"Let me guess," he said. "Holocaust news release."

Cass smiled. "You've been talking to Comrade Sterba." The Angel put an arm around Henry's shoulder and steered him into the office corridor. The talc and aftershave scent, with their faces inches apart, was pungent.

"We need to put out a release today. Headline: 'Peele Introduces Bill to Help Holocaust Victims Recover Damages.'"

"I hadn't heard about it." The Senate office alerted him to all of Peele's legislative action.

"It's a good bill," Cass said. "It makes certain countries prove they made full reparations to Holocaust victims, to their own people, who were put in camps, had their property seized. No more U.S. aid or trade without that proof."

Henry smiled. "What's the catch?"

Cass smiled back. "You're becoming such a cynic." Henry said nothing, and eventually Cass continued. "Well, there's an Austrian insurance company facing a lot of World War II claims. If the burden shifts to countries—which it should—then getting these insurance claims worked out would, appropriately, become less of a priority."

Henry shook his head. "And some of the old victims might die before their claims got resolved. Which would save the insurance company serious dough."

Cass shrugged.

"This Austrian insurance company, did it hire anybody in the U.S. to get this legislation passed?"

Cass smiled. "Could be."

He sighed. "Gil, what about justice?"

Cass glowered down at him. "There's no such thing as justice—in or out of court. You know who said that? Clarence Darrow. It's a world of smoke and mirrors. You should know that by now, Henry. You can leverage it, and have a closet full of cashmere suits. Or you can fight it, and spend your life punching a timecard, like a sap—like your father."

"Hey, Gil, my father's not a sap." He felt his arm tremble.

Cass shrugged. The nail-head fabric glimmered under a light fixture, as though silk had been woven into the wool. "Comrade," the Angel said, more softly. "You dig the ditch you're going to die in."

"You're going to have to help me with that one." He didn't have any patience for riddles. Not now.

Cass exhaled. "Lee Atwater, the late, great Republican visionary. What Lee meant was, in a campaign, you choose the issues that decide your fate. Now, you communists dug your ditch in the middle of the road. And there's only two things in the middle of the road: yellow lines and dead chickens." Cass stepped toward the open space and snatched the trench coat. "Freedom and prosperity."

Henry padded back to his little office and shut the door. He lifted a pencil and began doodling. So now Cass was saying that their centrist shift would cost them the nomination? Well, Cass had also dug a ditch. And maybe a grave. The Angel had kept him at the Des Moines office for half an hour the night Elizabeth died, kept him from the hotel until it was too late. He dug the pencil point across the notepad until it made an ugly black gash and broke. Rubbing a finger over the splattered graphite, his anger melted into depression. He reached for the phone and dialed from memory.

"Wish I could, but I'm halfway across the country," Fran said. That probably meant Omaha or Lincoln, fertile fields for digging up dirt on Peele. Whatever. "But I'll be in D.C. Wednesday night," she added, with what sounded like enthusiasm. "I'm staying at the Marriott in Roslyn; we can grab a bite there."

They arranged to meet at nine. He hit the release button, with a milder wave of the what-have-I-done apoplexy that had hit him after phoning Rensi.

He opened his office door and peered up and down the narrow corridor, making sure it was empty. He crept out of his hole and padded down the carpet to the large office at the end. He eased open the pressed-wood door. The room was empty, and bare. Cass operated mostly out of the corner office at his firm's downtown suite. Still, just being in this chamber where Cass had dispatched him to Iowa, and had decided so many others' fates, made Henry feel like a spy in a despot's sanctum.

Pressing the door closed behind him, he stepped to the desk and opened the top center drawer. Once he had begun, like picking up that first item from Elizabeth's toilet kit, he was committed, and he moved quickly and deliberately. The desk was nearly empty, with some stationery supplies in the center drawer and a few old campaign memos and briefing packages in the larger drawers below. He rifled through folders and papers, scribbled Post-it notes, business cards.

If Cass was involved in Elizabeth's death, if the Angel even had an inkling of what had happened, maybe he could find a clue. Finished with the desk, he flipped through some plastic binders on the bookshelf, finding only polling printouts and, ironically, some news releases he had drafted or approved.

He thought he heard a noise at the door and froze, holding his breath. His pulse pounded in his ears, but the door stayed shut. He stepped to a metal file cabinet, where he found a leather Coach briefcase in the bottom drawer that he had seen Cass carry. The case was empty, except for an issue of *Forbes* and a couple of paper clips wedged in the bottom folds. He had been moving so fast, he hadn't realized he was panting until he stood up too quickly, and a rush of blood left him dizzy, light points bouncing inside his skull. He breathed, rotated his neck, and settled.

Cass's computer was off and needed a password, so he

couldn't check the files or e-mails. He scanned the room. It looked as it had when he arrived, which felt like hours earlier. He cracked open the door. The corridor was empty. He stepped out and stole back to his little office, twenty feet that felt like a mile.

He arrived at the Rosslyn Marriott ten minutes early and settled into a booth. The sleepy business hotel across the river from D.C. was a smart place to meet Fran inside the Beltway, if there was any smart place to meet Fran.

As he fired off an e-mail to a *Meet the Press* producer, locking details for Peele's upcoming appearance on the Sunday show, he felt a tap on his shoulder. Fran slid into the booth, smiling. And why shouldn't she smile? If anybody caught her with him, she was researching the enemy, executing her mission to unearth dirt on Tom Peele. But what possible explanation could he offer? His meeting Fran was worse than any of Peele's or Cass's consorting. Peele had diddled a volunteer, a virtual outsider, not even on the payroll. Cass and Dagworth's pollster, Boggs, were also working together on an Ohio race: business as usual in the incestuous cesspool of Republican politics. He scanned the restaurant. Dark booths, salesmen, tourists. Okay. He'd done a few TV shows, but he wasn't kidding himself that he'd blossomed into a Beltway personality, a magnet for autograph hounds, fodder for *Washington Post* "Spotted" style-section pieces. But this was beyond reckless. Did he want to get caught?

She seemed to be waiting for a greeting. "Silly season?" he asked.

"Oh, man." On top of Dagworth, she said, she was working

congressional and statewide campaigns in Arizona, Texas, California, and Minnesota. "It's like playing six chessboards at once."

A platter of chilled shrimp dumplings arrived—even hotel chain restaurants were into fusion cuisine now—but didn't slow her war stories. In the Arizona race, she said, she had found four state officials, including the parks commissioner, who gave to the Governor's campaign shortly after being nominated. "They're buying the offices; it's a clear pay-to-play." She pressed a dumpling with her fork until the pasta skin burst, spilling its shredded innards.

"Very clever."

She smiled. She probably got few chances to talk. She was a lone assassin, profiling her targets, finding the best ways to take them out. She needed to recount her kills to others who could appreciate their beauty. In that sense, she was like Cass.

Some minutes later, she stopped mid-sentence, seeming to notice him gazing at a spot above her head. She reached across the table and placed a hand on his. The touch radiated through him. He looked down at her hand, tanned and warm, the nails glossed.

"Penny for your thoughts," she said.

"Going rate's a lot higher than that."

She squeezed the top of his fingers. Fatigue was beginning to tighten the vise on his temples and dull his brain, and part of him just wanted to crawl back to his own bed in Cleveland Park. But he didn't want to push her away, only to be left alone in the night with his demons and Elizabeth's ghost. He wanted Fran's touch, needed it, and was willing to pay for it. He returned the hand squeeze.

Upstairs, Fran's body was at once familiar and, after two

years, new. She was still firm and round; warm, soft, and dry; her areoles wide, almost perfect circles. A sweet, faintly citrus scent rose from the hot, downy flesh behind her ears.

When he reached down, she was wet, not just moist. A hot, syrupy wetness that glistened and coated his fingers and steamed his nostrils. When they locked, she gouged the back of his arm with the glossed nails and squeezed him in a leg scissors so tight that he worried a kidney would burst. After his breathing calmed, the depression returned. He curled into her, wrapped his arms around her, and buried his cheek in her side, the firm flare of a spherical breast pressing the orbital above his eye. The glossed nails stroked his scalp, then his back, and he drifted away.

29

★ ★ ★

GATE GUARDS

As the silver Lincoln passed the American History Museum, Peele could see the White House grounds in the distance. This was his twenty-third trip to the White House this year; he kept count. It would be nice to avoid the traffic in Marine One, or in a Secret Service motorcade.

"Good job setting this up, Mike," he said, twisting in the front seat to look at Sterba in the back. His chief of staff had been sulking for weeks, not the same old Mike, since he had brushed off Sterba's warnings and sat on the HHS nominee.

"Thanks, Senator." Well, that was underwhelming enthusiasm.

Sterba did do a nice job of getting these invitations; he was usually among only a few Republican senators at these things. His burly chief of staff had always had a touch. He had brought Sterba along today as a reward, let him get another photo with the President to cram onto that office wall.

"I'm going to ask the President about the juvenile diabetes bill, if I can get a moment," he called over the seat.

Sterba nodded.

"So little of what I do, especially since we announced, is really worth my time," he said. "You got to pick a few issues and throw yourself into them. It's all you're going to have time for. And saving kids from deadly diseases is pretty basic."

"The White House leg affairs folks know you want some face time," Sterba offered. "They should get it greased." The President's legislative affairs team could make things happen faster than anyone, even a senator. Good for Sterba for cultivating them.

He looked at his watch. "Come on, Joe, make this light, come on."

The kid gunned the engine and whipped through an orange light onto 14th Street.

His breathing was tightening, but not to the point that he needed the rescue inhaler. He worried about the strain on his heart, all those tough breaths. Maybe he'd croak during sex, performance anxiety and physical exertion converging on his overworked pump. Coming and going at the same time, like poor old Nelson Rockefeller, moderate Republican icon.

"This thing's going to be over in about ten minutes," he told Joe, as close to apologizing for his tone as he would get. "Really just a photo op." The President was making the announcement in the Roosevelt Room, which was so tiny the press would spill outside. He should be able to angle into the shot, at least get his head in. He had jumped on this event, to announce a new drug czar, for the same reason he went to the last one, to laud Biloxi Girl Scouts for making a sixteen-foot AIDS quilt, and most of the twenty-one others: because if he went to enough of these shows, he'd get four or five minutes with the President on a topic of his choice.

Ironic, here he was jockeying for a few minutes in another man's spotlight, the same way *Parkland* groupies begged him for photos. At the height of his popularity, he might have been more popular than the President was now. He had never planned on *Parkland*. He was going to do Broadway, serious film. He had studied at the Actors Studio, doing commercials and other crap to get by. And then the offer for a gig playing a western Barney Fife on a national park drama. The show would be lucky to last a full season, he figured, and the money was too good to pass up. Somehow, *Parkland* took off. The producers gradually made him more heroic, smoke-jumping into California wildfires, saving Bambi, and rescuing orphans stranded on nature hikes. America still seemed to want Ranger Roy; would it settle for a middle-aged Tom Peele?

At the White House Pennsylvania Avenue gate, a uniformed Secret Service guard peered around the Lincoln's windshield, flinched at recognizing him, and snapped to attention. He nodded, and the guard waved Joe through. At the parking lot, a Marine in dress blues snapped out a smart salute, elbow out and forearm up, fingers straight in white gloves.

"You gotta love this place," Sterba said. "It's a total stroke."

A few paces later, he stepped through a portal into the core of the White House. Bold hues and glossy white molding. The national security adviser passed by in a gray flannel suit, giving him a nod, followed a few seconds later by the First Lady, who shot a look like she owned the place, which he supposed she did. No bodyguards, no security, at least none hovering; this was the inner sanctum.

He glanced at Sterba. His chief of staff had already affected a jaded Washington façade, but you could tell Sterba was star-struck by it all, like a kid visiting the locker room after a big-league ball game. Sterba had looked that way ten years earlier in Lincoln, when the young artillery spotter, fresh off the Iraqi battlefields, had joined his gubernatorial staff. The ante had gone up; now it took the West Wing to dazzle him.

The Oval Office was just around the bend. That's probably where the national security adviser had come from, and maybe the First Lady. He stepped toward the corner and peered in, through a slit of the open doorway. There, standing and study-ing a piece of paper, was the President of the United States, the leader of the free world, the commander in chief. He tried to make himself feel the grandeur, the juice, even on this twenty-third trip of the year. Eventually, a tingle shot through his ribs.

"Senator Peele, the President will see you." A Secret Service type, coiled cord running from earpiece to collar, was at his side, beefy face all business. In a moment, he was walking around the bend and into the Oval Office. The three floor-to-ceiling windows, framed in gold drapes and valences behind a massive desk, made his Russell Building throne room look amateur. He peered through the open northeast door, into the President's secretary's office. Get used to it, he told himself; this may be yours soon.

The President's handshake was just a handshake from a guy in a slightly rumpled charcoal suit, no magic to it. But it was real. He felt comfortable, equal. He gave the President a quick summary of his juvenile diabetes bill, which he was trying to push through the HELP committee. The President nodded a couple of times as he talked, eyes locked on him, giving him full attention.

"Mr. President, I'd really like to sit down and talk to you at some length about our HELP bill."

"Well, Tom, I like what you guys have in it, and I like the Senate version. I'm not so keen on the House version."

"Let's sit down and talk about it, Mr. President; let's work on it." Already, he had enough to crow that he had discussed his bill personally with the President. If he could get a sit-down, he could build speeches and floor statements around it.

"Okay, Tom. My guys here . . . I'll have them call, we'll sit down next week."

He grinned. "Thank you, Mr. President."

During the drug czar event, he slid into the camera shot beside the President. The footage would make him look like a player on one of his new main issues, crime control. He could use the balance as he veered left on the other social stuff.

On the ride back to the Hill, he sat in the rear with Sterba, mostly to bask in the moment together. It was so nice to just ease back and feel good. "This is a great country," he said as they cleared the Pennsylvania Avenue gate, "where a farmer's son from Mead, Nebraska, can walk into the White House and talk to the President in the Oval Office."

"Yeah, home run." Sterba's heavy body shifted next to him. "Senator, something you need to know: I don't think you're being well served by Gil Cass."

The euphoria died, like that. He felt himself wilt. Couldn't Sterba have allowed him just five minutes to savor the moment? No, it was deliberate; he was being played. Sterba was leveraging the mood and the goodwill from the White House visit. He shook his head and gazed at the dome light. "Why do you say that, Mike?"

"For starters, he's self-dealing." Sterba gave a litany. So Cass was padding bills and steering contracts to friends. What a shocker, from a political consultant. When he brought Cass on board, he took on the Angel's baggage, too. He wrote it off as fringe benefits, a business expense. Just as long as the guy wasn't selling him out.

Joe was looking straight ahead, eyes on the road, but probably taking it all in. In an hour, his exchange with Sterba would be all over the Senate office and the campaign shop. He should have taken Joe into the White House instead of making the kid wait outside with the car. He could use the loyalty now.

"For your own benefit, Senator," Sterba was saying, "I need to weigh in on legislative stuff that Gil's been going to you with, directly." Sterba's eyes were wide in the big head. He knew that a week earlier, Sterba had asked Cass for a sit-down. And, if he could trust his sources, Cass had replied that Sterba was a substance geek and this was politics, so get out of the way.

"And that'll solve everything?" he asked, still staring at the roof.

"The leg stuff is only part of it, Senator. You need to add other voices to Gil's, across the board. Snake eaters who'll watch your six." Gutsy loyalists who had his back, he translated, thinking he needed subtitles when Sterba slipped into Army-speak.

He ran his tongue over his drying lips and let a small belch escape. He tasted the salmon filet he had eaten for lunch, stale now. "Mike, on any major issue, I already hear from two, three, four people, sometimes more—the L.A., the L.D., you, and maybe I ask Gil. Then I make a decision, and you carry it out, if it's a Senate matter. Or Gil carries it out if it's a campaign matter. I don't have time for this squabbling. I just do not. You and Gil work it out." He felt his anger rise. "Anything else?"

"Look, Senator," Sterba said after a time, pushing out each word. "I'm being ignored, I'm being marginalized. If that's the way you want it, you're the boss. I'm here to serve you. And if you don't think I'm serving you well anymore, then I'll move on."

The Lincoln had stopped at a light at 9th and Constitution, and Sterba gripped the door handle. The big mitt looked like it might be trembling. Was Sterba really ready to open that door and walk away, after ten years together? For months, maybe years, Sterba must have been picturing himself in a West Wing office. The guy probably already had his rug and curtains picked out. It was a lot to throw away.

"Jeez, Mike, we've been through too much together for this kind of talk now. You're doing a hell of a job, and if I haven't told you so recently, I'm telling you now. I don't have to worry about this place with you around, which takes an enormous burden off me. I want you to stay right where you are."

The big hand hesitated on the handle, and he was pretty sure he could read Sterba's thoughts. His chief wanted to demand a say on all major decisions, but worried he might reply that Sterba was in over his head in a national race. Which meant Sterba was also doubting himself, questioning his own qualifications to challenge Cass's judgment.

He had counted on Sterba's loyalty. What a letdown. Sterba, like the rest of them, was out for himself. Sterba would stay true only as long as it was in Sterba's own interest. Which meant Sterba was probably weighing his standing in the presidential polls, which remained too high to throw away.

Sterba's grip loosened on the handle. "Okay," his chief finally said, as the Lincoln eased ahead. "I'll talk to Gil."

Sterba was sticking around mostly for Sterba, not for him. Fine. But now he had Sterba by the short hairs. Now Sterba needed his support on any future clashes with Cass. Too many reversals would question whether Sterba was still the right fit.

Are you giving the boss the right guidance if you're always being ignored or overruled?

"You know what I'd like, Mike?" he asked. "I'd like to be able to sleep past three or four in the morning, even just once a week."

Sterba nodded, probably still trying to sort it all out. "Yuh."

"I wake up in the middle of the night knowing where there's an opening we should capitalize on, or where Dagworth or Sadler is going to hit us next, but I'm too tired to do anything about it."

"Yuh," Sterba repeated, softer, still in another world.

"I've got all kinds of thoughts buzzing through my head; I see openings for attacks and legislation, but I haven't got time to work them out, I'm on a roller coaster twenty-five hours a day. We're missing opportunities; we've got to *pounce*. This campaign has no sense of *urgency*. We're giving Dagworth free shots on crime, the death penalty . . . we should *own* those issues!" He exhaled. "But that's not my job; that's *your* job—all you guys. When are you guys going to wake up and give me some help around here?"

Sterba said nothing, probably fighting an instinct to assure him how hard the staff was working.

He felt better, getting all that off his chest, putting Sterba in his place. The fact was, he didn't want any rapprochement between Sterba and Cass. It was useful to keep your top aides divided, so they didn't conspire against you. The West Pointer was too prissy to think that way, or even recognize it.

The Lincoln stopped at the gate down the block from the Russell Building, and the Capitol Hill Police guard gave a friendly, if respectful, half-salute and waved them through. The Lincoln pulled to the curb. He told Sterba to go on, he was going to head to the Senate barber in a minute. He clapped his chief's heavy shoulder.

Sterba reached for the door handle and opened it slowly, then paused, probably desperate to say something to repair the mood, but not sure what. He stayed silent. Finally, Sterba stepped out. He watched his chief walk slowly but deliberately to the Russell Building door, head high. Worried but determined—just the mind-set he wanted. You could tell a lot from a person's gait.

"Joe, take the rest of the day off," he said. "You've been putting in the hours. I'll get Lance to drive me home tonight."

30

★ ★ ★

BOUILLABAISSE

wanted to let you know," the deep Jersey voice told Henry over the phone, "I'm working the Walmsley case."

"Jeff, that's great. Thanks." Well, no way of knowing what he had unleashed. But he'd had to do something. He pumped a fist.

"Just so you understand, now, it's the Iowa BCI's case. I'm just helping out."

"What is that, a state unit?"

"The Iowa Bureau of Criminal Investigation," Rensi said. "They've got jurisdiction over the county road where the woman was found. These are top-notch investigators, Henry, so don't go copping an East Coast attitude. The BCI brought the Des Moines police into the case. That's not unusual. We work together all the time."

"And you signed on."

"Actually, they asked for me personally."

"Sounds great, Jeff." Did Rensi expect him to be impressed?

"By the way," the sergeant said, "when we were talking the other day—if you hear anything or if you know anything, no matter how mundane it might appear, let me know . . . let me know everything."

"Okay."

Rensi paused. "If there's anything you know that you feel I should know, tell me now rather than it comes up later and embarrasses everyone."

Clearly, Rensi knew something. About Elizabeth and Peele, maybe. If the cop didn't already know as much as Burr, he probably soon would.

"Yeah, Jeff. Understood."

Rensi paused again. "Listen, let's get together. You're fairly close to the situation. Let's get together and have lunch."

Something was off in Rensi's tone. Henry didn't say anything. "We'll go somewhere nice," Rensi continued, "where cops and politicians don't go, so we can have some privacy. The French Bistro in West Des Moines. They make a nice bouillabaisse, with swordfish and scallops, and the sauce is light and just a little tart; they use orange peel, basil, and fennel. They make a pretty mean French onion soup, too."

When they hung up, Henry dialed the *Globe-Times* newsroom. He was poking a snake, but he needed some gauge on how much Burr knew. The reporter picked up on the first ring.

"Surprised I got you, Bill," he said. "I thought you might be out diving through Dumpsters."

"Listen, Henry, I'd love to jaw with you, but I gotta go. But let me give you a tip, okay? You should worry more about yourself and less about other people, okay? Because from what I hear, you got a lot of problems." And Burr hung up.

What did Burr mean, he had a lot of problems? What did the reporter know about him? That night at the Marriott, nestled in Fran's arms, he had bemoaned Elizabeth's death, careful not to mention her name. Had Fran made the connection and fed the lead to Burr? Was his pillow talk with Fran becoming Fran's pillow talk with Burr?

Secrets weren't staying secret in Peele-land. He needed to know who had hacked Peele's e-mail account and planted Elizabeth's missive in Eggert's Jeep, for Susan to find. A staffer who would rifle the boss's e-mails could leak anything. He made another phone call.

"Take three guesses, *boychick*," Fogel said.

He was making too many guesses already on too many crimes. He didn't say anything.

Fogel snorted. "Right out of Gil's playbook." Cass had known about Elizabeth almost from the beginning, the media man said. Mitch, the Des Moines driver, had dished to the scheduler after sitting through lunch with Peele and Elizabeth, Fogel said, and word didn't take long to reach Cass.

But why would Cass plant the printout?

"Two reasons," Fogel said. "First, he wanted the babe out of the way. She was a distraction and a time bomb. The wrong people were going to get wind if she and Peele kept canoodling in front of staffers."

Henry wanted to defend Elizabeth's honor, tell Fogel not to call her "the babe," but he stilled himself.

"So once Susan found out about the professor babe, Peele would have to break it off—the affair, that is." Fogel chuckled. "Second, if Gil was lucky, Susan would bail on Peele, and either Peele would fold the campaign or it would melt down. Then Gil could jump aboard Dagworth's campaign—the odds have been pretty good from the start that Dagworth's going to be the nominee—and get a top gig when Dagworth staffed up for the general election." A faint static rippled across the continent as Henry held the receiver, silent. "Hey, this is all just speculation, you understand," Fogel said.

"Yeah."

"But I'll tell you something else, though. If Gil's trying to get Peele to fold his tent, it ain't worked yet. So I'd watch out for him to escalate his tactics."

The French Bistro looked like a romantic escape: quilted floral seat covers on aged oak benches, candelabra, and impressionist oils. Rensi was already at a table toward the back when Henry arrived. The cop, in a glen plaid suit and rep tie, was reading the *Wall Street Journal*.

Soon after he took a chair, a waitress fluttered over, an Iowa farm girl made up like a Parisian coquette in a white ruffled blouse, black vest, and rouge. Rensi ordered the onion soup followed by the bouillabaisse along with a glass of Chateau des Tours blanc. He asked for the same, minus the wine. He needed to keep his head clear. Did Rensi expect him to drink up, too, a cop interrogation trick?

Henry scanned the restaurant. The next booth was empty, and nobody seemed in earshot, if he kept his voice low.

"New Jersey riverfront lots are going for as much as Park Avenue condos," Rensi said, tossing the *Journal* onto a chair. "Some of these Wall Street bankers like to commute in their private boats, across the Hudson River." The detective shrugged. "There goes the neighborhood."

They bantered about the Mets and the Yankees and graffiti-proof subway cars until the waitress returned. She set down two crocks of onion soup, each covered with a steaming mass of off-white cheese. He expected her to wish them "Bon appetit," but she just strode off.

Rensi raised a brimming spoon, stretching and breaking a strand of cheese without spilling any broth. "Very good," the detective pronounced. The cop leaned forward. "So how many volunteers has Senator Peele got in Iowa, people like me and Ms. Walmsley?"

He recognized the technique: ease the subject into the interview with simple factual questions. Then unload the ugly stuff. "Your best source on that is Phil Eggert," he said. "Or your friend Mary McCormick." A pang hit him. Mary had seen him hugging Elizabeth at the straw poll. What did it matter? Mary was at a retreat somewhere in Illinois, last he heard, probably in a straitjacket.

"How well did you know Ms. Walmsley?" Rensi's tone was neutral. The cop's eyes gave away nothing.

His cheese was congealing. He pressed the mass into the steaming broth and watched it swell and melt. He stabbed at the soup with his fork, gouging holes in the Gruyère-Parmesan alloy. Brown broth seeped through the wounds.

"Pretty well, given the limited time for socializing on a campaign. And given that I live in Washington." He had rehearsed these lines, these lies. But he looked away from Rensi as he spoke, rubbing his chin to feign thought, fixing on a framed Côte d'Azur travel poster behind the cop. The poster showed speedboats skipping on a deep turquoise sea. How wonderful, if he could trade Iowa and the rest of it for the Riviera. Even for a month. Even a week.

Rensi was eyeing him. "We've both been around the block a few times, Henry. Here's the story: attractive girl, smart girl, working on this campaign. I know there's a lot of hard work involved. I also know there's going to be a little extracurricular activity, recreation. And I have to know who was having any kind of relationship with her."

"Well, Jeff," he said, to make some sound, to buy some thinking time.

Mercifully, the waitress returned with a laden tray. She frowned at his abused, abandoned soup, opened a portable stand beside him and placed her tray on it. With calloused hands tipped by short peach fingernails, she set a bowl and plate in front of each of them, and in turn poured a chunky orange stew over slices of seasoned baguette. Despite the coquette uniform, she was all business, her hard little hands working quickly and precisely. She put the soup crocks on the cleared tray and marched off again.

"Jeff, she was my friend. I liked her." *She wuz ma fren. I like-ta.* Did the cop think he was mocking a Jersey accent? He breathed and concentrated on stifling the Queens-speak. "Listen, I know you're being thorough. But this isn't a direction I want to go." He pushed back his chair and crossed his arms.

Rensi stared at him for what felt like minutes, as a bouquet of exotic scents, saffron and basil, orange, wafted up around him.

"Jeff, if anybody was . . . involved in Elizabeth's death, you can start with two guys doing security work for our campaign." He pulled his chair back to the table, striking wood against wood. "Matt Moffat and Chris Gargano."

Rensi pulled a small leather-bound notepad and Parker pen from an inside pocket of the glen plaid coat. The cop shot him a glance, flipped some pages, and wrote.

31

★ ★ ★

THE HEARTLAND CAFÉ

enry took a booth at the back of the Heartland Café, where he was sure he had once sat with Fran. He waited five minutes, then ten. His BlackBerry buzzed. He asked a hovering waitress for some muffins, mostly to halt her anxious looks. Zabriskie had chosen the place, the restaurant at the hotel where they held the rally, saying he had to be in Des Moines for a meeting.

How smart was it to talk to Zabriskie? The Teamster boss might toast Elizabeth's death, if he knew she was Wife of Bath. Maybe Zabriskie had even helped dispatch her. But Zabriskie had pulled out of the stock scam months earlier, if Elizabeth had overheard correctly, and the Teamsters were at little risk if they just sat on their Western Pharmaceutical shares instead of selling them and giving profits to Peele's campaign.

As Henry squeezed lemon into his tea, a shadow passed over the table. He looked up. Zabriskie looked older than he recalled. The menace was in the stare. His father had affected the same blue-collar glare, at showdowns as mild as softball games in an Astoria schoolyard.

The Teamster boss eased into the booth with a grunt, the cushion squealing under the weight. The milky caramel eyes studied him. "Your father's good people," Zabriskie said.

Henry nodded. "Yeah."

"I never would have guessed. You looked like some stuck-up suit at Big Jim's place."

A waitress dropped off a basket of breads and jams, pastel drawings of various fruits on the labels and lids of the tiny jars.

"I didn't know how much time you had, so I thought I'd get us a head start."

Zabriskie glanced at the basket and then turned back to him.

"What I want to tell you needs to be strictly between us," he said. "The Senator might not like me getting you involved."

Zabriskie was looking at him, looking through him. It was the same look his father had cast when Henry lied about losing the football. "Henry, what's on your mind?"

How could Elizabeth call this guy a pussycat? "You met a woman at the Rigsdale Hotel one night a couple of months ago," he began. "Elizabeth Walmsley."

Zabriskie smiled. "The professor. Yeah."

"She told me she liked you. She called you a pussycat—her word, not mine."

"Yeah, actually, I told her that," Zabriskie said, maybe nodding at the memory.

"Elizabeth is dead."

The meaty head recoiled, as though it had been punched.

"It looked like a car wreck, but even the cops think there might be more to it than that. But who knows how seriously

284 | CHARLES ROBBINS

they're looking into it." The Teamster boss knew about killing local investigations.

Zabriskie plucked a roll from the basket, tore it, and mashed in blackberry jam.

"If anybody hurt her, I'm betting it was the two guys working as bodyguards at the rally here a couple of weeks ago. Maybe you noticed them."

Zabriskie gave a faint nod.

"The bigger question, if they were involved, is why? Someone should ask those guys some . . . *hard* questions."

Zabriskie chewed the roll.

He sipped some water, suddenly parched. "Well, I thought you'd like to know."

The Teamster boss tore another roll and studied it. In the silence, dishes clattered from a far table. Zabriskie drove a thick thumb into the dough. "Give me the names."

32

★ ★ ★

THE DEAD

A high-priority e-mail flashed on Henry's computer at the D.C. campaign office, with a news story attached: "Iowa Cops Probe Peele Aide's Death," by Bill Burr, *Globe-Times* Staff Writer.

> DES MOINES—Law enforcement officials have opened an investigation into the death of an Iowa State professor and political aide to U.S. Sen. Tom Peele (R-Neb.), authorities told the *Globe-Times*.
>
> Elizabeth M. Walmsley, 32, of Ames, an associate professor of English and an aide on Peele's presidential campaign, died Oct. 25. Walmsley, according to initial reports, died from blunt force trauma when the car she was driving swerved off Iowa Route 69 about 20 miles north of Des Moines and struck a tree.
>
> The matter was under investigation because authorities

had "gathered evidence that warranted further review," a Des Moines police detective told the *Globe-Times*. The officer asked not to be identified.

An autopsy revealed Ms. Walmsley was pregnant, officials said. Ms. Walmsley was divorced and living alone at the time of her death, officials said.

Elizabeth was pregnant? With his child? He pictured Elizabeth's midriff, her little paunch. He imagined a tiny pink creature inside with a huge head. His child. When was she going to tell him? *Was* she going to tell him? Yeah, it made sense. That night at the Rigsdale, when he had run out of condoms, and talked her into it. A thought hit him, and he gave the family snort. Peele would assume himself to be the father.

He dialed the Des Moines number from memory, no longer needing the yellow Post-it note. A receptionist told him, in a voice that could have passed for a mechanical recording, that Sergeant Rensi would report for the evening shift in four hours. When they finally connected, all Rensi offered was, "Kind of a pisser, huh?" The deep Jersey growl sounded more amused than alarmed.

"Jeff, did you talk to this reporter?"

"You'd make a hell of a detective, Hatten."

"This was all supposed to be confidential."

"Hey, look, the guy called us; I didn't call him. He said he had information relating to a case we're investigating. You're damn right I'm going to take his call. He gave me some pieces I didn't have, including your alleged relationship with the good professor." Rensi paused. "Which you're still not talking about, right?"

"Go on."

"I told the guy I'd follow up on his tips."

"Yeah, which gave him a story: cops investigating Walmsley death, looking at new angles."

"I got no problem with that. And I don't know why you got a bug up your ass. I thought you wanted the case investigated."

"Yeah, but *not in the media*," he practically screamed. In an even voice, he asked, "Jeff, you weren't spanking me, just a little, for not answering your question?"

"Hatten, I wouldn't *think* of doing something like that."

He clenched his jaw until it locked. Everybody guarded his turf, like dogs pissing on fence posts, and wanted to lead the pack. "Look, Jeff, whatever else, please look at the bodyguards."

"And I'll be very frank with you, Henry, as a friend. Right now, the evidence we're digging up doesn't point to Ostrow's goons."

"Well, where does it point? Toward me?"

"Well, let's just say it doesn't point toward Ostrow."

At Peele's North Capitol Street headquarters, their chief oppo researcher was popping in and out of a small office like a prairie dog, scanning and copying and shredding papers, bounding across the carpet. Henry had heard that the guy was assembling a haymaker for Peele to unload on Dagworth at a CNN debate the next week. Were they getting close enough for him to leak or release anything?

He found the oppo at the copier, feeding charts on various states' gun-possession laws into the machine's maw. "Getting close, getting close," the guy said. The oppo explained that a few years earlier, a Houston oil millionaire was caught with a loaded pistol in a church while stopping in a Texas town on the way to visit relatives. Nearly everybody had the right to transport a concealed weapon in Texas. But the town where the man had stopped, like other municipalities around the country and even some states, had banned weapons near churches and schools. The oilman was arrested and ultimately fined. The case made national headlines. Dagworth introduced a bill that said, essentially, that a citizen allowed to carry a weapon should be allowed to carry it anywhere. Dagworth's federal legislation, which would supersede state and local zoning laws, never came up for a vote.

It sounded to Henry like a jab, not a roundhouse. He stepped over to the scheduler.

"Gil around?"

"You just missed him," she said, seeming pleased to dispense the information. Knowledge was power. "He and Diane had a meeting downtown."

Good. He'd land his own haymaker. He stole over to the big office at the back of the corridor, his pulse pounding not quite so rapidly as before. His body was getting used to sneaking around. Besides, he felt almost authorized. This is what Cass would do, in his spot. This time, the Angel had left the computer on. He closed the door behind him and scurried over to wiggle the mouse, so the machine wouldn't time off.

The room smelled of Cass, talc with an undertone of exotic aftershave, intense at the desk. Typing felt awkward. He had to bend his wrists to reach the keys, sending an ache up his forearms. He realized the chair was set for a seven-foot man.

Cass had left four web browsers open. The first two sites were a Caribbean fishing boat rental and an outdoor gear supplier. A third browser showed Yahoo Mail, open to Cass's personal account. The Angel had more than six hundred messages in the inbox. He began scanning, looking for a subject or sender that might relate to Elizabeth.

Cass had received a spate of e-mails during the past week from a lawyer for a fireworks importer. Apparently, Cass had invested in the company, which was about to go bankrupt, and the CEO had vanished. He searched for messages containing "Walmsley" or "Elizabeth." Nothing. He searched for "Rigsdale." Nothing. He typed "Iowa." Forty-one messages appeared, but none seemed relevant. Three of the "Iowa" e-mails, though, were from Mark Boggs, Dagworth's pollster.

Cass and Boggs were teammates on an Ohio Senate race, so e-mails from Boggs seemed natural. But why were they discussing Iowa? He opened one of the messages, a Boggs reply to a Cass e-mail with the subject line "Numbers." The missive began with a harangue against the Iowa Republican Party. Toward the bottom, Cass wrote that Peele was flat in Iowa despite a recent direct-mail piece. Why would Cass share their internal polling with the enemy?

He forwarded all three Boggs e-mails to his own account. He deleted the sent versions, but the original e-mails now showed green "forwarded" arrows, which he couldn't erase. Fine; if Cass noticed, let him complain that somebody had hacked into his account and forwarded treasonous e-mails. Henry restored the screen to show the Caribbean fishing boat rental, slid the chair back in and walked to the men's room to wash the sweat off his temples and the scent off his hands.

Henry and Peele left for the CNN debate as the oppo was still bounding around the office, confirming facts. The silver Lincoln felt like the team van on the way to a wrestling tournament: the silence thick, with glory or defeat, fame or shame, awaiting. The debate offered what might be Peele's last big chance to pull ahead of Dagworth.

Henry leaned toward Peele in the backseat, Washington's marble grandeur passing in the windows. "Senator, I know this isn't the time, but I just thought you needed to know," he said just above a whisper. "A Des Moines cop called me about Elizabeth's death."

"You're right. This isn't the time."

Good. He'd tried to tell the boss, due diligence; he wouldn't have to try again.

By seven P.M., Henry was perched on a stool in a makeup room, feeling like a chicken in a microwave as six hundred watts bounced off mirrored walls. Peele sat on a barber chair in a smock as a woman in black knit pants dabbed beige powder on his forehead and nose.

They settled into a senior producer's office converted into a green room. Peele sat at the desk scanning notes and last-minute messages. Henry stood by a chrome armchair. Peele's name, laser-printed in block capitals, had been taped to the door over a nameplate, giving a makeshift feel. Photographs of two straw-haired boys, presumably the producer's sons, hung in metal frames, making Henry feel like an intruder. A TV with a security sticker on its side showed a wide shot of the CNN set.

Dagworth strode past, two feet away, grim handlers scurrying in tow. One of Dagworth's aides dropped some folders, spraying the floor with papers.

"The distinguished senior Senator from the great state of Virginia looks a little harried," Henry said.

Peele looked up and mouthed the words, "Fuck him."

Henry walked Peele to the set, following a production assistant through a carpeted labyrinth and two glass doors. The set, bathed in as much light as the makeup room, stung his eyes. Peele settled into a seat at a long table, next to a right-wing Oklahoma congressman.

Henry got back to their green room just as the TV zoomed in on Peele. He shut the door, leaned back in the producer's chair, and watched the screen pan the candidates. A moment later, the door opened and a figure filled the frame, to the top. Cass. The Angel folded into the chrome armchair, extending impossibly long legs in pinstriped pants nearly to the desk. Cass nodded at him. "Comrade."

He nodded back. "Gil." This was the first time he had been alone with the Angel in weeks, he realized. Since before Elizabeth's death.

Cass leaned back in the armchair as the moderator gave the welcome and rules. The producer's small office, with the door closed, soon took on Cass's musk. He watched Cass in his peripheral vision through the first round, brief opening statements, heavy on Republican red meat and laced with bows to Reagan, the Bible, and the flag. Cass snorted, the big Adam's apple bobbing in the long neck, when the Oklahoma congressman suggested bombing Tehran.

"Too conservative for you, Comrade Campaign Chairman?"

Cass straightened in the chair. "Dagworth's probably going to be the nominee. You should consider working for him in the general."

Mutinous talk, and so brusque. Why was he shocked? This was business; nothing to get sentimental about, like a broiled cat.

"I can put in a good word for you," the Angel continued. "I know some of Dagworth's top guys pretty well." Cass pushed himself fully up in the chair. "You won't be the communications director. But you might be a deputy or a regional director, something like that."

Whatever else, he could never work for Cliff Dagworth; it would be like the Mobile congressman all over again, stumbling on the agitprop. "So you think Comrade Press Secretary is redeemable?"

Cass shrugged. "Dagworth's going to be taking on a lot of people when he gets the nod."

On the screen, Peele was urging a fight against juvenile diabetes, citing his bill that had just cleared the HELP Committee. It really was a good bill, helping sick kids live full lives.

"What do you think, Gil, is it going to end with a bang or a whimper?"

Cass shrugged again. "What does it matter? Let the dead bury their dead."

On the TV, the contenders had moved onto the next round, which allowed freer exchanges. The second- and third-tier candidates sniped at Dagworth, also taking a few shots at Sadler, jumping at a chance to wound the frontrunners.

How could Dagworth call himself a fiscal conservative and lard appropriations bills with Virginia pork, the Oklahoma congressman demanded. Others flayed Dagworth for putting his brother on the campaign payroll and junketing to Maui and Barcelona.

Henry glanced across the room. Cass was leaning back in the armchair, eyes on the TV. Waiting. It was Henry's move.

With ten minutes left, Peele took what would probably be a last turn. "I believe in Americans' right to self-defense," the Senator began.

So Peele was going to throw the haymaker. Henry gave it a fifty-fifty chance of landing.

"But we can't turn our houses of worship into target ranges. Senator Dagworth doesn't seem to agree. He introduced legislation for the specific purpose of allowing guns in churches."

The TV whipped to Dagworth, whose eyes darted, mouth agape. Peele had done well, keeping it simple.

Peele went on. "Now, why would Senator Dagworth introduce such legislation?"

Henry craned toward the screen. This was new.

"Could it have anything to do with the fact that the man arrested for carrying a gun in a Texas church a month before Senator Dagworth introduced his bill was one of Senator Dagworth's biggest fund-raisers?"

Dagworth rose, flushed. "Senator Peele is playing politicians' games. Two of every American's most fundamental rights—the right to protect himself and his family, and the right to pray to his God—are being taken away. It's un-American."

As the camera zoomed in, Peele shook his head sadly.

Around two thirty A.M., Henry snapped awake to the buzzing of his BlackBerry. He found an e-mail from Fogel, apparently in the studio, cranking out scripts. The e-mail carried a long trail, beginning with a missive sent during the middle of the previous night from their pollster to Fogel: "Fuckety, fuckety, fuck, fuck." Fogel had replied, "What's up?" By the end of the candidates' debate, the two were spitballing by e-mail. Fogel was now polishing a script on extremism with guns, attacking . . . Sadler.

Henry was awake now, a needle threaded from one temple through both eyeballs and out the other temple. He dialed Fogel's studio. The media man picked up instantly. "Yeah!?"

"Ira, you got me a bit confused," Henry began. "The debate *I* saw had Dagworth pushing for guns in churches, not Sadler."

"Indirect approach, *boychick*," Fogel said, and Henry could hear keys clacking in the background. "B. H. Liddell Hart— famous British military historian—you should read his book,

Strategy. Basically, we need to play pool here, hitting one ball off the other."

"Can you be even more specific, Ira?"

Fogel paused, maybe annoyed. "The obvious play here is to attack Dagworth, who's already bleeding, and finish him off." More keys clacked. "But the most important question is, is a percentage of the people voting for Dagworth soft, and who is their second choice? We know from our polling that Dagworth's disaffected voters will go to Sadler, because they're both conservatives. So we use the Texas connection on the guns-in-church thing to attack Sadler, because we also know that Sadler's disaffected voters go to Peele. You follow?"

Henry thought his throbbing brain got it. "Yeah, Dagworth's already damaged, so you're basically killing two birds with one stone."

Fogel grunted. "The thing is, by the time one or the other figures out what we're doing, it's going to be too late."

The next afternoon, Fogel's spot, "Guns," went on the air. The Twitter-verse seemed to fixate on a single adjective: "Devastating."

33

★ ★ ★

CRAYFISH

Returning to the dark Presidential Suite at night felt like slipping into a recurring nightmare, a scene of lurid disarray and desperation. Using the small bathroom, all signs of struggle long washed away, made Henry feel like an accomplice.

This night, flipping on the lights, the place felt disturbed, even haunted. The wicker dining room chairs seemed in their proper places. Then he noticed footprints on the carpet, flattening the vacuumed nap. Somebody had been here after the maids finished. Peele was in Washington. The Iowa staff hadn't booked the suite, as now required. And if Eggert's crew had used the place, Henry would have faced a tableau of ground potato chips and stale tobacco. This looked like a lone invader.

He stepped into his bedroom cell. This room also felt violated. Then he saw two shoe prints by the dresser, about a foot apart. He pulled out the top drawer. The old wood creaked, maybe dried by the steam heat. His T-shirts and shorts lay folded and stacked, as he had left them.

He opened the second drawer. His socks, balled in pairs, had been pushed to one side. On the other side of the drawer was a blue-and-white Nike shoe box. A white sticker had been pasted askew at the bottom. Size 11. Not his size. And not his shoes. He slid two fingers under the lid and flipped it open.

"Whoa!" He jumped back, nearly toppling over a chair. He stepped, slowly, toward the open drawer and peered in the shoe box. A long gray rat, legs and paws splayed, tail curled around a corner, lay on its side, stiff and dead. White whiskers sprouted from its muzzle, off a pink nose. Coarse gray hair bristled on its flank.

Acid rose in his throat, his eyes watered, and he thought he would puke. He turned away, swallowed, and turned back. Looking to the side, he inhaled deeply through his mouth and held his breath. He turned back to the drawer and slid the lid back on the box. He exhaled and took several shallow breaths.

What was the message? That Gargano was going to get him for the thumping downstairs? Or maybe for ratting out Ostrow's thugs to Rensi? Or to Zabriskie? Or was it a warning? Lay off, or wind up a dead rat? Dead like Elizabeth. But how could the bodyguards know he had told anybody about them? Maybe it wasn't Gargano at all.

He felt naked, exposed, the planted rat like the snickers and sneers years earlier at Trinity. Taunt, belittle, frighten, make his life miserable. Well, cowing and conforming hadn't been the answer then, and weren't the answer now. He dashed into the kitchen, opened a cupboard above the sink, and ripped a plain black plastic bag from two bottles of Glenfiddich he had bought for Peele at a liquor store. He slid the bag over the Nike box, twisted the open end into two strands and tied them, cinching the knot.

Where was the trash chute in a hotel? He couldn't picture

one. He placed the bag in the corridor, then shoved it a few feet with his foot. He shut the door and scrubbed his hands.

How had the thugs gotten into his room? If they got in once, they could come back any time. Would they return in the middle of the night, when he was sleeping? They were nocturnal predators; they took out Elizabeth at night.

He looked around the suite for something he could use as rope, to tie the front door shut. Maybe cord from the Venetian blinds. Then he fixed on the wicker dining room chairs. He lifted one—was it the one Elizabeth had sat on their first night together? He wedged the chair under the front door's knob, letting two legs dig into the carpet for purchase, a technique he had seen on TV. It seemed to work.

That night in his little bed, he slipped into a stupor a few times, his mind conjuring childhood scenes from the Astoria row house and from gangster films, but he didn't sleep. He snapped alert around dawn, when his BlackBerry buzzed on the nightstand. His head was heavy, as though soaked, the dawn light stabbing his eyeballs and his brain behind them.

Another Burr story had landed: "Body of Iowa State Professor to be Exhumed." He scrolled through the text for his name, which he didn't see, then read. The piece said Iowa cops had convinced Elizabeth's parents to let them dig up her corpse. A medical examiner in Maine would examine her body and issue a report, probably within a few weeks. Burr noted that police had questioned "a senior aide" to Peele.

An image flashed across his mind of a limp and lifeless Elizabeth, her flesh gray and bloated, lying on an examining table. Would the Maine doctors do a DNA test on her unborn child? Their unborn child. Peele would probably also sweat that prospect. The Senator couldn't quash this investigation; this was bigger than a local Teamster boss smacking an underling.

He dressed slowly, gazing out the small bedroom window.
The lightness of autumn had chased the heavy summer. Soon
enough, the mercury would sink below zero. During Tyler's
run, his hands and face had dried and cracked by December,
leaving his cuticles and the corners of his mouth bleeding and
his fingertips raw, purple, and burning.

Heading to the campaign shop, the Black Baron's nineteen-
inch radials seemed to gobble the road. He turned left onto
Grand Avenue, hands light on the thick sport steering wheel.
Only a faint sanding sound gave away momentary loose trac-
tion. As he was straightening to accelerate, he heard a siren
and three electronic clacks, like a hand smacking a live mic. He
looked in his rearview mirror. A police cruiser filled the glass,
its roof rack flashing. He pulled to the curb.

"License and registration, please," the cop said, textbook.
He was a grizzled old vet with wavy gray hair, a bulbous red
nose, and a paunch. Not the kind of Iowa cop who would give
a break to a Washington sharpie driving a muscle car. The cop
ambled back to the cruiser, stepping almost daintily as Henry
watched in his side mirror.

He wanted to call the office on his BlackBerry, but you were
supposed to be respectful and remorseful at a traffic stop. He
sat studying the dash. About ten minutes later, the cop finally
came back, holding a wad of manila cards.

"I'm giving you three citations, Mr. Hatten. Failure to ob-
serve traffic lanes, for crossing the yellow line. Exceeding the
speed limit; you were traveling thirty-three miles per hour in a
thirty zone. And failure to give the proper signal, for failing
to engage your automatic turn signal when executing a turn."
A gloved hand extended the wad of cards through his open
window. The block capitals in blue carbon ink were already
smudged on one. He skimmed the cards and tallied the fines

as the cop recited options for pleading and paying by mail or in person.

"Officer, don't you think three tickets is kind of excessive for one harmless left turn?"

"Nothing harmless about breaking the law, Mr. Hatten. Have a nice day." The cop strutted back to the cruiser.

He wasn't surprised when Rensi called late that afternoon. A chat with the cop followed a Burr story, like a left hook after a straight right. "Let's get lunch tomorrow," the deep Jersey voice said.

"Somewhere else exotic?"

"Matter of fact, there's a new Scandinavian place downtown I've been meaning to try. It's basically Swedish, a family that kept grandma's recipes from the old country."

"A Swedish restaurant?" What did Swedes eat?

"Yeah," Rensi said, exuberant now. "They got a good review in the *Monitor*. The house specialty is fresh crayfish. They boil them, then refrigerate them overnight and serve them cold, garnished with dill flowers."

He was tempted to ask how you got fresh crayfish, or fresh fish of any kind, in Iowa. But he decided he really didn't care. "Sure, sounds good, Jeff."

Gota was modern and upscale, bleached wood and stainless steel, with a quiet crowd in business suits and designer casual. He spotted Rensi in a booth toward the back, face buried in the *Wall Street Journal*. The cop fit in the place, in a camel-hair blazer and painted tie. A shoulder holster was bulging slightly under the jacket. The grip on Rensi's Glock had looked worn that day at the station, used.

"Look what the cat dragged in." The detective extended a

big hand. Yeah, he knew he looked rough. The purple sacks under his eyes were so swollen they looked bruised. But the night
before, he had slept through, for the first time since finding the
rat.

Rensi ordered a house salad followed by the vaunted crayfish. He asked for the same. It was easier than going through
the menu. The place actually looked inviting and fresh. Maybe
he'd come back here in a lighter time. It would have been a
nice place to take Elizabeth.

"They're raising the fare on the New York City subway again,"
the cop said. "I remember when it was thirty-five cents."

"Yeah, it's obscene," he said. "You're much better off in Des
Moines, Iowa."

Rensi shot him a look.

The waiter returned with salads, dark leaves layered with
carrot and beet shavings and tomato wedges, all glistening with
vinaigrette. Rensi stabbed a tomato wedge and dangled it on a
fork, looking across the table at him. Not quite the same vibe
that Susan had projected.

Enough foreplay. "Nice story in the *Globe-Times* yesterday,"
Henry said. "About exhuming her body and questioning an
aide to the Senator."

Rensi waved a hand. "I asked you before if you had a relationship with Elizabeth and you never really answered the question."

That was the first time Rensi had referred to Elizabeth by
her first name. It felt like an invasion, a liberty the cop didn't
rate.

"Now we've seen the phone records and credit card bills,"
Rensi continued. "And some e-mails between you and her."

What credit card bills? Wine he bought in Ames? Room
service at the Rigsdale? No, Rensi must mean Elizabeth's bills.
What e-mails? They had exchanged a couple, mostly when she

was in Scotland, but they were tame, harmless. But their swapping *any* e-mails was probably enough. He shoveled the glistening greens with a fork.

"Were you screwing her?"

He looked up, his eyes probably wide. The cop was studying him.

"Listen, Henry. The medical examiner—the results are going to be coming back shortly. It would be best for you to tell me exactly what you know before that happens. If you don't, I won't be able to help you."

"What do you mean?" The cop was throwing too much at him; stall for thinking time.

"What I'm telling you is, it's going to come out. And they'll march you in front of a grand jury, and it's too late then. You'll get charged as an accessory to a felony, which carries the same penalty as the felony. And we're talking about murder here."

He met Rensi's brown eyes across the table. The cop just stared back, neutral.

"Jeff, did you look at Gargano and Moffat?" Stay on message.

"Henry, why are you so fixated on these guys? You have a run-in with them?"

Even before the dead rat, he had asked himself that. Moffat and Gargano were what he might have become, and to an extent had. He needed to immolate them, maybe, to exorcise some of his own demons. "They're bad guys, Jeff."

Rensi eyed him. "Yeah, rough around the edges."

He chewed a forkful of salad. It was pretty good, just enough dressing to give the greens a tang, with a symphony of textures, the leafy lettuce around the crisp vegetable shavings. He reached for the wire basket, lifted the white linen napkin and yanked off a hunk of bread, thick grainy crust over soft center, a hearty country loaf. He scraped a thin wedge of butter from his plate and ran it over the bread. Maybe he could just withdraw into himself and enjoy the meal.

"Think of the girl, the girl's parents," Rensi said. "You obviously cared about her. Don't you think you owe her something? Don't you think you owe her family something?"

He pictured Elizabeth the first time he had seen her, in the pink oxford shirt writing out name tags at the banker's barbecue, with her innocent smile. He felt Rensi studying him again. "If you were in my position, what would you do?"

"I'm not in your position. What can you live with? I'm telling you as a friend: don't go down the wrong road on this. You've got some decisions to make. If I can help you make those decisions, I will."

The waiter returned, scurrying to their table like a New York cabbie racing to a red light. He was pushing sixty but in shape, a shorn rim of hair mostly white. The waiter didn't look particularly Swedish, just white-bread Middle America, bland features in an oval face. He set down an elliptical plate before each of them. A paste coated the cold white crustaceans, fixing the dill chives to their bodies, maybe a natural slime that oozed in death.

When the waiter left, Rensi said, "If you tell me the truth, I'll help you out as much I can. As long as you're not involved in this."

So Rensi didn't think Henry was involved in Elizabeth's death, after all? Or the cop thought he was an accessory? Which was it? Oh, yeah, it was the unnamed "they" who were going to drag him into court and ruin him; Rensi was his pal. He breathed. "When do you think the medical examiner report's going to be in?"

"A few weeks."

"What do you think they'll find?"

Rensi shrugged. "Hard to say. But I can tell you what they'll be looking for: injuries inconsistent with an auto accident. That's the guidance we gave them. Examiners have a lot more success when they know what to look for." Rensi stabbed a crayfish and lifted it, keeping the brown eyes on him.

He leaned toward the cop, their faces now little more than a foot apart, his pulse pounding. "Jeff," he said, softly and evenly, "I'm telling you, you're wasting your time on me. But I can't give you proof because that would involve going into some stuff that I can't discuss."

Rensi slammed down the fork. "If you've got information about a crime that's been committed, you have an obligation to tell the police what you know. That's how it is."

Boy, this cop had zeroed in on him quickly. Clearly, Henry had misplayed this. How?

"You obviously want to get something off your chest," Rensi said. "You'll feel a lot better if you tell me about it."

He laughed, a cackle worthy of Bill Burr. A woman at a nearby table looked over. Come on, Jeff, give me some credit.

Rensi leaned back and waited.

"Jeff, I'd like to confide in you," he said, softer now. "But I don't want to do this on the record to a police officer."

"I've got to tell you, if you're going to tell me anything that implicates you in a crime, then all bets are off. I consider my-self a friend. But I'm not your priest."

He poked his fork at two crayfish clinging together. The dead creatures shifted their pasty bond as he pried them apart.

"Henry, it's obvious you're not leveling with me," Rensi said. "I'm not sure why you're not. Because I don't think you're involved in this. I don't think you did anything to her. But somewhere along the line, you're going to have to face up to reality. And at this point, I may be the only one who can help you, if you'll let me."

"I'll keep that in mind, Jeff." Okay, sounded like at least he had some time.

"You know, I don't even know if you're leveling with yourself. Or maybe you feel guilty. Sometimes, when people lose someone close, they come to believe it's their fault. They think they might have been able to prevent it, but subconsciously, they wanted to deny themselves this person they didn't deserve."

Suddenly, the deep Jersey voice was like nails clawing a chalkboard. Henry shoved his chair back, scraping the legs against the blond wood floor. That seemed to have become his signature move. He inhaled deeply, filling his lungs, and exhaled in a loud spasm. "Okay, Jeff," he said, avoiding Rensi's stare. "I gotta get back to the office."

34

★ ★ ★

PERP SHOT

In what had become a nightly ritual, Henry unlocked the Presidential Suite, scanned the carpet for footprints, leaped inside, and shut the door. He lifted a wicker dining room chair and wedged it under the doorknob, the back legs locking into now-deep grooves in the rug. As he set the chair, his BlackBerry rang in its holster. The call showed a 402 area code. Omaha. Fran? Susan? Burr?

"My associates had a talk with one of your friends tonight," a gravelly voice said.

He knew the voice. Then it came to him. Zabriskie. "You mean the friends we talked about over breakfast that day?" This was sounding like a mobster movie.

"Right. You didn't tell me how big this thing was, that it was in the papers. But that's okay. Anyway, they had this talk, but your friend didn't say much."

"Well, I appreciate the effort, and the call. It might help

just that my *friends* know . . . others are also concerned. Thank
you." He snapped the phone shut.

He pictured the bodyguards tethered to chairs in a dingy
warehouse, Ed's muscle interrogating them. Then a pang hit
him. Had the Teamster boss's "associates" told the bodyguards
that it was Henry who had sicced Zabriskie on them? Would
the thugs now attack, figuring their rat-in-the-dresser warning
hadn't worked?

A few minutes later, as Henry was urinating, his Black-
Berry rang again on his hip. Just for fun, as though to piss on
whoever was intruding, he reached across and pulled out the
device, keeping his stream within the bowl. The display showed
a familiar 703 number.

"Comrade Press Secretary."

"Gil." It was pushing midnight on the East Coast. Could
Cass hear the coda of his stream?

"The Des Moines cops are going to interview Peele about
the dead volunteer. Walmsley. Tomorrow in the campaign office. Rensi, a sergeant. That's the guy you talked to, right?"

"Yeah." He clamped the phone to his ear and zipped, feeling suddenly exposed.

"You tell nobody about this, understand?" Cass said. "This
is going to be in and out. The cop gets there at four, we give
him half an hour, and that's it. We're doing our civic duty helping them on a case, but the Senator's a busy man."

"Got it." He flushed the toilet and pictured Rensi looming
over Peele in a small office.

The next morning, Henry sidled over to Lynn, the Iowa scheduler. "When are the bodyguards staffing the Senator today, do
you know?" If Moffat or Gargano would be in the campaign

office that afternoon, maybe Rensi could do an impromptu interrogation. He reviewed a news release as he stood by her desk.

"Henry, did you look at the schedule?"

"Yeah. It doesn't say."

Lynn flicked through some papers. "Only public events today are the Rotary Club luncheon and the VFW banquet. If Chris is going to be around, that's when."

"Just Gargano?"

She looked up. "Yeah. You didn't hear? Matt's in the hospital. He got mugged last night."

"Our *bodyguard* got mugged?" He couldn't help grinning. Well, now the thugs had his answer to the rat. But Gargano was more dangerous than Moffat.

"Henry, it's not funny," Lynn said, reddening. "His skull got fractured. They had to operate, because of the pressure on his brain."

The one time he wanted Moffat around, and Zabriskie put the fireplug in intensive care. "Mugged, huh?"

She cocked her head. "He was coming out of a bar, some guys jumped him. I don't know the whole story. That's what I heard."

Henry ate a late lunch at the Lucky Dragon, the $7 special, wonton soup and chicken with snow peas. Dabbing his tongue against the roof of his mouth, he thought he could pick out the MSG, salt, starch, and sugar.

He jumped in the Black Baron to hit the state capitol. He'd work the reporters in the basement press room, just as he might be doing right now if he were Governor Tyler's press secretary. Poor Doug. Afterward, he'd stop downtown at WHO

Radio. WHO, a fifty-thousand-watt AM news station, was the venerable voice of the Midwest, where Ronald Reagan had begun as a sportscaster during the Depression. He should be able to avoid the campaign office until Rensi had come and gone.

He shifted into first and was going to peel out, but remembered his three tickets and eased onto Grand Avenue. The Mustang rolled through the gray gloom, past storefronts and empty lots, a left, and down the approach road. He steered into the capitol parking lot, the green and gold dome looming like the Emerald City castle. He was about to shoot into a spot when he heard a siren. A police cruiser filled his rearview mirror, lights flashing. Again.

He shifted into neutral and yanked the handbrake. In his mirrors, he saw two Des Moines cops in bulky uniform jackets step out of the cruiser, one on each side. One had yellow sergeant's stripes on his sleeve. They crouched and pulled pistols. Pistols? He slapped his hands on the steering wheel. In the side mirrors, the cops were creeping toward the Mustang. A moment later, the sergeant was at his window, and he was facing a Glock barrel.

"Step out of the vehicle, slowly," the sergeant commanded. The cop was blond going gray, with mottled skin that had turned pink in the chill. The eyes were narrow over blue irises, like a wolf's.

He gingerly pulled the metal lever and eased the door open. He slid one leg out and then the other. His feet felt bound in concrete. He reached a hand around the doorframe to pull himself upright. He didn't get the chance. The cop grabbed his wrist, yanked him, and spun him. His face slammed onto the Mustang's hood.

"Spread 'em!" the cop hollered, like something out of a bad

movie. He felt kicks on his insteps, then hands groping his body.

Were they arresting him for murdering Elizabeth? In a moment, would his arms be yanked back, cold metal cuffs tightened on his wrists as steel ratchets caught and locked? He thought he felt the Glock press against the back of his head, but it might just be a cop's knuckle. Looking up, across the Mustang's hood, he saw a few faces gaping at him.

"Mr. Hatten?"

He turned his head, but could see only the hood vent and a windshield wiper.

A hand on his shoulder lifted him onto his feet. The sergeant was looking at his wallet, flipped open, and then at him. "Henry Hatten?"

"Yes, sir."

The cop stared at him another couple of seconds, then flipped the wallet closed, and handed it to him.

"You matched the description of a suspect we're looking for," the cop said, now in a softer tone. "Regrets for any inconvenience."

He heard some clicking and turned. Across the hood, a photographer was pointing a giant lens at him, standing by a *Cedar Rapids Gazette* reporter. A WOI Radio reporter was frantically untangling cords with one hand, gripping a mic with the other.

He turned to the cop. "That's it?"

"Unless you want to file a complaint," the sergeant said, squaring to face him.

He pocketed the wallet with a nearly numb and weightless arm, and tugged his jacket straight. "No, no need."

As the cops walked back to their cruiser, he turned to the crowd, which gave the photographer a full frontal. His numbed legs made each step toward the car door an odd, disembodied event.

He wanted to climb into the Black Baron, lock the doors, and head for Interstate 80. If he drove twenty hours straight, he could be in Washington this time tomorrow, in his Cleveland Park condo with Walter. Instead, he slid the car into the parking spot, behind a dirt-caked pickup, and stepped out. Two mics were in his face before he could stand.

"No, no, I've got no problem with the police," he said, the words flat and even. "They're just doing their jobs, here to protect us. Honest mistake."

During the drive to WHO Radio, his BlackBerry began buzzing on his belt like a rattlesnake in a sack. He pulled over; no need to collect more tickets. He opened a link from Kyle on an e-mail headlined "Perp Shot." The *Cedar Rapids Gazette* popped up, showing him with hands splayed on the Black Baron's hood, looking dazed.

35

* * *

FRIENDS

In his Des Moines campaign office, Peele crossed his arms and leaned back in his desk chair. "Susan, you're giving these guys an excuse to sit around with their thumbs up their asses, and they don't need much of an excuse." Eggert and their Iowa finance guy were waiting to drive Susan to put the arm on some agribusiness execs. He needed his wife out of the campaign shop, but couldn't very well tell her that the cops were coming to interrogate him about his dead mistress.

"Jill Henson stopped me at the club and told me your plan to expand day-care subsidies is like the Italians paying couples to have kids," Susan said in her business tone. "I threw a few numbers at her, but I didn't have a good defense because, Tom, there *isn't* a good defense. That's because your starting point is Republican antichoice dogma. You're trying to make a silk purse out of a sow's ear."

He was a Nebraska Republican; did she expect him to be a poster boy for NARAL? The Midwest used to send progressive

Republicans to the Senate. Wisconsin's "Fighting Bob" La Follette and his son "Young Bob." Nebraska's own George Norris, immortalized in JFK's *Profiles in Courage*. Regulars scorned them as "sons of the wild jackass," but those enlightened ideals used to play in the Midlands. No more. He had inched as close as he could toward a decent stance on abortion, settling on libertarian, government-out-of-the-bedroom rhetoric and focusing on adoption and neonatal care. How many lines had that expediency etched on his Picture-of-Dorian-Gray face?

"Yeah," he said. "Let's celebrate female self-determinism, painted in bloody fetuses." Maybe he could annoy her out the door.

She shifted in a chair, away from him.

"Susan, you know the definition of a statesman? A dead politician."

She ignored him. He'd long since given up trying to recapture those early sappy romantic years. Those days had ended, for good, with her second pregnancy. For weeks, he had run his hand over her belly at night, grinning and even giggling. Then he came back from a New York trip to find her stomach flatter than his.

"Yeah, and let's keep abortion—*choice*—tied to privacy rights, so women can get scraped and tell their husbands it was a miscarriage."

She stormed out the door.

Ten minutes later, Peele was facing a tall police sergeant who dressed like a senator and a short cop with a mean, meaty little face and a crushing handshake. His door was shut, but if this got loud, the crew outside would hear. The walls were so thin he sometimes reached for his phone when the line rang in the next office.

He felt his chest tighten, couldn't fill his lungs to that satisfying point. His pulmonary specialist, maybe reading his mind, had been worried that the ongoing breathing strain was taxing his heart. So they X-rayed his chest. Good news, bad news, the doc had said. The heart looked fine, but they found an "abnormal density" under his sternum. Cancer? Don't know, the doc said in his usual impassive way, could be a mass of blood vessels, could be anything. So they sent him for a contrast CT, a nice term for flooding his veins with dye and feeding him through a giant microwave. The results were due by the end of the week.

Relax, he told himself. He had filmed dozens of *Parkland* scenes in which Roy interrogated poachers, squatters, firebugs, litterbugs, even a rapist and a murderer. He'd even written a couple. On the office-cabin set, he liked to sit on the edge of his desk and glare down at the perps, his gun belt creaking, his badge glinting. He indicated two metal-framed chairs.

"Senator, we know you haven't got much time, so we'll get right to the point," the sergeant, Rensi, said. "We're trying to build a profile of Elizabeth Walmsley. We're looking for any information, any details you can give us. What was your relationship with Ms. Walmsley?"

He had to say he knew her; too many entries on the official schedule to deny that. The model here was chess: face the cops across the desk the way he used to face challengers across the board in Washington Square Park. Show them nothing. Don't even picture Liz—the image could shatter his mask.

"A tragedy," he said. "A young life, so full of promise, snuffed out." He looked down, but only about fifteen degrees;

overdo it and you lose credibility. He met their eyes. "She was a volunteer on my campaign staff."

Rensi had a good poker face. The little cop, Porter, just looked mean, like a bulldog straining a leash. Clearly, they were at least sniffing around about him and Elizabeth.

"She became a friend," he said. That line sounded pregnant, as it were.

"How did you meet her?" Rensi pulled out a leather notebook and what looked like a Parker pen. Pretty fancy on a cop's pay, even a detective sergeant's.

"We met at one of my fund-raising events that she was staffing. In Sioux City."

"Senator," Rensi said, the voice even, "we know you took her to dinner, talked to her dozens of times on the phone. And we saw the antique bowl you gave her."

Oh, hell, the bowl. She didn't even seem to like the thing. He had thought she would throw her arms around him; instead she groused about the diplomatic pouch. "I talk to lots of people," he said. "I give gifts to lots of people."

Rensi shot a look at Porter and raised a hand, as though to still the smaller cop. "Yeah, but this Egyptian bowl is worth north of a thousand bucks," the sergeant said, turning back to him. "You give gifts like that to lots of people?"

"Some," he said. Not much of a comeback. But it wouldn't dig the hole any deeper, unless they wanted to subpoena old girlfriends.

"Senator," Rensi asked, "did you have an intimate relationship with Ms. Walmsley?"

Stay cool; show nothing. If they had to ask, they couldn't prove it. Maybe. Either way, no point helping them. "We're not going there," he said. "Infer what you want from that." He stood. "Anything else?"

Rensi stood, and the little cop followed. "We'll be in touch," the sergeant said.

After they left, he reached for his inhaler and took a long hit. Clearly, Tom Peele was in a multipart episode.

36

★ ★ ★

THIN CRUST

Henry steered the Black Baron off Interstate 80 at the Anita, Iowa, exit. The suspension felt stiff as the wide Goodyears bounced over some frozen roadkill, stringy strips of bright red flesh ripped from fur wrappings. Anita's main drag looked like an Edward Hopper scene. "Stanley's Diner, Nothing Finer" spouted steam next to a storefront bank. Farther along, fast-food franchises, motel chains, and gas stations sprouted. The homogenization of America. He steered into the Pizza Hut lot.

Fran was already there, nibbling a bread stick in a rear booth. They were halfway between Omaha, where she had been digging up who knew what about Peele, and Des Moines, an hour's drive for each.

The Pizza Hut was bustling, with a gaggle of plaid shirts and faded overalls at the salad bar, but their corner was empty. As he slid into the booth, the vinyl cushion gripped and bunched his khakis. He extended a leg under the table to press his topsider against her boot. She leaned her calf into his, and warmth spread through the cotton between them. This was the first time another human being had touched him with affection in weeks, since the last time he had seen Fran. He didn't count a chuck on the shoulder from Eggert.

A waitress came by and returned with their "pops." By the time the woman left with the empty breadbasket, Fran had rested her foot on his.

"Good to see you," he said. "I should expense this meal, since it's keeping you from whatever you're digging up on my guy."

"Actually, I'm just finishing," she said. "They extended my contract to follow up on some leads." She smiled. On Tyler's campaign, Fran had produced a 150-page book on the Iowa governor with a carton of supporting documents, including voting records, expense vouchers, invoices, and financial disclosure forms.

"Is Ed Zabriskie one of the leads you're following up on?" His latest odyssey with Fran had begun with the Teamster beating. But after Burr's initial burst of stories, Fran hadn't advanced the Zabriskie angle, at least not through Burr. But Fran never left a lead until she had picked the carcass clean.

He met her eyes, probed. She projected her poker face, school-girl innocent.

She might have made the connection to the stock scam. Zabriskie was already nervous, and she might have rattled him more. Ed would have done anything to protect himself, to avoid exposure. The union boss could have had Elizabeth beaten or killed, to shut her up, the same script he'd been working for decades on rogue Teamsters. Elizabeth said Ed had adopted her, but bears sometimes kill their young. That would explain why Zabriskie couldn't beat anything about Elizabeth out of Ostrow's goons; the Jersey toughs might not have had anything. Zabriskie could have had Moffat bludgeoned just as cover. But

Zabriskie couldn't have faked that reaction at the diner, could he? His head began to throb. Fran's voice pulled him out.

"Sorry, what's that?" he asked.

"I said, I did some research for you. Or mostly for you. No charge."

He gave her a wary look.

She leaned closer and said, barely above a whisper, "Elizabeth Walmsley's ex-husband, Evan Tabor, filed a claim in probate court against her estate. He's challenging their divorce settlement."

He tightened. Fran's poking felt like another violation of Elizabeth, what little remained of her. But Elizabeth's book-throwing, cokehead ex certainly deserved to be a suspect in her death.

"The cops are looking at Evan, now, too," Fran continued. "Partly because of his record, including a couple of drug-related arrests."

Well, good, at least Rensi was doing something right. Wait. "How do *you* know what the cops are looking at? From your little bearded friend at the *Globe-Times*? You know, it's funny, Fran, how things I tell you pop up in his stories."

She withdrew her leg. "I may have given him a nudge in the right direction, but he did the rest himself. He's better than you think."

Where did you nudge him, he wanted to ask. He gave the family snort.

"Henry, you don't win campaigns with moderation. I'm not talking about your middle-of-the-road . . . values. I'm talking about your whole approach. You know, I've never heard you raise your voice."

He was tempted to bleat out a Howard Dean scream, right there in the Anita Pizza Hut.

"Oh, let's not sandbag the Governor's son just because he sold a little dope. That wouldn't be moral. That wouldn't be moderate. Even your new guy, Peele, his big thing is reaching across the aisle and working with the Ds. It's nothing bold. Nothing radical. Today, all that buys you is a ticket to the political graveyard, with your friend Tyler."

The waitress lumbered over, granting reprieve. Fran ordered a small pie with mushrooms and he asked for a plain thin crust and the salad bar. Rensi would be appalled. He found himself dipping his knife into his water glass and painting swirls on the green Formica table. A few large drops leaned toward neighboring swirls until they rushed together. The key to keeping the swirls apart was moving the knife fast enough that the water didn't clump, yet slow enough to draw a solid strand. He went back and sharpened the swirls with his fork tines, separating gobs that had joined. He dabbed one blot with a corner of his paper napkin, but it left a sloppy streak in the divide between two swirls. He was trying to loop a stream around his water glass when Fran took his hand in hers.

"Hey, you all right?"

He looked up. "Yeah."

"Maybe it would help to talk about it," she said. "Off the record."

She was still holding his hand. He felt his face tighten and thought he might cry. He swallowed and breathed. He looked down at his evaporating artwork. Gaps had formed in several of the thinner strands. The water left a dull residue where it receded. What chemicals had he been drinking all these months in Iowa tap water?

She seemed to know that all she had to do was wait long enough.

"Well," he began, "you know most of the pieces already."

37

★ ★ ★

LEAKS

Diane waved Henry into her office as he was heading for the men's room. He couldn't even take a leak without getting derailed.

"Close the door," she said. Her green-and-gold neckerchief was tangled in her collar.

He shoved the pressed-wood panel shut. What now?

"Dagworth's campaign manager called the boss last night," she said. "On the Senator's emergency line. You know anything about that?" She was trying to read his face, the way Rensi did.

He returned her stare. "No," he said evenly. He was one of only four or five aides, that he knew of, who had Peele's break-glass-in-case-of-emergency phone number.

She studied him again. "Dagworth offered a deal: the boss withdraws from the race and endorses Dagworth, and Dagworth makes the boss health secretary. If he wins." She paused. "Thing is, Dagworth's guy knew our polls, that we'd begun to slip again in Iowa. I've never seen the boss this pissed."

About time Peele sweated. He curbed an impulse to say something glib. "What did the Senator say?"

"The boss hung up on the guy." She shook her head. "Lord help whoever leaked those numbers."

"What did Gil say?"

"That Dagworth's people were probably bluffing about having our numbers. That they also have to be polling in Iowa, and must have figured our polls showed what theirs did."

He cocked his head. "Could be."

An hour later, a *Washington Post* reporter phoned Henry about Dagworth's offer. She wouldn't reveal her source. "We're in it to win it," he said, and aped some other lines he had vetted with Diane.

After hanging up, he printed the three e-mails between Cass and Boggs that he had sent himself from Cass's computer. An image from childhood appeared in his head, of his father smashing a giant water bug crawling up their kitchen wall, using a bare hand. He had nearly puked. "You've got to kill the enemy," his father had growled, seeing his distress, and wiping yellow ooze off a hand. Henry sealed the pages in a manila envelope, which he slid into a pocket of his briefcase.

The next morning just after six, Henry's BlackBerry wrenched him from a rare deep sleep, in his own bed in Cleveland Park. He fumbled with the device to find himself on the line with an ABC-TV producer.

"Do you have any comment on the *Post* piece?" she asked in a quick, crisp alto. No apology for the hour; flacks didn't rate courtesy.

"I'll call you back in ten minutes," he said.

"I just need—"

"I'll call you back in ten minutes," he hissed. "What's your number?"

He fired up his desktop and found a headline in the *Post*'s on-line version, "Peele Vows to Stay in Race." He scanned the piece for his name. Not there. But Cass was, saying Dagworth's offer was like Lee demanding Grant's surrender. Not bad.

His BlackBerry blared. The 703 number. "Gil?"

"Peele's going to go ape-shit," Cass said. "I just got a call from Andrea Swain at CNN. How do these twats get my cell number?"

"I just got a call from ABC. I told her I'd call her back."

"Okay," Cass said. "You tell me what you told the *Post* reporter, and I'll tell you what I told him." Cass's words were tumbling out, the voice higher than usual. He had never heard Cass nervous before. The Angel was looking for a fall guy.

"I just told him that 'we're in it to win it,'" he said. "I used just those words. I remember thinking it was pretty cliché."

"Wait a minute, let go!" Cass hollered. Then, softer: "Not you. I was talking to somebody else." Who was Cass with at six A.M.? Jeannine the call girl? "You tell him anything off the record?" Cass asked, back in the harried business voice.

"Nope. Not on this." In fact, he had told the *Post* reporter, off the record, that Peele had hung up when Dagworth's man made the offer.

"Who else knows about this thing, the HHS sec deal?" Cass asked. "Who else has Peele talked to?"

"I don't know if he talked to anybody, apart from Diane. He was in New Hampshire all day yesterday."

"Perfect," Cass said, sounding like the old Angel. "He must have talked to that twit Brian Natter. I'll call you right back."

Ten minutes later, Cass's number blared on his BlackBerry.

"Swain at CNN is looking for Natter's home number," Cass said. "If she calls you, tell her you don't have it."

Swain phoned Henry five minutes later. He let the message to go voice mail. He needed to figure out how to play this.

He dressed and stood in front of his bedroom closet, admiring the suit from Mr. Yang. He felt rich just looking at it. The brown tortoiseshell buttons lay flat and perfectly aligned on the lustrous gray pinstriped wool. The stitching was flawless. He grazed the back of his fingers against the cloth. Liquid smooth. He had been waiting for an occasion to wear it. He had even laid it out one day, but the radio said chance of rain. Slipping two fingers under the rosewood hanger, he draped the suit over his shoulder and headed for the elevator.

In the lobby, he stopped at the desk. He slid Mr. Yang's suit on the marble counter. "That old clothes drive is still on, right?" he asked the clerk. "Add this to the pile, will you?"

When Henry reached the North Capitol Street office, calls about the *Post* story were clogging his voice mail. He chanted that Peele was in it to win it. As for any offer Dagworth may have made, he said, "Senator Dagworth has made a lot of odd proposals during the course of this campaign."

At eight fifteen, Cass phoned him. "No worries, Comrade," the Angel sang. "Swain called the New Hampshire office, and one of the dweebs there confirmed that Peele and Natter were talking about our Iowa numbers yesterday."

"Congratulations."

"Natter probably *was* the leak," Cass said. "Gotta go. Freedom and prosperity."

He shut his office door and punched the number Andrea Swain had left in his voice mail.

"This needs to be strictly not for attribution," he told the CNN producer. "You can say 'sources within the Peele campaign,' but nothing more specific than that. Okay?"

When she agreed, he said, "Contrary to what you may have been told, it was Peele's campaign chairman, Gil Cass, who arranged the Dagworth call to Peele and Cass who leaked the story to the *Post*. Cass is collaborating with Dagworth's pollster, Mark Boggs."

He pulled the manila envelope from his briefcase, opened his door, and strode to the big office at the end of the corridor. The room was empty. He spied Peele's leather briefcase on a table. He slipped inside and shut the door behind him until it just met the frame. He rubbed his palm against his pants leg and lifted the flap of Peele's bag. Wiping his hand again, he slid the envelope into the main section. He snapped the hasp shut, took a breath, and stepped outside. He jogged back to his office.

In fifteen minutes, CNN updated its story. The network was now reporting that sources in both campaigns had said that Cass had arranged Dagworth's offer.

He printed the CNN.com story, stapled the pages, and placed it in a folder. He trotted down the corridor to the big offices. Peele's office was still empty, but he heard voices from Cass's. Peering in, he saw the Senator and the Angel at a table, chatting. Since the previous afternoon, Peele had been serene, after getting what Henry had heard was a good medical diagnosis. He knocked, waited, and walked in. He placed the printout on the table by Cass, but facing Peele. "CNN just posted this."

Cass looked at him and then down at the printout.

"That's bullshit!" the Angel said, backhanding the pages off the table.

"Yeah?" Peele asked.

"Hey, Tom, sure. The CNN twat talked to Dagworth's people, it says so in the story. Somebody there set me up. That's all that makes sense."

Peele turned to him. "Excuse us, would you, Henry?"

He stepped out, raced back to his little office, and shut the door. He signed onto a dummy gmail account he had created the night before and pulled up the Cass-Boggs e-mails. He dialed the phone.

The *Des Moines Monitor* political editor picked up on the first ring.

"I'm going to send you some e-mails, which are self-explanatory," he began. "But only on your assurance you won't divulge how you got them." He pressed some keys and waited.

"Interesting," the editor pronounced. "You're not such a Boy Scout anymore."

Henry heard a knock and looked up to see Fogel in his doorframe. The media man was wearing a natty check sport coat nicely tailored around the expanding gut. Fogel had apparently conceded the battle with the tortellini and moo shoo pork.

"Tough day for Uncle Gil," Henry said. He couldn't help grinning.

Fogel stepped in. "Tough day for the whole Peele-palooza."

"Ira, you're the last guy I expected to see crying over Cass's grave. You said chairmen were all Machiavellian creeps."

"*Boychick*, how do you think this campaign started? Gil wrote a plan for a moderate to win the Republican nomination."

"Fine. Cass wrote the campaign plan. That's what consultants do."

"No, you're missing the point. Gil wrote the plan *before*

Peele was even thinking about running. He wrote it for Zach Lowe. But Lowe turned him down. Huge fight. So Gil fished around and came up with Peele. Tom was his second or third choice."

Cass's "you-work-for-me" rebukes, the Angel's vendetta against Lowe; now it all made sense.

"Well, the Romanovs survived after Rasputin checked out," Henry said. "At least for a while."

Fogel raised an eyebrow.

38

★ ★ ★

THE GOLDEN RULE

Rensi's number was flashing on Henry's D.C. office phone, and it was barely noon, three hours before the cop's shift started. Henry breathed and lifted the receiver.

"We just got the medical examiner's report in from Maine on Elizabeth Walmsley." The Jersey voice paused, stretching the suspense. "Blunt force trauma inconsistent with injuries from an automobile accident. The Walmsley case is now officially a homicide."

The cop was waiting for him to speak. "Okay," he said.

"Anything you want to say now?"

"Yeah. I'm getting the sense that Des Moines's finest is giving me special treatment. I got a collection of traffic tickets, and a couple of gorillas with badges used my face to shine the hood of my car the other day. You know anything about that?"

"Henry, I told you I consider myself a friend. Maybe your only friend. I'm trying to help you. Because if I don't, you're just going to damn yourself."

"You're making me a liability to the people I work for."

"Like I say, I'm trying to help you."

"Yeah, well, thanks, friend." He slammed down the receiver.

Scanning his day planner, Henry noticed a circled item, "Walter—food." He pulled up an online supplier and entered an order for grilled-tuna-and-egg-flavor dried cat food and a canned variety pack. He typed his address and MasterCard information and hit Pay Now. A message in red capitals appeared: "Credit Card Not Valid." He checked his card number and expiration date and hit the "back" button. He moved the arrow over Pay Now and clicked it again, harder. The red message appeared again. He read his card again, then flicked it across the office. "Goddamnit, Jeff!"

The walls of his little windowless cell were closing in. He grabbed his jacket and stormed out, his head pounding until he reached the lobby and the pavilion outside. He walked the garden path, the Capitol on his right, toward the Senate office buildings. The bushes and flower beds, vibrant in spring with a pallet of violet, yellow, ochre, and deep red, were bare and brittle, like skeletons.

Was he burning out? For months, he had been looking for signs. Would he soon be unable to spew Peele's message points, the way he had choked on Morris's agitprop? No, that wasn't burnout. That was just disgust. Burning out, he now saw, was a gradual deadening, in which emotion atrophies into reflexes from political stimuli. You begin to assess people in terms of their needs, wants, and agendas to better manipulate them, and eventually you lose the ability to plumb another soul and connect. His slide had accelerated since Elizabeth's death. Was it already too late?

———

A few nights later, Henry steered the Black Baron out of the Des Moines campaign lot onto Ingersoll Avenue and headed south, toward the Rigsdale. The streets were dark, silent, and empty, gray ice hanging from lampposts and parked cars' underbellies.

A set of headlights ignited behind him as he neared 27th Street, lighting the Mustang's cabin and searing his eyeballs. He tapped his brakes, but the car stayed with him. Squinting into the mirror, he could make out two forms in the front seat, large, wide men, maybe bulked by parkas. Squinting further, he made out the car's square muzzle, heavy grille, and chrome bumpers: a 1970s muscle car.

He whipped left onto 25th Street and accelerated, off his usual route and away from the Rigsdale. The headlights disappeared. Then they reappeared on one side, and then flush behind him again.

Were these Rensi's men, in an unmarked cruiser, "helping" him? The car didn't have any search lights, long antennas, or other cop trappings. Were they Ostrow's thugs, Gargano and a replacement for Moffat?

He turned right at the corner, hand-over-hand, now gripping the wheel at the ten and two, textbook driver's ed. The headlights vanished, then appeared again. Then they slid off the left side of his mirror.

A moment later, he heard an engine whine, and turned to his left to see the muscle car beside him, chrome trim glinting in the streetlamps. He tried to make out the passenger's features, while still watching the dark street. The car edged toward him, crowding him. He eased the Mustang right, half into the curb lane. The bigger car kept nudging him over. Is this how they killed Elizabeth, forcing her off the road?

He was about to turn his head to yell at the men, when he

saw a parked car ahead, blocking his path and closing fast. He was facing a green minivan, seventy feet away, now fifty, aglow in the wash of his headlights. He jammed both feet down on the pedals. He heard a squeal, felt the antilock brakes kick in and the Black Baron skid to the right as its Goodyears burned on the asphalt. Anticipating the collision, he whipped his head to the side, to shield his eyes from a spray of glass. He felt the Mustang stop, but heard no crash. He turned. The Black Baron had come to rest at an angle, less than two feet from the minivan.

The street was empty. The muscle car was gone.

When Henry reached the Presidential Suite, he wedged a wicker chair under the doorknob and poured a glass of Peele's Glenfiddich. As he was draining it, his BlackBerry rang, showing a 515 number. Rensi.

"Listen, I've got some new information; we're going to have to meet on it." The deep Jersey voice was East Coast quick. "Where are you now?"

Maybe Rensi knew exactly where he was. Had the goons in the muscle car reported to their sergeant? "Rigsdale Hotel."

"Okay, let's meet down at the bar. In twenty minutes."

No exotic restaurant? No Balinese or Ethiopian places open this late?

He arrived before Rensi this time and took a table away from the television. He scanned the bar. The crowd was thin, mostly middle-aged out-of-towners. The Rigsdale buzzed most weekends with traffic from the nearby civic center. The state wrestling tourney, dart championship, nutritionists' convention, high school basketball tournament, even the high school power-lifting tourney, all passed through.

He asked for a club soda, to keep his head clear. The place was dim, the dark wood paneling absorbing the meager light, lending an odd aura of privacy. He found his heel circling a table leg, his mind counting the rotations.

Rensi arrived and took the chair next to him, about a foot away, instead of the one across the table. The cop loomed over him, sitting straight. Rensi's navy suit and white shirt stood out in the bar, but probably said executive more than cop. A waiter came over and the sergeant ordered an Amstel.

"We've got information that Elizabeth Walmsley was killed here, at this hotel," Rensi began. "And the body was moved later. The car wreck looks like a setup."

He felt the detective's eyes probing him, measuring his re-action. It was a maddening way to have a conversation. He was tempted to say so, or to shove his chair back again. He grunted, mostly to make some sound.

Had Fran spoon-fed the Rigsdale to Rensi, though Burr? Was she trying to help him, placing the bodyguards closer to the crime scene? Or was she just trying to torpedo Peele? He hadn't really expected her to keep quiet. If Fran was involved, another Burr story was probably coming, this one saying a Peele aide was murdered in the Senator's hotel room. On a story like that, Burr would have to call him first for comment. He could almost hear his BlackBerry ring.

The waiter swept by, set an Amstel on the table, and contin-ued past. Rensi glanced at the bottle but didn't reach for it. "Anything you want to tell me?"

He circled the chair leg again with his heel. "Well, that's interesting, Jeff. That's interesting because, the night Elizabeth died, some of her stuff was left in kind of a mess in the hotel bathroom." He clamped his jaw, bracing. One side of his face began tingling, nearly numb, where Rensi's eyes were boring at it. "She kept some stuff, clothes and toothpaste and such, for when she got stuck in Des Moines and had to stay over. And that night, the stuff in her toilet kit was kind of strewn around one of the bathrooms."

"Strewn around?"

"Yeah. So I cleaned it up."

"You cleaned it up?"

"Yeah. It was kind of a mess. So I cleaned it up."

Rensi just stared at him. "What else are you not telling me?" the cop finally asked, in a voice loud enough to carry. "What the hell else are you lying about?"

He didn't look to see if anybody was listening. He didn't want to know, didn't want to meet the eyes. The numbness had spread to his entire face. His interview voice kicked in, but at low decibel, the most he could muster. "I've been telling you for weeks to check the bodyguards. Well, those guys stay at the hotel. Maybe now you've got enough reason to check them out." He thought about mentioning Zabriskie as a second possibility. No, keep it simple.

Rensi was looking at him the way his father had looked at him when the old man caught him in the lost-football lie. "First, Henry, you tell me everything," the cop said. "The truth."

"Jeff, I'm telling you all I can."

Rensi pushed back the chair, harder than Henry had ever shoved back a chair, and stood. More eyes were probably on them by now than on the TV newscast.

"I tried to help you out," Rensi said. "You're on your own. Whatever will be will be." Rensi reached into the dark suit coat. For a moment, Henry thought the cop was going for the Glock. But Rensi pulled out a ten-dollar bill and tossed it on the table. And then the detective stalked out of the bar.

Back upstairs, alone in the Presidential Suite, Henry dialed a preprogrammed Virginia number on his BlackBerry that he hadn't used in more than a year.

"Hen-ry," the familiar voice pronounced, hitting both syllables, an emphatic statement of fact. But there was something else in Doug Tyler's voice, the way it projected his name, as though rolling its tongue over a prized, rarely used word. He smiled.

"Yes, sir. Good quote in the *Times* the other day, on prescription drug funding." Tyler had recently landed a spot as CEO of a health-care advocacy group.

"A lot of sound and fury. But nice to be noticed. How's life in the fast lane?"

He almost laughed. "Doug, I need some advice," he said. "Wearing your congressman hat and your lawyer hat." He gave a summary, the way he used to on media queries.

The line crackled with static. Had Tyler hung up?

"Okay," Tyler said. "Look, we never had this conversation."

"Doug who?"

"Very good."

He told Tyler most of it. Several times, he thought his old boss would cut him off, tell him to find a good criminal lawyer.

"So I cleaned it up," he said. "I know you might say that wasn't too smart."

"I'm glad you saved me the trouble," Tyler said. "Okay, look, let's figure out what to do now. We can talk later about how dumb it all was."

He liked that prospect, talking to Tyler again later, reconnecting.

"See, what's worrying me," Henry said, "I don't want to get

334 | CHARLES ROBBINS

charged as an accessory to murder for withholding facts from
the police."

"This isn't a confessional. You don't have to connect the dots
for them, or give them the most likely story. All you have to
give them is the barest facts that you know, so that you've come
clean, as a matter of law."

"Okay." He scribbled notes on a pad.

"I think your story to the cops should be what you've identified, which is that she threw the stuff around. Remember, one
advantage of cleaning the stuff up is that no one can say that it
looked like the work of an intruder or her own fit of anger. You
can describe it however you want. But remember the golden
rule, that it's hard to remember the same lie twice. You're better off coming clean with the barest facts you can present. It's
the only way to keep a story straight."

"Okay, that works." He wanted to hug the guy. "Doug,
thanks so much."

He reached for the disconnect key, but Tyler wasn't done.
"It would be one thing if it was the FEC looking for campaign
contribution snafus," Tyler continued. "But you're describing
something that involves pointing a very sharp finger, ultimately, at somebody. You just better make sure it's not at you."

"Yeah."

"If you keep getting grilled by the cops, you want to revisit
this. If there's someone you think the cops should be talking to
instead, the day may come, sooner rather than later, that you
say to the cops, 'Hey, I know who would be happy to talk to
you.'"

He pictured one such person. "Thanks. That's a big help."

"I don't know, and I'm not sure I want to know, what or
whom you're covering for," Tyler said. "But you seem close to
deciding that, for whatever reason, it isn't worth sticking your

neck out anymore, and that's usually a good decision to make."

"You're a clever guy, Doug."

"Clever is as clever does, Henry," Tyler said, with a note of sadness. "Be careful."

He splayed on the living room recliner for an hour in the dark, a warm respite when his BlackBerry buzzed only sporadically in the small bedroom, a distant hum. Switching on a lamp, he drafted a script, editing until the page looked almost as worn as Peele's Kennedy School Address. At twelve thirty A.M., he dialed Rensi's cell. "I want to give you some answers to the questions you asked me tonight."

"That's good," the cop said.

He read his script, hitting the highlights: ". . . Elizabeth told only two people directly, that I know of, that she would be at the hotel that night: Peele, who had arranged her visit, and me. . . . But there was a third person who certainly knew: Gil Cass . . . Cass kept me away from the suite with a pretext that night. Cass is the guy you should be looking at." What about Zabriskie? *The barest facts.*

"Listen, you told me; that's good," Rensi said. "But you're going to have to come forward."

"Okay." He felt lighter, looser, nearly ecstatic. Free. "But I need some time to work out some things with some people."

"I can give you a few days."

39

✴ ✴ ✴

THE MOSAIC

Henry began the next morning, shortly after six, with Peele at the Des Moines YMCA. He felt like Judas, waiting for Jesus to discover his betrayal. He'd file his statement with Rensi in a few days, and Peele would be on the cross. But he also felt violated; the Y had been his escape and sanctuary, his recharging cocoon, and now Peele had commandeered it, resplendent in bright red Nebraska sweats.

As Peele showered, Henry found a quiet corner by a trophy case and dialed Zabriskie's cell. He needed to rule the union boss in or out. Gazing at a tarnished men's basketball cup, he reviewed his script a final time.

When the deep voice barked "Yeah?" the exercise seemed futile, maybe dangerous, like trying to rope a bear. But too late now.

"The authorities are getting close to catching whoever took the actions we discussed, involving the woman," he began. He heard a grunt and waited for more. Nothing came. "The focus still seems to be on the two gentlemen whom your associates met that night. But the authorities also seem concerned about recent injuries to one of your colleagues, and about similar injuries to another of your colleagues some years ago." He paused, but could hear only his own pulse pounding in his ears. "The authorities might ask you about those events, and I just thought you needed to know."

Another grunt. Then, "All right. Thanks."

The line went dead.

Henry sat on a stool amid heaping carts in the small studio as Fogel worked the console. Figures appeared on the three screens, arms flailing and lips vibrating, and vanished.

"I did a film for the Navy once, a promo on fast-attack submarines," Fogel said, sharpening the focus on a close-up of Peele. "Everything on those boats was secret or top secret. I was careful not to show any dials, readouts, and nothing near the reactor and turbines." Fogel zoomed in closer on Peele, until Henry could see the pores in the Senator's nose. "They rejected my film. The admiral said it gave out too much information. He said no image in itself was compromising, but the mosaic was. The *mosaic*."

Henry rotated his neck, trying to loosen a knot of muscle.

"I'm going to show you some raw footage from the last few months." Fogel twisted to face him. "Call it a mosaic." The playful glint was gone from the eyes. "I put this together after I heard about your phone stunt with Zabriskie. I told you, you can figure out who people are by watching them on tape. In this case, I didn't find what I expected."

The large screen came to life, showing a brilliant outdoor scene, lush grass and a striped tent. Peele's tent at the Iowa Straw

Poll. The screen flashed to Henry wrapping a TV interview and a woman in a wide-brimmed hat stepping toward him. Elizabeth. His mouth went dry. The screen followed them to a pole at the rear of the tent.

"I didn't know you had a camera there."

"Eyes everywhere, Henry. Watch."

On the screen, he was smiling. He stepped forward and gave Elizabeth a long hug. He could almost feel her pressing against him again, and thought he might choke up. On screen, he and Elizabeth separated, then he gave her another hug, draping his arms over her shoulders.

Henry swallowed.

"That first segment was just to pique your interest," Fogel said.

The screen flashed to a different outdoor event. Peele was working a crowd. The Senator approached a russet-haired woman. Elizabeth again. They hugged, a bit too long. Henry felt his stomach churn, but forced himself to watch. He didn't recognize the event; it wasn't one he had attended. It looked summery, judging by the clothing. The frame flashed to Susan Peele, standing alone by a picnic table and glaring. The camera panned from Susan, across the crowd, back to Peele and Elizabeth. Now the two lovers were standing by a punch bowl, patting arms and shoulders as they chatted.

The screen flashed to an indoor crowd scene, which Henry recognized as the rally at the Des Moines Holiday Inn. In a wide shot, he found the back of his father's and Zabriskie's gray heads. So Zabriskie *was* involved in whatever this was. The camera zoomed in on two figures against a wall. Susan and Gargano the bodyguard, talking intensely. The screen jumped to another event, a Peele open-house meeting in a light-bathed town hall. Henry hadn't been at that one, either. It looked like Iowa. The screen froze on a glimmering russet head in the front row, hair pulled back in a tortoiseshell clip. Elizabeth again. Then the camera flashed to three figures in the same room, by a sun-lit wall. Susan and Gargano again, this time also with the blond thug, Moffat. Susan, an intense look on her face, pointed an index finger. Her lips formed words that he couldn't make out. The screen panned to the back of Elizabeth's head again, and held for a few seconds.

Now an outdoor scene, Peele walking to the silver Lincoln on a bustling downtown street. Washington. Gargano and Moffat hovering. The frame froze on Gargano's face, and zoomed in. One of the bodyguard's large brown eyes was slightly shut, the flesh bruised in the corner.

"That last sequence was shot two days after she died," Fogel said and hit a switch. The screen went black.

Henry's temples were squeezing his brain, clamping his thoughts.

Fogel came toward him, extending a jewel case. "This is a DVD of what you just saw, minus that first segment. You decide what you want to do with it."

That night, Henry found himself at Reagan National Airport. He didn't remember hailing a cab; he seemed to just materialize at the terminal. He caught the last connection to Des Moines, through Chicago. The flights would give him time to think. And sanctuary. By federal law, he had to turn off his BlackBerry.

Susan? Okay, she'd gotten pissed at finding the printout of directions to Elizabeth's house. But Susan must have known that Elizabeth was just one of many. Peele was so brazen, some of his paramours even appeared on the schedules e-mailed to staff each morning, listed for meetings in the Senator's office. And Susan wasn't exactly madly, desperately in love with Peele.

Or particularly faithful herself. The face-holding at the Manchester restaurant made that pretty clear. So why would Susan take such drastic action to stifle just another of Peele's flings? At worst, you walk out on hubby, which was what Cass was hoping for when he planted the e-mail, at least by Fogel's reckoning. No, it didn't make sense. Unless . . .

Henry breathed deeply, expelling loud streams of air at the porthole. Unless Susan had figured out that Elizabeth was also Wife of Bath, who had scotched Susan's seat on Western Pharmaceutical's board and jeopardized her shot at First Lady.

Henry sipped club soda and stared through the porthole into darkness, somewhere above the Great Plains. Then a pang shot through his innards. *Cass.* Henry had torpedoed the Angel with Rensi. On a murder case. And Cass had nothing to do with it. Well, nothing directly. Cass *had* brought the two thugs into Peele's camp, through Ostrow. Maybe it was poetic justice, for Cass's trying to frame Natter over the leaked poll numbers, and for countless other sins.

Why destroy Susan, and Peele? Why explode his own world? To do justice by Gil Cass? He could shatter Fogel's DVD and drop the shards into a dozen O'Hare trash bins. What did the footage really prove, anyway?

The Iowa caucuses were weeks away; he might still get Peele on the cover of *Time.* While Rensi fenced with Cass, or groped for new suspects, Peele could win the presidency, and change the world. For the better. It was still possible. Elizabeth was gone; nothing could bring her back. He could go on. All he'd have to do was live with it the rest of his life.

The next morning, Henry turned off his BlackBerry and shoved the electronic leash into his briefcase. He climbed into the Black Baron and drove out 6th Avenue, to Mercy Medical Center. He strode the hospital corridors as though in charge, a Washington gait. He followed the signs to the room. Hospitals were laid out so clearly, navigable even by the distressed and desperate.

He stepped through the doorway into a four-patient chamber. Industrial beds with computer caddies and fluid-drip stands beside them, computer displays flashing and beeping. Everything on wheels, ready to rush along the gleaming vinyl tiles. At a central desk, a nurse was flipping pages on a metal clipboard. An attendant was leaning over the patient nearest Henry, shifting the man like a broken doll to reach bandaged ribs.

In the far corner, by a window, he saw a stocky form with its head wrapped in a gauze turban. One arm was in a cast. He pranced over with a smile, as though spotting his brother. "How you doing, Matt?" he asked Moffat. "You got the best view in the place." He looked out the window. "Course, it's still Des Moines."

The karate man, face puffy and bruised, looked up at him, and a flash of recognition crossed the dull blue eyes. Moffat tried to raise himself on the bed, but it seemed too much effort, and the bodyguard just lay there, watching warily.

Henry felt an urge to gouge the dull, gazing eyes. Thumbs against the bridge of the nose, press into the sockets and flick outward, like popping eggs out of a carton. He might be able to stride out of the room and back down the corridor before anybody figured out what had happened, amid the screams, or had time to look for him.

He powered up his laptop and slid the DVD into the port. "Came to show you something, buddy." He placed the computer on the bed, the screen a foot from Moffat's face. He hit Play. "You and your friend Chris are both going down."

When the disc finished, he rewound and paused on a frame of an intense Susan pointing, flanked by the two bodyguards. He placed the screen back in front of Moffat. The attendant was watching them, from the neighboring bed. Henry smiled and gave a thumbs-up. The man turned back to the other patient.

"You'll make out a lot better if you tell your side first, before Gargano." He looked at his watch. "Who's probably sitting down with the cops just about now." He shoved the computer so the base hit Moffat's chin, bouncing the bandaged head. He locked his eyes on Moffat's, the way he used to try to stare down opponents at wrestling weigh-ins.

Moffat turned his head a few degrees away, maybe all he could. After what seemed minutes, the karate man said, "We were only going to scare her."

"Yeah?" Henry leaned in. "So what happened, Matt?"

Moffat closed his eyes and shook his head a few degrees. Henry stared at the puffy, almost childlike face. He clicked off the digital recorder in his shirt pocket and folded the laptop into its case.

He began to step away, then turned back. "By the way," he said, inches from Moffat's ear, "the dead rat, and the car running me off the road—that didn't scare me; it just pissed me off, made me work even harder to nail you."

The blue eyes gave a vacuous, confused look. And then it hit him. It wasn't the bodyguards, after all, who had been terrorizing him. Now he saw who had planted the rat and sent the muscle car after him. He should have figured it out long ago. The rat appeared two days after he had forwarded e-mails from Cass's computer, and the car appeared after he had set up Cass with CNN. It was the Angel.

An hour later, Henry stepped into the Anderson Erickson Dairy on University Avenue in Des Moines. He scanned the store and spotted the tall figure, in an Air Force sweatshirt and jeans, by a shelf of onion sour cream dips.

"Another errand for the boss?" he asked.

Rensi smiled. "Yeah."

Henry pulled two jewel cases from a coat pocket and handed them to Rensi, one containing Fogel's DVD, the other a CD of his hospital chat with Moffat.

Six hours later, striding into the Des Moines detective bay, Henry felt none of the anxiety that had hit him that first night, when he came looking for handgun statistics. He marched to the third office on the left. Rensi was at the desk, leafing through forms. The Glock pressed against a crisp white shirt. Henry sat in the vinyl chair.

"The timing turned out to be good," Rensi said. "Gargano flew into Des Moines this afternoon and went right to the hotel. We had uniforms waiting for him."

He nodded.

"Moffat was a lot easier to get hold of, as you know. By the way, you have any idea how he got banged up?"

Henry shrugged.

"Well, it didn't take long. Each of them said the other did it, but it doesn't really matter. Basically, the way they both tell it, they were told to deliver a message to the good professor: 'Stay away from the campaign, stay away from the Senator, and keep your mouth shut.'"

"Nice."

"They said she went nuts, they wound up tussling, and she cracked her head on the wall."

He pictured Elizabeth wrestling the two apes in the Rigsdale bathroom, their hands on her, smashing her delicate, already abused face. The bathroom where he had showered that morning.

"They stuffed her in a duffel bag and loaded the bag into the trunk of a rental car," Rensi continued. "Then they walked to a bar, had a few rum and Cokes, went to a movie, went back to the bar for a nightcap. Then, around one A.M., one of them took off in the rental car and the other followed in the professor's Honda. About halfway to Ames, they put her in the Honda and sent it into a tree."

"Okay, Jeff," he said, squirming in the chair.

"Two guys from Jersey, one of them Italian." Rensi shook his head.

"And Susan?"

Rensi looked at his watch. "Should be here in an hour. Couple of uniforms are driving her in from Omaha."

40

★ ★ ★

DARK SHADOWS

Henry rifled through files in his Des Moines office, tossing odd papers, a glo-lite Iowa Pork Producers pen, and other trinkets into his gym bag. Anything he might want, he needed to take now. A Judas call could come from Peele at any moment, banishing him. A wave of sadness swept him, like sifting through his dead mother's photo albums, picking the prints he wanted. What might have been.

His desk phone rang, flashing the Washington "224" Senate number for the fourth time in fifteen minutes.

"Okay, here's the SitRep," Sterba said. "FUBAR, FUBB really. ThreatCon Delta."

"That sounds bad, Mike, whatever it means."

"It means Susan's making a statement to the cops now; she wouldn't lawyer up. She's going to admit she was involved in popping the boss's Iowa squeeze."

Is that how Elizabeth would be remembered? Not for her scholarship, her teaching, her warmth and kindness? Or even for her knockout smile? Elizabeth Walmsley, Tom Peele's Iowa Squeeze. "So how did the cops find out Susan did it?" He braced.

"I don't know," Sterba said, annoyed. "Look, the boss is going to make an announcement in half an hour. At the office there, as soon as he gets to Des Moines. He wants you to set it up."

He hung up and stepped into the main space. The scheduler was pecking at her keyboard. One of the organizational directors was on the phone, leaning back in a chair. He spotted the Iowa press secretary. "Kyle!" He told the kid to put out a media alert. "Head is, 'Senator Peele to Make Major Announcement.' That's all you need to say."

He turned off his BlackBerry, grabbed his coat and gym bag, and headed out the back door to the Black Baron. Nobody noticed, or said anything. In ten minutes, he was at the Rigsdale. He opened the Presidential Suite's paint-slathered front door, knowing it was also for the last time. With the lights off, the place was dark, before six P.M. Winter was only a few weeks off. With the windows shut against the cold, the sour antiseptic scent with the moldy undertone was stronger. The aqua carpet showed the dark vacuum swaths. The place looked and smelled as it had that night. But Elizabeth's ghost no longer seemed to lurk.

He yanked his suitcase from the back of a closet and tossed in his clothing, toilet kit, a sci-fi novel he had been reading in his few free minutes before passing out at night. Anything he might need, or that was worth keeping. He raced through the place, checking each room. He stopped at the hall closet, on the chance that somehow it had all been a dream, and Elizabeth's red Iowa State tote was still atop the linen. White sheets and a yellowed pillow stared back at him.

He paused outside the master bedroom, where he had so

rarely ventured. He stepped in, feeling none of the old angst. Just an empty room. He rifled through the desk, sifting hotel stationery and a few coins. Then, in the back of one of the drawers, he spotted a sheaf of yellow sheets, heavy with smudged blue ink. Peele's draft of the Kennedy School Address. The Senator's statement of principles. He flipped the pages. Toward the end, he noticed Peele had written a Bible verse, Mark 8:36, but crossed it out: "For what shall it profit a man, if he shall gain the whole world, and lose his own soul?"

Henry parked the Black Baron behind the airport Quality Inn, by a trailer-sized Dumpster. The digital dash clock read 6:10 as he killed the engine. Across town, Peele would be holding his news conference. Maybe his last news conference. Henry walked to the entrance and up to the reception desk. The lobby was Formica, track lighting, and mass-market floral prints. None of the Rigsdale's faded charm.

"A single, for three days, please," he told the clerk. He placed his MasterCard and driver's license on the counter.

"Oh, hey!" he said, as she typed. "There might be a problem running that card."

She looked up. "No problem, Mr. Hatten. I'm just printing your receipt now."

He ordered a pizza with onions from a take-out service. The thing arrived in his room an hour later, warm in a soggy cardboard box. It tasted bland, the onions just dry shavings. He hadn't expected New York pizza in Des Moines, but this wasn't even Pizza Hut. He watched a weekly football update on cable. He hadn't seen any of the games that season, and the playoffs were approaching. The Jets were out, but the Giants were still alive. He watched a few movies on cable, careful not to even flip through a news channel, and passed out sometime after eleven.

The next morning, almost for amusement, he turned on his BlackBerry. The device showed 259 new e-mails. Its voice mail had filled the previous evening. He flipped through the headers. At least two dozen news alerts, most beginning "Peele Withdraws." A dozen more from Sterba. One from Fran, headed "U OK? Pls Call." A couple of messages were marked "Susan's Confession," courtesy copies of e-mails fired among Peele staffers. He scrolled to the original. Apparently, a Des Moines police employee had sold a copy of Susan's statement to a pay-for-gossip website. By morning, it had gone viral.

Susan's statement ran only four paragraphs. Essentially, she said she had asked Ostrow's men to pass on a message to the professor: Stay away from her husband. "Tom has been too indiscreet for too long, flouting our marriage and making a fool of me," she wrote. "The stakes had grown too high." Susan wrote that she had been shocked and saddened to learn Elizabeth had been killed. As far as she knew, the karate men delivered her message, and a day or two later Elizabeth wrapped her car around a tree driving home. But Susan was willing to pay the price. No more lying, no more cheating, no more hiding.

Henry waited outside the courthouse, pulling up his collar against a stinging Plains breeze. Whenever a question was shouted at him, he just shook his head, without looking. When he did glance, he saw more cameras, reporters, and mics than he had ever drawn, even for Peele's announcement at the Washington Monument. Portable lights, like miniature suns, baked his face and his eyes. He said nothing. Just stood there. Eventually, the horde tired. About twenty feet away, he spotted Bill Burr, mop of orange hair, crazed eyes, chewing an unlit cigar. The newshound looked like he was flying on a case of Jolt.

The media scrum erupted. He widened his stance to keep his balance amid the stampede. Looking up, he saw the pack swarming a graying head. Peele had emerged from the courthouse. The Senator was flanked by Eggert, Kyle, and half a dozen other aides. But it didn't take the reporters long to bust through the blockers. He edged closer, fighting for inches.

"I said everything I had to say last night" Peele was chanting. But the questions kept coming, about Elizabeth, Susan, the bodyguards. What did Peele know when?

The Senator just stood there, declining to say more. And then not saying anything. Just standing, watching the doors like the rest of them.

A minute later, Peele turned, and the intense blue eyes spotted him and glared. Peele waved him over. He tried to push through the crowd, but could advance only a few feet. He looked at Peele, shrugged, and turned away. Peele's last look, maybe the last time they would ever see each other, seemed pained by betrayal. It was a look Henry knew would haunt him.

A second eruption went off. The courthouse doors were opening again. A phalanx of cops burst through, two with arms extended. Behind them, flanked by two beefy officers, a thin, dark-haired figure shuffled in a tan trench coat.

The crowd parted as the cops charged down the steps, girth and gravity on their side. As Susan moved toward the police cruiser that would bear her away, her stride became lighter. Her shoulders unbowed. Her posture straightened. She seemed to become young again, as young as Fran.

Henry felt himself straining toward her, wishing he had

taken her when she offered. If he had, none of this might ever have happened. She might have chosen him as her emissary to Elizabeth. Once again, he had been decent for the wrong reasons. Once again, people were ruined through his decency.

He turned to his left, and saw the same wistful look in Peele's eye. Had Peele also fallen in love with Susan again, as she went away from him forever?

Henry smiled as the deep Jersey voice grunted, "Homicide, Rensi."

"Jeff, I just called to say good-bye. I'm going back to D.C. tomorrow."

"What are you doing for dinner tonight?"

"Delivery pizza and Diet Dr Pepper. I'm going to try the mushrooms this time."

"No, Hatten. You need a fitting last supper. There's a German place I haven't been to in months. They make a sauerbraten, a beef stew, blow your mind. They put in crumbled ginger snaps; it really gives it bite. That's not a joke, that's really how they make it. Be there at seven."

The restaurant, in suburban North Des Moines, had a Bavarian tavern intimacy. A long dark-wood bar ran the length of a narrow dining room, shields and crests lining the walls. Rensi arrived with his trademark *Wall Street Journal*.

"I've got to tell you, Henry," the detective said, lifting a glass of Rhine Valley white, "you're really in a scummy business. You going to do this the rest of your life?"

Elizabeth had asked him the same question, their first night together. He shook his head. "I'm a pariah, Jeff. Or going to be." He sipped the wine, cool with an afterburn. He poked the plate of sauerbraten. "The process does work, Jeff. It's just a little ugly sometimes, like making sausage."

Rensi smiled. "We come from the same background. But one place where we differ, I've spent my career trying to find the truth, wherever it takes me. People in your business, you obscure the truth."

He let images dance across his brain. Tyler's denuded House office. Cass, tall and intense at a staff meeting when they still lived in a world of possibilities. And Susan striding toward the police cruiser.

"Politics is a game won in the margins, so you've got to play on the edge," Henry said. He bit a ginger snap. It was chewy with beef sauce, with a satisfying give and sting as his molars clamped. "The problem comes when you step over the edge."

Rensi forked some stew with deft hands.

"Somehow, nobody seems to have connected me to this mess. Which is baffling. But I suppose you had something to do with that, Jeff."

The cop gave an almost imperceptible nod.

"If you can keep my name out, you'll save my career—any career."

Rensi dabbed a napkin at his mouth. "I've been in this business a long time. I've found that even with good people, no matter how careful they try to be, sometimes they step into the wrong area. Everybody's got dark shadows that they keep hidden, and I don't hold that against people."

"Well, it's—"

Rensi raised an empty fork. "I never had much use for stationhouse gossip. And I don't see how it would help things if I tied you in."

Could he really get out of this with his career intact, even his name? Henry had resigned himself to being a "disgraced" flack, in or out of jail. Peele was already joining the growing ranks of "disgraced" senators. A favorite Beltway word, "disgraced." He raised his wineglass. "I'm going to miss you, Jeff. And I'm going to miss these meals."

Rensi smiled. "A varied order leads to success."

"Shakespeare?"

"No, *Bristol's Guide to Rotisserie Baseball*. The A-shift sergeant left it open on the desk the other day."

EPILOGUE
ANTEATERS AND GIBBONS

Henry made a final sweep of the Quality Inn room and dialed Sterba on his BlackBerry. They hadn't yet cut off his service. "I'm not going back on the Senate staff," he said. Peele was hanging on to his seat, for now.

"Your call, buddy," Sterba said flatly. "Can't say I'm surprised." The chief of staff must have been distraught over Peele's implosion. Henry had lost a dimming shot at the White House podium. Sterba probably lost the keys to the universe.

"I'll send Peele a letter. So, you're sticking?"

"No, actually, you just beat me out of the hooch. I've had an offer on the table to lobby for the meat-packing industry. Yesterday, I took it. I got twelve days and a wake-up."

He smiled. It was a good fit; Sterba even looked like a meatpacker. He congratulated the old nose guard. "You going to miss it, Mike, at least the chance to fight the good fight?"

"Ah, it's all bullshit; doesn't matter how you come at it."

He didn't want to talk to Peele, but brightened when the

Senator phoned. After everything, he didn't want to end it with a glare across courthouse steps. Unless this was going to be worse. As he lifted the receiver, his pulse pounded and his palms moistened, reflexes Peele hadn't triggered in months.

"I thought you were in for the duration." Peele seemed wounded.

"Well, this is the duration, Senator. We lived a lifetime in Iowa."

By the time he returned the Black Baron to the Des Moines airport and climbed aboard a flight to D.C., Cass had landed as Dagworth's deputy chairman. The leaked poll numbers, so devastating only a week earlier, were forgotten, buried with Peele's campaign. He had barely bruised the water bug.

Henry crawled into his Cleveland Park condo and slept for six weeks. His body tried to recoup a year of adrenaline-charged days and sleepless nights, of marathons and sprints. Each morning, he took four hours to accomplish what used to take fifteen minutes. He needed two hours just to wake, shower, spoon some cereal, and prepare Walter's bowls. It was usually past one P.M. before he walked down Connecticut Avenue to the grocery store or organic market, or for a turkey sub at Quiznos or a Southwestern salad at California Tortilla. Sometimes he wandered to the zoo. He stood unshaven among the tourists, retirees, and fellow jobless, watching the anteaters plow the turf, the gibbons swing, and the tigers pace. Then he climbed back into his fifth-story hole. He woke in the evening to order Chinese delivery or eat peanut butter and jam sandwiches, watch a cable movie, and then slog into bed. Somehow he filled the days, or floated through them.

Occasionally, he scanned on-line election coverage. Dagworth won the Iowa caucuses and was cruising toward the Republican nomination. Anticipating the general election, Dagworth hired another veteran media whiz, Ira Fogel.

Bill Burr's stories soon grew sparse on the *Globe-Times* website. The Omaha paper shrank its political coverage after its home-state senator quit the race, and shrank it further after the caucuses. Then, in February, Burr's bylines stopped entirely. Henry called the newsroom and was told Burr no longer worked there. Jimmy Olsen had moved back to Los Angeles, another reporter told him, to attend law school.

The bodyguards moved toward court dates, he read in stories by new reporters, but were expected to plea bargain. Ostrow seemed to have trouble recalling Moffat and Gargano. They were just two of the thousands of students who had passed through his dojo over the years, and a couple of bad apples were inevitable in a big enough barrel. Ostrow noted that every student, at the first class, had to sign a pledge to use the techniques only in self-defense. By February, the karate magnate seemed headed for Capitol Hill.

Susan had pleaded not guilty, finally convinced to hire a top pro from an Arlington criminal law firm. She might avoid doing time.

After two months, Henry's checking account was hovering at the balance floor and he still hadn't thought about another job.

An envelope arrived with a printed Tyler for Governor Iowa address but a Washington postmark. A single sheet inside screamed in giant, blood-red uppercase, "URGENT RE-QUEST / PLEASE REPLY IMMEDIATELY." At bottom, in tiny type, "Paid for by Tyler for Governor." He vaguely remembered that letterhead, from a final fund-raising appeal. A local phone number was typed on the page, nothing more.

He dialed the number. She answered on the first ring.

"You're in D.C. now?" he asked.

"Yeah," Fran said. "I'm the Smithsonian's new director of government relations. It's a good cause, and they need the help."

He smiled. "I didn't realize the Smithsonian needed help so urgently. What can I do?"

"No, pal," she said. "The urgent help is for *you*."

"So you think you can save me?"

"No promises; you're pretty far gone," she said. "It might take me thirty or forty years."

They met for dinner that night.